GEORGETTE HEYER

Faro's Daughter

D0204412

Mandarin

A Mandarin Paperback
FARO'S DAUGHTER

First published in Great Britain 1941
by William Heinemann Ltd
This edition published 1992
by Mandarin Paperbacks
Michelin House, 81 Fulham Road, London SW3 6RB

Mandarin is an imprint of the Octopus Publishing Group,
a division of Reed International Books Limited

Copyright © Georgette Heyer 1941

A CIP catalogue record for this title
is available from the British Library
ISBN 0 7493 0513 4

Printed and bound in Great Britain
by Cox & Wyman Ltd, Reading, Berks

CHAPTER I

Upon her butler's announcing the arrival of Mr Ravenscar, Lady Mablethorpe, who had been dozing over a novel from the Circulating Library, sat up with a jerk, and raised a hand to her dishevelled cap. 'What's that you say? Mr Ravenscar? Desire him to come upstairs at once.'

While the butler went to convey this message to the morning-caller, her ladyship tidied her ruffled person, fortified herself with a sniff at her vinaigrette, and disposed herself on the sofa to receive her guest.

The gentleman who was presently ushered into the room was some twenty years her junior, and looked singularly out of place in a lady's boudoir. He was very tall, with a good pair of legs, encased in buckskins and topboots, fine broad shoulders under a coat of superfine cloth, and a lean, harsh-featured countenance with an uncompromising mouth and extremely hard grey eyes. His hair, which was black, and slightly curling, was cut into something perilously near a Bedford crop. Lady Mablethorpe, who belonged to an older generation, and herself continued to make free use of the pounce-box, in spite of Mr Pitt's iniquitous tax on hair-powder, could never look upon the new heads without a shudder. She shuddered now, as her affronted gaze took in not only her nephew's abominable crop but also the careless set of his coat, his topboots, the single spur he wore, and the negligent way he had tied his cravat, and thrust its ends through a gold-edged button-hole. She raised the vinaigrette to her nostrils again, and said in a fading voice: 'Upon my word, Max! Whenever I clap eyes on you I fancy I can smell the stables!'

Mr Ravenscar strolled across the room, and took up a

1

position with his back to the fire. 'And can you?' he enquired amiably.

Lady Mablethorpe chose to ignore this exasperating question. 'Why, in the name of heaven, only one spur?' she demanded.

'That's the high kick of fashion,' said Ravenscar.

'It makes you look for all the world like a postilion.'

'It's meant to.'

'And you know very well that you do not care a snap for the fashion! I beg you will not teach Adrian to make such a vulgar spectacle of himself!'

Mr Ravenscar raised his brows. 'I'm not likely to put myself to so much trouble,' he said.

This assurance did nothing to mollify his aunt. She said severely that the fashion of waiting upon ladies in garments fit only for Newmarket was not one which she had until this day encountered.

'I've this instant ridden into town,' said Mr Ravenscar, with an indifference which robbed his explanation of all semblance of apology. 'I thought you wanted to see me.'

'I have been wanting to see you these five days and more. Where in the world have you been, tiresome creature? I drove round Grosvenor Square, only to find the house shut up, and the knocker off the door.'

'I've been down at Chamfreys.'

'Oh, indeed! Well, I'm sure I hope you found your Mama in good health—not but what it's the height of absurdity to call Mrs Ravenscar your mother, for she's no such thing, and of all the foolish——'

'I don't,' said Ravenscar briefly.

'Well, I hope you found her in good health,' repeated Lady Mablethorpe, a trifle disconcerted.

'I didn't find her at all. She is at Tunbridge Wells, with Arabella.'

At the mention of her niece, Lady Mablethorpe's eyes

2

brightened. 'The dear child!' she said. 'And how is she, Max?'

The thought of his young half-sister appeared to afford Mr Ravenscar no gratification. 'She's a devilish nuisance,' he replied.

A shade of uneasiness crossed her ladyship's plump countenance. 'Oh, indeed? Of course, she is very young, and I daresay Mrs Ravenscar indulges her more than she should. But——'

'Olivia is as big a fool as Arabella,' responded Ravenscar shortly. 'They are both coming up to town next week. The 14th Foot are stationed near the Wells.'

This grim pronouncement apparently conveyed a world of information to Lady Mablethorpe. After a somewhat pensive pause, she said: 'It is time dear Arabella was thinking of marriage. After all, *I* was married when I was scarce——'

'She never thinks of anything else,' said Ravenscar. 'The latest is some nameless whelp in a scarlet coat.'

'You ought to keep her more under your eye,' said his aunt. 'You are as much her guardian as Mrs Ravenscar.'

'I'm going to,' said Ravenscar.

'Perhaps if we could marry her suitably——'

'My dear ma'am,' said Mr Ravenscar impatiently, 'Arabella is no more fit to be married than if she were still in long coats! I have it from Olivia that she has been head over ears in love with no fewer than five aspiring gentlemen in as many months.'

'Good God, Max! If you don't take care, we shall have some dreadful fortune-hunter running off with her!'

'It wouldn't surprise me at all.'

Lady Mablethorpe showed slight signs of agitation. 'You are the most provoking creature! How can you talk in that cool way about such a disastrous possibility?'

'Well, at least I should be rid of her,' said Mr Ravenscar

3

callously. 'If you're thinking of marrying her to Adrian, I can tell you now that——'

'Oh, Max, that is what I wanted to see you about!' interrupted his aunt, recalled by the mention of her son's name to the more pressing problem of the moment. 'I am quite distracted with worry!'

'Oh?' said Ravenscar, with casual interest. 'What's the young fool been doing?'

Lady Mablethorpe bristled instinctively at this uncomplimentary description of her only child, but a moment's reflection brought the unwelcome conviction that the slighting term had been earned. 'He thinks he is in love,' she said tragically.

Mr Ravenscar was unmoved. 'He'll think it a good many times for the next five or six years. How old is the cub?'

'Considering you are one of his trustees, you surely know that he is not yet twenty-one!'

'Forbid the banns, then,' recommended Mr Ravenscar flippantly.

'I wish you will be serious! This is no laughing matter! He will be of age in a couple of months now! And before we know where we are we shall have him married to some scheming hussy!'

'I should think it extremely unlikely, ma'am. Let the boy alone. Damme, he must cut his milk teeth sometime!'

Lady Mablethorpe flushed angrily. 'It is all very well for you to stand there, talking in that odious way, as though you did not care a fig, but——'

'I'm only responsible for his fortune,' he said.

'I might have known you would have come here only to be disagreeable! Wash your hands of my poor boy by all means: I'm sure it's only what I expected. But don't blame *me* if he contracts the most shocking misalliance!'

'Who is the girl?' asked Mr Ravenscar.

'A creature—oh, a *hussy*!—out of a gaming-house!'

'*What?*' demanded Ravenscar incredulously.

'I thought you would not be quite so cool when you heard the full sum of it!' said her ladyship, with a certain morbid satisfaction. 'I was never so appalled in my life as when I heard of it! I went immediately to your house. Something must be done, Max!'

He shrugged. 'Oh, let him amuse himself! It don't signify. She may cost him less than an opera-dancer.'

'She will cost him a great deal more!' said her ladyship tartly. 'He means to marry the creature!'

'Nonsense! He's not such a fool. One does not marry women out of gaming-houses.'

'I wish you will tell him so, for he will pay no heed to anything I say. He will have us believe that the girl is quite something out of the common way, if you please. Of course, it is as clear as daylight. The dear boy is as innocent as a lamb, and full of the most nonsensical romantic notions! That hateful, vulgar, scheming woman lured him to her house, and the niece did the rest. You may depend upon it she meant to have him from the start. Sally Repton tells me that it is positively absurd to see how Adrian worships the wench. There is no doing anything with him. She will have to be bought off. That is why I sent for you.' She observed a distinctly saturnine look in Mr Ravenscar's eye, and added with something of a snap: 'You need not be afraid, Max! I hope I know better than to expect you to lay out any of *your* odious wealth on the business!'

'I hope you do, aunt, for I shall certainly do no such thing.'

'It would be a very odd thing if anyone were to ask you to,' she said severely. 'Not but what you would scarcely notice the expenditure, as wealthy as you are. Indeed, I cannot imagine how you contrive to spend the half of your income, and I must say, Max, that nobody would

5

suppose, from the appearance you present, that you are quite the richest man in town.'

'Are you complimenting me upon my lack of ostentation, ma'am?'

'No, I am not,' said her ladyship acidly. 'There is nothing I have ever felt the least desire to compliment you on. I wish to heaven there were someone other than yourself to whom I could turn in this fetch. You are hard, and unfeeling, Max, and excessively selfish.'

He sought in the recesses of his pocket for his snuff-box, and drew it out, and opened it. 'Try Uncle Julius,' he suggested.

'That old woman!' exclaimed Lady Mablethorpe, disposing of her brother-in-law in one contemptuous phrase. 'Pray, what could he do to the purpose?'

'Sympathize with you,' said Mr Ravenscar, taking snuff. He saw the vinaigrette come into play, and shut his snuff-box with a snap. 'Well, you had better tell me who this Cyprian of Adrian's is.'

'She is that vulgar Lady Bellingham's niece—or so they pretend,' answered Lady Mablethorpe, abandoning the vinaigrette. 'You must know Eliza Bellingham! She keeps a gaming-house in St James's Square.'

'One of the Archer-Buckingham kidney?'

'Precisely so. Well, I don't say she is as bad as that precious pair, for, indeed, who could be?—but it's all the same. She was Ned Bellingham's wife, and I for one never thought her good *ton* at all, while we all know what Bellingham was!'

'I seem to be singularly ignorant.'

'Oh well, it was before your day! It doesn't signify, for he's been dead these fifteen years: drank himself into his grave, though they called it an inflammation of the lungs— fiddle! Of course he left her with a pile of debts, just as anyone might have expected. I'm sure I don't know how

6

she contrived to live until she started her wretched gaming-house: I daresay she might have rich relatives. But that's neither here nor there. You may see her everywhere; she rents her box at the opera, even! but no person of *ton* will recognize her.'

'How does she fill her house, then? I suppose it is the usual thing?—Discreet cards of invitation, handsome supper, any quantity of inferior wine, E.O. and faro-tables set out above-stairs?'

'I was referring to ladies of breeding,' said his aunt coldly. 'It is well known, alas, that gentlemen will go anywhere for the sake of gaming!'

He made her a slight, ironical bow. 'Also, if my memory serves me, Lady Sarah Repton.'

'I make no excuse for Sally. But duke's daughter or not, I should never think of describing her as of good *ton*!'

He looked faintly amused. 'I wish you will enlighten me: do you recognize her?'

'Don't be absurd, I beg of you! Naturally Sally has the entrée everywhere. Eliza Bellingham is quite another matter, and you may depend upon it that although Sally may go to her house, she does not set foot in Sally's! It was Sally who warned me of what was going forward. As you may suppose, I immediately taxed Adrian with it.'

'That is what I supposed,' agreed Mr Ravenscar, looking sardonic.

Lady Mablethorpe cast him a glance of scornful dislike. 'You need not imagine that I am a fool, Max. Of course I went tactfully about the business, never supposing for an instant that I should discover the affair to be more than a—than a —— Well, you know what anyone would expect, hearing that a young man had become enamoured of a wench from a gaming-house! You may conceive my dismay when Adrian at once, and without the least hesitation, informed me that he was indeed madly in love with

7

the girl, and meant to marry her! Max, I was so taken aback that I could not utter a word!'

'Has he taken leave of his senses?' demanded Mr Ravenscar.

'He is just like his father,' said Lady Mablethorpe, in a despairing way. 'Depend upon it, he has taken some romantic maggot into his head! You know how he was for ever reading tales of chivalry, and such nonsense, when he was a boy! This is what comes of it! I wish I had sent him to Eton.'

Mr Ravenscar raised his eyes, and thoughtfully contemplated the portrait which hung on the wall opposite to him. It depicted a young man in a blue coat, who looked out of the picture with a faint smile in his fine eyes. He was a handsome young man, hardly more than a boy. He wore his own fair hair tied in the nape of his neck, and supported his chin on one slender, beautiful hand. His expression was one of great sweetness, but there was a hint of obstinacy in the curve of his lips, at odd variance with the dreamy softness of his eyes.

Lady Mablethorpe followed the direction of her nephew's gaze, and herself studied, with misgiving, the portrait of the 4th Viscount. A despondent sigh escaped her; she transferred her attention to Mr Ravenscar. 'What's to be done, Max?' she asked.

'He can't marry the wench.'

'Will you speak to him?'

'Certainly not.'

'It is very difficult to do so, I own, but he might be brought to attend to you.'

'I can conceive of nothing more unlikely. What figure will you go to to buy the girl off?'

'No sacrifice would be too great to save my son from such an entanglement! I shall rely on you, for I know nothing of such matters. Only rescue the poor boy!'

'It will go very much against the grain,' said Ravenscar grimly.

Lady Mablethorpe stiffened. 'Indeed! Pray, what may you mean by that?'

'A constitutional dislike of being bled, ma'am.'

'Oh!' she said, relaxing. 'You may console yourself with the reflection that it is I, not you, being bled.'

'It is a slight consolation,' he admitted.

'I have not the least doubt that you will find the girl rapacious. Sally tells me that she is at least five years older than Adrian.'

'She's a fool if she accepts less than ten thousand,' said Ravenscar.

Lady Mablethorpe's jaw dropped. 'Max!'

He shrugged. 'Adrian is not precisely a pauper, my dear aunt. There is also the title. Ten thousand.'

'It seems wicked!'

'It is wicked.'

'I should like to strangle the abominable creature!'

'Unfortunately, the laws of this land preclude your pursuing that admirable course.'

'We shall have to pay,' she said, in a hollow voice. 'It would be useless, I am persuaded, to appeal to the woman.'

'You would make a great mistake to betray so much weakness.'

'Nothing would induce me to speak to such a woman! Only fancy, Max! she presides over the tables in that horrid house! You may imagine what a bold, vulgar piece she is! Sally says that all the worst rakes in town go there, and she bestows her favours on such men as that dreadful Lord Ormskirk. He is for ever at her side. I daresay she is more to him than my deluded boy dreams of. But it is useless to suggest such a thing! He fired up in an instant.'

'Ormskirk, eh?' said Ravenscar thoughtfully. 'That

settles it: any attempt to bring to reasonable terms a lady in the habit of encouraging his attentions would certainly be doomed to failure. I had thought better of Adrian.'

'You can't blame him,' said Lady Mablethorpe. 'What experience has he had of such people? Ten to one, the girl told him some affecting story about herself! Besides, she is quite lovely, according to what Sally Repton says. I suppose there is no hope of her deciding in Ormskirk's favour?'

'Not the smallest chance of it, I imagine. Ormskirk won't marry her.'

Lady Mablethorpe showed signs of dissolving into tears. 'Oh, Max, what is to be done if she won't relinquish him?'

'She must be made to relinquish him.'

'If it were not for the unsettled state of everything on the Continent, I should feel inclined to send him abroad! Only I daresay he would refuse to go.'

'Very likely.'

Lady Mablethorpe dabbed at her eyes. 'It would kill me if my son were to be caught by such a female!'

'I doubt it, but you need not put yourself about, ma'am. He will not be caught by her.'

She was a little comforted by this pronouncement. 'I knew I could rely upon you, Max! What do you mean to do?'

'See the charmer for myself,' he replied. 'St James's Square, you said?'

'Yes, but you know how careful these houses have to be, Max, on account of the law-officers. I daresay they won't admit you, if you have no card.'

'Not admit the rich Mr Ravenscar?' he said cynically. 'My dear aunt! I shall be welcomed with open arms.'

'Well, I hope they won't fleece you,' said Lady Mablethorpe.

'On the contrary, you hope they will,' he retorted. 'But I am a very ill bird for plucking.'

'If Adrian meets you there, he will suspect your purpose. He will certainly think that I sent you.'

'Deny it,' said Ravenscar, bored.

Lady Mablethorpe started to deliver herself of an improving lecture on the evils of deception, but, finding that her nephew was quite unimpressed, stopped, and said with a somewhat vindictive note in her voice: 'I beg that you will take care, Max! They say the girl is like a honeypot, and I'm sure I've no wish to see *you* caught in her toils.'

He laughed. 'There is not the slightest need for you to concern yourself about me, ma'am. I am neither twenty years of age, nor of a romantic disposition. You had better not tell Adrian that I have been here. No doubt I shall see him in St James's Square this evening.'

She held out her hand to him, a good deal mollified. 'You are a most provoking man, Max, but indeed I don't know what I should do without you! You will manage it all: I depend entirely upon you!'

'For once,' said Mr Ravenscar, raising her hand formally to his lips, 'you may quite safely do so.'

He took his leave of her, and departed. She opened her book again, but sat for a few moments gazing into the fire, her mind pleasantly occupied with daydreams. Once extricated from his present predicament, she had great hopes that her son would have learnt his lesson, and keep clear of any further entanglements. The account Ravenscar had brought of his half-sister's activities had not been entirely palatable, but Lady Mablethorpe was a broadminded woman, disinclined to set much store by the vagaries of a young lady of only eighteen summers. To be sure, it was unfortunate that Arabella should be such a flirt, but what, in another damsel, would have been a shocking fault, was, in such a notable heiress, a mere whimsicality of youth. Flirt or not, Lady Mablethorpe had every intention of seeing Arabella married to her son. Nothing, she thought, could be more suitable. Arabella had birth, fortune, and prettiness; she had known her cousin intimately since babyhood, and would make him a very good wife. Lady Mablethorpe had not the smallest objection to the child's liveliness: she thought it very taking, coupled, as it had always been, with a graceful, playful deference towards her aunt.

The recollection of the nameless suitor in a scarlet coat momentarily disturbed her ladyship's complacent dream. She soon banished it, reflecting that Max could be counted upon to put a stop to any such nonsense. Callous he might be, but he was not at all the man to stand idle while Arabella bestowed herself and her eighty thousand pounds on some nobody in a line regiment. For herself, Lady Mablethorpe was obliged to admit that it would be a shocking thing for Arabella to bestow these rich gifts on any other man than young Lord Mablethorpe.

She was not, she insisted, a mercenary woman, and if her dearest boy disliked his cousin she would be the last to urge him into matrimony with her. But eighty thousand pounds, safely invested in the Funds! Any woman of common prudence must wish to see this fortune added to the family coffers, particularly since (if Max were to be believed) the staggering sum of ten thousand pounds would shortly have to be disgorged from the amassed interest of Adrian's long minority. In this connection, thought her ladyship, it was a fortunate circumstance that the conduct of all the business of the Mablethorpe estate had been left in Max's capable hands rather than in the Honourable Julius Mablethorpe's. There was no doubt that Max had a very shrewd head on his shoulders. Thanks, in a great measure, to his management, Adrian would find himself when he came of age (and in spite of the loss of that ten thousand pounds) the master of a very pretty fortune. It would not compare, of course, with the Ravenscar wealth, a melancholy circumstance which had for years caused her ladyship a quite irrational annoyance. She had even, upon occasion, wished that she had a daughter who might have married Max.

She could have borne it better if she could have had the satisfaction of seeing him squandering his wealth. But this solace was denied her. Mr Ravenscar had simple tastes. He kept up a large house in Grosvenor Square, to be sure, and his country estate, Chamfreys, was a noble mansion, with a deer-park, some very good shooting, and a vast acreage attached to it, but he held no magnificent house-parties there, which he might, thought his aggrieved aunt, very well have done, with his stepmother to play hostess. That would have given the second Mrs Ravenscar something better to think about than her health. The second Mrs Ravenscar's health was a subject which, while it in no way concerned her, never failed to irritate Lady Mable-thorpe. Her ladyship inhabited a very pretty house in Brook Street, but would infinitely have preferred to live in Grosvenor Square, where she could have entertained on a large scale. It was thus a source of continual annoyance to her that her sister-in-law should declare that the delicate state of her nerves could not support the racket of London, and should spend the best part of her time at Bath, or Tunbridge Wells. Such parties as Max gave, therefore, were either bachelor gatherings, or of a nature which must preclude his asking his aunt to act as hostess for him. She wondered that he should care to live in solitary state in such a barrack of a house!

She wondered too, being herself a woman of gregarious tastes, that he should care so little for all the accepted pleasures of his world. You might look in vain for

Mr Ravenscar at balls, ridottos, and masquerades: ten to one, he would be at a cockfight, or rubbing shoulders with prize-fighters in some vulgar tavern in Whitechapel. He was a member of a number of fashionable clubs, but rarely visited most of them. His aunt had heard that he played a good deal at Brooks's, where the play was very deep, and she knew that his horses were the envy of his friends; but these were positively his only extravagances. While the town swarmed with Bucks and Jessamies, and even men who did not aspire to these heights of fashion would spend hours on the designing of a waistcoat, and fortunes on rings, fobs, shoebuckles, and pins, Mr Ravenscar wasted neither time nor money on anything but his boots (which were admittedly excellent), and had never been seen to wear any other ornament than the heavy gold signet ring which adorned his left hand.

He was thirty-five years of age, and it was now a considerable time since any but the most optimistic of matchmaking mothers had entertained hopes of his casting the handkerchief in her daughter's direction. There had been a time when he had been the most courted man in London; invitations had showered upon him; the most wily traps had been laid for him; but the indifference with which he regarded all eligible females (an indifference which he was never at any pains to hide), his cold reserve, and his habit of pleasing himself upon all occasions, had at last convinced the disappointed matrons that there was nothing whatever to be hoped for from him, not even some pretty, expensive trinket to mark his regard for those ladies who thought themselves his friends. Mr Ravenscar gave nothing away. No use thinking that he would gallantly offer to frank you at whist, or silver loo: he was far more likely to arise from the table further enriched by your losses. It was small consolation to reflect that ladies of easier virtue with whom his name had been coupled from time to time had never been able to flaunt jewels of his bestowing: it merely showed him to be abominably tight-fisted, a shocking fault! He was held to be a proud, disagreeable man; his manners were not conciliating; and although the gentlemen said that he was a good sportsman, meticulous in all matters of play and pay, the ladies were much inclined to think him a rakish fellow, with a pronounced taste for low company.

Lady Mablethorpe, who relied upon his help, and had for years trusted his advice, condemned his rudeness, deplored his coldness of heart, stood just a little in awe of his occasionally blistering tongue, and hoped that somebody one day would teach him a much-needed lesson. It would serve him right if he were to lose a great deal of money in St James's Square, for instance: ten thousand pounds, perhaps, which any man less odiously selfish would have offered to put up on behalf of his unfortunate young cousin.

CHAPTER II

Mr Ravenscar was spared the necessity of trading upon his name and fortune, by encountering upon the doorstep of Lady Bellingham's house in St James's Square an acquaintance who was perfectly willing to introduce him to her ladyship. Mr Berkeley Crewe prophesied that the old girl would be delighted to welcome him, assured him that the play was fair, the wine very tolerable, and the suppers the best in town; and said that Lady Bel had quite cast Mrs Sturt and Mrs Hobart into the shade. The door being opened to them by a stalwart individual with a rugged countenance and a cauliflower ear, they passed into the lofty hall, Mr Crewe nodding in a familiar manner to the porter, and saying briefly: 'Friend of mine, Wantage.'

Mr Wantage favoured the stranger with an appraising and a ruminative stare before offering to help him off with his greatcoat. Mr Ravenscar returned this with interest. 'When were you in the Ring?' he asked.

Mr Wantage seemed pleased. 'Ah, it's a long time ago now!' he said. 'Afore I joined the army, that was. Fancy you a-spotting that!'

'It wasn't difficult,' replied Ravenscar, shaking out his ruffles.

'I was thinking you'd peel to advantage yourself, sir,' observed Mr Wantage.

Mr Ravenscar smiled slightly, but returned no answer. Mr Crewe, having adjusted his satin coat to his satisfaction, given a twitch to his lace, and anxiously scrutinized his appearance in the mirror on the wall, led the way to the staircase. Ravenscar, after glancing about him, and noting that the house was furnished in the first style of elegance, followed him up to a suite of saloons on the first floor.

Entering the gaming-rooms by the first door they came to, they found themselves in an apartment given over to deep basset. About a dozen persons were seated round a table, most of them so intent upon the cards that the entrance of the newcomers passed unnoticed. A deathly hush brooded over the room, in marked contrast to the cheerful hubbub in the adjoining saloon, towards which Mr Crewe led his friend. This was a noble apartment in the front of the house, hung with straw-coloured satin, and furnished with a number of chairs, tables, and stands for the punters' rouleaus, and their glasses. At one end of the room a faro-bank was in full swing, presided over by a somewhat raddled lady in purple satin, and a turban lavishly adorned with ostrich plumes; at the other end, nearer to the fire, a vociferous knot of persons was gathered round an E.O. table, which was being set in motion by a tall young woman with chestnut hair, glowing in the candlelight, and a pair of laughing, dark eyes set under slim, arched brows. Her luxuriant hair was quite simply dressed, without powder, being piled up on top of her head, and allowed to fall in thick, smooth curls. One of these had slipped forward, as she bent over the table, and lay against her white breast. She looked up as Mr Crewe approached her, and Mr Ravenscar, dispassionately surveying her, had no difficulty at all in understanding why his young relative had so lamentably lost his head. The lady's eyes were the most expressive and brilliant he had ever seen. Their effect upon an impressionable youth would, he thought, be most destructive. As a connoisseur of female charms, he could not but approve of the picture Miss Grantham presented. She was built on queenly lines, carried her head well, and possessed a pretty wrist, and a neatly turned ankle. She looked to have a good deal of humour, and her voice, when she spoke, was low-pitched and pleasing. On one side of her, lounging over a chairback, an exquisite in a striped coat and a powdered wig watched the spin of the table in a negligent, detached fashion; on the other, Mr Ravenscar's cousin had no eyes for anything but Miss Grantham's face.

Miss Grantham, seeing a stranger crossing the room in Mr Crewe's wake, looked critically at him. Trained by necessity to sum up a man quickly, she was yet hard put to it to place Mr Ravenscar. His plain coat, the absence of any jewels or furbelows, did not argue a fat bank-roll, but his air was one of unconscious assurance, as though he was accustomed to going where he chose, and doing what he pleased in any company. If at first glance she had written him down as a country bumpkin, this impression was swiftly corrected. He might be carelessly dressed, but no country tailor had fashioned that plain coat, she decided.

She turned her head towards the middle-aged exquisite leaning on the chairback. 'Who is our new friend, my lord? A Puritan come amongst us?'

The exquisite languidly raised a quizzing-glass, and levelled it. Under its elaborate *maquillage* his thin, handsome face was curiously lined. His brows went up. 'That is no Puritan, my dear,' he said, in a light, bored voice. 'It is a very fat pigeon indeed. In fact, it is Ravenscar.'

This pronouncement brought young Lord Mablethorpe's head round with a jerk. He stared incredulously at his cousin, and ejaculated: 'Max!'

There was astonishment in his tone, not unmixed with suspicion. His fair countenance flushed boyishly, making him look younger than ever, and not a little guilty. He stepped forward, saying rather defensively: 'I did not expect to see you here!'

'Why not?' asked Ravenscar calmly.

'I don't know. That is, I did not think—— Do you know Lady Bellingham?'

'I am relying upon Crewe to present me to her.'

'Oh! It was Crewe who brought you!' said his lordship, a little relieved. 'I thought—at least, I wondered—— But it doesn't signify!'

Mr Ravenscar eyed him with a kind of bland surprise. 'You seem to be most unaccountably put-out by my arrival, Adrian. What have I done to incur your disapproval?'

Lord Mablethorpe blushed more hotly than ever, and grasped his arm in a quick, friendly gesture. 'Oh, Max, you fool! Of course you haven't done anything! Indeed, I'm very glad to see you! I want to make you known to Miss Grantham. Deb! This is my cousin, Mr Ravenscar. I dare say you will have heard of him. He is a notable gamester, I can tell you!'

Miss Deborah Grantham, encountering Mr Ravenscar's

hard grey eyes, was not sure that she liked him. She acknowledged his bow with the smallest of curtseys, and said lightly: 'You are very welcome, sir, and have certainly come to the right house. You know Lord Ormskirk, I believe?'

The middle-aged exquisite and Ravenscar exchanged nods. A large, loose-limbed man, standing on the other side of the table, said, with a twinkle: 'Don't be shy, Mr Ravenscar: we're all mighty anxious to win your money! But, I warn you, Miss Grantham's luck is in—isn't it, me darlin'?—and the bank's been winning this hour and more.'

'It's commonly the way of E.O. banks—to win,' remarked a metallic, faintly sneering voice at Ravenscar's elbow. 'Servant, Ravenscar!'

Mr Ravenscar, responding to this salutation, made a mental vow to rescue his cousin from the society into which he had been lured if he had to knock him out and kidnap him to do it. The Earl of Ormskirk, Sir James Filey, and—as a comprehensive glance round the room had informed him—all the more hardened gamesters who frequented Pall Mall and its environs were no fit companions for a youth scarcely out of swaddling-bands. It would, at that moment, have given Mr Ravenscar great pleasure to have seen Miss Grantham standing in the pillory, together with her aunt, and every other *brelandière* who seduced green young men to ruin in these polite gaming-houses.

Nothing of this appeared in his face as he accepted Miss Grantham's invitation to make his bet. E.O. tables held not the slightest lure for him, but since he had come to St James's Square for the purpose of getting upon easy terms with Miss Grantham, and judged that the quickest way of doing this was to spend as much money as possible in her house, he spent the next half-hour punting recklessly on the spin of the table.

Meanwhile, the dowager at the faro-table, who was Lady Bellingham, had discovered his identity, and was pleasantly fluttered. One of her neighbours informed her that Ravenscar had twenty or thirty thousand pounds a year, but tempered these glad tidings by adding that he was said to have the devil's own luck at all games of chance. If this were so, it was out to-night. Mr Ravenscar went down to the tune of five hundred guineas in the short time he spent at the E.O. table. While affecting an interest he was far from feeling in the gyrations of the little ball, he had the opportunity he sought of observing Miss Grantham. He was obliged also to observe his cousin's lover-like attentions to the lady, a spectacle which made him feel physically unwell. Adrian's frank blue eyes openly adored her; he paid very little attention to anyone else; and his attitude towards Lord Ormskirk reminded Ravenscar strongly of a dog guarding a bone.

Ormskirk seemed faintly amused. Several times he addressed some provocative remark to Adrian, as though he derived a sadistic pleasure from baiting the boy. Several times Adrian seemed to be on the verge of bursting into intemperate speech, but on each such occasion Miss Grantham intervened, turning his lordship's poisoned rapier aside with considerable deftness, tossing a laughing rejoinder to him, soothing Adrian by a swift, intimate smile which seemed to assure him that between him and her there was a secret understanding which Ormskirk's sallies could not impair.

Ravenscar allowed her to be a very clever young woman, and liked her none the better for it. She was holding two very different lovers on the lightest of reins, and so far she had not tangled the ribbons. But although Adrian might be easy to handle, Ormskirk was of another kidney, reflected Ravenscar, with grim satisfaction.

His lordship, who was nearer fifty years of age than forty, had been twice married, and was again a widower. It was popularly supposed that he had driven both his wives into their graves. He had several daughters, none yet having emerged from the schoolroom, and one son, still in short coats. His household was presided over by his sister, a colourless woman, prone to tears, which perhaps accounted for the fact of his lordship's being so seldom to be found at home. Both his marriages had been prudent, if unexciting, and since he had for years been in the habit of seeking his pleasures in the arms of a succession of fair Cyprians, it was in the highest degree unlikely that he was contemplating a third venture into matrimony. If he were, he would not look for his new bride in a gaming-house, Mr Ravenscar knew. His designs on Miss Grantham were strictly dishonourable; and, judging by his cool air of ownership, he was very sure of her, too sure to be discomposed by the calf-love of a younger suitor.

But Ravenscar knew Ormskirk too well to feel easy in his mind. If Miss Grantham were to decide that marriage with Adrian would be better worth her while than a more elastic connection with Ormskirk, Adrian would have acquired a very dangerous enemy. No consideration of his youth would weigh for an instant with one whose pride it was to be considered deadly either with the small-sword, or the pistol. It was perfectly well known to Ravenscar that Ormskirk had thrice killed his man in a duel; and he began to perceive that the extrication of his cousin from Miss Grantham's toils was a matter of even greater urgency than he had at first supposed.

The third gentleman who appeared to have claims on Miss Grantham was the man who had so cheerfully hailed him upon his first approaching the table. He seemed to be on intimate terms with the lady, but was resented neither by Adrian nor by Lord Ormskirk. He was a pleasant

21

fellow, with smiling eyes, and an engaging address. Mr Ravenscar would have been much surprised to have found that he was not a soldier of fortune. Miss Grantham called him Lucius; he called Miss Grantham his darling, with an easy familiarity that indicated long friendship, or some fonder relationship. Miss Grantham, thought Mr Ravenscar, was altogether too free with her favours.

At one in the morning she relinquished the E.O. table, calling upon Mr Lucius Kennet to take her place at it. 'Ah, I'm tired, and want my supper!' she said. 'My lord, will you take me down to supper? I swear I'm famished!'

'With the greatest pleasure on earth, my dear,' said Lord Ormskirk, in his weary voice.

'Of course I will take you down, Deb!' said Lord Mablethorpe, offering his arm.

She stood between them, laughing dismay in her eyes, looking from one to the other. 'Oh, I am overwhelmed, but indeed, indeed——'

Ravenscar walked forward. 'Madam, you stand between two fires! Allow me to rescue you! May I have the honour of taking you down to supper?'

'Snatching a brand from the burning?' she said, in a rallying tone. 'My lords!' She swept them a deep curtsey. 'Pray forgive me!'

'Mr Ravenscar wins all,' said Sir James Filey, with one of his mocking smiles. 'It is the way of the world!'

There was a flash of anger in her eyes, but she pretended not to hear, and passed out of the room on Ravenscar's arm.

There were already several people in the dining-room on the ground-floor, but Ravenscar found a seat for Miss Grantham at one of the smaller tables arranged beside the wall, and, having supplied her with some pickled salmon, and a glass of iced champagne, he sat down opposite her, picked up his own knife and fork, and said: 'You must allow me to tell you, Miss Grantham, that I count myself fortunate in their lordships' misfortune.'

The corners of her mouth lifted. 'That's mighty pretty of you, sir. I had the oddest fancy that you were not much in the way of making pretty speeches.'

'That depends on the company in which I find myself,' he replied.

She eyed him speculatively. 'What brought you here?' she asked abruptly.

'Curiosity, Miss Grantham.'

'Is it satisfied?'

'Oh, not yet, ma'am! Let me give you some of these green peas: they are quite excellent!'

'Yes, we pride ourselves on the quality of our suppers,' she said. 'Why did you play at E.O.? Is not faro your game?'

'Curiosity again, Miss Grantham. My besetting sin.'

'Curiosity to see a female elbow-shaker, sir?'

'Just so,' he agreed.

'Was that why you came?'

'Of course,' he said coolly.

She laughed. 'Well, I did not think when I saw you that you were a gamester!'

'Did you take me for a flat, Miss Grantham?'

Her eyes twinkled rather attractively. 'Why, yes, for a moment I did! But Lord Ormskirk put all my hopes to flight. The rich Mr Ravenscar's luck at the bones or the cards is proverbial.'

'It was out to-night.'

'Oh, you do not care a fig for that silly game! I wish you may not break my aunt's faro-bank.'

'If you will inform the stalwart person at your door that I am free to enter the house, I promise I shall endeavour to do so when I come again.'

'You must know that all doors are open to the rich Mr Ravenscar—particularly such doors as this.'

'Make it plain, then, to your henchman, or you may have a brawl upon your doorstep.'

'Ah, Silas is too knowing a one! Only law-officers and their spies are refused admittance here, and he would smell one at sixty paces.'

'What a valuable acquisition he must be to you!'

'It would be impossible to imagine an existence without him. He was my father's sergeant; I have known him from my cradle.'

'Your father was a military man?' said Mr Ravenscar, slightly raising his brows.

'Yes, at one time.'

'And then?'

'You are curious again, Mr Ravenscar?'

'Very.'

'He was a gamester. It runs in the blood, you observe.'

'That would account for your presence here, of course.'

'Oh, I have been familiar with gaming-houses from my childhood up! I can tell a Greek, or a Captain Sharp, within ten minutes of his entering the room; I could play the groom-porter for you, or deal for a faro-bank; I can detect a bale of flat cinque deuces as quickly as you could yourself; and the man who can fuzz the cards when I am at the table don't exist.'

'You astonish me, Miss Grantham. You are indeed accomplished!'

'No,' she said seriously. 'It is my business to know those things. I have no accomplishments. I do not sing, or play upon the pianoforte, or paint in water-colours. *Those* are accomplishments.'

'True,' he agreed. 'But why repine? In certain circles they may be *de rigueur*, but they would be of very little use to you here, I imagine. You were wise to waste no time on such fripperies: you are already perfect for your setting, ma'am.'

'For my setting!' she repeated, flushing a little. 'The devil! Your cousin is more complimentary!'

'Yes, I dare say he is,' replied Ravenscar, refilling her wine-glass. 'My cousin is very young and impressionable.'

'I am sure you, sir, are certainly not impressionable.'

'Not a bit,' he said cheerfully. 'But I am perfectly ready to pay you any number of compliments, if that is what you wish.'

She bit her lip, saying, after a moment, with a suggestion of pique in her voice: 'I don't wish it at all.'

'In that case,' said Ravenscar, 'I feel that we shall deal extremely together. Do you play picquet?'

'Certainly.'

'Ah, but I mean do you play well enough to engage in a rubber with me?'

Miss Grantham eyed him with considerable hostility. 'I am thought,' she said coldly, 'to have a reasonably good understanding.'

'So have many others I could name, but that does not make them good card-players.'

Miss Grantham sat very straight in her chair. Her magnificent eyes flashed. 'My skill at cards, Mr Ravenscar, has never yet been called in question!'

'But you have not played with me yet,' he pointed out.

'That is something that can be mended!' she retorted.

He lifted an eyebrow at her. 'Are you sure you dare, Miss Grantham?'

She gave a scornful laugh. 'Dare! I? I will meet you when you choose, Mr Ravenscar, the stakes to be fixed by yourself!'

'Then let it be to-night,' he said promptly.

'Let it be at once!' she said, rising from her chair.

He too rose, and offered his arm. His countenance was perfectly grave, but she had the impression that he was secretly laughing at her.

25

On the staircase they met Lord Mablethorpe, on his way down to supper. His face fell when he saw Miss Grantham. He exclaimed: 'You have not finished supper already! I made sure of finding you in the dining-room! Oh, do come back, Deb! Come and drink a glass of wine with me!'

'You are too late,' said Ravenscar. 'Miss Grantham is promised to me for the next hour.'

'For the next hour! Oh, come now, Max, that's too bad! You are quizzing me!'

'Nothing of the sort: we are going to play a rubber or two of picquet.'

Adrian laughed. 'Oh, poor Deb! Don't play with him: he'll fleece you shamefully!'

'If he does, I have a strong notion that it will rather be shame*lessly*!' Miss Grantham smiled.

'Indeed it will! There is not an ounce of chivalry in my cousin. I wish you will have nothing to do with him! Besides, it is so dull to be playing picquet all night! What is to become of me?'

'Why, if E.O. holds no charms for you, you may come presently and see how I am faring at your cousin's hands.'

'I shall come to rescue you,' he promised.

She laughed, and passed on up the stairs to the gaming-saloons. In the larger room, one or two small tables were set out; Miss Grantham led the way to one of these, and called to a waiter for cards. She looked speculatively at Ravenscar, as he seated himself opposite to her; his eyes met hers, and some gleam of mockery in them convinced her that he had been laughing at her. 'You are the strangest man!' she said, in her frank way. 'Why did you talk *so* to me?'

'To whet your curiosity,' he responded, with equal frankness.

'Good God, to what end, pray?'

'To make you play cards with me. You have so many noble admirers, ma'am, who pay you such assiduous court, that I could not suppose that a conciliating address would answer my purpose.'

'So you were rude to me, and rough! Upon my word, I do not know what you deserve, Mr Ravenscar!'

He turned to pick up the picquet-packs the waiter was offering him on a tray, and laid some card-money down in their place. 'To be plucked, undoubtedly. What stakes do you like to play for, Miss Grantham?'

'You will recall, sir, that the decision was to rest with you.'

'Well,' he said, 'let us make it ten shillings a point, since this is a mere friendly bout.'

Her eyes widened a little, for this was playing deep, but she said coolly: 'What you will, sir. If you are satisfied, it is not for me to cavil.'

'What humility, Miss Grantham!' he said, shuffling one of the packs. 'If you should find it insipid, we can always double the stakes.'

Miss Grantham agreed to it, and in a moment of bravado suggested that they should play for twenty-five pounds the rubber, in addition. On these terms they settled down to the game, the lady with her nerves on the stretch, the gentleman abominably casual.

It was soon seen that Mr Ravenscar was a much more experienced player than his opponent; his calculation of the odds was very nice; he played his cards well; and had a disconcerting trick of summing up Miss Grantham's hands with sufficient accuracy to make him a very formidable adversary. She went down on the first rubber, but not heavily, taking him to three games. He agreed that the balance of the luck had been with him.

'I'm emboldened to think you don't find my play contemptible, at all events,' Miss Grantham said.

27

'Oh, by no means!' he replied. 'Your play is good, for a lady. You are weakest in your discards.'

Miss Grantham cut the pack towards him with something of a snap.

In the middle of the third rubber, Lord Mablethorpe came back into the saloon, and made his way to Miss Grantham's side. 'Are you ruined yet, Deb?' he asked, smiling warmly down at her.

'No such thing! We have lost a rubber apiece, and this one is to decide the issue. Hush, now! I am very much on my mettle, and can't be distracted.'

He drew up a frail, gilded chair, and sat down astride it, resting his arms on the back. 'You said I might watch you!'

'So you may, and bring me good fortune, I hope. Your point is good, Mr Ravenscar.'

'Also my quint, Miss Grantham?'

'That also.'

'Very well, then; a quint, a tierce, fourteen aces, three kings, and eleven cards played, ma'am.'

Miss Grantham cast a frowning glance at the galaxy of court cards which Ravenscar spread before her eyes, and a very dubious glance at the back of the one card remaining in his hand. 'Oh, the deuce! All hangs upon this, and I swear there's nothing to tell me what I should keep!'

'Nothing at all,' he said.

'A diamond!' she said, throwing down the rest of her hand.

'You lose,' said Ravenscar, exhibiting a small club.

'Piqued, repiqued, and capotted!' groaned Lord Mablethorpe. 'Deb, my dearest, I warned you to have nothing to do with Max! Do come away!'

'I am not so poor-spirited! Do you care to continue, sir?'

'With all my heart!' said Mr Ravenscar, gathering up the cards. 'You are a good loser, Miss Grantham.'

'Oh, I don't regard this little reverse, I assure you! I am not rolled-up yet!'

As the night wore on, however, she began to go down heavily, as though Ravenscar, trifling with her at first, had decided to exert his skill against her. She thought the luck favoured him, but was forced to acknowledge him to be her master.

'You make me feel like a greenhorn!' she said lightly, when he robbed her of a pique. 'Monstrous of you to have kept the spade-guard! I did not look for such usage, indeed!'

'No, you would have thrown the little spade on the slim chance of picking up an ace or a king, would you not?'

'Oh, I always gamble on slim chances—and rarely lose! But you are a cold gamester, Mr Ravenscar!'

'I don't bet against the odds, I own,' he smiled, beckoning to a waiter. 'You'll take a glass of claret, Miss Grantham?'

'No, not I! Nothing but lemonade, I thank you. I need to have my wits about me in this contest. But this must be our last rubber. I see my aunt going down to the second supper, and judge it must be three o'clock at least.'

Lord Mablethorpe, who had wandered away disconsolately some time before, came back to the table with a tale of losses at faro to report, and a complaint to utter that his Deb was neglecting him for his tiresome cousin. 'How's the tally?' he asked, leaning his hand on the back of her chair.

'Well, I am dipped a trifle, but not above two or three hundred pounds, I fancy.'

He said in an undervoice: 'You know I hate you to do this!'

'You are interrupting the game, my dear.'

He muttered: 'When we are married I shan't permit it.'

She looked up, mischievously smiling. 'When we are

married, you foolish boy, I shall of course do exactly as you wish. Your deal, Mr Ravenscar!'

Mr Ravenscar, on whom this soft dialogue had not been wasted, picked up the pack, and wished that he had Miss Grantham's throat in his strong, lean hands instead.

The last rubber went very ill for Miss Grantham. Ravenscar won it in two swift games, and announced the sum of her losses to be six hundred pounds. She took this without a blink, and turned in her chair to issue a low-voiced direction to Mr Lucius Kennet, who, with one or two others, had come to watch the progress of the game. He nodded, and moved away towards the adjoining saloon. Sir James Filey said mockingly: 'How mistaken of you, my dear, to play against Ravenscar! Someone should have warned you.'

'You, for instance,' said Ravenscar, directing a glance up at him under his black brows. 'Once bit twice shy, wasn't it?'

Miss Grantham, who detested Sir James, cast her late opponent a grateful look. Sir James's colour darkened, but the smile lingered on his lips, and he said equably: 'Oh, picquet's not my game! I will not meet you there. But in the field of sport, now——! That is a different matter!'

'Which field of sport?' enquired Ravenscar.

'Have you still a pair of match grays in your stable?' said Sir James, drawing out his snuff-box.

'What, are you at that again? I still have them, and they will still beat any of the cattle you own.'

'I don't think so,' said Sir James, taking snuff with an elegant turn of his wrist.

'I wouldn't bet against them,' said a man in a puce coat, and a tie-wig. 'I'd buy them, if you'd sell, Ravenscar.'

Mr Ravenscar shook his head.

'Oh, Max wins all his races!' Lord Mablethorpe declared. 'He bred those grays, and I'll swear he wouldn't part with them for a fortune. Have they ever been beaten, Max?'

'No. Not yet.'

'They have not yet been evenly matched,' said Sir James.

'You thought they were once,' remarked Ravenscar, with a slight smile.

'Oh, admittedly!' replied Filey, with an airy gesture. 'I underrated them, like so many other men.'

Mr Lucius Kennet came back into the room, and laid some bills and a number of rouleaus on the table. Miss Grantham pushed them towards Mr Ravenscar. 'Your winnings, sir.'

Mr Ravenscar glanced at them indifferently, and, stretching out his hand, picked up two of the bills, and held them crushed between his fingers. 'Five hundred pounds on the table, Filey,' he said. 'I will engage to drive my grays against any pair you may choose to match 'em with, over any distance you care to set, upon a day to be fixed by yourself.'

Lord Mablethorpe's eyes sparkled. 'A bet! Now what do you say, Filey?'

'Why, this is paltry!' said Sir James. 'For five hundred pounds, Ravenscar? You don't take me seriously, I fear!'

'Oh, we multiply the stake, of course!' said Ravenscar carelessly.

'Now I am with you!' said Sir James, putting his snuff-box back into his pocket. 'Multiply it by what?'

'Ten,' said Ravenscar.

Miss Grantham sat very still in her chair, glancing from one man to the other. Lord Mablethorpe gave a whistle. 'That's five thousand,' he said. 'I wouldn't accept it! We all know your grays. Flying too high, Filey!'

'You'd accept it if I offered you odds,' said Ravenscar.

The man in the puce coat gave a laugh. 'Gad's life,

there's some pretty plunging in the wind! Do you take him, Filey?'

'With the greatest readiness in life!' said Sir James. He looked down at Ravenscar, still lying back in his chair with one hand thrust deep into his pocket. 'You're very sure of your grays and your skill! But I fancy I have you this time! Did you say you would offer me odds?'

'I did,' replied Mr Ravenscar imperturbably.

Lord Mablethorpe, who had been watching Sir James, said quickly: 'Careful, Max! You don't know, after all, what kind of a pair he may be setting against your grays!'

'Well, I hope they may be good enough to give me a race,' said Ravenscar.

'Just good enough for that,' smiled Sir James. 'What odds will you offer against my unknown pair?'

'Five to one,' replied Ravenscar.

Even Sir James was startled. Lord Mablethorpe gave a groan, and exclaimed: 'Max, you're mad!'

'Or drunk,' suggested the man in the puce coat, shaking his head.

'Nonsense!' said Ravenscar.

'Are you serious?' demanded Filey.

'Never more so.'

'Then, by God, I'll take you! The race to be run a week from to-day, over a course to be later decided on. Agreed?'

'Agreed,' nodded Ravenscar.

Mr Kennet, who had been following the discussion with bright-eyed interest, said: 'Ah, now, we'll record this bet, gentlemen! Waiter, fetch up the betting-book!'

Mr Ravenscar glanced at Miss Grantham, his lip curling. 'So you even have a betting-book!' he remarked. 'You think of everything, don't you, ma'am?'

CHAPTER III

MR RAVENSCAR left Lady Bellingham's house while his young relative was still engaged at the faro-table, having himself declined to hazard any of his winnings at his favourite game. As he was shrugging his shoulders into his drab overcoat, he was joined, rather to his surprise, by Lord Ormskirk, who came sauntering down the stairs, swinging his quizzing-glass between his white fingers.

'Ah, my dear Ravenscar!' said his lordship, with a lift of his delicately pencilled brows. 'So you too find it a trifle flat! My hat, Wantage; my cloak! If you are going in my direction, Ravenscar, I am sure you will bear me company. My cane, Wantage!'

'Yes, I'll bear you company willingly,' said Mr Ravenscar.

'So obliging of you, my dear fellow! Do you find the night air—ah, the morning air, is it not?—invigorating?'

'Immensely,' said Mr Ravenscar.

His lordship smiled, and passed out of the house, drawing on a pair of elegant, lavender gloves. A link-boy ran up with his flaring torch, with offers of a chair or a hackney.

'We'll walk,' said Ravenscar.

It was past four o'clock, and a ghostly grey light was already creeping over the sky. It lit the silent square sufficiently for the two men to see their way. They turned northwards, and began to traverse the square in the direction of York Street. A couple of sleepy chairmen roused themselves to proffer their services; a melancholy voice in the distance, proclaiming the hour, showed that the Watch was abroad; but there seemed to be no other signs of life in the streets.

'I recall a time,' remarked Ormskirk idly, 'when it was positively dangerous to walk the town at night. One took one's life in one's hands.'

'Mohocks?' asked Mr Ravenscar.

'Such desperate, wild fellows!' sighed his lordship. 'There is nothing like it nowadays, though they tell me the footpads are becoming a little tiresome. Have you ever been set upon, Ravenscar?'

'Once.'

'I am sure you gave a good account of yourself,' smiled Ormskirk. 'You are such a formidable fellow with your fists. Now, that is a sport in which I have never been able to interest myself. I remember that I was once compelled to be present at a turn-up on some heath, or Down— really, I forget: it was abominably remote, and the mud only remains clearly imprinted on my memory! There was a greasy fellow with a nose, whom everyone seemed to be united in extolling. Yes, none other than the great Mendoza: you cannot conceive the depths of my indifference! He was matched with a fellow called Humphries, who bore, quite inexplicably, the title of Gentleman. I do not recollect the outcome; possibly I may have slept. It was very bloody, and crude, and the scent of the *hoi polloi*, in spite of all that a most disagreeable east wind could do, was all-pervading. But I am speaking, I believe, to one of Mendoza's admirers!'

'I've taken lessons from him,' replied Mr Ravenscar. 'I suppose you did not choose to walk home with me to discuss the Fancy. Let's have it, my lord: what do you want of me?'

Ormskirk made a deprecating gesture. 'But so abrupt, my dear Ravenscar! I am walking with you as a gesture of the purest friendliness!'

Mr Ravenscar laughed. 'Your obliged servant, my lord!'

'Not at all,' murmured his lordship. 'I was about to

34

suggest to you—in proof of my friendly intentions, be it understood—that the removal of your—ah—impetuous young cousin, would be timely. I am sure you understand me.'

'I do,' replied Ravenscar rather grimly.

'Now, don't, I beg of you, take me amiss !' implored his lordship. 'I am reasonably certain that your visit to Lady Bellingham's hospitable house was made with just that intention. You have all my sympathy; indeed, it would be quite shocking to see a promising young gentleman so lamentably thrown away ! For myself, I shall make no attempt to conceal from you, my dear fellow, that I find your cousin a trifle *de trop*.'

Mr Ravenscar nodded. 'What's the woman to you, Ormskirk ?' he asked abruptly.

'Shall we say that I cherish not altogether unfounded hopes ?' suggested his lordship blandly.

'Accept my best wishes for your success.'

'Thank you, Ravenscar, thank you ! I felt sure that we should see eye to eye on this, if upon no other, subject. I should be extremely reluctant, I give you my word, to be obliged to remove from my path so callow an obstacle.'

'I can understand that,' said Mr Ravenscar, a somewhat unpleasant note entering his level voice. 'Let me make myself plain, Ormskirk ! You might have my cousin whipped with my good will, if that would serve either of our ends, but when you call him out you will have run your course ! There are no lengths to which I will not go to bring you to utter ruin. Believe me, for I was never more serious in my life !'

There was a short silence. Both men had come to a standstill, and were facing each other. There was not light enough for Mr Ravenscar to be able to read his lordship's face, but he thought that that slim figure stiffened under its shrouding cloak. Then Ormskirk broke the silence with a soft laugh. 'But, my dear Ravenscar!' he protested. 'One would say that you were trying to force a quarrel on to me!'

'If you choose to read it so, my lord——?'

'No, no!' said his lordship gently. 'That would not serve either of our ends, my dear fellow. I fear you are a fire-eater. Now, I am quite the mildest of creatures, I do assure you! Let us have done with this—I fear we shall have to call it bickering! We are agreed that we both desire the same end. Are you, I wonder, aware that your impulsive cousin has offered the lady in question matrimony?'

'I am. That is why I came to see the charmer for myself.'

Lord Ormskirk sighed. 'You have the *mot juste*, my dear Ravenscar, as always. Enchanting, is she not? There is—you will have noticed—a freshness, excessively grateful to a jaded palate.'

'She will do very well for the rôle you design for her,' said Mr Ravenscar, with a curl of his lip.

'Precisely. But these young men have such romantic notions! And marriage, you will allow, is a bait, Ravenscar! One cannot deny that it is a bait!'

'Especially when it carries with it a title and a fortune,' agreed Ravenscar dryly.

'I felt sure we should understand one another tolerably well,' said his lordship. 'I am persuaded that the affair can be adjusted to our mutual satisfaction. Had the pretty creature's affections been engaged it would have been another matter. There would, I suppose, have been nothing left for me to do than to retire from the lists—ah—discomfited! One has one's pride: it is inconvenient, but one has one's pride. But this, I fancy, is by no means the case.'

'Good God, there's no love there!' Ravenscar said scornfully. 'There is a deal of ambition, I will grant.'

'And who shall blame her?' said his lordship affably. 'I feel for her in this dilemma. What a pity it is that I am not young, and single, and a fool! I was once both young and single, but never, to the best of my recollection, a fool.'

'Adrian is all three,' said Mr Ravenscar, not mincing matters. 'I, on the other hand, am single, but neither young nor a fool. For which reason, Ormskirk, I do not propose either to discuss the matter with my cousin, or to attempt to remove him from the lady's vicinity. The rantings of a youth in the throes of his first love-affair are wholly without the power of interesting me, and although I do not pique myself upon my imagination, it is sufficiently acute to enable me to picture the result of any well-meant interference on my part. The *coup de grâce* must be delivered by Miss Grantham herself.'

'Admirable!' murmured his lordship. 'I am struck by the similitude of our ideas, Ravenscar. You must not suppose that this had not already occurred to me. Now, to be plain with you, I regard your entrance upon our little stage as providential—positively providential! It will, I trust, relieve me of the necessity of resorting to the use of a distasteful weapon. Instinct prompts me to believe that you have formed the intention of offering the divine Deborah money to relinquish her pretensions to the hand of your cousin.'

'Judging from the style of the establishment, her notions of an adequate recompense are not likely to jump with mine,' said Mr Ravenscar.

'But appearances are so often deceptive,' said his lordship sweetly. 'The aunt—an admirable woman, of course!—is not, alas, blessed with those qualities which distinguish other ladies in the same profession. Her ideas, which are charmingly lavish, preclude the possibility of the house's being run at a profit, in the vulgar phrase. In a word, my dear Ravenscar, her ladyship is badly dipped.'

'No doubt you are in a position to know?' said Mr Ravenscar.

'None better,' replied Ormskirk. 'I hold a mortgage on the house, you see. And in one of those moments of generosity, with which you are doubtless familiar, I—ah—acquired some of the more pressing of her ladyship's debts.'

'That,' said Mr Ravenscar, 'is not a form of generosity with which I have ever yet been afflicted.'

'I regarded it in the light of an investment,' explained his lordship. 'Speculative, of course, but not, I thought, without promise of a rich return.'

'If you hold bills of Lady Bellingham's, you don't appear to me to stand in need of any assistance from me,' said Mr Ravenscar bluntly. 'Use 'em!'

A note of pain crept into his lordship's smooth voice. 'My dear fellow! I fear we are no longer seeing eye to eye! Consider, if you please, for an instant! You will appreciate, I am sure, the vast difference that lies between the surrender from—shall we say gratitude?—and the surrender to—we shall be obliged to say *force majeure*.'

'In either event you stand in the position of a scoundrel,' retorted Mr Ravenscar. 'I prefer the more direct approach.'

'But one is, unhappily for oneself, a gentleman,' Ormskirk pointed out. 'It is unfortunate, and occasionally tiresome, but one is bound to remember that one is a gentleman.'

'Let me understand you, Ormskirk!' said Mr Ravenscar. 'Your sense of honour being too nice to permit of your holding the girl's debts over her by way of threat, or bribe, or what you will, it yet appears to you expedient that some-one else—myself, for example—should turn the thumb-screw for you?'

Lord Ormskirk walked on several paces beside Mr Ravenscar before replying austerely· 'I have frequently deplored a tendency in these days to employ in polite conversation a certain crudity, a violence, which is offensive to persons of my generation. You, Ravenscar, prefer the fists to the sword. With me it is otherwise. Believe me, it is always a mistake to put too much into words.'

'It doesn't sound well in plain English, does it?' retorted Ravenscar. 'Let me set your mind at rest! My cousin will not marry Miss Grantham.'

His lordship sighed. 'I feel sure I can rely on you, my dear fellow. There is positively no need for us to pursue the subject further. So you played a hand or two at picquet with the divine Deborah! They tell me your skill at the game is remarkable. But you play at Brooks's, I fancy. Such a mausoleum! I wonder you will go there. You must do me the honour of dining at my house one evening, and of giving me the opportunity to test your skill. I am considered not inexpert myself, you know.'

They had reached Grosvenor Square by this time, where his lordship's house was also situated. Outside it, Ormskirk halted, and said pensively: 'By the way, my dear Ravenscar, did you know that Filey has acquired the prettiest pair of blood-chestnuts it has ever been my lot to clap eyes on?'

'No,' said Mr Ravenscar indifferently. 'I supposed him to have bought a better pair than he set up against my grays six months ago.'

'What admirable sangfroid you have!' remarked his lordship. 'I find it delightful, quite delightful! So you actually backed yourself to win without having seen the pair you were to be matched with!'

'I know nothing of Filey's horses,' Ravenscar responded. 'It was quite enough to have driven against him once, however, to know him for a damnably cow-handed driver.'

His lordship laughed gently. 'Almost you persuade me

to bet on you, my dear Ravenscar! I recall that your father was a notable whip.'

'He was, wasn't he?' said Mr Ravenscar. 'If Filey's pair are all you say, you will no doubt be offered very good odds.' He raised his hat as he spoke, nodded a brief fare-well, and passed on towards his own house, at the other end of the square.

He was finishing his breakfast, several hours later, when Lord Mablethorpe was announced. Coffee, small-ale, the remains of a sirloin, and a ham still stood upon the table, and bore mute witness to the fact that Mr Ravenscar was a good trencherman. Lord Mablethorpe, who was looking a trifle heavy-eyed, grimaced at the array, and said: 'How you can, Max——! And you ate supper at one o'clock!'

Mr Ravenscar, who was dressed only in his shirt and breeches, with a barbaric-looking brocade dressing-gown over all, waved a hand towards a chair opposite to him. 'Sit down, and have some ale, or some coffee, or whatever it is you drink at this hour.' He transferred his attention to his major-domo, who was standing beside his chair. 'Mrs Ravenscar's room to be prepared, then, and you had better tell Mrs Dove to make the Blue Room ready for Miss Arabella. I believe she took a fancy to it when she was last here. And take the dustsheets off the chairs in the drawing-room! If there is anything else, you will probably know of it better than I.'

'Oh, are Aunt Olivia and Arabella coming to town?' asked Adrian. 'That's famous! I haven't seen Arabella for months. When do they arrive?'

'To-day, according to my latest information. Come and dine.'

'I can't to-night,' Adrian said, his ready blush betraying him. 'But tell Arabella I shall pay her a morning-call immediately!'

Mr Ravenscar gave a grunt, nodded dismissal to his

major-domo, and poured himself out another tankard of ale. With this in his hand, he lay back in his chair, looking down the table at his cousin's ingenuous countenance. 'Well, if you won't come to dine to-night, come to Vauxhall Gardens to-morrow,' he suggested. 'I shall be escorting Arabella and Olivia there. There's a ridotto, or some such foolery.'

'Oh, thank you! Yes, indeed I should like it of all things! That is, if—but I don't suppose——' He stopped, looking a little conscious. 'I am glad I have found you at home,' he said. 'I particularly wanted to see you!'

'What is it?' Ravenscar asked.

'As a matter of fact, I came to ask your advice!' replied Adrian, in a rush. 'At least, no, not that exactly, for my mind is quite made up! But the thing is that my mother depends a good deal upon your judgment, and you've always been devilish good to me, so I thought I would tell you how things stand.'

There was nothing Mr Ravenscar wanted less than to hear his cousin explain his passion for Miss Grantham, but he said: 'By all means! Are you coming to watch my race, by the way?'

This question succeeded in diverting Lord Mablethorpe for the moment, and he replied, with his face lighting up: 'Oh, by Jove, I should think I am! But what a complete hand you are, Max! I never heard you make such a bet in your life! I suppose you will win. There is no one like you when it comes to handling the ribbons! Where will it be run?'

'Oh, down at Epsom, I imagine! I left it to Filey to settle the locality.'

'I hate that fellow!' said Lord Mablethorpe, frowning. 'I hope you will beat him.'

'Well, I shall do my best. Do you go to Newmarket next month?'

'Yes. No. That is, I am not sure. But I didn't come to talk of that!'

Mr Ravenscar resigned himself to the inevitable, made himself comfortable in his chair, and said: 'What did you come to talk of?'

Lord Mablethorpe picked up a fork, and began to trace patterns with it upon the table. 'I hadn't the intention of telling you about it,' he confessed. 'It is not as though you were my guardian, after all! Of course, I know you are one of my trustees, but that is quite a different thing, isn't it?'

'Oh, quite!' agreed Ravenscar.

'I mean, you are not responsible for anything I may do,' said Adrian, pressing home his point with a little anxiety.

'Not a bit.'

'In any event, I shall come of age in a couple of months. It is really no concern of *anyone's*!'

'None at all,' said Ravenscar, betraying no trace of the uneasiness his relative evidently expected him to feel. 'In fact, you may just as well keep your own counsel, and have some ale.'

'No, I don't want any,' said Adrian, rather impatiently. 'As I said, I had no intention of telling you. Only you happened to visit—to visit Lady Bel's house last night, and —and you met Her.'

'I did not exchange more than half a dozen words with Lady Bellingham, however.'

'Not Lady Bellingham!' said Adrian, irritated by such stupidity. 'I mean Miss Grantham!'

'Oh, Miss Grantham! Yes, I played picquet with her, certainly. What of it?'

'What did you think of her, Max?' asked his lordship shyly.

'Really, I don't remember that I thought about her at all. Why?'

42

Adrian looked up indignantly. 'Good God, you surely must at least have seen how—how very beautiful she is!'

'Why, yes, I suppose she is tolerably handsome!' conceded Ravenscar.

'Tolerably handsome!' ejaculated Adrian, in dumbfounded accents.

'Yes, certainly, for one who is not in the first blush of youth. A little too strapping for my taste, and will probably put on flesh in middle age, but I will allow her to be a well-looking woman.'

Adrian laid down the fork, and said, with a considerably heightened colour: 'I had better make it plain to you at once, Max, that—that I mean to marry her!'

'Marry Miss Grantham?' said Ravenscar, raising his brows. 'My dear boy, why?'

This unemotional way of receiving startling tidings was damping in the extreme to a young gentleman who had braced himself to encounter violent opposition, and for a moment Adrian seemed to be at a loss to know what to say. After a slight pause, he said with immense dignity: 'I love her.'

'How very odd!' said Ravenscar, apparently puzzled.

'I see nothing odd in it!'

'No, of course not. How should you, indeed? But surely someone nearer your own age——?'

'The difference in our ages doesn't signify in the least. You talk as though Deb were in her thirties!'

'I beg pardon.'

Adrian eyed him with considerable resentment. 'My mind is irrevocably made up, Max. I shall never love another woman. I knew as soon as I saw her that she was the only one in the world for me! Of course, I don't expect you to understand *that*, because you are the coldest fellow —well, I mean, *you* have never been in love!'

Ravenscar laughed.

'Well, not in the way I mean,' amended his lordship.

'Evidently not. But what has all this to do with me?'

'Nothing at all!' replied Adrian, with emphasis. 'Only that since you have met Deb I thought I would tell you. I do not wish to do anything *secretly*. I am not in the least ashamed of loving Deb!'

'It would be very odd if you were,' commented Ravenscar. 'I apprehend that Miss Grantham has accepted your offer?'

'Well, not precisely,' Adrian confessed. 'That is, she will marry me, I know, but she is the most delightfully teasing creature———! Oh, I can't tell you, but when you know her better you will see for yourself!'

Ravenscar set down his tankard. 'When you say "not precisely", what do you mean?'

'Oh, she says I must wait until I come of age before I make up my mind—as though I could ever change it! She did not wish me to say anything about it yet, but someone told my mother that I was entangled—*entangled!*—by her and so it all came out. And that is "in part" why I have come to you, Max.'

'Oh?'

'My mother will listen to you,' said Adrian confidently. 'You see, she has taken an absurd notion into her head that Deb is not good enough for me. Of course, I know that her being in Lady Bel's house is a most unfortunate circumstance, but she is not in the least the sort of girl you might imagine, Max, upon my word she is not! She don't even like cards above a little! It is all to help her aunt.'

'Did she tell you so?'

'Oh no, it was Kennet who told me! He has known her since her childhood. Really, Max, she is the dearest, sweetest—oh, there are no words to describe her!'

Mr Ravenscar could have found several, but refrained.

'She is not like any other woman I have ever met,'

pursued his lordship. 'I wonder that you were not struck by it!'

'Well, I have met rather more women than you have as yet had time to,' said Ravenscar apologetically. 'That might account for it.'

'Yes, but I should have thought that even *you*—however, that's neither here nor there! What I want you to understand, Max, is that I mean to marry Deb, whatever anyone may choose to say about it!'

'Very well; and now that I understand that, what do you expect me to do about it?'

'Well, Max, I thought I could talk to you so much more easily than to my mother. You know how it is with her! Just because Deb has been in the habit of presiding in a gaming-house, she will not listen to a word I say! It is monstrously unjust! It is not Deb's fault that she is obliged to be friendly towards men like Filey, and Ormskirk: she cannot help herself! Oh, I can scarcely wait to take her away from it all!'

'I see,' said Ravenscar. 'I must own that you have taken me by surprise. No doubt I quite mistook the matter, but I should have said that it was Ormskirk's suit which the lady favoured, rather than yours.'

Adrian looked troubled. 'No, no, you don't understand! It is that which makes me so anxious—in short, Lady Bel is under an obligation to Ormskirk—a monetary obligation, you know—and Deb dare not offend him. It is an intolerable position for her! If only I had control of my fortune *now*, I would put an end to it on the instant!'

Mr Ravenscar experienced no difficulty at all in believing this, and could only be thankful that there were still two months to run of his cousin's minority. 'May I ask if the source of your information is again Mr Kennet?' he enquired.

'Oh, yes! Deb will not say a word about it! But Kennet knows all the circumstances.'

'Miss Grantham is happy in the possession of so devoted a friend,' remarked Ravenscar ironically.

'Well, yes, I suppose—except that—— Well, he is not quite the sort of fellow who—— But that will all be changed when we are married!'

'Miss Grantham's parentage, I need hardly ask, is respectable?' said Ravenscar, in a matter-of-fact voice.

'Oh, yes! The Granthams are related to Amberley, I believe. They are some sort of cousins: I am not precisely informed. Deb's father was a military man, but he sold out.' Lord Mablethorpe looked up with a disarming smile. 'Well, the truth is he was a gamester, I suppose. His *birth* was respectable, but from all I can discover he was not quite the thing. But he is dead, after all, and *his* sins are not to be visited upon Deb. There is also a brother. I have not met him yet, but there is talk of his getting leave: he is stationed somewhere in the south. He is a military man too, and was at Harrow, so you see there is nothing to take exception to *there*.' He paused, waiting for his cousin to make some comment. Ravenscar, however, said nothing. His lordship drew a beath. 'And now that I have explained. it to you, Max, I wish—that is, I should be very much obliged to you if you would but speak to my mother!'

'I?' said Ravenscar. 'What would you have me say to her?'

'Well, I thought you could make her understand that it is not such a bad match after all!'

'No, I don't think I could do that,' replied Ravenscar. 'I doubt if anyone could.'

'But, Max——'

'I should wait until I had come of age, if I were you.'

'But if Mama could only be brought to consent, I should not have to wait! And there is that fellow, Ormskirk, to be thought of! I want Mama to give her consent, so that Deb need have no scruples. Then the engagement could be announced, and I dare say there would be no trouble about advancing me some of my fortune.'

'Impossible!'

'But, Max, if you and Uncle Julius both agreed to it——'

'What makes you think that we should?'

'But I have *explained* it all to you!' said his lordship impatiently.

Mr Ravenscar got up, and stretched his long limbs. 'Wait until you are of age,' he said. 'You may then do as you please.'

'I did not think you would behave so shabbily!' exclaimed Adrian.

Ravenscar smiled. 'But surely you know that I am abominably close-fisted?'

'It is not *your* money,' Adrian muttered. 'I suppose the truth is that you are as bad as Mama, and don't wish me to marry Deb!'

'I won't conceal from you that I am not enthusiastic over the match. You had better approach your Uncle Julius.'

'You know very well he is as bad as Mama! I made sure you would help me to talk Mama over! I have always depended upon you! I did not think you would fail me in the most important thing in my life!'

Ravenscar walked round the table, and dropped a hand on to Adrian's shoulder, gripping it for an instant. 'Believe me, I don't mean to fail you,' he said. 'But you must wait! Now I am going to exercise those grays of mine. Come with me!'

It spoke volumes for the love-sick state of Adrian's mind that he shook his head, saying disconsolately: 'No, I think I won't. I have no heart for it now. I must be going. If you knew Deb better you would soon change your mind!'

'Then you must hope for a closer acquaintanceship between us,' said Ravenscar, moving to the fireplace, and jerking the bell-push beside it.

Adrian rose. 'Anyway, I *shall* marry her!' he said defiantly.

Ravenscar accompanied him out into the hall. 'By all means, if you are still of the same mind in two months' time,' he agreed. 'My compliments to my aunt, by the way.'

'I don't suppose I shall tell her that I have been with you,' replied Adrian, sounding much like a thwarted schoolboy.

'That will teach me a lesson,' said his cousin.

Adrian was never sulky for many minutes at a time. A reluctant grin put his scowl to flight. 'Oh, damn you, Max!' he said, and departed.

Mr Ravenscar returned to his breakfast-parlour, and stood for a moment or two, leaning his arm on the mantelpiece, and looking fixedly out of the window. His thoughts were not kindly towards Miss Grantham, and as they dwelled upon her his expression grew a little ugly. Very clever of the wench to set the convenient Mr Kennet to tell her pathetic story to Adrian! So she would not have him announce his betrothal to her until he came of age? Well, that was clever too, but not quite clever enough. Miss Grantham should have the honour of trying a fall with one Max Ravenscar, and maybe she would learn something from that encounter.

'You rang, sir?'

Mr Ravenscar turned his head. 'Yes, I rang. Send word to the stables, please, that I want the grays brought round in half an hour.'

CHAPTER IV

MISS GRANTHAM, sleeping late into the morning, did not leave her room until past eleven o'clock. The servants, in green baize aprons and shirt-sleeves, were still sweeping and dusting the saloons, and Miss Grantham presently found her aunt in her dressing-room, seated before a table on which her toilet accessories were inextricably mixed with bills, letters, pens, ink, and wafers.

Lady Bellingham had been a very pretty woman in her youth, but there was little trace of a former beauty to be detected in her plump countenance to-day. A once pink-and-white complexion had long been raddled by cosmetics; there were pouches under her pale blue eyes; her cheeks had sagged; and it could not have been said that a golden wig became her.

Some traces of hair-powder still clung to this erection, but the monstrous plumes she had worn in it on the previous evening had been removed, and a lace cap set in their place, with lilac ribbons tied under her little chin. A voluminous robe, with a quantity of ruffles and ribbons, enveloped her stout form, and she wore, in addition, a trailing Paisley shawl, which was continually slipping off her shoulders, or getting its fringe entangled in the pins and combs which littered the dressing-table.

She looked up, when her niece entered the room, and said in a distracted way: 'Oh, my dear, thank heavens you are come! I am in such a taking! I am sure we are ruined!'

Miss Grantham, who was looking very neat in a chintz gown, with her hair dressed plainly, bent over her to kiss her cheek. 'Oh no! Don't say so! I had some deep doings myself last night.'

49

'Lucius told me you had gone down six hundred pounds,' said Lady Bellingham. 'Of course, it can't be helped, but why would not Mr Ravenscar play faro? People are so tiresome! My love, nothing could be worse than the fix we are in. Just look at this bill from Priddy's! Twelve dozen of Fine Hock at thirty shillings the dozen, and such nasty stuff as it is! Ditto of Claret, First Growth, at forty-two shillings the dozen—why, it is robbery, no less! Ditto of White Champagne, at seventy shillings—I cannot conceive how the half of it can have been drunk, and here is Mortimer telling me that we shall be needing more!'

Miss Grantham sat down, and picked up the bill from Priddy's Foreign Warehouse and Vaults. 'It does seem shocking,' she agreed. 'Do you think we should buy cheaper wine?'

'Impossible!' said Lady Bellingham, with resolution. 'You know what everyone says about the inferior stuff that Hobart woman gives her guests to drink! But that is not the worst! Where is that odious bill for coals? Forty-four shillings the ton we are paying, Deb, and that not the best coal! Then there's the bill from the coachmakers—here it is! No, that's not it—— Seventy pounds for green peas: it doesn't seem *right*, does it, my love? I dare say we are being robbed, but what is one to do? What's this? Candles, fifty pounds, and that's only for six months! Burning wax ones in the kitchen, if we only knew. Where *is* that?—oh, I have it in my hand all the time! Now, do listen, Deb! Seven hundred pounds for the bays and a new barouche! Well, I can't think where the money is to come from. It seems a monstrous price.'

'We might let the bays go, and hire a pair of job horses,' suggested Miss Grantham dubiously.

'I can't and I won't live in Squalor!' declared her aunt tearfully.

Miss Grantham began to gather up the bills, and to sort them. 'I know. It would be horrid, but we should be spared these dreadful bills for repairs. What is K.Q. iron, Aunt Lizzie?'

'I can't imagine, my love. Do we use that, too?'

'Well, it says here, *Best K.Q. iron, faggotted edgways—* oh, it was for an axle-tree!'

'We had to have *that*,' said Lady Bellingham, comforted. 'But when it comes to eighty pounds for liveries which are the most hideous colour imaginable, and not in the least what I wanted, we have reached the outside of enough!'

Miss Grantham looked up with an awed expression in her eyes. 'Aunt, do we really pay four hundred pounds for a box at the opera?'

'I dare say. It is all of a piece! I am sure we have not used it above three times the whole season.'

'We must give it up,' said Miss Grantham firmly.

'Now, Deb, do pray be sensible! When poor dear Sir Edward was alive, we always had our box at the opera. Everyone did so!'

'But Sir Edward has been dead these dozen years, aunt,' Miss Grantham pointed out.

Lady Bellingham dabbed at her eyes with a fragile handkerchief. 'Alas, I am a defenceless widow, whom everyone delights to impose upon! But I will *not* give up my box at the opera!'

There did not seem to be anything more to be said about this. Miss Grantham had made another, and still more shocking discovery. 'Oh, aunt!' she said, raising distressed eyes from the sheaf of bills. 'Ten ells of green Italian taffeta! That was for that dress which I threw away, because it did not become me!'

'Well, what else is one to do with dresses which don't become one?' asked her aunt reasonably.

'I might at least have worn it! Instead of that, we bought all that satin—the Rash Tears one, I mean—and had it made up!'

'You never had a dress that became you better, Deb,' said her ladyship reminiscently. 'You were wearing that when Mablethorpe first saw you.'

There was a short silence. Miss Grantham looked at her aunt in a troubled way, and shuffled the bills in her hand.

'I suppose,' said Lady Bellingham tentatively, 'you could not bring yourself——?'

'No,' said Deborah.

'No,' agreed Lady Bellingham, with a heavy sigh. 'Only it would be such a splendid match, and no one would dun me if it were known that you were betrothed to Mablethorpe!'

'He is not yet twenty-one, ma'am.'

'Very true, my dear, but so devoted!'

'I'm his calf-love. He won't marry a woman out of a gaming-house.'

Lady Bellingham's mouth drooped pathetically. 'I meant it all for the best! Of course, I do see that it puts us in an awkward position, but how in the world was I to manage? And my card-parties were always so well-liked—indeed, I was positively renowned for them!—that it seemed such a sensible thing to do! Only, ever since we bought this house our expenses seem to have mounted so rapidly that I'm sure I don't know what is to become of us. And here is dearest Kit, too! I forgot to tell you, my love. I have a letter from him somewhere—well, never mind, I must have mislaid it. But the thing is that the dear boy thinks he would be happier in a cavalry regiment, and would like to exchange.'

'Exchange!' exclaimed Kit's sister, aghast. 'Why, I dare say it would cost seven or eight hundred pounds at the least!'

'Very likely,' said Lady Bellingham in a despondent tone. 'But there's no denying he would look very well in Hussar uniform, and I never did like his being in that horrid line regiment. Only where the money is to come from I don't know!'

'Kit can't exchange. It would be absurd! You must explain to him that it is impossible.'

'But I promised poor dear Wilfred I would always look after his children!' said Lady Bellingham tragically.

'So you have, dearest Aunt Lizzie,' said Deborah warmly. 'We have never been anything but a shocking charge on you!'

'I am sure no one ever had a better nephew and niece. And if you won't have Mablethorpe, I dare say someone richer will offer for you.'

Miss Grantham looked down at her shapely hands. 'Lord Ormskirk is making very precise offers, aunt.'

Lady Bellingham picked up the haresfoot, and began to powder her face in an agitated way. 'There you are, then! If only you would have Mablethorpe, there would be an end to Ormskirk's pretensions! I can't deny, Deb, that we are very awkwardly situated there. Don't, for heaven's sake, quarrel with the man! I daresay he would clap us up in a debtors' prison in the blink of an eye!'

'How much money do we owe Ormskirk?' asked Deborah, raising her clear gaze to her aunt's face.

'My love, don't ask me! I had never the least head for figures! There's that odious mortgage on the house, for one thing. I have been quite misled! I made sure we should make a great deal of money, if only we could set up in a modish establishment. But what with green peas, and two free suppers every night, not to mention all that champagne and claret, and the faro-bank's being broke twice in one week, I'm sure it is a wonder we can still open our doors! And now what must you do, my love, but play

53

picquet with Ravenscar; not that I blame you, for I am sure you did the right thing, and if only he may be induced to try his hand at faro it will have been worth the outlay. Did he seem pleased, my dear?'

'I don't know,' answered Deborah candidly. 'He is a strange creature. I had the oddest feeling that he did not like me, but he chose to play with me all the evening.'

Lady Bellingham laid down the haresfoot, and turned a brightening countenance upon her niece. 'Do you suppose perhaps he may offer for you, Deb? Oh, if that were to happen——! I declare I should die of very joy! He is the richest man in London. Now, don't, *don't*, I implore you, take one of your dislikes to him! Only think how our troubles would vanish!'

Deborah could not help laughing, but she shook her head as well, and said: 'My dear aunt, I am persuaded no such thought has entered Mr Ravenscar's head! I wish you will not think so much about my marriage. I doubt I was born to wear the willow.'

'Never say so, Deb! Why, you are so handsome you have even turned Ormskirk's head—not that I should like you to become his mistress, because I am sure it is not the sort of thing your poor father would have wished for you at all, besides putting you in an awkward situation, and quite ruining all your chances of making a good match. Only if it is not to be Ormskirk, it must be marriage.'

'Nonsense! Put all these bills away, ma'am, and forget them. We have had a run of bad luck, it's true, and have been monstrously extravagant besides, but we shall come about, trust me!'

'Not with Indian muslin at ten shillings the yard, and wheatstraw for bedding a crown the truss, or the bushel, or whatever it is,' said Lady Bellingham gloomily.

'Wheatstraw?' asked Miss Grantham, wrinkling her brow.

'Horses,' explained her aunt, with a heavy sigh.

Miss Grantham seemed to feel the force of this, and once more bent her head over the bills in her hand. After a prolonged study of these, she said in a daunted voice: 'Dear ma'am, do we never eat anything but salmon and spring chickens in this house?'

'We had a boiled knuckle of veal and pig's face last week,' replied Lady Bellingham reflectively. 'That was for our dinner, but we could not serve it at the suppers, my love.'

'No,' agreed Miss Grantham reluctantly. 'Perhaps we ought not to give two suppers every night.'

'Anything of a shabby nature is repugnant to me!' said her aunt firmly. 'Sir Edward would not have approved of it.'

'But ma'am, I daresay he would not have approved of your keeping a gaming-house at all!' Deborah pointed out.

'Very likely not, my love. I'm sure it is not at all the sort of thing I should choose to do, but if Ned didn't wish me to do so he should not have died in that inconsiderate way,' said Lady Bellingham.

Miss Grantham abandoned this line of argument, and returned to her study of the bills. Such items as Naples Soap, Patent Silk Stockings, Indian Tooth-brushes, and Chintz Patches, mounted up to a quite alarming total; while a bill from Warren's, Perfumiers, and another from a mantua-maker, enumerating such interesting items as One Morning Sacque of Paris Mud, Two Heads *Soupir d'étouffes*, and One Satin Cloak trimmed *Opera Brûlée* Gauze, made her feel quite low. But these were small bills compared with the staggering list of household expenses, which it was evident Lady Bellingham had been trying to calculate. Her ladyship's sprawling handwriting covered several sheets of hot-pressed paper, whereon Servants'

55

Wages, Liveries, Candles, Butcher, Wine, and Taxes jostled one another in hopeless confusion. The house in St James's Square seemed to cost a great deal of money to maintain, and if there were nothing to cavil at in the Wages of Four Women Servants, £60, it did seem that two waiters at twenty pounds apiece, an Upper Man at fifty-five, and the coachman at forty were grossly extortionate.

Miss Grantham folded these depressing papers, and put them at the bottom of the sheaf.

'I am sure I am ready enough to live a great deal more frugally,' said Lady Bellingham, 'but you may see for yourself, Deb, how impossible it is! It is not as though one was spending money on things which are not necessary.'

'I suppose,' said Deborah, looking unhappily at a bill from the upholsterers, 'I suppose we need not have covered *all* the chairs in the front saloon with straw-coloured satin.'

'No,' conceded Lady Bellingham. 'I believe that was a mistake. It does not wear at all well, and I have been thinking whether we should not have them done again, in mulberry damask. What do you think, my love?'

'I think we had better not spend any more money on them until the luck changes,' said Deborah.

'Well, my dear, *that* will be an economy at all events,' said her ladyship hopefully. 'But have you thought that if the luck *don't* change——?'

'It must, and shall!' said Deborah resolutely.

'I am sure I hope it may, but I do not see how we can recover, with peas at such a price, and you playing picquet with Ravenscar for ten shillings a point.'

Miss Grantham hung her head. 'Indeed, I am very sorry,' she apologized. 'He *did* say he would come again, to let me have my revenge, but perhaps I had better make an excuse?'

'No, no, that would never do! We must hope that he

will presently turn to faro, and make the best of it. Mable-thorpe has sent you a basketful of roses this morning, my love.'

'I know,' replied Deborah. 'Ormskirk sent a bouquet of carnations in a jewelled holder. I have quite a drawerful of his gifts to me. I would like to throw them in his painted face !'

'And so you could, if only you would take poor young Mablethorpe,' her aunt pointed out. 'I am sure he has the sweetest of tempers, and would make anyone a most amiable husband. As for his not being of age yet, that will soon be a thing of the past, and if you are thinking about his mother—not that there is the least need, for though she can be very disagreeable, she is not a bad-hearted creature, Selina Mablethorpe——'

'No, I was not thinking of her,' said Deborah. 'And I will not think of Adrian either, if you please, aunt ! I may be one of faro's daughters, but I'll not entrap any unfor-tunate young man into marrying me, even if my refusal means a debtors' prison !'

'You don't feel that Ormskirk would be better than a debtors' prison ?' suggested Lady Bellingham, in a desponding voice.

Deborah broke into laughter. 'Aunt Lizzie, you are a most shocking creature ! How can you talk so ?'

'Well, but, my dear, you will be just as surely ruined for ever in prison as under Ormskirk's protection, and far less agreeably,' said her ladyship, with strong common sense. 'Not that I wish for such a connection, for I don't, but what else is to be done ?'

'Oh, I have the oddest notion that something will hap-pen to set all to rights, ma'am ! Indeed, I have !'

'Yes, love,' said Lady Bellingham, without much hope. 'We both of us had that notion when we laid five hundred guineas on Jack-Come-Tickle-Me at the Newmarket races, but it turned out otherwise.'

'Well,' said Miss Grantham, thrusting all the bills into one of the drawers of a small writing-table by the window, 'I have a very good mind to back Mr Ravenscar to win his curricle-race against Sir James Filey. *He* was offering odds at five to one on himself.'

'What is all this?' demanded Lady Bellingham. 'Lucius did say something about an absurd bet, but I was not attending.'

'Oh, Sir James was being as odious as ever, and it seems he was beaten in a race against Ravenscar six months ago, and is as wild as fire to come about again. The long and the short of it is that Ravenscar offered to run against him when and where he chose for a stake of five thousand pounds. And as though that were not enough, he laid odds at five to one against Sir James! He must be very sure of himself.'

'But that is twenty-five thousand pounds!' exclaimed Lady Bellingham, who had been doing some rapid multiplication.

'If he loses!'

'I never heard of anything so provoking!' declared her ladyship. 'If he has twenty-five thousand pounds to lose, pray why could he not do so at my faro-bank? But so it is always! Men have never the least spark of consideration for anything but their own pleasure! Well, I recall that his father was a very disagreeable, selfish kind of a man, and I dare say the son is no better.'

Miss Grantham returned no answer to this. Her aunt, dissatisfied with her appearance, picked up a pot of Serkis-rouge, and began to apply this aid to beauty with a ruthless hand. 'It is the oddest thing,' she remarked, 'but all the richest men are the most odious creatures imaginable! Only think of Filey, and now Ravenscar!'

'Good God, ma'am, you cannot mean to couple Mr

Ravenscar with that vile man!' cried Miss Grantham, flushing a little.

Lady Bellingham set the rouge-pot down. 'Deb, never say you have taken a fancy to Ravenscar?' she exclaimed. 'It would be the most wonderful thing if he could be got to offer for you, but I have been thinking it over, my dear, and I believe it won't answer. He is turned thirty-five, and has never asked any female to marry him that I ever heard of. Besides, he is said to be abominably *close*, and that would not do for us at all.'

'Offer for me indeed! Of course he won't, or I accept him, believe me, aunt! And as for *fancies*—pooh, what nonsense! I liked him for taking Sir James up so swiftly, and for something about him that was different from all those other men, but he was quite rude to me, you know. I am very sure he despises me for presiding at gaming-tables. I cannot conceive what should have brought him to the house, unless it was to see what kind of a harpy his cousin had fallen in love with.'

'Oh dear!' sighed Lady Bellingham. 'I daresay that would be it! We shall have him whisking poor Adrian off, and then we shall have no one but Ormskirk to fall back upon!'

Miss Grantham laughed. 'He may whisk him off with my good-will, I assure you, ma'am, but he seemed to me much like a sensible man, and will no doubt have seen that the foolish boy will come to no harm in this house. Why, I will not even permit him to put down a rouleau of above ten guineas at a time!'

'No,' said her ladyship regretfully. 'And he is not at all a lucky punter. It does seem a pity, my love.'

'Now, you know very well, ma'am, you don't wish to be plucking schoolboys!' Deborah said, laying an arm about her aunt's shoulders.

Lady Bellingham agreed to this, but without much

conviction. A small black page scratched on the door for admittance, and announced that Massa Kennet was below-stairs. Deborah kissed her aunt, recommended her not to worry her head over the bills, and went off to join this friend of her childhood in the small back-room behind the dining-room.

If to live by one's wits and a dice-box was to be a soldier-of-fortune, Mr Ravenscar had summed Mr Lucius Kennet up correctly. Although considerably his junior, he had been one of the late Captain Wilfred Grantham's closest friends, wandering about Europe with him, and generally sharing his fluctuating fortunes. Like Silas Wantage, at present engaged in cleaning silver in the pantry, while Mortimer, Lady Bellingham's expensive butler, slept with the current number of the *Morning Advertiser* spread over his face, Lucius Kennet had always formed a part of Miss Grantham's background. He had never been above mending a broken doll, or tying up a cut finger; and when Deborah reached adolescence he had constituted himself an easy-going protector. Captain Grantham had not been one to put himself out for a parcel of plaguey brats, the greatest effort he had ever made on his son's and daughter's behalf having been to place them in his sister's care, upon the death of his long-suffering wife.

Lady Bellingham, childless, and devoted to a brother who recalled her existence only when he found himself in straits from which it was in her power to rescue him, was delighted with the charge, and could not imagine that a boy of twelve, and a girl of fifteen could be the least trouble in the world. She had been a widow for some few years, living a somewhat hand-to-mouth existence, and she had very soon discovered that a boy of school age, and a girl requiring a governess, were expensive luxuries. She had a small fortune of her own, besides a much smaller join-ture, and generally relied upon her luck at all games of chance to bridge the gap between her income and her expenditure. She gave charming little parties at her house in Clarges Street, and was so successful at the faro-table that the idea of turning her propensity for cards to good account gradually took root in her mind. Mr Lucius Kennet, appearing suddenly in London with the news of Captain Grantham's death in Munich, was happy to lend her ladyship the benefit of his experience and advice, and even to deal for her, at her first faro-bank. It had really answered amazingly well, and had even provided funds for the purchase of a pair of colours for Mr Christopher Grantham, upon that young gentleman's leaving school.

At the outset, it had been no part of Lady Bellingham's plan to admit her niece into her gaming-saloon. She could never be quite certain how it had happened that within a month of being emancipated from the schoolroom Deborah had made her appearance at one of those cosy evening-parties, but it had happened, and the girl had been such an instant success with her aunt's male guests, and had brought such a rush of new visitors to the house that it would clearly have been folly to have excluded her.

The card-parties in Clarges Street had been held during a peak period of gaming. Gentlemen had thought nothing of staking rouleaus of fifty guineas on the turn of a card, and the profits of the modest little house had really quite justified the acquiring of a much larger establishment in St James's Square. But whether it was because there had been a great deal of absurd stuff written in the daily papers about the wickedness of such gaming-houses as Mrs Sturt's, and Lady Buckingham's, which might have caused the attendances to fall off a trifle; or whether because the expenses of the house in St James's Square were much heavier than Lady Bellingham had anticipated, there had not been any profits to enjoy for several months. Of course, quite large sums of money found their way into

Lady Bellingham's pockets, but somehow or other these were always swallowed up by the tide of bills, which so inexplicably threatened to engulf the house. For the past few weeks, too, the establishment had been suffering from a run of most persistent ill-luck. The faro-bank had been broken for six thousand pounds on one disastrous evening, and a misfortune such as that was hard to recover from. Lady Bellingham had done her best by introducing the game of E.O. into her rooms, but even this had not gone very far to set matters to rights, since serious gamesters were inclined to despise it, and it certainly could not be said to improve the tone of the house. In fact, as Deborah said bitterly, it reduced it to the ranks of quite common gaming-hells.

It had been one of Lucius Kennet's ideas, well-meant, of course, but very displeasing to Miss Grantham. He had lately been talking of the new game of *roulet*, which seemed to be played on much the same principles as E.O., but Miss Grantham was determined that no *roulet* board should make its appearance in St James's Square.

Mr Kennet, when Miss Grantham joined him, was idly engaged in casting the dice, right hand against left, on a small table in the centre of the room. 'Good morning, me darlin',' he said cheerfully, not desisting from his occupation. 'Will you look at the fiend's own luck of my left hand, now? Upon my soul, it can't lose!' He cast a shrewd glance at Miss Grantham's rather pensive expression, and added: 'What's the trouble, me dear? Is it Ormskirk again, or will it be the suckling?'

'It isn't either,' replied Deborah, sitting down on the opposite side of the table. 'At least, no more than I'm used to. Lucius, what is to become of us?'

'Why, what should become of you at all?'

'My aunt is quite distracted. There are nothing but bills!'

'Ah, throw them in the fire, me dear!'

'You know well that won't answer! I wish you will stop casting the bones!'

He gathered them up into the palm of one hand, tossing them into the air, and catching them as they fell. There was a smile in his eyes as he answered: 'Your heart's not in this, is it?'

'Sometimes I think I hate it,' she admitted, sinking her chin into her cupped hands, and glowering. 'Oh, the devil, Lucius! I'm no gamester!'

'You chose it, me darlin'. I'd say 'twas in your blood.'

'Well, and so I thought, but it's tedious beyond anything I ever dreamed of! I think I will have a cottage in the country one day, and keep hens.'

He burst out laughing. 'God save the hens! And you supping off lobsters every night, and wearing silks, and fal-lals, and letting the guineas drip through the pretty fingers of you!'

Her eyes twinkled; the corners of her humorous mouth quivered responsively. 'That's the devil of it,' she confessed. 'What's to be done?'

'There's the suckling,' he drawled. 'I doubt he'd be glad to give you your cottage, if it's that you want, so you might play at keeping farm, like the sainted French Queen, God rest her soul!'

'You know me better!' she said, with a flash. 'Do you think I would serve a romantic boy such a turn as that? A rare thing for him to find himself tied to a gamester five years his elder!'

'You know, Deb,' he said, watching the rise and fall of his dice through half-shut eyes, 'there are times I've a mind to run off with you meself.'

She smiled, but shook her head. 'When you're foxed, maybe.'

His hand shut on the dice; he turned his head to look at

her. 'Be easy; I'm sober enough. What do you say, me darlin'? Will you throw in your lot with a worthless fellow that will never come to any good in this world, let alone the next?'

'Are you offering for me, Lucius?' she demanded, blinking at him.

'Sure I'm offering for you! It's mad I am entirely, but what of that? Come adventuring with me, me love! I'll swear you've the spirit for it!'

She gave him one of her clear looks. 'If I loved you, Lucius. I don't, you see. Not as your wife, but only as your good friend.'

'Ah well!' he said, tossing up the dice again, 'I doubt it's all for the best!'

'Indeed, I don't think you would make a very good husband,' she said reflectively. 'You would be wishing me at the devil before a year was out.'

'I might,' he agreed.

'Besides,' she said practically, 'how should marriage with you help Aunt Lizzie out of her difficulties?'

'Ah, to hell with the old woman! You're too young to be worrying your head over her troubles, me dear, believe you me!'

'It's when you talk like that I like you least, Lucius,' she said.

He shrugged. 'Have it as you will. What's it to be? Will you have a *roulet* table or the noble Earl of Ormskirk?'

'I will have neither!'

'Tell that to your aunt, Deb, and see how she takes it.'

'What do you mean?' she asked fiercely.

'God bless us all, girl, if she were not playing his lordship's game for him, what possessed the silly creature to borrow money from him?'

'You are thinking of the mortgage of this house! She had no notion——'

'That, and the bills his lordship bought up, all out of the goodness of his heart, you'll be asking me to believe.'

Her cheeks whitened. 'Lucius, he has not done that?'

'Ask the old lady.'

'Oh, poor Aunt Lizzie!' she exclaimed. 'No wonder she is so put-about! Of course she would never have the least notion that that horrid man would use them to force me to become his mistress! And I won't! I'll go to prison rather!'

'Prison is a mighty uncomfortable place, me dear.'

'He'd not do that!' she said confidently. 'This is all conjecture! He has used no threats to me. Indeed, I am very sure he is too proud. But, oh, I would give anything to get those bills out of his hands!'

He threw her an ironical glance. 'I'm thinking you'd best ask your rich new friend to buy 'em back for you, me darlin'. It's delighted I'd be to help you, but my pockets are to let, as well you know.'

'I wish you will not be absurd!' she said crossly. 'It's ten to one I shall never set eyes on Ravenscar again, and if I did—oh, don't be a fool, Lucius, for I'm in no funning humour!'

The door opened to admit Mortimer. 'Mr Ravenscar has called, miss, and desires to see you. I have shown him into the Yellow Saloon.'

'Faith, it's heaven's answer, Deb!' said Mr Kennet, chuckling.

'Mr Ravenscar?' repeated Miss Grantham incredulously. 'You must have mistaken!'

The butler silently held out the salver he was carrying. Miss Grantham picked up the visiting-card on it, and read in astonishment its simple legend. *Mr Max Ravenscar* ran the flowing script, in coldly engraved letters.

CHAPTER V

MR RAVENSCAR was standing by the window in the Yellow Saloon, looking out. He was dressed in topboots, and leather breeches, with a spotted cravat round his throat; and a drab-coloured driving coat with several shoulder-capes reached to his calves. He turned, as Miss Grantham entered the room, and she saw that some spare whip-lashes were thrust through one of his buttonholes, and that he was carrying a pair of driving-gloves of York tan.

'Good morning,' he said, coming a few paces to meet her. 'Do you care to drive round the Park, Miss Grantham?'

'Drive round the Park?' she repeated, in a surprised tone.

'Yes, why not? I am exercising my grays, and came here to beg the honour of your company.'

She was conscious of a strong inclination to go with him, but said foolishly: 'But I am not dressed to go out!'

'I imagine that might be mended.'

'True, but——' She broke off, and raised her eyes to his face. 'Why do you ask me?' she asked bluntly.

'Why, from what I saw here last night, ma'am, it would appear to be impossible to be private with you under this roof.'

'Do you wish to be private with me, Mr Ravenscar?'

'Very much.'

She was aware of a most odd sensation, as though an obstruction had leapt suddenly into her throat on purpose to choke her. Her knees felt unaccountably weak, and she knew that she was blushing. 'But you barely know me!' she managed to say.

66

'That is another circumstance that can be mended. Come, Miss Grantham, give me the pleasure of your company, I beg of you!'

She said with a little difficulty: 'You are very good. Indeed, I should like to! But I must change my dress, and you will not care to keep your horses standing.'

'You will observe, if you glance out of this window, that my groom is walking them up and down.'

'You leave me nothing to say, sir. Grant me ten minutes' grace, and I will gladly drive out with you.'

He nodded, and moved to open the door for her. She glanced up at him under her lashes as she passed him, and was once more baffled by his expression. He was the strangest creature! Too many men had been attracted to her for her to fail to recognize the particular warm look in a man's eyes when they fell upon the woman of his fancy. It was not in Mr Ravenscar's eyes; but if he had not fallen a victim to her charms what in the world possessed him to invite her to drive out with him?

It did not take her long to change her chintz gown for a walking dress. A green bonnet with an upstanding poke, and several softly curling ostrich plumes, admirably framed her face, and set off the glory of her chestnut locks. She was conscious of looking her best, and hoped that Mr Ravenscar would think that she did him credit.

Lady Bellingham, informed of the proposed expedition, wavered between elation, and a doubt that her niece ought not to drive out alone with a gentleman she had met but once before in her life; but the obvious advantages of Deborah's fixing Mr Ravenscar's interest soon outweighed all other considerations. Lucius Kennet chose to be amused, and to quiz Miss Grantham unmercifully on having made such an important conquest, but she answered him quite crossly, telling him it was no such thing, and that she thought such jests extremely vulgar.

It was consequently with a slightly heightened colour that she presently rejoined Ravenscar in the Yellow Saloon. Glancing critically at her, he was obliged to admit that she was a magnificent creature. He accompanied her downstairs to the front door, where they were met by Kennet, who came lounging across the hall to see them off.

Ravenscar and he exchanged a few civilities, and the groom led the grays up to the door. Mr Kennet inspected them with a knowledgeable eye, while Ravenscar gave Miss Grantham his hand to assist her to mount into the curricle, and said that he should back them to beat Filey's pair.

They were, indeed, beautiful animals, standing a little over fifteen hands, with small heads, broad chests and thighs, powerful quarters, and good, arched necks.

'Ah, I'll wager they are sweet goers!' Mr Kennet said, passing a hand over one satin neck.

'Yes,' Ravenscar acknowledged. 'They are beautiful steppers.'

He got up into the curricle, while the groom still stood to the grays' heads, and spread a rug over Miss Grantham's knees. Taking his whip in his hand, and lightly feeling his horses' mouths, he nodded to the groom. 'I shan't need you,' he said briefly. 'Servant, Mr Kennet!'

Both the groom, and Kennet stepped back, and the grays, which were restive, plunged forward on the kidney-stones that paved the square.

'Don't be alarmed!' Ravenscar told Miss Grantham. 'They are only a little fresh.'

'I wonder you can hold them so easily!' she confessed, repressing an instinctive desire to clutch the side of the curricle.

He smiled, but returned no answer. They swept round the corner into King Street, turned westwards, and bowled along in the direction of St James's Street.

There was sufficient traffic abroad to keep Mr Ravenscar's attention fixed on his task, for the grays, though perfectly well-mannered, chose to take high-bred exception to a wagon which was rumbling along at the side of the road, to shy playfully at a sedan, to regard with sudden misgiving a lady's feathered hat, and to decide that the lines of white posts, linked with chains, that separated the footpaths from the kennels and the road, menaced them with a hitherto unsuspected danger. But the gates leading into Hyde Park were reached without mishap, and once within them the grays settled into a fine, forward action, satisfied, apparently, to find themselves in surroundings more suited to their birth and lineage.

There were several other equipages in the Park, including some phætons, and a number of barouches. Mr Ravenscar touched his hat every now and then to acquaintances, but presently, drawing away from the other vehicles, he was able to turn his attention to his companion.

'Are you comfortable, Miss Grantham?'

'Very. Your carriage is beautifully sprung. Do you drive it in your race?'

'Oh, no! I have an especially built racing-curricle for that.'

'Shall you win?' she asked, looking up at him with a slight smile.

'I hope so. Do you mean to hazard your money on my grays?'

'Oh, I must certainly do so! But I have never the least luck, I must tell you, and shall very likely bring you bad fortune.'

'I am not afraid of that. Your luck was out last night, but I hope you may come about again.'

'That is very pretty of you, Mr Ravenscar, but I fear it was my skill rather than my luck which was at fault,' she owned.

'Perhaps.' He looped his rein dexterously as the grays

69

overtook a gig, and let it run free again as they shot past. 'It is to be hoped that your ill-luck is not consistent. It would surely be disastrous to the success of your delightful establishment if this were so.'

'It would indeed,' she agreed somewhat ruefully. 'The world is too apt to imagine, however, that a gaming-house must be a source of enormous wealth to its proprietors.'

'I collect that this is not so, Miss Grantham?'

'By no means.'

He turned to look down at her, saying with the abruptness which she found disconcerting: 'Are you in debt, Miss Grantham?'

She was quite taken aback, and did not answer for a moment. She said then, in a stiffened voice: 'What prompts you to ask me such a question, sir?'

'That is no answer,' he pointed out.

'I know of no reason why I should give you one.'

'I should have set your scruples at rest at the outset by informing you that I am not entirely ignorant of your circumstances,' he said.

She regarded him in astonishment. 'I cannot conceive how you should know anything about my circumstances, sir!'

'You—or should I say your amiable aunt?—are in debt to Lord Ormskirk.'

'I suppose he told you so,' she said in a mortified tone.

'On the contrary, my young cousin told me.'

'Adrian told you?' she exclaimed. 'You must be mistaken! Adrian knows nothing of Lord Ormskirk's dealings with my aunt!'

He reined in his horses to a walk. He thought her a remarkably good actress, but her artlessness irritated him, and it was with a sardonic inflexion that he said: 'It is you who are mistaken, Miss Grantham. Mablethorpe seemed to me to be singularly well-informed.'

'Who told him?' she demanded.

He raised his brows. 'You would have preferred him to remain in ignorance of your indebtedness to Lord Ormskirk? Well, I can appreciate that.'

'I should prefer everyone to remain in ignorance of it!' she said hotly. 'Am I to understand that Ormskirk took your cousin into his confidence? I must tell you that I find it incredible!'

'No, I apprehend that your friend, Mr Kennet, was the source of my cousin's information.'

She bit her lip, and was silent for a few moments, a good deal discomfited. When she spoke again, it was with studied lightness. 'Well! And if this is so I do not immediately perceive why you should interest yourself in the matter, Mr Ravenscar.'

'I might help you out of your difficulties.'

She suffered from a momentary dread that he was about to make her a dishonourable proposal, and gripped her hands together in her lap. It would not be the first time she had been the recipient of such proposals; she was aware that her position in her aunt's house laid her open to such attacks, and had never permitted herself to receive them in the tragic manner, rather turning them off with a laugh and a jest; but she found herself desperately hoping that Mr Ravenscar was not going to prove himself to be just like other men. Then she recalled the hard light in his eyes, and felt so sure that whatever his motive might be it was not amorous that she dared to ask: 'Why?'

'What would you wish me to reply?' he enquired. 'I will endeavour to oblige you, but the truth is that I am no fencer.'

She was by now quite bewildered, and said in as blunt a manner as his own: 'I don't understand you! We met for the first time last night, and I did not suppose that—in short, I fancied that you were much inclined to dislike

71

me, sir! Yet to-day you tell me that you might help me out of what you call my difficulties!'

'Under certain circumstances, Miss Grantham.'

'Indeed! And what circumstances are these?'

'You must be as well aware of them as I am myself,' he said. 'I am perfectly willing to be more explicit, however. I am prepared to recompense you handsomely, ma'am, for whatever disappointment you may suffer from the relinquishment of all pretensions to my cousin's hand and heart.'

She had been so much in the habit of regarding Lord Mablethorpe's infatuation for her as an absurdity that this forthright speech fell upon her ears with stunning effect. She was quite unable to speak for several moments. A tumult of emotion swelled her bosom, and her brain seethed with a jumble of thoughts. The deepest chagrin battled with a furious desire to slap Mr Ravenscar's face, to assure him, without mincing her words, that she would rather die a spinster than marry his cousin, and, after telling him her opinion of his manners, morals, and abysmal stupidity, to demand to be set down instantly. A strong inclination to burst into tears accompanied these more violent ambitions, and was followed almost immediately by a resolve to punish Mr Ravenscar in the most vindictive way open to her, and a perfectly irrational determination to show him that she was every bit as bad as he imagined her to be, if not worse. To relinquish her pretensions, as he had the insolence to call them, to Lord Mablethorpe's hand and heart for the mere asking, was no way of punishing him. She perceived that she must forgo the pleasure of slapping his face. Overcoming the constriction in her throat, she said, with very tolerable command over her voice: 'Pray what do you think a handsome recompense, Mr Ravenscar?'

'Shall we say five thousand pounds, ma'am?'

She gave a tinkle of rather metallic laughter. 'Really, sir I am afraid you are trying to trifle with me!'

'You rate your claims high,' he said grimly.

'Certainly. Your cousin is quite devoted to me.'

'My cousin, Miss Grantham, is a minor.'

'Oh, but not for long!' she said. 'I am not impatient: I can afford to wait for two months, I assure you.'

'Very well,' he said. 'I do not choose to haggle with you, ma'am. I will give you exactly double that sum for my cousin's release.'

She leaned back in the curricle, very much at her ease, schooling her lips to smile. Mr Ravenscar observed the smile, but failed to notice the dangerous glitter in the lady's eyes. 'Paltry, Mr Ravenscar,' she said gently.

'Come, Miss Grantham, that won't serve! You will get not a penny more out of me, so let us waste no time in haggling!'

'But only consider, sir!' said Miss Grantham, smoothing her lemon kid gloves over her wrists. 'You would remove from my grasp at one stroke a fortune and a title!'

'Rest assured, ma'am, that there is not the slightest possibility of your enjoying the possession of that particular fortune or title!' said Ravenscar unpleasantly.

'My dear sir, you underrate my intelligence, believe me!' said Miss Grantham, softly chiding. 'You would not have offered me money had it been possible to detach Adrian from me by any other means. You are quite in my power, you know.'

'If you refuse my terms, you will discover your mistake!' said Ravenscar, anger hardening his voice.

'Nonsense!' said Miss Grantham coolly. 'Do, I beg of you, be reasonable, sir! You cannot, I am persuaded, think me so big a fool as to let such an advantageous marriage slip through my fingers for the sake of a mere ten thousand pounds!'

'How old are you?' he demanded.

'I am twenty-five, Mr Ravenscar.'

'You would do well to accept my offer. Nothing but unhappiness could be the sequel to your marriage with a boy barely out of his tutor's hands. Think this over carefully, Miss Grantham! Adrian's calf-love will not endure, I assure you.'

'It is very possible,' she acknowledged. 'But I do not anticipate that it will wane within the next two months. I shall be at *such* pains, you see, to keep it alive.'

She had the satisfaction of knowing that she had succeeded in putting him in a rage. A muscle twitched at the corner of his mouth; she thought the expression in his eyes quite murderous, and wondered indeed if her body would be found in some secluded corner of the Park one day.

'Let me make it plain to you, Miss Grantham, since you will have it, that there is nothing I will not do to prevent my cousin's marrying a women of your order!'

She gave a gasp, but rallied enough to retort: 'Very fine talking, Mr Ravenscar! In fact, there is nothing you can do.'

'You will see, ma'am!'

She yawned. 'I protest, you are unreasonable, sir! Pray, what is to become of me if I whistle your cousin down the wind? I have made up my mind to it that it is time I became eligibly settled in the world.'

'As to eligibility, ma'am,' said Ravenscar, through his teeth, 'I apprehend that Ormskirk has plans for your future which should answer the purpose admirably!'

The palm of Miss Grantham's hand itched again to hit him, and it was with an immense effort of will that she forced herself to refrain. She replied with scarcely a tremor to betray her indignation. 'But even you must realize, sir, that Lord Ormskirk's obliging offer is not to be thought of beside your cousin's proposal. I declare, I have a great fancy to become Lady Mablethorpe.'

'I don't doubt it!' he said harshly. 'By God, if I had

my way, women of your stamp should be whipped at the cart's tail!'

'Why, how fierce you are!' she marvelled. 'And all because I have a desire to turn respectable! I daresay I shall make Adrian a famous wife.'

'A wife out of a gaming-house!' he ejaculated. 'One of faro's daughters! You forget, ma'am, that I have been privileged to observe you in your proper milieu! Do you imagine that I will permit the young fool to ruin himself by marriage with you? You'll learn to know me better!'

She shrugged. 'This is mere ranting, Mr Ravenscar. It would be well if you learned to know *me* better.'

'God forbid!' he said with a snap. 'I have learnt enough this morning to assure me that no greater disaster could befall my cousin than to find himself tied to you!'

'And is ten thousand pounds all you are prepared to offer to save your cousin from this horrid fate?' she enquired.

He looked at her in a measuring way, as though he were appraising her worth. 'It would be interesting to know what figure you set upon yourself, Miss Grantham.'

She appeared to give this matter her consideration. 'I do not know. *You* regard the affair in so serious a light that I feel I should be very green to accept less than *twenty* thousand.'

He turned his horses, and they broke into a trot again. 'Why stop at that?' he asked, with a short bark of laughter.

'Indeed, I daresay I shan't,' said Miss Grantham cordially. 'My price will rise as Adrian's birthday approaches.'

He drove on in silence for some little way, frowning heavily at the road ahead.

'How pretty the trees are, with their leaves just on the turn!' remarked Miss Grantham, in soulful accents.

He paid no heed to this sally, but once more looked down at her. 'If I engage to pay you twenty thousand

75

pounds, will you release my cousin?' he asked abruptly.

Miss Grantham tilted her head on one side. 'I own, twenty thousand pounds is a temptation,' she said. 'And yet . . . !' she added undecidedly. 'No, I think I would prefer to marry Adrian.'

'You will regret that decision, ma'am,' he said, dropping his hands, and letting the grays shoot.

'Oh, I trust not, sir! After all, Adrian is a most amiable young man, and I shall enjoy being his wife, and having a great deal of pin-money. I hope,' she added graciously, 'that you will be one of our first guests at Mablethorpe. You will see then what a fine ladyship I mean to be.'

He vouchsafed no answer to this, so after a thoughtful pause she said airily: 'Of course, there will be a good many changes to be made at Mablethorpe before I shall be ready to receive visitors. I collect that everything is shockingly old-fashioned there. The London house too! But I have a great turn for furnishing houses, and I do not despair of achieving something very tolerable.'

The contemptuous curl of Mr Ravenscar's mouth was all the sign he gave of having heard this speech.

'I mean to set up a faro-bank of my own,' pursued Miss Grantham. 'It will be very select, of course: admission only by card. To make a success of that sort of thing, one must have a certain position in the world, and *that* Adrian can give me. I will wager that my card-parties become the rage within a twelvemonth!'

'If you think, ma'am, to force up the price by these disclosures, you are wasting your time!' said Ravenscar. 'Your plans for the future come as no surprise to me.' He reined in his horses to a more sober pace, as the gates of the Park came into sight. 'You have had the chance to enrich yourself, and you have seen fit to refuse it. My offer is no longer open to your acceptance.'

She was surprised, but took care not to let it appear.

'Why, now you talk like a sensible man, sir!' she said. 'You accept the inevitable, in fact.'

They passed through the gates, and turned eastwards, bowling along with a disregard for the convenience of all other traffic which drew curses from two porters, a hackney-coachman, and a portly old gentleman who was unwise enough to try to cross the street ahead of the curricle. 'No,' said Ravenscar. 'Once more you are out in your reckoning, Miss Grantham. You have chosen to cross swords with me, and you shall see how you like it. Let me tell you that it was with the greatest reluctance that I made my offer! It goes much against the grain with me to enrich harpies!' He glanced down at her as he spoke, and encountered such a blaze of anger in her eyes that he was momentarily taken aback. But even as his brows snapped together in quick suspicion, the long-lashed lids had veiled her eyes, and she was laughing.

The rest of the drive back to St James's Square was accomplished in silence. When the curricle drew up outside her door, Miss Grantham put back the rug that covered her knees, and said with deceptive affability: 'A most enjoyable drive, Mr Ravenscar. I must thank you for having given me the opportunity to make your better acquaintance. I fancy we have both of us learnt something this morning.'

'Can you get down without my assistance?' he asked brusquely. 'I am unable to leave the horses.'

'Certainly,' she replied, nimbly descending from the high carriage. 'Good-bye, sir—or should I say *au revoir*?'

He slightly raised his hat. '*Au revoir,* ma'am!' he said, and drove on.

The door of the house was opened to Miss Grantham by Silas Wantage, who took one look at her flushed countenance, and said indulgently: 'Now, what's happened to put you into one of your tantrums, Miss Deb?'

'I am not in a tantrum!' replied Deborah furiously. 'And if Lord Mablethorpe should call, I will see him!'

'Well, that's a good thing,' said Wantage. 'For he's been here once already, and means to come again. *I* never saw anything like it, not in all my puff!'

'I wish you will not talk in that odiously vulgar way!' said Deborah.

'Not in a tantrum: oh, no!' said Mr Wantage, shaking his head. 'And me that's known you from your cradle! Your aunt says as how Master Kit's a-coming home on leave. What do you say to that?'

Miss Grantham, however, had nothing to say to it. She was an extremely fond sister, but for the moment the iniquities of Mr Ravenscar possessed her mind to the exclusion of all other interests. She ran upstairs to the little back-parlour on the half-landing, which was used as a morning-room. Lady Bellingham was writing letters there, at a spindle-legged table in the window. She looked up as her niece entered the room, and cried: 'Well, my love, so you are back already! Tell me at once, did——' She broke off, as her eyes met Miss Grantham's stormy ones. 'Oh dear!' she said, in a dismayed voice. 'What has happened?'

Miss Grantham untied her bonnet-strings with a savage jerk, and cast the bonnet on to a chair. 'He is the vilest, rudest, stupidest, horridest man alive! Oh, but I will serve him out for this! I will make him sorry he ever *dared*—I'll have no mercy on him! He shall *grovel* to me! Oh, I am in such a rage!'

'Yes, my love, I can see you are,' said her aunt faintly. 'Did he—did he make love to you?'

'Love!' exclaimed Miss Grantham. 'No, indeed! His thoughts did not lie in *that* direction! I am a harpy, if you please, Aunt Lizzie! Women like me should be whipped at the cart's tail!'

'Good heavens, Deb, is the man out of his senses?' demanded Lady Bellingham.

'By no means! He is merely stupid, and rude, and altogether abominable! I hate him! I wish I might never set eyes on him again!'

'But what did he *do*?' asked Lady Bellingham, wholly bewildered.

Miss Grantham ground her white teeth. 'He came to rescue his precious cousin from my toils! *That* was why he invited me to drive out with him. To insult me!'

'Oh dear, you thought it might be that!' said her aunt sadly.

Miss Grantham paid no heed to this interruption. 'Deb Grantham is not a fit bride for Lord Mablethorpe! To marry me would be to ruin himself! Oh, I could scream with vexation!'

Lady Bellingham regarded her doubtfully. 'But you said as much yourself, my dear. I remember distinctly——'

'It doesn't signify in the least!' said Miss Grantham. '*He* had no right to say it!'

Lady Bellingham agreed to this wholeheartedly, and after watching her niece pace round the room for several minutes, ventured to enquire what had happened during the course of the drive. Miss Grantham stopped dead in her tracks, and replied in a shaking voice: 'He tried to bribe me!'

'Tried to bribe you not to marry Adrian, Deb?' asked her aunt. 'But how very odd of him, when you had never the least intention of doing so! What can have put such a notion into his head?'

'I am sure I don't know, and certainly I don't care a fig!' replied Deborah untruthfully. 'He had the insolence to offer me five thousand pounds if I would relinquish my pretensions—my pretensions!—to Adrian's hand and heart!'

Lady Bellingham, over whose plump countenance a hopeful expression had begun to creep, looked disappointed, and said: 'Five thousand! I must say, Deb, I think that very shabby!'

'I said that I feared he was trying to trifle with me,' recounted Miss Grantham with relish.

'Well, and I am sure you could not have said anything better, my love! I declare, I did not think so meanly of him!'

'Then,' continued Miss Grantham, 'he said he would double that figure.'

Lady Bellingham dropped her reticule. 'Ten thousand!' she exclaimed faintly. 'No, never mind my reticule, Deb: it don't signify! What did you say to that?'

'I said, Paltry!' answered Miss Grantham.

Her aunt blinked at her. 'Paltry . . . Would you— would you call it *paltry,* my love?'

'I did call it paltry. I said I would not let Adrian slip through my fingers for a mere ten thousand. I *enjoyed* saying that, Aunt Lizzie!'

'Yes, my dear, but—but was it wise, do you think?'

'Pooh! what can he do, pray?' said Miss Grantham scornfully. 'To be sure, he flew into as black a temper as my own, and took no pains to conceal it from me. I was excessively glad to see him so angry! He said—about Ormskirk—— Oh, if I were a man, to be able to call him out, and run him through, and through, and through!'

Lady Bellingham, who appeared quite shattered, said feebly that you could not run a man through three times. 'At least, I don't think so,' she added. 'Of course, I never was present at a duel, but there are always seconds, you know, and they would be bound to stop you.'

'Nobody would stop *me!*' declared Miss Grantham blood-thirstily. 'I would like to carve him into mincemeat!'

'Oh dear, I can't think where you get such unladylike notions!' sighed her aunt. 'I do trust that you did not say so?'

'No, I said that I thought I should make Adrian a famous wife. That made him angrier than ever. I thought he might very likely strangle me. However, he did not. He asked me what figure I set upon myself.'

Lady Bellingham showed a flicker of hope. 'And what answer did you make to *that*, Deb?'

'I said I should be very green to accept less than twenty thousand!'

'Less than—— My love, where are my smelling-salts? I do not feel at all the thing! Twenty thousand! It is a fortune! He must have thought you had taken leave of your senses!'

'Very likely, but he said he would pay me twenty thousand if I would release Adrian.'

Lady Bellingham sank back in her chair, holding the vinaigrette to her nose.

'So then,' concluded Miss Grantham, with reminiscent pleasure, 'I said that after all I preferred to marry Adrian.'

A moan from her aunt brought her eyes round to that afflicted lady. 'Mablethorpe instead of twenty thousand pounds?' demanded her ladyship, in quavering accents. 'But you told me positively you would not have him!'

'Of course I shall not!' said Miss Grantham impatiently. 'At least, not unless I marry him in a fit of temper,' she added, with an irrepressible twinkle.

'Deb, either you are mad, or I am!' announced Lady Bellingham, lowering the vinaigrette. 'Oh, it does not bear thinking of! We might have been free of all our difficulties! Ring the bell; I must have the hartshorn!'

Deborah looked at her in incredulous astonishment. 'Aunt Eliza! You did not suppose—you *could* not suppose that I would allow that odious man to buy me off?' she gasped.

'Kit might have bought his exchange! Not to mention the mortgage!' mourned her ladyship.

'Kit buy his exchange out of—out of *blood-money*? He would prefer to sell out!'

'Well, but, my love, there is no need to call it by such an ugly name, I am sure! You do not want young Mablethorpe, after all!'

'Aunt, you would not have had me accept a bribe!'

'Not an *ordinary* bribe, dear Deb! Certainly not! But twenty thousand——Oh, I can't say it!'

'It was the horridest insult I have ever received!' said Deborah hotly.

'You can't call a sum like that an insult!' protested her ladyship. 'If only you would not be so impulsive! Think of poor dear Kit! He is coming home on leave too, and he says he has fallen in love. Was ever anything so unfortunate? It is all very well to talk of insults, but one must be practical, Deb! Seventy pounds for green peas, and here you are throwing twenty thousand to the winds! And the end of it will be that you will fall into Ormskirk's hands! I can see it all! The only comfort I have is that I shall very likely die before it happens, because I can feel my spasms coming on already.'

She closed her eyes as she spoke, apparently resigning herself to her approaching end. Miss Grantham said defiantly: 'I am not in the least sorry. I will make him sorry he ever dared to think I was the kind of creature who would entrap a silly boy into marrying me!'

This announcement roused Lady Bellingham to open her eyes again, and to say in a bewildered way: 'But you told me you said you would marry him!'

'I said so to Ravenscar. *That* is nothing!'

'But I don't see how he can help thinking it if you told him so!'

'Yes, and I told him also, that I meant to set up my own faro-bank when I am Lady Mablethorpe,' nodded Miss Grantham, dwelling fondly on these recollections. 'And I said I should change everything at Mablethorpe. He looked as though he would have liked to hit me!'

Lady Bellingham regarded her with a fascinated stare. 'Deb, you were not—you were not *vulgar*?'

'Yes, I was. I was as vulgar as I could be, and I shall be more vulgar presently!'

'But *why*?' almost shrieked her ladyship.

Miss Grantham swallowed, blushed, and said in a small-girl voice: 'To teach him a lesson!'

Lady Bellingham sank back again. 'But what is the use of teaching people lessons? Besides, I cannot conceive what he is to learn from such behaviour! I do hope, my dearest love, that you have not got a touch of the sun! I do not know how you can be so odd!'

'Well, it is to punish him,' said Miss Grantham, goaded. 'He will not like it at all when he hears that Adrian is going to marry me. I daresay he will try to do something quite desperate.'

'Offer you more money?' asked Lady Bellingham, once more reviving.

'If he offered me a hundred thousand pounds I would fling it in his face!' declared Miss Grantham.

'Deb,' said her aunt earnestly, 'it is *sacrilege* to talk like that! What—*what*, you unnatural girl, is to become of me? Only remember that odious bill from Priddy's, and the wheatstraw, and the new barouche!'

'I know, Aunt Lizzie,' said Deborah, conscience-stricken. 'But indeed I could not!'

'You will have to marry Mablethorpe,' said Lady Bellingham despairingly.

83

'No, I won't.'

'My head goes round and round!' complained her aunt, pressing a hand to her brow. 'First you say that Ravenscar will be sorry when he hears you are to marry Mablethorpe, and now you say you won't marry him!'

'I shall pretend that I am about to marry him,' explained Miss Grantham. 'Of course I shall not do so in the end!'

'Well!' exclaimed Lady Bellingham. 'That is shabby treatment indeed! I declare it would be quite shocking to serve the poor boy such a trick!'

Miss Grantham looked guilty, and twisted her ribbons. 'Yes, but I don't think that he will mind, Aunt Lizzie. In fact, I daresay he will be very glad to be rid of me presently, because ten to one he will fall in love with someone else, and I assure you I don't mean to be *kind* to him! And in any event,' she added, with a flash of spirit, 'it serves him right for having such an abominable cousin!'

CHAPTER VI

WHEN Lord Mablethorpe was admitted to the house in St James's Square, he was quite as much surprised as delighted to find Miss Grantham in a most encouraging mood. He was so accustomed to her laughing at him, and teasing him for his adoration of her, that he could scarcely believe his ears when, in response to his usual protestations of undying love, she allowed him to take her hand, and to press hot kisses on to her veined wrist.

'Oh, Deb, my lovely one, my dearest! If you would only marry me!' he said, in a thickened voice.

She touched his curly, cropped head caressingly. 'Perhaps I will, Adrian.'

He was transported with rapture immediately, and

caught her in his arms. 'Deb! Deb, you are not funning? You mean it?'

She set her hands against his chest, holding him off a little. He was so young, and so absurdly vulnerable, that she felt compunction stir in her breast, and might have abandoned this way of punishing his cousin had she not recalled Ravenscar's prediction that this youthful ardour would not last. She knew enough of striplings to be reasonably sure that this was true; and indeed wondered if it would even endure for two months. So she let him kiss her, which he did rather inexpertly, and gave him to understand that she was perfectly serious.

He began at once to make plans for the future. These included a scheme for a secret wedding to be performed immediately, and it took Deborah some time to convince him that such hole-in-corner behaviour was not to be contemplated for an instant. He had a great many arguments to put forward in support of his plan, but was presently brought to abandon it, on the score of its being very uncomplimentary to his bride. This notion, once delicately instilled into his brain, bore instant fruit. He was resolved to follow no course that could suggest to his world that he was in any way ashamed of Miss Grantham. At the same time, he continued to be urgent with Deborah to permit him to announce their betrothal in the columns of the *London Gazette*, and was with difficulty restrained from running off to arrange for the insertion of his advertisement then and there. Miss Grantham would not hear of it. She pointed out that, as a minor, it would lie in the power of his mother to contradict the advertisement in the next issue of the paper. He agreed to it that this would be very bad, and was obliged to admit that Lady Mablethorpe would be quite likely to take such prompt and humiliating action. But he thought it would be proper to advise his relations of the impending marriage, and begged

Deborah's permission to do so. She was half-inclined to refuse it, but a suspicion that Lady Mablethorpe had probably been behind Mr Ravenscar's abominable conduct induced her to relent. She said that Adrian might tell his mother, but in strict confidence.

'I daresay there will be a great deal of unpleasantness,' she pointed out, 'and you would not wish to lay me open to anything of that nature, would you?'

No, indeed! He wished nothing less. She was right, as always. 'Only, Deb, I should like to tell Max. You will not object to that?'

'Not in the least!' said Deborah, with quite unnecessary emphasis. 'I wish you will tell him!'

'Oh, that is famous!' he said, catching her hand to his lips again. 'I knew you could not mind Max's knowing! In point of fact, he knows my feelings: he is a good fellow, Max! He always gets me out of scrapes, you know, and he don't preach, like my uncle. I always tell him things.'

'Oh!' said Miss Grantham.

'You will like him excessively,' his lordship assured her. 'He is quite my best friend. He is one of my trustees, you know.'

'Oh?' said Miss Grantham again.

'Yes, and that is in part why I told him about you, my dearest. Well, I did hope that he might be brought to explain it all to my mother, but he would not. I was devilish angry with him at the time, but I daresay he was right. I told him I did not think that *he* would fail me, but he promised me that he did not mean to, so you will see that everything will come about famously!'

'He said that, did he?' said Miss Grantham, in an odd voice. 'Indeed!'

His lordship's blue eyes smiled into hers with such an unclouded look of innocence that she shut her lips tightly

86

on the words that were hovering on the tip of her tongue. 'Why do you say it like that, Deb? Don't you like Max?'

Miss Grantham was obliged to exercise her powers of self-restraint to the utmost. She would have been very happy to have poured the whole story of the insults she had endured into Lord Mablethorpe's ears. That would shatter for ever Adrian's blind trust in his cousin, and destroy whatever influence Ravenscar possessed over the boy. If he were fond of Adrian, which he seemed to be, it might even make him as unhappy as he deserved to be. Unfortunately, it was certain that it would make Adrian unhappy too. Miss Grantham resolved, with real heroism, to keep her dealings with Ravenscar secret. She said that she was not yet much acquainted with him.

'You will soon know him better,' promised Adrian. 'You shall meet Arabella too—she is his half-sister. She is coming up to town to-day, and Max is actually going to take her to the ridotto at Vauxhall Gardens to-morrow! You must know that Max is a sad case, and will never go to such parties in the ordinary way!'

'A ridotto?' Deborah exclaimed, forming another resolve. 'Oh, how much I should like to go!'

'Would you? Would you indeed, Deb?' Mablethorpe said eagerly. 'I did not ask you, because you never will consent to go anywhere with me! But I should like of all things to escort you there! We will take sculls at Westminster, I'll bespeak a box at Vauxhall, and we will spend the jolliest evening!'

He was not quite so enthusiastic about Miss Grantham's suggestion that Lucius Kennet, and some other lady, should join the party, but upon its being pointed out to him that it would not be seemly for his adored Deborah to be seen alone with him, he acquiesced with a good grace, and very soon went off to make all the preparations imaginable to ensure the evening's being a success.

Miss Grantham also made preparations, the first of these being to sally forth to Bond Street to buy herself some coquelicot ribbon, and a headdress quite as startling as any which her aunt could show. Poppy-coloured ribbons with a *vive bergère* gown of green and white stripes would, she fancied, present a shockingly garish picture. If that failed to introduce the desired note of vulgarity, the head, which was constructed of a wisp of lace, a bunch of ribbons, and three of the tallest, most upstanding ostrich plumes ever seen, could not but achieve its object.

Mr Lucius Kennet did not put in a second appearance in St James's Square until an advanced hour in the evening. When he did stroll into the gaming-saloon, Miss Grantham, who was standing behind the dealer at the faro-table, moved across the floor to meet him, and at once drew him aside. 'Lucius,' she said anxiously, 'do you know a vulgar widow?'

He burst out laughing. 'Sure, what would you be wanting with the same, me darlin'?'

'Well, she need not be a widow,' conceded Deborah. 'Only my aunt said that it was a pity you were acquainted with so many vulgar widows, that I thought—— The thing is that I am going to Vauxhall with Mablethorpe tomorrow, and I shall need you. And the widow too, of course.'

It was not to be expected that Lucius Kennet would refrain from demanding an explanation of this odd request. Miss Grantham, who had been in the habit of confiding all her troubles to him, then took him into the adjoining saloon, and gave him a fluent account of the day's events. He whistled when he heard of her refusal to accept twenty thousand pounds, but he had a very lively sense of humour, and her scheme for revenging herself appealed to him so strongly that he vowed he did not blame her for

88

choosing it in preference to sordid gold. He promised to present himself at Mablethorpe's box at Vauxhall with a widow who should be everything that was desired, and went off, still chuckling, to join a number of gentlemen seated round a table, and intent upon hazard.

Mr Ravenscar, meanwhile, had driven away in a towering rage, quite as heartily resolved as Miss Grantham to be revenged. To be crossed was a new experience, for from the circumstances of his father having died when he was still a very young man, and of his having come into the possession of the Ravenscar fortune, he had been used for a number of years to have everything very much as he chose. He was, in fact, accustomed to flattery, and downright sycophancy, both of which he despised; and since they had discovered from experience that he had a decided will of his own, neither his stepmother nor his aunt ever made any but half-hearted attempts to influence him. To be out-faced, therefore, by a girl from a gaming-house was something he had never anticipated, nor, consequently, made any plans to counter. He had been as surprised as he was enraged by the intransigent attitude assumed by Miss Grantham; his pride, bruised at the outset by the necessity of buying off such a creature, had now received a wound from which it would be long before it recovered. The thoughts he cherished about the lady were quite as unkind as any she indulged towards him; and his will was now set on rescuing Adrian from her toils without enriching her by as much as a farthing.

But although Mr Ravenscar's imperious temper was hot, it was by no means ungoverned, since he was, as Miss Grantham had at first supposed, a sensible, even a hardheaded man. After dwelling grimly upon every circumstance of his encounter with Deborah, he was obliged to confess that her behaviour was not only unexpected, but almost inexplicable. His dislike of not getting his own way, coupled with the conviction of an infuriated moment that no price would be too heavy to pay to extricate Adrian from such an entanglement, had prompted him to make his final offer. The offer was regretted as soon as it was made, for twenty thousand pounds was a fantastic figure, and Mr Ravenscar disliked being swindled as much as he disliked having his will crossed. But the very magnitude of the sum ought at least to have given Miss Grantham pause. She had indeed pretended to consider the matter, but he was convinced that this was the merest affectation. She had never the smallest intention of relinquishing Adrian.

Having observed her demeanour towards his cousin, Ravenscar was perfectly certain that she did not feel a spark of love for him. He could only suppose that she had set her heart on acquiring a title, and a position in the world of *ton*. He acknowledged that he had not, at their first meeting, thought this of her. Reflecting, he admitted that on the whole he had been rather pleasantly surprised by her. She had a frank way of looking at one, and very easy, unaffected manners, quite at variance with the airs she had assumed during their drive together. Mr Ravenscar remembered the flash he had seen in her eyes, and frowned again. Had the circumstances been other than they were, he would almost have suspected her of being very angry. Her position in her aunt's house, her enslavement of a green boy out of the schoolroom, her connection with such a notorious rake as Ormskirk, must, however, put such a possibility out of count. He decided that she was playing a deep game, and registered a mental oath to frustrate her. But while he was turning over plans in his head, still that seed of doubt troubled his mind, and was presently fostered by a hurried visit from Lord Mable-thorpe.

His lordship paid his second morning call in Grosvenor

Square scarcely an hour after Ravenscar reached the house again, after taking his grays to Kensington and back. Hearing that his cousin was in his library, he declined being announced, but erupted upon Ravenscar without ceremony, saying impetuously as he entered the room: 'Max! I am very sorry—you won't mind, I am persuaded!—I find I cannot go with you to Vauxhall to-morrow!'

'Very well,' replied Ravenscar. 'Have a glass of Madeira!'

'Well, really I ought to be on my way! However, perhaps—I have a toast to drink, Max!'

Ravenscar poured out the wine into two glasses. 'Is it a momentous one? Shall I send for the Burgundy?'

Adrian laughed. 'No, I like your Madeira. I must tell you that I have just come this instant from St James's Square.'

Ravenscar paused in the act of picking up his glass. He shot a quick, frowning look at his cousin. 'Indeed!'

'Yes, and so I came on here at once. I had to see you!'

Ravenscar stiffened, and turned to face his lordship. 'Yes?'

'Max, she has consented at last!' Adrian said joyfully. 'She says she will marry me as soon as I come of age!'

Ravenscar's eyes remained fixed on the handsome young face confronting him, a startled expression in them. 'Is that all she said?' he demanded.

'Good God, what more could I desire to hear from her? What a fellow you are, to be sure! She considers it would be unwise to announce the betrothal, but she made no objection to my telling you, and my mother, of course.'

'Oh, she made no objection to that? You said, in fact, that you would tell me?'

'Yes, certainly, and she said I might do so with her goodwill. Max, I am the happiest man alive! And that is why I cannot go with your party to Vauxhall. I knew you would understand! Deb has a great fancy to go there, and I am to escort her. I am off now to bespeak a box, and supper. But first we must drink to my betrothal!'

Ravenscar picked up his glass. 'I will drink to your future happiness,' he said.

Adrian tossed off his wine, and set the glass down. 'Well, that is the same thing. I must be off! I shall see you in a day or two, I daresay.'

'At Vauxhall, no doubt. Do you value my advice?'

'Why, you know I do!' Adrian said, pausing, with his hand on the door, and looking back.

'Say nothing of this to your mother.'

'Oh, you are too late! I have told her! Of course, she don't like it, but only wait until she is acquainted with Deb! She will very soon change her opinion.'

It was fortunate that he was in haste to be off, and so did not wait long enough to see the expression in his cousin's face. A look of contemptuous disbelief made Mr Ravenscar appear rather saturnine, and must have startled his unsuspicious relative. But he went away in happy ignorance of Ravenscar's thoughts, bent only on making every arrangement for Miss Grantham's entertainment on the following evening.

He left his cousin a prey to conflicting emotions. Rage at Miss Grantham for having countered his attack so swiftly, rage at her impudence in encouraging Adrian to inform him of the engagement, struggled with the first tiny shoots of that seed of doubt in his mind. It might be that Deborah was seeking to force up her price: but could she possibly hope for a larger sum than had already been offered to her? Considering this, he recalled that she had rallied him, on their first meeting, on being the rich Mr Ravenscar. She had heard him lay a preposterous bet; perhaps she imagined that his fondness for Adrian would induce him to lay out some vast sum for his redemption.

She should discover her mistake! But she had not told Adrian of her drive with him in the Park that morning. He was unable to find a motive to account for this forbearance. In his present white-hot ardour, Adrian would most assuredly have taken up the cudgels in her defence. She could have had nothing whatsoever to fear through laying bare the whole to Adrian, and she must have known this. What the devil was the wench up to? She might have destroyed at a blow any influence he had ever had over Adrian, and, incalculably, she had refrained from doing it. Mr Ravenscar began, reluctantly, to feel interested in the workings of Miss Grantham's mind.

The knowledge that Adrian had informed his parent of Deborah's acceptance of his hand prepared Ravenscar for the inevitable sequel. Before the day was out, Lady Mablethorpe's lozenge-carriage had drawn up in Grosvenor Square, and her ladyship, awe-inspiring in purple lustring and nodding plumes, was demanding to see her nephew.

Her call followed hard upon the arrival from Tunbridge Wells of Mrs and Miss Ravenscar, and she entered the house to find herself in a hall piled high with cloak-bags, portmanteaus, and bandboxes, which several harassed servants were endeavouring to remove with all possible despatch. She was annoyed to find that she had mistimed her visit, but after a moment's hesitation she decided to remain, and requested the butler to send in her card to Mrs Ravenscar.

She was almost immediately desired to step upstairs to the drawing-room, where she found her sister-in-law lying on a satin sofa, with her smelling-salts in her hand, and a glass of ratafie-and-water on a small table beside her. Chattering animatedly to Ravenscar, by the window, her niece, Arabella, presented an agreeable picture in a flowered gown with fluttering ribbons, and a demure fichu round her neck.

Miss Ravenscar bore very little resemblance to her mother, who was a classically beautiful woman of pale colouring, and rather expressionless features. Miss Ravenscar was a tiny brunette, with the most vivid, mischievous little face imaginable. She was quite as dark as her half-brother, and much better-looking. Her short upper lip had the most enchanting lift; her pansy-eyes sparkled as she talked, and a pair of dimples played at hide-and-seek at the corners of her mouth. When she caught sight of her aunt, she came running across the room to meet her, crying: 'Oh, my dear Aunt Selina, how pleased I am to see you again! Oh, *dearest* aunt, I declare I never saw such a terrifying bonnet! It makes me quite frightened of you! I wonder my cousin will let you wear such an abominable thing!'

'Arabella, my love!' expostulated Mrs Ravenscar, in feeble accents.

But Arabella's lilting smile and warm embrace quite robbed her impertinent speech of offence. Lady Mablethorpe patted her indulgently, calling her a naughty puss, and trod over to the sofa to kiss her sister-in-law's faded cheek. Privately, she considered that Olivia might very well have risen to welcome her, but she made no comment, merely remarking that she was sorry to see her looking so poorly.

'It was the journey,' explained Mrs Ravenscar, in a gently complaining tone. 'I have been telling Max he must positively have the coach-springs attended to. I thought I should have been shattered by the jolting. You must excuse my receiving you upon my sofa, but you know how the least exertion prostrates me, my dear Selina. Do, pray, be seated! How noisy it is in town! I do not know how my nerves will support it. I am conscious of all the bustle already.'

Lady Mablethorpe had little patience with such fancies,

but she was a civil woman, and for the next few minutes she listened with outward sympathy to a description of the many and varied ailments which had overtaken her sister-in-law since their last meeting.

Arabella broke in presently on her mother's lamentations, exclaiming: 'Oh, Mama, you know it is quite decided that you are not going to find London too fatiguing for you this time! I am so happy to be here again! I mean to go to all the balls, and the ridottos, and the masquerades, and the theatres, and—oh, everything! And you know you are to go with me to all the best warehouses to choose the stuffs for my new dresses, for I declare I have not a rag to my back, and no one has such good taste as you, dearest!'

Mrs Ravenscar smiled faintly, but said that she feared her health would break down under the strain.

'Well, if it does, Arabella knows she may count upon me,' said Lady Mablethorpe bracingly. 'Nothing would give me more pleasure than to take the child about a little. I have often been sorry that I had never a daughter.'

This was not strictly true, but it had the effect of making Arabella hug her ruthlessly, and call her her darling aunt. Lady Mablethorpe was more than ever convinced that it would be the greatest shame if the sweet child were not to be her daughter-in-law.

This reflection brought to her mind the purpose of her visit, and she cast a glance towards Ravenscar, so fraught with meaning that he could scarcely have remained oblivious of it. He contrived, however, to appear unaware of the silent message thus conveyed to him, and her ladyship was obliged to request the favour of a few words with him.

'Certainly,' he said. 'Will you come down to the library, ma'am?'

She accepted this not very cordial invitation, and made

her excuses to Mrs Ravenscar, promising to visit her again when she should have had time to settle down.

Ravenscar led the way downstairs, and ushered his aunt into the library. She barely waited for him to close the door before saying: 'I would not for the world mention the matter before that dear child! But the most shocking thing has happened, Max!'

'I know it,' he replied. 'Miss Grantham has accepted Adrian's offer.'

'You told me you would see the woman, Max!'

'I did see her.'

'But you did nothing! I quite depended on you! I was never so mortified!'

'I'm sorry, ma'am. My efforts on your behalf have so far been entirely unavailing. Miss Grantham will not be bought off.'

'Good God!' said her ladyship, sinking down on to the nearest chair. 'Then we are lost indeed! What is to be done?'

'I do not see that you can do anything to the purpose. You had better leave it in my hands. I am determined Adrian shall not lead that woman to the altar.'

Lady Mablethorpe shuddered. 'Is she dreadful?'

'She is an impudent strumpet!' said Mr Ravenscar coldly.

'Really, Max! Not that I doubt it! I always knew she was a hateful creature. Tell me about her! Is she beautiful, or is that poor Adrian's folly?'

'No, she is extremely handsome,' responded Ravenscar.

'In a vulgar style, I conclude? A painted hussy?'

'No. She is not painted. I cannot say that I found her vulgar at our first meeting. She has a pleasant way; her manners are a little free, but not disagreeably so; her voice is good; her air and countenance quite distinguished. As far as appearances go, she will do very well.'

'Have you taken leave of your senses?' gasped his aunt.

'No, I haven't. I said, *as far as appearances go.* Under this not unprepossessing exterior, she is a harpy.'

'Heaven help my poor boy!' moaned Lady Mablethorpe.

'I hope heaven may do so; I most certainly shall. Leave her to me, ma'am! If I have to kidnap Adrian, she shall not get her talons into him!'

She seemed to consider this suggestion on its merits, and to be not ill-pleased with it. 'Do you suppose that would answer?' she asked.

'No.'

'Then what in the world is the use of thinking of such a thing?' she demanded crossly.

'I am not thinking of it. I would sooner kidnap the girl.'

'Max!' exclaimed his aunt, as an unwelcome thought entered her brain. 'Do not tell me that she has got *you* under her odious spell!'

'You may rest perfectly at ease on that score, ma'am,' he said harshly. 'I do not recall when I have met any woman whom I disliked more!'

She was relieved in a slight measure, but said: 'Do you think her determined to marry my unfortunate boy?'

'I am not sure. It may well be that she is trying to frighten us into offering her more money. Adrian's birthday is all too close at hand, and she knows it. Her behaviour in coming into the open points that way.'

'We shall have to give her whatever she asks,' said Lady Mablethorpe gloomily.

'I have already offered her twenty thousand,' he said, in a curt tone.

Her ladyship changed colour. 'Twenty thousand! Are you mad? The estate can never stand it!'

'Don't alarm yourself!' he said ironically. 'I was not proposing to pledge Adrian's fortune.'

She stared at him, quite astonished. 'Well, I must say, Max, I never looked for such generosity from you! I am very grateful, I assure you, but——'

'You have nothing to thank me for,' he interrupted. 'She refused.'

'She must be out of her senses!'

'I know nothing of that, but she has certainly mistaken her man.'

She moved restlessly in her chair. 'I wish I might see the woman!'

His lips curled. 'So you may, if you care to accompany us to Vauxhall to-morrow. Adrian is to take her there, to the ridotto.'

'Flaunting him in the eyes of the world!' she cried indignantly.

'Precisely. Or in my eyes: I cannot be certain which.'

She got up with an air of resolution. 'Well, I will go with you. I daresay Olivia will be glad to let me take her place. Perhaps my deluded boy may be brought to a sense of his folly if he sees his mother when he has that creature on his arm!'

'I hope he may,' responded Ravenscar. 'I would not myself be willing to hazard a penny on it, however.'

CHAPTER VII

LADY BELLINGHAM'S emotions when she beheld her niece on the following evening threatened for a moment or two to overcome her. She could only stare at her with horrified eyes, and open and shut her mouth in an ineffective way.

Miss Grantham had come into her dressing-room to borrow her rouge-pot, and some patches. The *vive bergère* dress had always been arresting, for its green stripes were quite an inch broad, but until its owner had embellished it with knots of coquelicot ribbons it had been quite unexceptionable. It was amazing, thought poor Lady Bellingham, what a difference a few yards of ribbon could make! But even those shocking ribbons faded into insignificance beside the atrocity which Deborah had chosen to pin on to her elaborate coiffure. Fascinated, Lady Bellingham blinked at those three upstanding plumes, springing from a bed of gauze, and ribbon, and lace.

'I should like,' said Miss Grantham blandly, 'to borrow your garnets, Aunt Lizzie, if you please.'

Lady Bellingham found her voice. 'Garnets? With that dress? You cannot! Deb, for the love of heaven!'

'They are just what I need,' said Deborah, going to the dressing-table, and opening the jewel-casket that stood on it. 'You'll see!'

Lady Bellingham covered her eyes with her hand. 'I don't want to see!' she said. 'You look—you look like some dreadful creature from the stage!'

'Yes, I think I do too,' replied her niece, apparently pleased. 'Oh, do but look, aunt! Nothing could be more vulgar!'

Lady Bellingham permitted herself one glance at the garnets flashing round Deborah's throat, and in the lobes of her ears, and gave a groan. 'You cannot mean to go out looking such a figure of fun! I implore you, Deb, take off that shocking head!'

'Not for the world!' said Deborah, clasping a couple of bracelets round her wrists. 'But I must paint my face a little, and put on just one patch.'

'No one wears patches now!' protested her aunt. 'Oh, Deb, what are you about? And why did you have your hair powdered, pray? It makes you look thirty years old at least! For heaven's sake, child, if you must wear a patch let it be a *small* one, not that great vulgar thing!'

Miss Grantham gave a gurgle of laughter, and stood back to survey her image in the mirror. 'Dear Aunt Lizzie, I told you that I was going to be vulgar! I look famous!'

'Deb!' said her aunt, in anguished accents. 'Do but think of that poor young Mablethorpe! How can you be so unfeeling as to go out in his company looking so odd? He will very likely be ready to sink into the ground!'

'I daresay he will notice nothing amiss,' said Miss Grantham optimistically. 'And if he does, it won't signify.'

Lord Mablethorpe was in a condition when he might have been expected to be blind to any shortcomings in the dress of his adored Deborah, but not even his infatuation was strong enough to make him oblivious of that astonishing head. It obtruded itself upon his notice at the outset, since it seriously impeded Miss Grantham's entrance to the carriage which was to carry them to Westminster. She was obliged to duck her head as low as she could to get through the door, and when she sat down on the seat, the feathers brushed against the roof of the carriage. Lord Mablethorpe cast them a doubtful glance, but was too respectful to make any comment.

They took sculls at Westminster, to carry them across the river, and that nothing should be wanting to add to Miss Grantham's pleasure, and give consequence to the expedition, his lordship had lavishly arranged for a boat of French horns to attend them. Miss Grantham was touched by this boyish piece of extravagance, but could not help laughing a little.

Vauxhall Gardens, which were enjoying a run of extreme popularity, were soon reached. It was a very fine autumn evening, but although there was still daylight the walks and the alleys were already lit by a quantity of lanterns, and lamps burning in innumerable golden globes. Lord Mablethorpe piloted Miss Grantham towards the centre of the pleasure-gardens where, in a large, open space, a number of booths, or boxes, for refreshment were arranged in two wide semi-circles. The booths presented a festive appearance, being well-lit, and adorned with gay paintings on their backs. In the middle of the open space an orchestra was playing, and couples strolling about to meet and greet acquaintances, or to show off smart toilettes. Dancing was going forward in the big rotunda near at hand, and at a more advanced hour in the evening a Firework Display was promised.

The booth which Mablethorpe had hired for the night being reached, it was found that Mr Kennet and his fair partner had already arrived there, and were enjoying a somewhat noisy flirtation. One glance informed Miss Grantham that Mrs Patch was all that she had hoped. She was an improbable blonde of uncertain years, with a very much painted face, a singularly penetrating voice, and a laugh which made Mablethorpe wince. Lucius Kennet called her Clara, and seemed to be on terms of the greatest familiarity with her. He was engaged in taking snuff from her dimpled wrist when Deborah and his host joined them, and as he turned to greet the newcomers he winked once, very broadly, at Deborah.

Mrs Patch, upon being made known to Adrian, treated him with a kind of arch flattery that quite set Deborah's teeth on edge. If his lordship were momentarily taken aback by the company in which he found himself, he was far too well-bred to betray it, and at once did his best to fall in with Mrs Patch's notions of convivial behaviour. He succeeded well enough to make her hide her supposed blushes behind her fan, rap him playfully over the knuckles with it, and declare that she vowed he was the wickedest creature alive.

Under cover of this raillery, Deborah said in an awed voice to Kennet: 'Good God, Lucius, where did you find such a person?'

He removed her cloak from her shoulders. 'Why, isn't she what you told me you wanted, me dear? And me thinking I'd hit upon the very thing!'

Her lips twitched. 'Indeed, she could not be better! But how shabby it is of us to subject that poor boy to such vulgarity!'

Mr Kennet, who had had time to assimilate the full glory of Miss Grantham's dress, gave vent to one of his low whistles. He eyed her with considerable respect. 'If it's vulgarity you're talking of, me darlin'———'

She bit back a laugh, 'I know, I know! Poor Aunt Lizzie is in despair! Tell me, is Ravenscar here? Have you seen him?'

'No, but we shall have the best view of him, and he of us, God help him! for I've prowled round the booths, and found his card on the door of that empty box over there. There's little he will miss, I'm thinking.'

'Good!' said Deborah, moving forward to the front of the booth.

The green stripes, now first seen by Lord Mablethorpe, hit him most forcibly in the eye, and almost caused him to change colour. He was too inexperienced in the niceties of female fashions to think his Deborah's dress vulgar, but he did wish that she had chosen a more sober combination of colours than grass-green and coquelicot. He did not think, either, that the dusting of powder on her hair became her very well. It made her look old, almost like a stranger; while the over-large patch at the corner of her mouth he did not admire at all. As for the feathers in her headdress, he supposed, vaguely, that they must be quite the thing, but he could not help wishing that she had worn her hair simply dressed, in the way she was accustomed to.

He asked her if she would like to go into the pavilion, to dance, but she declined, saying that it was more amusing to watch the crowd passing and repassing the box. So he pulled a chair forward for her, and established himself at her elbow, while Lucius Kennet took Mrs Patch to stroll about the grounds, and to see the waterworks.

There were quite a number of fashionable people parading about the gardens, and Miss Grantham soon recognized most of the habitués of her aunt's house. The boxes began to fill up, and presently, in the one beside Ravenscar's, she observed Sir James Filey, gorgeous in a coat of puce brocade, and leaning over a chair in which a scared-looking child with pale golden ringlets, and forget-me-not blue eyes sat bolt upright, clutching a fan between her mittened hands.

The child, who was as pretty as a picture, Miss Grantham saw, could not have been more than eighteen or nineteen, and to watch a roué of Filey's years and experience leering down at her made Miss Grantham long to be able to box his ears, and send him to the right-about. There was a formidable dowager in the booth, who seemed to look upon Filey's advances with an approving eye; a harassed-looking man with a peevishly pursed mouth, who might be her husband; a young woman, whom Miss Grantham judged to be the pretty child's sister; and a stout, middle-aged man with a dull face, and an air of consequence.

Miss Grantham directed Lord Mablethorpe's attention to this party, and asked him if he knew who the child was. He did not, but after glancing at the dowager, he said: 'Oh, she must be one of the Laxton girls! That's Lady Laxton, horrid old wretch! Laxton, too. I suppose the other lady to be the eldest daughter. She was married last year to some nabob or other. My mother says Lady Laxton don't care whom she marries them to as long as there's money. Poor as church mice, the Laxtons. I know the two sons slightly. I believe there are five daughters.'

'That is certainly a cross for any mother to bear, but I hope she does not mean to marry that poor child to Filey.

Do but see how frightened the little thing looks! I wish I sat in her place! She is no match for him!'

He laughed. 'No! *You* would soon send him about his business! I have heard you give some famous set-downs!'

As he spoke, the door leading into Ravenscar's box was opened, and he saw his mother enter it, closely followed by Arabella and Ravenscar. He exclaimed: 'Good God, there is my mother! I had no notion she was to be here! She said nothing of it to me. I suppose Aunt Olivia has the spasms again, and would not come. Look, Deb! that is Arabella: isn't she a rogue?'

He waved to the party, trying to attract their attention, but although Ravenscar perceived him, and returned the salutation, Lady Mablethorpe was too busy directing one of the waiters where to place her chair, and when to serve supper, to pay any heed. But Arabella saw her cousin, and at once blew him an airy kiss. Miss Grantham thought that Arabella was rather a sweet little creature, and wondered that Adrian's fancy should have alighted on a woman five years his senior when such a charming and eligible cousin stood ready, surely, to be fallen in love with.

Adrian turned to her. 'Deb, I want to take you over, and make you known to my mother! Do please come!'

'Certainly!' replied Deborah, rising from her chair, and shaking out her full skirts.

Mr Ravenscar, meanwhile, had enjoyed only the briefest glimpse of her. This had sufficed to make him acutely aware of her headdress, but it was not until he saw her approaching the front of his box on Adrian's arm that he had the opportunity of taking in the full enormity of the green stripes, poppy-red ribbons, and crimson garnets. He was not a man who wasted much thought on female dress, but the difference between Miss Grantham's appearance to-night and her appearance on the previous two occasions when he had been in her company struck him most forcibly. He had, in fact, thought her a woman of taste, so he was a good deal astonished at the flamboyance of her attire. Recalling that he had told his aunt that Miss Grantham was not vulgar, he touched her arm, saying somewhat grimly: 'You had better be prepared to meet your future daughter-in-law, ma'am. Adrian is bringing her towards the box now.'

Lady Mablethorpe looked round immediately, and stiffened in outraged dismay at the approaching vision. She had no time to do more than throw one fulminating glance at her nephew before Adrian was leaning over the front of the box to shake hands with Arabella, saying: 'I am so glad to see you again! I had meant to call in Grosvenor Square this morning, but something happened to prevent me. Mama, I did not know you meant to come here to-night! I have brought Deb over to see you!'

The affronted matron bowed slightly, and said in frigid tones that she was happy to make Miss Grantham's acquaintance. Miss Grantham, to the uneasy surprise of her betrothed, simpered, and turned away her head, and uttered a memorable speech.

'Oh, la, ma'am—your ladyship, I *should* say!—I am sure you are monstrous good to say so! I declare I am quite of a-tremble to be standing in front of one who is to be my Mama-in-law! But Adrian would have me come across to speak to you, and I thought to myself, Well, I thought, if it *must* be, let it be at once, for I was always one to rush upon my fate, as the saying is! But there! I am sure we shall deal extremely, after all!'

'Indeed!' said Lady Mablethorpe icily.

'Oh, la, yes, ma'am! I made sure you was a dragon, and my knees quite knocked together when Adrian said you was here, but I vow and declare the instant I clapped eyes on you I knew I should love you as though you were my own Mama! And then the affability with which you said you was happy to meet me—la, I'm sure I never looked for such a degree of condescension in one so far above me!'

A muscle twitched at the corner of Mr Ravenscar's mouth. Nothing could exceed his dislike of Miss Grantham, but he had a sense of humour, and was hard put to it not to burst out laughing. If her object were to convince Lady Mablethorpe that no price would be too high to pay to rescue her son from such a woman as herself, it would certainly succeed, for her ladyship's face was rigid with disgust, and she could barely bring herself to answer with at least a semblance of civility.

Arabella, meanwhile, was watching Miss Grantham in the liveliest astonishment. 'Good gracious, are you going to marry Adrian?' she exclaimed, with that impetuosity so much regretted by her mother. 'No one said a word about it to me!'

Miss Grantham recollected Mrs Patch's arch use of a fan, and unfurled her own, and hid behind it. 'Oh, I protest, Miss Ravenscar! You must spare my blushes!'

'But are you?' asked Arabella.

'That will do, child!' said her aunt.

'Of course she is going to marry me!' Adrian declared stoutly. 'Won't you wish us happy?'

'Yes, indeed I do,' Arabella responded, with a doubtful look at Miss Grantham. 'I wish you *very* happy!'

'Adrian!' said his parent, in majestic tones. 'I should like to talk to Miss Grantham. Do you take your cousin to dance while she sits with me for half-an-hour!'

Lord Mablethorpe, hoping that the extraordinary manners which Miss Grantham had assumed upon being presented to his mother had their origin in nervousness which would wear off as the two ladies became better acquainted, readily agreed to this suggestion, and said that he would bring Miss Grantham round to the door of the box. Miss Grantham giggled, and said that it seemed absurd to be obliged to go round to the back of the booths when she was sure she could jump over the low wall in front, if only Adrian would give her his hand. Then she said that she supposed that she would have to learn to behave respectably since she was to become a Viscountess, and consented to be led round to the back of the boxes.

When she made her entrance, in the correct manner, Mr Ravenscar left the booth. He would try a fall with her himself before very long and enjoy doing it, but it was no part of his plan to join his aunt in whatever scheme she might have in mind for the discomfiture of the minx.

He returned to the box a few minutes before Adrian led Arabella back to it. One glance at the two ladies was enough to assure him that it was not Miss Grantham who had suffered discomfiture. Lady Mablethorpe was looking crushed, and the glance she cast up at her nephew was one of pathetic entreaty.

She had sustained the most shattering half-hour of her life. She had subjected Miss Grantham to a catechism which had been intended to show that young woman how very far she stood from Adrian, and how very uncomfortable she would feel in Polite Society. It had apparently failed in this laudable object. Miss Grantham had replied with the greatest readiness, and the most appalling frankness to all the searching questions put to her. She had remained throughout wholly oblivious of the most patent disapproval. She had been voluble, expansive, and shockingly vulgar; had confessed to a passion for all forms of gaming; described in quite imaginary detail the events of several horse-races she said she had attended; and expressed a desire to set up a select faro-bank in Brook Street. She had also ogled several bucks who had strolled past the box, and had claimed intimate acquaintance with three of the most notorious rakes in town. Her ladyship felt herself to be passing through a nightmare, and hailed the return of her nephew with heartfelt relief. Miss Grantham assured him that she and Lady Mablethorpe were now the greatest of friends.

He received this information with raised brows, smiled slightly, and turned to address some idle remark to his aunt. Adrian and Arabella then came back to the box, and the two parties separated.

'How could you tell me she was not vulgar!' was all her ladyship could at first bring herself to say, and that in accents of bitter reproach.

'I told you the truth. She was not vulgar when I met her. Her manner to-night was certainly assumed.'

'Assumed! In heaven's name why, if she wishes to win my consent to the match?'

'I am reasonably sure that she has no such wish. This is no doubt her way of trying to force up the price, ma'am.'

'Whatever it is it must be paid!' said her ladyship, in great agitation.

'Whatever it is it shall not be paid!' said Mr Ravenscar. 'Oh, don't put yourself in a taking, my dear aunt! I shan't let her marry Adrian!'

'How he *could*——!' she shuddered. 'Look at her now! Look at that dreadful woman with her!'

Arabella, who had been attending to this with an air of lively interest, said: 'Well, of course she was shockingly vulgar, Aunt Selina, but I could not help liking her a little, because she has such laughing eyes! And Adrian told me that she was not generally ill-at-ease, so perhaps she is not so very bad after all!'

'Ill-at-ease!' ejaculated Lady Mablethorpe. 'I saw no sign of *that*! Do you call her behaviour at this moment ill-at-ease?'

Miss Grantham was seated by this time in the front of her own box, and was laughing immoderately at something

Lucius Kennet had said to her. Her troubled swain laughed too, but in a perfunctory manner. She could do no wrong in his enamoured eyes, but he did wish that she would not laugh so loudly, or flirt so much with her fan. Ably assisted by Kennet and Mrs Patch, she contrived to make their box the most stared at of any in the circle, so that he was glad when his carefully chosen supper had been eaten, and he was able to suggest a stroll through the gardens.

Miss Grantham, who was feeling quite exhausted by this time, went with him willingly, and behaved so prettily that he was soon in a fair way towards forgetting her previous conduct. He supposed her to have been excited, and nervous at being presented to his mother, and thought no more about it. Except for the coquelicot ribbons and that towering headdress, she was again his own dear Deb, and he spent a blissful half-hour, walking with her down the many paths of the gardens, and telling her how much he loved her.

It had grown dark by this time, and the coloured lights showed up brightly against the black sky. Lord Mablethorpe found a seat in a secluded alley, and persuaded Deborah to sit down for a few minutes. He began to describe his home to her, shyly expressing the hope that she would not find it very flat in the country; and had just asked her if she would not drive out with him one day to visit Mablethorpe, which was at no great distance from London, when the sound of a sob interrupted him.

He broke off, looking about him, but he could see no one. 'I thought I heard someone crying,' he told Miss Grantham. 'Did you hear anything?'

She had not, but even as she said so, the sound came again, and from no great distance.

'Do you think we had better go away?' whispered his lordship, looking alarmed.

'Go away? Certainly not! Someone is in trouble!' replied Miss Grantham, getting up, and peering down the alley.

Yet another heavy sob reached their ears. It seemed to come from one of the small summer-houses which were dotted about the grounds. Miss Grantham walked up to it, and entered, her tall figure silhouetted by the lights behind her. A frightened gasp greeted her arrival, followed by a breathless silence.

'Is anyone here?' she asked, trying to pierce the gloom. 'Can I help you?'

A very young and scared voice answered: 'Please go away!'

By now Miss Grantham's eyes had become more accustomed to the darkness, and she was able to discern a pale form, huddled in a chair against the far wall. She made her way to this ghost-like figure, and said kindly: 'But, my dear, indeed I cannot go away and leave you in such unhappiness! Come, can I not be of assistance?'

There was a tense pause; then the voice said desolately: 'No one can help me! I wish I were dead!'

'Oh dear, is it as bad as that?' Miss Grantham asked, sitting down beside the pale figure, and drawing it into her arms. 'Won't you tell me what it is?'

Instead of complying with this request, the figure laid its head upon her shoulder, and burst into tears.

While Miss Grantham was endeavouring to soothe this grief, Lord Mablethorpe had unhooked one of the coloured lanterns from its stand outside the summer-house, and brought it inside. Its roseate light illuminated the figure in Miss Grantham's arms, a woebegone face was turned towards his lordship, and he saw that it belonged to the fair child in Lord Laxton s box.

'Why, you must be Miss Laxton!' he exclaimed.

Miss Laxton was one of the fortunate few whom tears

did not much disfigure. They sparkled on the ends of her lashes, and drowned her blue eyes, but they made no unsightly blotches on her fair skin, and did not turn the tip of her little nose red. She said, with a catch in her voice: 'Yes, I am Phœbe Laxton. Who are you, please?'

'I'm Mablethorpe,' responded his lordship, setting his lantern down on a rustic table, and drawing nearer. 'I am a little acquainted with your brothers. I wish you will tell us how we may help you!'

Miss Laxton's lip trembled, and her eyes filled again. She turned her face away. 'You cannot help me. No one can! I am very sorry to be so tiresome! I did not think anyone would find me here.'

'Don't cry!' said Miss Grantham. 'Were you hiding from Sir James Filey?'

Miss Laxton looked startled, and stammered: 'Oh, how did you know?'

'Our box is opposite yours, my dear. I saw him leaning over your chair, and I did not think you enjoyed having him so close.'

Miss Laxton shuddered, and pressed her handkerchief to her lips. 'I meant to be good!' she managed to say. 'Indeed, I did! But I hate him so! And when he took me to walk about the gardens, I—I made up my mind I would do my duty. But when he offered for me, and—and kissed me, I c-couldn't bear it, and I ran away! Oh, what shall I do?'

'You shall not marry Filey, that's certain!' declared Lord Mablethorpe, revolted by the thought.

'You don't understand,' said Miss Laxton mournfully. 'There are three more of us at home, and Mama—and Mama—you see, she will make me!'

'No one can make you marry against your will,' Miss Grantham assured her. 'You have only to be firm, my dear!'

Even as she said it, she realized that although there was great sweetness in Miss Laxton's flower-like countenance, there was not an ounce of decision. It was plain that Phœbe Laxton was a gentle little thing, easily led, and still more easily bullied.

'You do not know my Mama,' Phœbe said simply. 'She will be so dreadfully angry, and I cannot bear people to be angry with me! Even Papa says it is my duty. You see, Sir James is very rich, and he will make a most g-generous settlement, and—and—only, I am *afraid* of him, and when he kissed me I knew I could not do it!'

Lord Mablethorpe sat down on the other side of her, and took her hand. 'I should think not, indeed! But is there no one who will take your part?'

Her hand trembled a little in his, but she did not withdraw it. 'There is only my Aunt Honoria, and she lives such a long way away, and is a great invalid beside and could not come to London. Papa is a little afraid of her, and she did write to him, but—but he does not care much for letters. I thought if I could only run away to aunt, she would hide me from Papa and Mama, or—or contrive something. But then I remembered that I haven't any money, and it all seemed hopeless, and—and that's why I cried.'

Over her head Adrian's and Deborah's eyes met. 'Deb, can't we——? It's horrible to think of such a child's being tied to that devil!'

The hand stirred in his. 'Oh, do you mean you will help me? I thought no one could!' gasped Miss Laxton.

'If she goes back to the Laxtons she will be lost!' said Adrian.

'Yes, I think she will,' admitted Miss Grantham. 'I must say, I should like to throw a little rub in Filey's way.'

'We must take her away from here,' said Adrian decidedly. He bent his head over that other fair one. 'You will be quite safe with Miss Grantham, you know. She will take care of you, and we will contrive to convey you to your aunt.'

Miss Laxton sat up, a tinge of colour creeping into her cheeks. 'Oh, will you really hide me? Oh, I did not think anyone cared what became of me! How good you are! How *very* kind!'

Adrian coloured too, and said in a low voice: 'It's no such thing! Anyone would be glad to be of service to you! You may trust us to take care of you. I promise you, Filey shall not pester you again!'

'I feel so *safe* with you!' sighed Miss Laxton, lifting worshipful eyes to his face.

Miss Grantham, who had been looking pensive for some minutes, now took a decision of her own, and said with a strong suggestion of a laugh in her voice: 'Well, that is settled! You will come home with me, my dear, and we will make up our minds presently what is to be done for the best. Adrian, can we slip out of the gardens unobserved?'

He threw her a warm look of gratitude. 'There is no one like you, Deb! I knew you would not fail! Trust me, I will take you out by the gate at this end of the place!'

It was plain that his confident air greatly impressed Miss Laxton. To her, he appeared as the god in the machine, and she seemed content to leave her fate in his hands. It was left, however, to Miss Grantham to arrange the more practical details of the escape, and this she did by directing his lordship to return to their box for her cloak, and to inform Mr Kennet and Mrs Patch that she had the migraine, and was returning home immediately.

While he was performing this errand, the two ladies remained in the summer-house, Miss Laxton quite dazed by her unexpected rescue, and Miss Grantham weaving plans in her head which might have surprised, though possibly not displeased, her companion, had she been aware of them.

Adrian returned presently with Miss Grantham's cloak, and his own roquelaure. Miss Grantham wrapped Miss Laxton up in the cloak, which was by far too big for her, and drew the hood up over her pale curls. She herself accepted the roquelaure, informing his lordship that knight-errantry entailed sacrifice. They then made their way out of the gardens, without encountering any acquaintances, took sculls across to Westminster, and there picked up a hackney, which carried them safely to St James's Square. Here his lordship took leave of them, promising, however, to call early on the following morning. He kissed both their hands on the doorstep, and Miss Laxton said shyly that she did not know how to thank him for all his kindness. Miss Grantham, who thought privately that if matters had been left to his lordship, Miss Laxton would have been allowed to sob her heart out in the summer-house while he beat a strategic and alarmed retreat, waited indulgently for this touching leave-taking to come to an end, and did not knock on the door until his lordship had said his last farewell.

Silas Wantage, opening the door to admit his mistress, looked with surprise at the muffled figure of her companion, and directed an enquiring glance at Deborah. 'Now, what's to do?' he asked.

'I have brought a friend home with me, Silas. Are there many here to-night?'

'There's a few. Don't tell me you're not up to your tricks again, Miss Deb, for I wouldn't believe you!'

'Never mind that!' said Miss Grantham, with the quiver of a smile. 'You need not tell anyone that I am in the house. I don't mean to go into the saloons to-night. Tell Betty I want her in my bedchamber immediately! Come, my dear! We will slip up the backstairs, and no one will see you. Oh, Silas, remember! There was no one with me when I came home!'

'No one with you,' repeated Mr Wantage obediently. 'You'll be happy when you end in gaol, I daresay, but I won't, and that's the truth! Oh well! Be off with you, missie, and trust old Silas!'

Miss Grantham then led her guest up to her room on the second floor, by the backstairs, and was very soon joined by her maid, who carried a taper, and lit the candles for her. This damsel seemed a little surprised to discover that the unexpected visitor had come without so much as a night-bag, but accepted her mistress's involved story of trunks, bandboxes, and a fraudulent coachman, and made no demur at being requested, at this hour of the night, to prepare the spare bedchamber, and to slip a hot brick between the sheets.

Miss Laxton, meanwhile, had shed the cloak, and was trying to straighten her dishevelled locks. When Betty left the room, she turned, saying impulsively: 'Dear ma'am, I know I am putting you to a shocking deal of trouble, and I ought not to be here, but oh, I do thank you so *very* much!'

'Nonsense, child!' said Miss Grantham. 'I have had a grudge against Filey these many months. But whether I should have brought you to this house is another matter. Perhaps I ought to have explained that my aunt holds— well, gaming-parties.'

Contrary to her expectations, Miss Laxton seemed to regard this circumstance as being romantic rather than deplorable. She asked a great many questions about the house, and said wistfully that she wished that she too could preside over an E.O. table. Nothing of that nature, she explained, had ever come in her way. She had had a very dull life, sharing a horridly strict governess with her sisters, and being bullied by Mama. She thought she might do very well in a gaming-saloon, for she was excessively fond of cards, and had very often played at lottery or quadrille for hours together. It was true that she knew nothing of faro, but she thought (hopefully) that she would soon learn. Only the information that Sir James Filey patronized Lady Bellingham's house induced her to abandon the idea of offering her services in the saloons.

Miss Grantham, who had been searching in her cupboard, turned, with one of her own nightgowns over her arm. 'I am afraid you will be lost in this,' she said, 'but it must serve for to-night. To-morrow I will see about procuring clothes for you.'

'Oh, I never thought of that!' exclaimed Phœbe. 'To be sure, I have nothing in the world now but what I stand up in, and how can I travel to Wales in my party dress? Oh dear, I shall be such a charge on you, dear ma'am! But indeed my aunt will pay you back, I promise!'

'I wish you will call me Deb,' said Miss Grantham. 'As to travelling into Wales, do you know, I have been thinking it over, and I fancy I have a better scheme in my head than that?'

'What is it?' asked Phœbe, sitting down on the edge of the bed, and clasping her hands in her lap. 'I will do anything which you and Lord Mablethorpe think right.'

'Well, it seems to me,' said Miss Grantham, 'that if you go to your aunt your Papa will very likely fetch you back. It would be much better if he did not know where you were. In the morning, we will write him a letter between us. You will explain that you do not wish to marry Sir James——'

'But he knows that!'

'Very well, you will remind him of it. You will say that you have sought refuge with friends, who are taking you into the country, and that you won't return to your home unless he inserts an advertisement in the *Morning Post,* signifying that he will not ask you to marry Sir James.'

Phœbe looked a little doubtful. 'Yes, but my Papa is so obstinate that I don't suppose he will do it.'

'Fiddle! If he cannot find you, and he will not, he must do so.'

'He will be dreadfully angry,' said Phœbe, with a shiver.

'No, he will be too glad to have you restored to him. Besides, he would be just as angry if you went to your aunt, would he not?'

'Yes, indeed he would! Oh dear, do you think I ought not to have run away at all? It happened so quickly that I had scarcely time to think, and now I see that whatever I do they will be angry with me. Besides, I have no friends, so where am I to go?'

'Nowhere, silly puss! You will stay here with me until your parents relent, or until I—until Lord Mablethorpe and I think what is to be done with you.'

'Oh!' cried Phœbe, jumping up. 'If only I could! And then perhaps I could become a governess, or an actress, or something of that nature, and never, never go home again!'

'As to that,' said Miss Grantham diplomatically, 'we shall have to consult Lord Mablethorpe.'

'Oh yes! *He* will know what I ought to do!' agreed Phœbe confidently.

Miss Grantham, having no such faith in his lordship's wisdom, mentally resolved to prime him well, and led Miss Laxton away to the spare bedchamber, helped her to undress, and tucked her up snugly for the night.

CHAPTER VIII

WHEN Lady Bellingham, sipping her early chocolate in bed on the following morning, was informed by her niece that she had brought home a guest to stay, she not unnaturally demanded to know who the visitor might be. When she learned that she was none other than the Honourable Phœbe Laxton, and that her visit would be for an indefinite time, she laid down her cup and saucer and regarded Deborah with real concern.

'Deb, my love, are you feeling quite the thing?' she asked anxiously. 'You never told me that you were acquainted with the Laxtons, and why in heaven's name should one of them wish to come and stay here, when they have a very good house of their own?'

'I am not acquainted with the Laxtons,' replied Miss Grantham, with a twinkle. 'I never saw this child in my life until yesterday. I am helping her to escape from gross persecution, you must know.'

'Oh dear, as though we had not trouble enough!' groaned her aunt. 'I'm sure I don't know what you mean, you unnatural girl!'

Deborah laughed, and, sitting down beside the bed, gave Lady Bellingham an account of the events of the evening. Her ladyship was quite horrified, and told her that she was little better than a kidnapper. She then begged her to consider the danger she courted in offending a man of Filey's standing in the world, not to mention Miss Laxton's parents, and expressed herself as being fully satisfied now that she was out of her mind.

'Besides, Deb, what are we to do with the girl if her parents don't relent?' she asked reasonably.

Miss Grantham's eyes danced. 'Well, dear ma'am, I

have a little plan of my own for Phœbe's future,' she said.

Lady Bellingham looked at her uneasily. 'I don't trust you, Deb. I *know* you have some dreadful scheme in your head when you look like that! What am I to say if Lady Laxton comes here demanding her daughter?'

'Dearest Aunt Lizzie, this must surely be the last house in London where Lady Laxton would think of looking for her daughter! While she remains with us, by the way, she is to be known as Miss Smith, in case the servants should talk.'

'Yes, but how long *is* she to remain with us?' asked her ladyship. 'If it is not just like you, Deb, to fill the house with guests when there is no money to pay the coal-bill! And poor Kit is coming next week besides! We shall be ruined! And I must tell you that Ormskirk was here last night, and when he asked me where you were I declare I hardly knew how to answer him! But I daresay he guessed, for he said in a very dry voice that he saw Mablethorpe was absent too. Oh dear, what a tangle we are in, my love, and you making it so much the worse with all this nonsense about Miss Laxton, let alone enraging Ravenscar, and behaving so abominably at Vauxhall that I declare I feel quite ashamed to own you! Where is this girl?'

Miss Grantham then offered to fetch Phœbe for inspection. Lady Bellingham said that she had no wish to see her, but if she were to be compelled to house her for the rest of her life, as she had little doubt would turn out to be the case, she supposed she had better make her acquaintance. So Miss Laxton was brought into her hostess's room, clutching one of Deborah's wrappers round her small person, and Lady Bellingham said that she understood nothing, but Deborah had better put on her hat at once; and go out to buy the poor child something to wear and, as for Filey's thinking that he would be permitted to gobble up such a morsel as that, it would give her much pleasure to be able to bestow a piece of her mind upon him, which she very likely would do, one fine day, for she was sure he was a disagreeable creature with a bad heart, and she had never liked him, no, not from the start!

This rambling speech gave Miss Grantham to understand that her aunt was resigned to the unexpected addition to her household, so she kissed that long-suffering lady's cheek, and went off to replenish Phœbe's wardrobe. By noon, Phœbe, dressed in pale blue muslin, was able to emerge from the seclusion of her bedchamber; and when Lord Mablethorpe arrived to pay his promised call, she was sitting with Deborah in the small back-parlour half-way up the stairs.

Lord Mablethorpe heartily approved of Deborah's plan to keep Phœbe in St James's Square, and he could not help feeling rather flattered by her dependence on his judgment. She made him feel quite old, and responsible, and by the time he had endorsed all his Deborah's suggestions, he was in a fair way to believing that he had thought of them for himself. He helped to draft a suitable letter to Lord and Lady Laxton, which Phœbe copied out in her best copyplate handwriting, and he said that he would give a monkey to see their faces when they received it. This made their undutiful daughter giggle. His lordship then asked if it were true that the Honourable Arnold Laxton had been rolled-up at Epsom, and Miss Laxton said, yes, it was all so dreadful because Arnold always backed horses which fell down, or crossed their legs, and that was why it was so important that she should make a good match. This exchange led to others and, since both lived in the same circle, and knew very much the same people, it was not many minutes before they were on the most comfortable terms, pulling most of their relatives' characters to shreds, and laughing a great deal over the business.

Lady Bellingham, coming into the room presently, and seeing her niece sewing quietly by the window, while, on the sofa, Lord Mablethorpe and Miss Laxton had their heads close together, was quite dismayed. She seized the earliest opportunity of warning her niece that if she did not take care she would lose Mablethorpe as well as the twenty thousand pounds she had so recklessly refused.

'Well, I don't want Mablethorpe,' said Miss Grantham, maddeningly placid. 'I think it would be a charming thing if he were to fall out of love with me, and into love with Phœbe.'

'It might be a very charming thing if we had twenty thousand pounds,' said Lady Bellingham, with strong common sense. 'When we have nothing but debts, it is a disaster! Do you know, my love, I have been trying to add up my accounts, and do what I will I cannot alter the truth! We lost seven thousand pounds last year by bad debts!'

'I daresay we might have,' said Miss Grantham. 'It all comes of letting people run upon tick at the faro-table. I knew we ought not to do it.'

'Everything is so difficult!' sighed her ladyship. 'No one can feel more conscious of the awkwardness of your situation than I, Deb, but if Ravenscar were to make his offer again, which I daresay he will, if you behaved as badly as you tell me you did, do you think you might——?'

'No,' said Miss Grantham resolutely. 'Nothing would induce me to accept a farthing from that man! Besides, he assured me his offer was no longer open to my acceptance, and I am convinced he meant it. I *think* he is going to try to worst me by some other means.'

'Good heavens!' cried her ladyship, aghast. 'Never say so, my love! He might set about to ruin us! He would be the most dangerous enemy!'

'So am I a dangerous enemy,' retorted Miss Grantham.

'He will soon find *that* out! Whatever he does, I shall counter with something worse.'

Lady Bellingham moaned, and tottered to her dressing-table to fortify herself with hartshorn-and-water. Her hand shook quite pitiably as she poured the drops into her glass, and she again gave it as her opinion that her niece was mad. 'Some dreadful fate will befall us!' she prophesied. 'I know it. It is flying in the face of Providence to throw everything to the winds, as you are bent on doing! And I will tell you something else, Deb, though I daresay you won't care for that any more than for the rest. It is all over town that Ormskirk is done-up. Beverley told me last night that he has had some deep doings these last months, and the cards running against him five nights out of seven. And *we* know how badly that odious horse of his did at Newmarket! Ten to one, he will call in that mortgage, for you know his estates are entailed! And all you will do is to talk of countering Ravenscar! The very man you should have made a push to turn into a friend instead of an enemy!'

'I make a friend of that man?' exclaimed Miss Grantham, flushing hotly. 'I will starve rather!'

'Very well, my love, I am sure I do not wish to interfere with you, but *I* don't want to starve!' said her ladyship indignantly.

'I won't let you, ma'am. If we were to be faced with *that*, I would—I would make a bargain with Ormskirk! I would do anything rather than be beholden to Ravenscar!'

'Well, if you would do anything, you had better send that Laxton child home, and make sure of Mablethorpe.'

'Oh, poor Adrian, no!' said Miss Grantham quickly.

Lady Bellingham sank into a chair, and closed her eyes. 'Go away!' she begged faintly. 'I shall have the vapours in a minute!'

Miss Grantham laughed. 'Oh, there are a dozen things

we might do to be saved! Lucius was talking of going to Hanover the other day, and trying his fortune there. What do you say to our closing this house, and running off with him?'

'Now I *am* going to have the vapours!' said Lady Bellingham, with conviction.

'Only I won't leave England until I have settled my score with Ravenscar,' said Miss Grantham, a sparkle in her eyes. 'I wish I knew what he means to do next!'

'If it would bring you to your senses, I wish you might know!' said her aunt. 'I daresay it would kill *me*, but you will not care for that!'

But a knowledge of Mr Ravenscar's activities that morning would scarcely have occasioned Lady Bellingham any great discomfort of mind. Mr Ravenscar had gone to White's Club.

He was a member of several clubs, but Brooks's was known to be his favourite, so that some surprise was felt at his appearance at White's. The porter told him that he had become quite a stranger to the place; and an acquaintance whom he encountered on the stairs said: 'Why, Ravenscar, don't tell me you've abandoned Brooks's at last! We thought you was wholly lost to us!'

'No, not wholly,' Ravenscar replied. 'Who's upstairs?'

'Oh, the usual set!' said his friend airily. 'I must tell you the odds are shortening on your race, by the way! Beverley's seen Filey's pair in action, and he says they are rare steppers.'

'Yes, so I hear,' Ravenscar said, unperturbed.

He passed on up the stairs to the room overlooking the street. Here he found several friends gathered, but after staying for a few minutes with them, he strolled over to the window, where Ormskirk was seated, glancing through the *Morning Post*.

Ormskirk lowered the paper. 'So you have decided not

to desert the club!' he remarked. 'And how—may I ask?
—are your plans for your ingenuous cousin's rescue pro-
gressing, my dear Ravenscar?'

'So far, the honours go to the lady,' answered Ravenscar.

'Ah!' said his lordship, gently polishing his quizzing-
glass. 'Somehow, I apprehended that your efforts had not
been attended by success. Am I, I wonder, correct in
assuming that the lady was in your cousin's company last
night?'

'You are. They were at Vauxhall together.'

His lordship looked pensive. 'At Vauxhall, were they?
That seems a rather public spot, does it not? One might
almost infer that the die was cast.'

'Don't disturb yourself! I have reason to think Miss
Grantham has little or no intention of marrying my
cousin. Unless I am much mistaken, she is playing deep.'

Ormskirk sighed. 'But how sordid!' he complained.
'I hope you may not have misjudged your powers of—
persuasion, my dear fellow.'

'I don't despair because the dice fall against me in the
first throw,' responded Ravenscar.

'I am sure you are a hardened gamester,' agreed Ormskirk, smiling.

'Talking of gaming,' said Ravenscar, 'when do you
mean to permit me to measure my skill against yours at the
game which, I confess, I regard as peculiarly my own?'

'Peculiarly your own?' murmured Ormskirk, raising his
brows. 'Can you mean picquet, my dear Ravenscar?'

'Why, yes!' acknowledged Ravenscar. 'You threw a
most delicate challenge in my way the other night. I must
confess my curiosity and my self-esteem were stirred. I
did not think I had my match, but I fancy you think
otherwise, my lord.'

'To be sure,' sighed his lordship, 'I have not been used
to consider my own skill contemptible.'

'Come and dine at my house, and let us discover which of us has met his match!'

Ormskirk did not answer immediately. The bored smile still lingered on his lips, but seemed to have grown a little rigid. He went on polishing his glass with his lace-edged handkerchief, his eyes veiled.

'No?' Ravenscar said, the faintest suggestion of mockery in his voice.

Ormskirk lifted his eyes, and also his quizzing-glass. 'My dear Ravenscar! My very dear Ravenscar! I never refuse a challenge. By all means let us measure our skill! But my recollection is that I invited you to come to *my* house. Give me the pleasure of your company at dinner to-night, I beg of you!'

Mr Ravenscar accepted this invitation, stayed for a few moments in idle conversation, and presently withdrew, perfectly satisfied with the results of his visit to the club.

He dined *tête-à-tête* with his lordship, the faded sister who presided over the establishment having gone to spend the evening with friends, his lordship explained. Ravenscar guessed that she had had orders to absent herself, for it was well known that she never received anything but the most cavalier treatment from her brother. Dinner was good, and the wine excellent. Mr Ravenscar, calmly drinking glass for glass with his host, was glad to think that he had a hard head. He might almost have suspected Ormskirk of trying to fuddle his brain a little, so assiduous was he in keeping his guest's glass filled.

A card-table had been set out in a comfortable saloon on the ground-floor of the house. Several unbroken packs stood ready to hand, and it was not long before the butler carried into the room a tray loaded with bottles and decanters, which he placed upon a side-table. Lord Ormskirk directed him to move a branch of candles nearer to the card-table, and with a smile, and a slight movement of one white hand, invited Ravenscar to be seated.

'What stakes do you care to play for, my dear Ravenscar?' he enquired, breaking open two of the packs at his elbow, and beginning to shuffle the cards.

'It is immaterial to me,' Ravenscar replied. 'Let the stakes be what you choose, my lord: I shall be satisfied.'

Lady Bellingham had been correct in saying that his lordship had been having deep doings during the past weeks. He had had a run of ill-luck which had pursued him even into the racing-field, and had gone down to the tune of several thousands. Ravenscar's challenge could not have been worse timed, but it was not in his lordship's character to draw back, particularly from an adversary towards whom he felt a profound animosity. It was this animosity, coupled with a gamester's recklessness, which prompted him to reply: 'Shall we say pound points, then?'

'Yes, certainly,' Ravenscar answered.

Ormskirk pushed the pack across to him; he cut for the deal, and lost it. 'I hope not an ill-omen!' Ormskirk smiled.

'I hope not, indeed.'

The game opened quietly, no big hands being scored for some little time, and each man bent more upon summing up his opponent than upon the actual winning of points. The rubber went to Ormskirk, but the luck seemed to be running fairly evenly, and there was not much more than the hundred points for the game in it. Ormskirk was inclined to think Ravenscar an over-cautious player: an impression Mr Ravenscar had been at some pains to give him.

At the end of an hour, a glance at the score by his elbow showed his lordship that Ravenscar was steadily creeping ahead. He was too good a card-player not to know when he had met his match, and he recognized in the younger man one who combined his own *flair* for cards with a greater degree of cool caution. Lord Ormskirk, always playing for the highest prize, too often failed to defeat the major hand by the retention of some small card; again and again, Ravenscar, holding the minor hand, sacrificed a reasonable chance of scoring to spoil a pique which his lordship had felt sure of winning.

In temperament, Ravenscar had the advantage over his opponent. Trying, as a gamester must, to put all thought of his losses out of mind, Ormskirk was yet bitterly conscious of a tightening of the nerves, and still more bitterly aware of Ravenscar's imperturbable calm. It mattered nothing to a man of his wealth, Ormskirk reflected, whether he won or lost; he could have cursed the misfortune that had caused Ravenscar to challenge him to this meeting at a moment when his own affairs stood in such confusion. The knowledge that he was in a tight corner, and might find himself facing ruin if the evening's play went heavily against him, could not but affect his nerves, and, through them, his skill. He knew his judgment to be impaired by his desperate need, allowed Ravenscar to win a capotte through a miscalculation, and got up to pour himself out some brandy.

Ravenscar's eyes flickered towards him, and then dropped again to the pack he was shuffling.

'Brandy?' his lordship said, holding the decanter poised.

Ravenscar pushed his empty Burgundy glass a little away from him. 'Thank you.'

'You should not have had that capotte,' Ormskirk said abruptly.

'No.'

'I must be out of practice,' Ormskirk said, with a light laugh. 'A stupid error to have made! Do not hope for another like it.'

Ravenscar smiled. 'I don't. Such things rarely happen twice in an evening, I find. It is your deal, my lord.'

Ormskirk came back to his chair, and the game proceeded. Once the butler came into the room, to make up the fire. His master, his attention distracted from the play of his cards by the man's movements, looked up, and said sharply: 'That is all! I shall not need you again!'

Outside, in the square, an occasional carriage rumbled over the cobbles, footsteps passed the house, and link-boys could be heard exchanging personalities with chairmen; but as the night wore on the noise of traffic ceased, and only the voice of the Watch was heard from time to time, calling the hour.

'One of the clock, and a fair night!'

It was not a fair night for his lordship, plunging deeper and ever deeper into Ravenscar's debt. Under his *maquillage,* his thin face was pale, and looked strained in the candlelight. He knew now that his ill-luck was still dogging him; the cards had been running against him for the past two hours. Only a fool chased his own bad luck, yet this was what he had been doing, hoping for a change each rubber, risking all on the chance of the big *coup* which maddeningly eluded him.

A half-consumed log fell out on to the hearth, and lay smouldering there. 'I make that fifteen hundred points,' said Ravenscar, adding up the last rubber. He rose, and walked over to the fire to replace the log. 'Your luck is quite out: you held wretched cards, until the very last hand.'

'You are a better player than I am,' his lordship said, with a twisted smile. 'I am done-up.'

'Oh, nonsense! Play on, my lord; your cards were better at the end. I daresay you will soon have your revenge on me.'

'Nothing would give me more pleasure, I assure you,' said Ormskirk. 'But, unhappily, my estates are entailed.'

'Is it as bad as that?' Ravenscar asked, as though in jest.

'Another hour such as the last, and it certainly would be,' replied Ormskirk frankly. 'I don't play if I cannot pay.'

Ravenscar came back to the table, and sat down, idly running the cards through his hands. 'If you choose to call a halt, I am very willing. But you hold certain assets I would be glad to buy from you.'

Ormskirk's thin brows drew together. 'Yes?'

Mr Ravenscar's hard grey eyes lifted from the cards, and looked directly into his. 'Certain bills,' he said. 'How many? and what are they worth?'

'Good God!' said Ormskirk softly. He leaned back in his chair, wryly smiling. 'And how came you by that knowledge, my dear Ravenscar?'

'You yourself told me of them, when we walked away from St James's Square together the other night.'

'Did I? I had forgotten.'

Silence fell. Ormskirk's eyes were veiled; one of his white hands rhythmically swung his quizzing-glass to and fro on the end of its ribbon. Mr Ravenscar went on shuffling the cards.

'I have a handful of Lady Bellingham's bills,' his lordship said at last. 'Candour, however, compels me to say that they would not fetch quite their face-value in the market.'

'And that is?'

'Fifteen hundred,' said his lordship.

'I am ready to buy them from you at that figure.'

Ormskirk put up his quizzing-glass. 'So!' he said. 'But I do not think I wish to sell, my dear Ravenscar.'

'You had much better do so, however.'

'Indeed! May I know why?'

'Put brutally, my lord, since your sense of propriety is too nice to allow of your using these bills to obtain your ends, it will be convenient to you, I imagine, to put them into my hands. I shall use them to extricate my cousin from his entanglement. Once that is accomplished, I cannot suppose that Miss Grantham will continue to reject your offer.'

'There is much in what you say,' acknowledged his lordship. 'And yet, my dear Ravenscar, and yet I am loath to part with them!'

'Then let us say good night,' Ravenscar replied, rising to his feet.

Ormskirk hesitated, looking at the scattered cards on the table. He was a gambler to the heart's core, and it irked him unbearably to end the night thus. Ill-luck could not last for ever; it might be that it was already on the turn: indeed, he had held appreciably better cards in that last hand, as Ravenscar had noticed. He hated having to acknowledge Ravenscar to be his superior, too. He could conceive of few things more pleasing than to reverse their present positions. It might well be within his power to do so. He raised his hand. 'Wait! After all, why not?' He got up, picked up one of the branches of candles, and carried it over to his writing-table at the end of the room. Setting it down there, he felt in his pocket for a key, and unlocked one of the drawers in the table, and pulled it out. He lifted a slim bundle of papers out, and brought it back to the table, tossing it down on top of the spilled cards. 'There you are,' he said. 'How fortunate it is that you are less squeamish than I!'

Ravenscar picked up the papers, and slipped them into the wide pocket of his coat. 'Very fortunate,' he agreed. 'You are fifteen hundred pounds in hand, my lord. Do you care to continue the game?'

Ormskirk raised his brows mockingly. 'Had you not better count them? You will find there are six in all, for varying sums.'

'I'll take your word for it,' replied Ravenscar. 'Shall we continue?'

'By all means!' Ormskirk said, and sat down again. 'We may find that this—ah, transaction—has changed my luck.'

'We may,' agreed Ravenscar, cutting the cards towards him.

It seemed, in the next rubber, that the luck had indeed veered in his lordship's favour. He played cautiously for a while, grew bolder presently, won a little, lost a large rubber, refilled his glass, and allowed all other considerations than his overmastering desire to get the better of Ravenscar to fade from his mind. As the fumes of the brandy mounted to his brain, not clouding it, but exciting him, he ceased to keep an eye on the sum of his losses.

It was three o'clock when Ravenscar said: 'It is growing late. I make it four thousand, my lord.'

'Four thousand,' Ormskirk repeated blankly. He looked at Ravenscar, not seeing him, wondering which of his horses he would be obliged to sell, knowing that if he sold all he would yet be unable to extricate himself from his embarrassments. Mechanically he opened his delicate Sèvres snuff-box, and took a pinch. 'You will have to give me time,' he said, hating the need to speak these words.

'Certainly,' Ravenscar replied. One of the candles was guttering; he snuffed it. 'Or you might prefer to let me purchase from you the mortgage on Lady Bellingham's house,' he said coolly.

Ormskirk stared at him for a moment. His eyes narrowed suspiciously. He said with an edge to his smooth voice: 'What's your object, Ravenscar?'

'I have told you.'

'The mortgage is for five thousand: it may be worth something over four.'

'We need not haggle over the figure, I suppose. I will give you five thousand for it.'

'You would appear to cherish an unusual degree of affection for your young relative,' Ormskirk said, his lips curling in a faint sneer.

Ravenscar shrugged. 'The boy is in some sort my responsibility.'

'It is gratifying to meet with such a sense of duty in these days. Yet it seems to me that you are paying high for his salvation, my dear Ravenscar!'

'You are mistaken: I am acting for Lady Mablethorpe.'

'Do you know,' said Ormskirk softly, 'I have the oddest idea in my head? I cannot rid myself of the notion that you have some other motive in acquiring this hold over Deb Grantham.'

'It is not love, if that is what you mean, my lord.'

'Indeed? Then what may it be?'

A smile flickered in Ravenscar's eyes. 'A strong dislike of being worsted in a fight.'

Ormskirk regarded him fixedly for a few moments, tapping the lid of his snuff-box with one polished finger-nail. A short laugh broke from him; he rose from his chair, and once more trod over to his writing-table. 'After all, why not?' he said, with one of his airy gestures. He pulled open the drawer, took from it a folded document, and tossed it to his guest. 'Take it! You have it all now, have you not? I suppose you meant to have it from the start. Do not think me unkind if I say that I hope she worsts you again, my dear Ravenscar: it would do you so much good!'

CHAPTER IX

MISS LAXTON's letter having been delivered to her parents through the medium of the post, she had nothing to do but to await events, not omitting, of course, to scan the advertisement columns of the *Morning Post*. No intimation of surrender on her father's part made its appearance there immediately, but this, Miss Grantham pointed out, was not surprising, as no doubt the Laxtons would first prosecute enquiries amongst their acquaintances. She was able to report, on the evening following Miss Laxton's escape, that Sir James Filey was playing faro in the Yellow Saloon, and seemed to be in the devil's own temper. Miss Laxton, curled up with an exciting novel from the lending library in Lady Bellingham's boudoir, giggled, and said she did not care a button, and only wished that she could remain in St James's Square for the rest of her life. Possibly out of regard for her aunt's quite different wishes, Miss Grantham took what steps she could to prevent this from coming to pass by descending again to the saloons, and suggesting softly to Lord Mablethorpe that he might go upstairs to sit with the poor child for a while, to save her from dying of boredom. His lordship was perfectly ready to obey this, or any other behest, and slipped away presently, to spend a comfortable hour playing at cribbage with Phœbe. In between games he extolled Deborah's virtues to Miss Laxton, and Miss Laxton agreed with him that she was a wonderful woman, and said that she was not at all surprised at his being determined to make her his wife. She was quite shocked to hear from him of his mother's opposition, and in general showed herself to be so sympathetic that his lordship found himself confiding far more to her than he had meant to. When the conversation veered towards Miss Laxton's future, he found his part in it more difficult to sustain, for he could not think what was to be done if her parents remained obdurate. He was firm, however, on three points: on no account must Phœbe marry Sir James, apply for a post as governess, or tread the boards. Phœbe said that if he thought it wrong of her to become an actress or a governess, she would not do it, because she knew well that he was more worldly-wise than she and she meant to be guided by his judgment. His lordship was conscious of a strong conviction that some well-disposed person ought to take Miss Laxton under his wing, and protect her from the buffets of the world, but try as he would he was unable to think of anyone who would be at all suitable to fill the post. He made up his mind to consult Deborah on this point. Meanwhile, he assured Phœbe that while he remained in some part responsible for her well-being she had nothing to fear from Filey, or, indeed, from anyone else. Miss Laxton, looking up into his face with dewy eyes, said simply that she knew she was safe with him, had known it from the first moment of seeing him.

It was not to be expected that Lord and Lady Laxton would advertise their loss to the world, and as Deborah did not move in their circle she had no means of learning what their emotions might be upon receipt of their daughter's politely worded ultimatum. Lady Mablethorpe was acquainted with the family, but a few casual questions put to her by her son merely elicited the information that she had always considered Augusta Laxton to be an odious woman, with an overbearing nature, and grasping ways, and that how she hoped to marry a pack of girls respectably was a mystery to everyone. Asked if she were in the habit of visiting the Laxton establishment, she replied that she never went there unless she was obliged to.

Lady Bellingham, although resigned, she said, to any conceivable folly on the part of her niece, wished to know what was to be done with her guest if her parents failed to insert the desired notice in the *Morning Post*. 'For the girl cannot spend the rest of her days in hiding,' she pointed out, without the least hope of being attended to. 'I am sure it must be very bad for her to walk out only at dusk, and then heavily veiled; and unless Augusta Laxton has changed since I knew her, which I cannot credit, she will very likely be glad to be rid of at least one of her brood of daughters, and not make the least push to discover her whereabouts.'

'Well, I hope you may be right,' said Miss Grantham. 'My only fear is that she may have hired the Bow Street Runners to find Phœbe.'

This suggestion was so appalling that Lady Bellingham sank plump into a chair. 'My love, don't say such a thing! Oh dear, what have you done? Only think of the scandal if the law-officers were to come to this house! We shall all be prosecuted!'

'My dear ma'am, there is not the least likelihood of such a thing happening. No one knows of any circumstance connecting me with Phœbe, and Adrian must be quite above suspicion.'

But the idea, once instilled into Lady Bellingham's brain, took such strong possession of it that it might well have brought on her dreaded spasms had it not been ousted by a far more pressing threat.

The following morning's post brought Miss Grantham a curt communication from Mr Ravenscar.

It was handed to her as she sat at breakfast with her aunt, and her protégée. She did not recognize the handwriting, which was very black and firm, and the crest on the seal was equally strange to her. She turned it over idly, broke open the seal, and spread out the single, crackling sheet of paper.

She was eating a slice of bread-and-butter as she ran her eye down the missive, and startled her aunt by choking suddenly. She let a hasty exclamation escape her, swallowed a stray crumb, which found its way into her windpipe, and fell into helpless coughing. By the time she had been restored by having her back briskly slapped by her aunt, all the impropriety of disclosing the contents of her letter in Miss Laxton's presence had been recollected, and she sat with it in her lap throughout the rest of the meal. Lady Bellingham noticed that she was unusually silent, and saw that her eyes were smouldering and her cheeks unduly flushed. Her heart sank, for she knew these signs. 'My love, I do trust you have not received some bad news?' she said nervously.

'Bad news, ma'am?' said Miss Grantham, sitting very straight in her chair. 'Oh, dear me, no! Nothing of that nature!'

Lady Bellingham's alarms were not in the least allayed by this assurance, and she sat fidgeting until Phœbe presently left the table. When the door had shut behind her, her ladyship fixed her eyes on Deborah's martial countenance, and demanded: 'What is it? If I am not to be laid upon my bed with the vapours, tell me the worst at once! The Laxtons have discovered that child's whereabouts?'

'This obliging letter,' said Deborah, looking at it with loathing, 'does not come from the Laxtons. It comes from Mr Ravenscar.'

'Never say so, my love!' cried her ladyship, reviving fast. 'Well, now, this time, don't you think, dearest Deb, that you should compound with him? What does he offer you?'

'You are mistaken, ma'am; he does not offer me anything. He threatens me instead!'

'Threatens you?' exclaimed her aunt. 'For heaven's sake, child, what with?'

'Mr Ravenscar,' said Deborah, through her teeth, 'begs leave to inform me that he has acquired—*acquired!*—certain bills of exchange drawn by you, and a mortgage on this house.'

'What?' almost screamed Lady Bellingham. 'He can't have acquired them! Ormskirk holds them! You know he does! It must be a trick to frighten you!'

'No, it isn't, and I am not in the least frightened!' said Miss Grantham indignantly. 'He has got them from Ormskirk; that much is plain.'

'I can't believe such a thing! Ormskirk would never give them up, I am persuaded!'

'You said he was badly dipped, Aunt Lizzie,' Deborah reminded her. 'If Ravenscar offered to buy them from him, I daresay he may have been glad to agree to sell them.'

'I never heard of such treachery in my life!' declared her ladyship. 'It passes everything! Besides, if he does not hold the bills any longer, what hope can Ormskirk have of persuading *you*, my love?'

Miss Grantham thought this over, wrinkling her brow over the problem. 'I daresay he might think he had no hope of me,' she said at last. 'If he believes I am about to marry Adrian, that would be it, no doubt.'

'I shall go distracted!' said Lady Bellingham, clasping her head in her hands, and sadly disarranging her cap. 'Nothing could be worse! You have now lost them both through your tricks! I do not know how you can be so improvident, Deb, indeed I don't! You must marry Adrian at once!'

'Nonsense! He is not of age, ma'am. Besides, I do not mean to marry him at all.'

'No! You mean to fob him off with this Laxton child, which is so downright *wasteful* of you I cannot bear to think of it! But if Ravenscar holds those dreadful bills, there is nothing to be done (unless you choose to give

Adrian up altogether) but to marry him secretly at once! I know you will say these Gretna marriages are not at all the thing, but it can't be helped now! Matters are desperate!'

'I must get them into my hands,' said Deborah, who had not been paying much heed to this speech.

'Get what into your hands?' demanded her ladyship.

'The bills, and the mortgage, ma'am; what else?'

'Do you mean you will agree to give Adrian up?' asked Lady Bellingham. 'I own, it may come to that, but I do think it would be better if you married him.'

'Ravenscar and Lady Mablethorpe would have the marriage annulled if I did anything so foolish. Oh, he thinks he has me in a pretty corner, but I shall show him!'

'No, no, don't show him anything more, Deb, I implore you!' begged her aunt, agitated. 'You see what has come of showing him things! If only you would be a little conciliating!'

'Conciliating! I mean to fight him to the last ditch!' said Miss Grantham. 'The first thing is to get those bills away from him!'

'You can't get them away from him,' said Lady Bellingham despairingly. 'What does he say in his letter?'

'Why, that he will be happy to restore them to me in return for his cousin's freedom! How *dare* he insult me so? Oh, I will never forgive him!'

'Says he will restore them? Well, I must say, my dear, that is very handsome of him! To be sure, it is not as good as twenty thousand pounds, but it would be a great relief to be rid of some of our debts!'

'And if I *don't* send Adrian about his business, he will foreclose on you,' added Miss Grantham.

Lady Bellingham gave a moan. 'The brute! I cannot possibly pay him! I suppose he wants me to go upon my knees to him, but I won't do it! I won't!'

'Go on your knees to him?' cried Miss Grantham. 'No,

indeed! I would never speak to you again if you did!'

'Very likely no one will ever speak to me again—no one I care to speak to, at all events—for I shall be in a debtors' prison, and shall end my days there. Oh, Deb, how can you be so heartless?'

Miss Grantham put her arms round the afflicted matron. 'I'm not heartless, dearest, indeed I'm not, and you shan't be put into any prison! It is not *you* that hateful man wishes to punish, but *me*! He thinks to frighten me, but I have still a trick or two up my sleeve, and so he shall find! I'll get those bills back, and I won't give Adrian up—at least, I will really, but Ravenscar shall not know of it until he owns himself beaten—and——'

'Don't!' begged her aunt. 'I cannot bear it! Nothing will do for you but to ruin us all, and that is the matter in a nutshell! And I do think Ravenscar must be the most disagreeable man in the world, besides the oddest-behaved! If he means to foreclose, why don't he tell me so? I am sure it is not your business!'

'Oh, he wrote to me because I made him so angry that he wants to punish me! I am sure he has no quarrel at all with you, aunt, so pray do not put yourself in a taking! This is all wicked spite! But I will teach him a lesson!'

Since no arguments of hers seemed likely to prevail against this determination, Lady Bellingham gave up any attempt to induce her niece to see reason, and tottered away to spend a melancholy morning trying to discover an error in her dressmaker's bill, and to convince Mortimer that the stubs of the candles used in the saloons could quite well be lit again for kitchen purposes. As she succeeded in neither of these objects, her spirits underwent no change for the better, and might indeed have borne her down utterly had she been privileged to know what her niece was planning to do. This knowledge, however, was prudently kept from her, so that she was able to go out for her usual drive in the Park in ignorance of the events which were brewing above her unfortunate head.

For quite some time, Miss Grantham was unable to think of an adequate counter to Mr Ravenscar's last move. It really seemed to be unanswerable, but she was by this time so determined to fight him that the idea of surrender never entered her head. The time for signifying to him that she had not the least intention of marrying his cousin would come only when he was beaten out of every position. Miss Grantham would then be able to derive great satisfaction from her magnanimity. To give way to bribes or threats would be so spiritless a course that she naturally could not entertain it for a moment.

After dwelling wistfully on all the exceedingly unpleasant things she would like to do to Mr Ravenscar, but which circumstances unhappily prevented her from doing, her brain presently turned resolutely from these impractical daydreams, and grappled the problem in a more serious spirit. It was not long before a scheme, so dazzlingly diabolical as almost to take her breath away, was born in her mind. She sank her chin in her hands, pondering the plan with a rapt look on her face, and was discovered in this absorption by Lucius Kennet, who strolled in towards noon to see how she did.

'Faith, what devilment will you be up to, me darlin'?' asked Mr Kennet, regarding her with a sapient twinkle.

Deborah jumped up. 'Lucius, you are the very man I need! You must help me!'

'Sure and I will!' responded Kennet promptly.

'And Silas too,' decided Miss Grantham. 'You will not mind a little risk, will you, Lucius?'

'Me sword's at your service, Deb!'

'Oh no! It has nothing to do with swords—at least I do hope it has not! I just want you to kidnap Ravenscar for me.'

He burst out laughing. 'Is that all? Whisht, it's a mere nothing! And what will I be doing with him when I've kidnapped him?'

'I want you to put him in the cellar,' said Miss Grantham remorselessly.

'What cellar?' enquired Kennet.

'This one, of course. It has a very stout lock on the door, and it is not at all damp—not that that signifies, and in any event he will be tied up.'

'It's a grand plan you have there, me dear, but what will you be doing with him when you have him in the cellar, and what the devil ails you to want him there at all?'

'Oh, to be sure, you do not know what he has done! Read that!' said Deborah, thrusting Mr Ravenscar's letter into his hand.

He read it with lifting brows of astonishment. 'The old dog!' he ejaculated.

'Old? He isn't old!' said Deborah, unaccountably annoyed.

'Not Ravenscar: Ormskirk!'

'Oh, him! Well, yes, I must say I think it very shabby of him to serve poor Aunt Lizzie such a trick, but he is of no account, after all.'

'How did Ravenscar know he had the bills?' demanded Kennet.

Miss Grantham looked at him, suddenly frowning a little. 'Yes, how did he know? I had not thought of that! He must have made it his business to find out, I suppose. It is the vilest piece of work! But he will be sorry, I promise you!'

'I dare swear he will. Does it mean you are going to marry the young sprig at the latter end, me dear?'

'No, indeed!'

He shook his head ruefully. 'You go beyond me, Deb, upon me soul you do! If you don't mean to have Mablethorpe, why, for any sakes, will you not say so, and be done with it?'

'Lucius, I made sure *you* would understand!' said Deborah reproachfully. 'Do you think I will give in as tamely as that? You do not know what language he used towards me! He insulted me, and now he dares to threaten me, and nothing—*nothing!*—would induce me to yield to him! What! Am I to have a pistol held to my head, and submit to such conduct? I won't! I will get the better of him if I die for it!'

'When you put it like that, me darlin', it's not meself that has the heart to gainsay you. Sure, he's a black villain, and deserves to be put in the cellar! But I'd say, from the little I've seen of him, that he's devilish obstinate. Do you mean to keep him in the cellar until he hands over the bills to you? I'm thinking he may be a charge on you for a weary while!'

'I have thought of all that,' said Miss Grantham triumphantly. 'I fancy he will not stay in the cellar above an hour or two. Lucius, he is delivered into my hands by his own act! I want you to kidnap him on Wednesday evening!'

'On Wednesday——' His jaw dropped suddenly. 'No, by the powers, you can't do that, Deb! His race is to be run on Thursday!'

'Exactly so!' nodded Deborah. 'You may depend upon it, he will agree to do anything rather than lose the race by default.'

'Faith, me dear, if he didn't murder you, and me too, he'd have the pair of us clapped up in gaol!' Kennet said, awed. 'What's more, I couldn't find it in me heart to blame him.'

This gave Miss Grantham a moment's pause, but after thinking it over she said: 'I do not *think* he would murder us, Lucius, and I am quite sure he would not have us clapped up, because he is too proud to admit to the world that one of *faro's daughters* got the better of him, and in *such* a fashion! No, he will do nothing, and then, when he is smarting, I will tell him that he might have spared himself his trouble, for I would not marry his cousin if he were the last to offer for me!'

'I'm thinking,' said Kennet slowly, 'that while you have him tied up in the cellar, Deb, you might get that twenty thousand out of him.'

Miss Grantham flushed. 'I will do nothing of the sort! How dare you think I would touch his horrid money, much less force him to give it to me?'

'After all, me dear,' said Kennet reasonably, 'you've no objection to forcing him to hand over the mortgage, and that's worth a cool five thousand, let alone the bills.'

'That,' said Miss Grantham, with dignity, 'is a very different matter. The other—— Why, what a wretch I should be! You cannot have considered!'

Kennet smiled wryly. 'It's you who are too quixotic for me, Deb. However, it's your own affair. Now, how are we to kidnap my fine gentleman?'

'I thought very likely you would be able to arrange for that,' said Miss Grantham hopefully. 'Silas will help you and between you you should be able to overpower him, I imagine.'

'Ah, there's no difficulty about that! But do you suppose I am to walk into his house, or club him in the open street, me darlin'?'

Miss Grantham looked rather anxious. 'I don't want him to be hurt, you know. At least, not *much*. Couldn't you catch him after dark, when he is coming away from his club, or some such thing?'

Mr Kennet pursed up his lips disparagingly. 'Too chancy, Deb. It won't do to bungle it. I'm thinking you should write to him, appointing a meeting-place in some quiet spot, and I'll keep the tryst for you.'

Once more Miss Grantham's tiresome conscience intervened. 'No!' she said, revolted. 'I won't win by such a horrid trick! Besides, he thinks I am an odious woman who would do any vile thing, and I am not! We must think of something else.'

Mr Kennet cast her a sidelong, appraising glance. 'Ah well!' he said diplomatically, 'you'd best leave the manner of it to me. I shall contrive somehow, I daresay.'

'And what am I to do about this wicked letter?' asked Miss Grantham, her eyes kindling as they alighted on it. 'I should like to write to him, and tell him that he may go to the devil, but I suppose that would spoil everything. I must fob him off until Wednesday. Only I don't know what to say!'

'Give me a pen!' said Kennet. 'It will be better if I reply to it for you. You must play for time, me dear.'

'Why should you reply to it?' asked Deborah suspiciously. 'If you mean any mischief, Lucius——'

'Devil a bit!' he said, cheerfully lying. 'You shall look over me shoulder while I write it, and seal it yourself. 'Twill be better for the gentleman to see that you think too little of him to answer with your own hand. Besides, you must plead with him a trifle, me dear, and that you'll never bring yourself to do. I'll write it for you in the third person.'

'What do you mean to say?' asked Miss Grantham, a little doubtful still, but bringing him some notepaper, and a pen.

He drew the paper towards him, and dipped the pen in the standish. 'How will this answer?' he said, and began to write in flowing characters, slowly reading the words aloud as he did so. *'Miss Grantham is obliged to Mr Ravenscar for his letter, and begs to inform him that she is astonished that any gentleman——* We'll underline that word, Deb!—*could address a defenceless female in such terms.'*

'I am not defenceless!' objected Miss Grantham.

'Whisht, now! *She is persuaded that Mr Ravenscar cannot mean to put his barbarous threat into execution, since Lady Bellingham has done nothing to incur his enmity. Miss Grantham cannot but believe that a Compromise might yet be reached, and begs the favour of a reply to this suggestion at Mr Ravenscar's Earliest Convenience.* And we'll underline that too, to make him think it's frightened you are, Deb. How's that?'

'I suppose it will answer,' said Deborah, in a discontented voice. 'But I hate to sue for mercy!'

Mr Kennet shook some sand over the letter, read it through, and folded it, and reached for a wafer. 'You'll have your revenge on him presently, me darlin', but till Wednesday we must keep him quiet, or it's ruined all our fine plans will be.'

'Very well: send it!' said Deborah.

CHAPTER X

WHEN Mr Ravenscar received Mr Kennet's letter, his emotions were very much what the writer had hoped they would be. He was not surprised that Miss Grantham should show signs of weakening. He had expected her to be thrown into a flutter by his brief communication, and he lost no time in giving a turn to the screw by sitting down to indite a second curt note to her.

'*Mr Ravenscar presents his compliments to Miss Grantham, and desires to inform her that no Compromise being in any way agreeable to him he must beg her to make her decision within the next three days, at the end of which time he will consider himself free to act in a manner which he has reason to believe must cause Miss Grantham a degree of*

embarrassment which he would be loath to inflict upon any
female, defenceless or otherwise.'

'There!' exclaimed Miss Grantham indignantly, when
she read this unamiable communication. 'I said I wished
you would not call me a defenceless woman! I knew he
would sneer at me!'

'He'll not sneer for long,' promised Lucius Kennet.

'I will answer for that!' said Miss Grantham fiercely.
'Only bring him here on Wednesday night!'

'I'll do that, me dear, never fear!'

'Yes, but do you know how you will contrive to do
it?'

'Leave it to me, Deb: that's my part in the business.'

She was not quite satisfied with this answer, but since
he only laughed when she pressed him to tell her what his
plan was, she was obliged to accept it, merely stipulating
that no severe harm should befall the victim. 'Not that I
care,' she explained. 'I should not care if you killed him,
but it would be bound to lead to trouble, and we don't
want *that*!'

Mr Kennet agreed that they did not want trouble, and
went away to compose another letter to Mr Ravenscar, in
the same flowing hand. But this letter he had no intention
of showing to Miss Grantham, concurring to the full in
Mr Wantage's dictum, that what Miss Deb knew nothing
about she'd not grieve over.

Meanwhile, there was nothing further for Deborah to
do but to await the coming of Wednesday evening, and to
nourish thoughts of the direst vengeance. She had no
expectation of receiving any more news of Mr Ravenscar,
and was consequently much astonished to see, on looking
out of the window on the following day, a carriage draw up
outside the house, bearing the Ravenscar crest on the
panel. As she stared at it, the footman sprang down to open
the door, and let down the steps. But the figure that

146

alighted from the carriage was not Mr Ravenscar's. Miss Grantham recognized Arabella Ravenscar's trim form, and felt almost ready to faint from surprise.

Miss Ravenscar tripped up the steps to the front door, and sent in her card. Silas Wantage brought this to his mistress, and handed it to her, saying darkly that he doubted it was all a trick, and recommending that he should be allowed to send the young party about her business. Miss Grantham, however, felt a good deal of curiosity to know what could have brought Arabella to see her, and directed her henchman to desire Miss Ravenscar to step upstairs.

A few moments later, Arabella was ushered into the room, a charming vision in a sprigged muslin dress with a pink tiffany sash, a pink silk coat, and a ravishing hat tied under her chin with pink ribbons. She paused on the threshold, eyeing her hostess with her head tilted a little, like a bird, Miss Grantham thought. The big, pansy-brown eyes were half-doubtful, half-mischievous.

Miss Grantham, herself very prettily dressed in a pale green saque, and with her hair in simple ringlets, moved forward to greet her visitor, quite forgetting that she had previously appeared to Miss Ravenscar in a most vulgar guise. 'How do you do?' she said politely.

The doubt vanished from Arabella's face. She ran forward, and caught Deborah's hands, exclaiming: 'There! I *knew* I should like you! Oh, how badly you did behave, to be sure! But I told my aunt you had such laughing eyes that I could not but like you! Do you mind my coming to see you without my Mama? She will never go anywhere, you know, and besides that, she is against you, just like all of them! Only Adrian said you were not like that in the general way, and I made up my mind I would come and see you for myself.'

Deborah coloured, and said: 'You should not have

come, Miss Ravenscar. I am persuaded your brother would not wish you to visit this house.'

'Oh, pooh! Who cares for Max?' said his sister scornfully. 'He will know nothing about it, in any event. And if you are going to be my cousin, there can be no objection to my visiting you. I must tell you that I am very glad you are to marry Adrian.'

'Are you?' asked Deborah, surprised. She led Arabella to the sofa. 'I cannot think why you should be!'

'Well, I am glad *now*, because I like you,' replied Arabella, seating herself, and turning towards Deborah with a pretty, confiding air. 'I was glad *before*, because my Mama, and Aunt Selina, had made the stupidest plan to marry *me* to Adrian, which is a thing neither of us wanted in the very least. Of course, they could not have prevailed with us, because we decided long ago that we should not suit, but you have no idea how tiresome it is to have people making such schemes for one!'

'Your brother too, no doubt, desired this marriage?'

'I daresay he does, not that he has ever said a word to me about it, for the only thing he said to me about being married was that I am too young and silly to think of such a thing, which is absurd. But I don't care for what Max says, in any event. I shall marry *whom* I choose, and *when* I choose! I have very nearly run away to be married several times already.'

Miss Grantham could not help laughing at this. 'Do you change your mind so often, Miss Ravenscar?'

'Yes, isn't it dreadful?' sighed Arabella, shaking her head. 'I have been in love a score of times already! And the odd thing is that each time it happens I do truly feel quite sure that it is for always. But somehow it never is. That is why Mama has brought me to London. She has such poor health, you see, that she finds me a sad trial. She said Max must look after me, and naturally I was transported, because I like being in London, and going to parties. In fact, it is just what I hoped would happen!'

'You do not anticipate, I collect, that your brother may look after you too strictly?'

'Oh no!' said Arabella blithely. 'Max is a great dear, and he is *never* unreasonable! He does not like to be crossed, of course, but we deal delightfully together, I assure you.'

'I fear that he would be very angry if he knew you had come to visit me.'

'Max is never angry with me,' replied Miss Ravenscar confidently. 'Besides, why should he care? You are charming!'

Miss Grantham blushed. 'Thank you! I beg you will not tell him that you have been here, however. You must be aware that he dislikes me very much.'

'Yes, I am, of course, and I cannot conceive why he should! I thought it might be a good thing if I were to tell him that he is quite mistaken in you.'

'No, no!' said Deborah quickly. 'I beg you will not do so! It must sound odd to you, I know, but I have a very particular reason for not wishing him to be informed of this visit!'

'Well, I won't say a word about it, then,' said Arabella obligingly. 'I daresay I had better not, indeed, for if he has taken one of his stupid dislikes to you he won't listen to anything anyone says. But why did you behave in that shocking way at Vauxhall? Do tell me! You made me want to laugh so!'

Miss Grantham, finding herself quite unable to explain her conduct at Vauxhall, said vaguely that she had had a reason, which she could not well divulge. Arabella looked as though she would have liked to have probed farther into the mystery, but was too well-bred to do so. Instead, she remarked that she was acquainted with a Mr Grantham, and wondered if he might be related to Deborah.

'I met him at the Assemblies at Tunbridge Wells,' she said. 'He is in the 14th Foot.'

'Indeed!' Deborah said. 'Then you have met my brother, Miss Ravenscar. Do you know him well?'

'Oh, I have danced with him several times!' responded Arabella carelessly. 'Tunbridge Wells was abominably flat, you know, until the 14th were stationed there!'

She was interrupted by the entrance of Lucius Kennet, who had been told by Silas who was abovestairs, and had come up in a spirit of the liveliest curiosity to behold the guest with his own eyes.

Miss Grantham was not quite pleased at his having come into the room. It was evident, from Arabella's artless disclosures, that that young lady was extremely susceptible, and Mr Kennet, besides being a good-looking man, had more than his share of male charm. She was obliged to present him to Arabella, but gave him a somewhat minatory look as she did so, which he received with the blandest of smiles. He sat down opposite to the sofa, and engaged both ladies in conversation. His manners were pleasing, and his address very easy and assured, while the smile that lurked in his eyes had been more than one lady's undoing. However, Miss Grantham was relieved to see that he was behaving with perfect propriety towards her guest, treating her, in fact, in a way that almost bordered on the avuncular.

But nevertheless Miss Grantham was not sorry when Arabella got up to take her leave. She could not think Lucius Kennet a fit companion for a volatile young lady not yet nineteen years of age, and she was a little afraid that his knowledge of the world, the gay stories he told, the cosmopolitan air that clung to him, might have an extremely undesirable effect upon Miss Ravenscar. When Arabella exclaimed that he must have led the most romantic life, and expressed a wish to be a vagabond herself, she said in a damping fashion that vagabondage was not at all romantic, but, on the contrary, tedious beyond words.

'Oh, I should love to be a gamester, and to travel, and to have adventures!' declared Arabella, drawing on her gloves again. 'I must go now, but pray let me come to see you again, dear Miss Grantham! I shan't say a word to Max, or to Mama, I promise.'

But although Miss Grantham had thought of a number of ways of punishing Mr Ravenscar, the introduction of his half-sister into gaming circles was not one of them, and she told Arabella that she could not permit her to visit the house while her relatives continued to disapprove of its inmates. 'It would not be right, my dear,' she said, taking Arabella's hand, and patting it. 'You must do what your Mama and—and your brother think proper.'

Arabella pouted. 'Oh, that is so stuffy, and I did not think you would be *that*! When you are married to Adrian, I shall visit you often, I warn you!'

'Ah, then!' said Deborah, smiling. 'That is another matter.'

So Arabella went away, and was handed into her carriage by Mr Kennet, who told her that he for one was very sorry to think he should not see her in St James's Square again, since he had had the oddest feeling, when he had entered the saloon, that the sun had got into it.

'It is a very sunny day,' said Arabella demurely.

'But the saloon looks north,' Mr Kennet reminded her. 'Sure, there's no accounting for it at all!'

Arabella's dimples peeped out. 'It is very strange indeed,' she agreed, as innocent as a kitten.

'I wonder, now, do you ever walk in the Park?' asked Kennet.

'Why, sometimes I do!' said Arabella. 'In the morning, with my maid.' She paused, and added, with the naughtiest gleam in her eye: 'The most *discreet* creature!'

He was still holding her tiny, gloved hand in his, and he pinched one of her fingers, and said, chuckling: 'Miss Ravenscar, you're the prettiest rogue I've clapped eyes on this many a day! It will be a queer thing, so it will, if we do not meet in the Park, one of these fine days.'

'Oh, do you walk there too?' asked Arabella ingenuously. 'Then I daresay we shall meet—one of these fine days!'

She withdrew her hand, and Mr Kennet laughed, and signed to the coachman to drive on.

Mr Ravenscar, meanwhile, in happy ignorance of his half-sister's activities, had received another letter from St James's Square, written in the same sloping characters as the first, but in far more agitated language. The letter hinted at unforeseen complications, held out a vague hope of capitulation, but expressed a desire on the part of the writer to meet him for the purpose of explaining the awkwardness of the situation. Mr Kennet, improvising freely in the guise of Miss Grantham, wrote that it was imperative that Lady Bellingham should know nothing either of this correspondence or of the proposed negotiations, and desired Mr Ravenscar to be so obliging as to reply under cover to Mr Lucius Kennet, at 66 Jermyn Street.

Mr Ravenscar found himself at a loss to understand either the mysterious references in the letter, or the need for discussion of his ultimatum, and wrote, as requested, to say so. This brought forth a distracted note, the gist of which left him with the impression that Lady Bellingham, and not Miss Grantham, was the prime mover in the plot to entrap Lord Mablethorpe; and indicated a fear of her aunt on Miss Grantham's part which would have astonished both ladies, had they been privileged to see this remarkable letter. It ended by begging Mr Ravenscar to do Miss Grantham the favour of meeting her at a rendezvous in the Park, on Wednesday afternoon, at dusk, when she engaged herself to explain fully to him how matters stood, and to do what lay in her power to comply with his wishes.

Mr Ravenscar, being almost wholly unacquainted with Lady Bellingham, saw nothing incredible in the suggestion that her niece might be acting under her compulsion. He was even conscious of a faint feeling of satisfaction, and was not entirely averse from meeting Miss Grantham again. Mr Kennet, accordingly, was gratified to receive, on the following day, a brief intimation from Mr Ravenscar that he would present himself at the rendezvous.

Silas Wantage, informed of the success of a stratagem which had had his full support, grunted, and said that Mr Kennet might leave the rest to him.

'My good man, Ravenscar's no Jessamy!' Kennet said impatiently. 'He boxes with Mendoza!'

'Handy with his fives, is he?' said Silas. 'I thought when he walked in here that night as how he'd strip to advantage. Well, it'll suit me fine to have a turn-up with him. I haven't had a good set-to since I don't know when.'

'Understand, Silas, this is no sporting event!' said Kennet. 'Miss Deborah wants Ravenscar delivered to her without commotion. There will be no turn-up.'

Mr Wantage seemed dissatisfied with this ruling, and shook his head disapprovingly at Lucius Kennet's plan of clubbing the victim into insensibility. But when it had been shown to him that an impromptu turn-up in the Park, even at dusk and in a little-frequented locality, could scarcely fail to attract attention, he yielded the point, and promised to assist Kennet to accomplish the business with the least possible amount of uproar.

Lady Bellingham's thoughts were diverted upon Wednesday afternoon, by the arrival from Kent of Mr Christopher Grantham, in all the glory of his scarlet regimentals.

Kit Grantham was three years younger than his sister. He was a pleasant-looking young man, fairer than Deborah, and without her brilliance of eye. From the circumstance of his having been granted every indulgence by his doting aunt, he had grown up to be rather spoilt, and not much inclined to consider the wishes of other people, but this selfishness arose more from thoughtlessness than from any badness of disposition, and he was in general very well-liked, having amiable manners, a good seat on a horse, and an openhanded nature which led him to spend a great deal of money in the sort of hospitality appreciated by his friends in the regiment.

He had not been to London on leave for above a year, so that his aunt and sister were delighted to see him, and could not fail to notice many changes in him, due to his advancing years. They hung about him in the fondest way, and found him all that a young officer should be. He was glad to be with them again, kissed them both most affectionately, and did his best to answer all their eager questions. But Deborah's asking him if he were happy in his career, and liked the other officers in the 14th, recalled to his mind its most pressing preoccupation, and he immediately adverted to the desirability of his exchanging into a cavalry regiment.

Deborah said at once that he must put such an idea out of his head, since the cost of it would be too great.

'Oh, but it would not be above eight hundred pounds, and very likely less, with the exchange money!' Kit assured her. 'I have a particular reason for wishing to be in a better regiment. You know, it is shabby work to be in a Line regiment, Deb! Only think how well a Hussar uniform would become your only brother!'

Miss Grantham, however, was impervious to his cajolery, and replied: 'Indeed, Kit, it would be impossible! Poor Aunt Lizzie has had such losses lately that you would not wish her to be put to extra expense on your account.'

'Oh no! But you are bound to come about again, ma'am, I am persuaded! *You* would like to see me in a pelisse and silver lace, now, wouldn't you?'

'Yes, but I do not know how it may be managed, dearest,' said Lady Bellingham, looking very much distressed. 'You have no idea what a charge this house is upon me! And now here is——' She broke off, as she encountered a warning glance from her niece, and said hurriedly: 'But that we shall say nothing about! We will talk of it later, Kit.'

'But you are living in such famous style here!' he said, looking about him critically. 'I never saw anything to equal it. It must have cost a fortune to furnish this house!'

'Well, that is just it,' replied his aunt. 'It did cost a fortune, not that it is paid for yet, because no one could possibly pay such bills as the wretched people are for ever dunning me with, but the thing is that everyone wants to run upon tick nowadays, and the times are so bad I declare it is a rarity to see a rouleau of as much as twenty guineas! And the E.O. table does not answer as well as we had hoped, besides being not quite the style of thing I like to have in my house.'

'An E.O. table!' he repeated, in astonished accents. 'My dear ma'am, you do not have *that* here, surely?'

'Why not?' asked his sister, in rather a hard voice. 'This is a gaming-house, Kit.'

He stirred uneasily in his chair, and began to talk about private parties.

'Oh, we send out cards of invitation, but we turn no one away from our door who has a few guineas to risk at the tables!' Deborah said.

It was evident that he could not like this, but as he stood a little in awe of his sister he did not say much until she had left the room. He turned then to Lady Bellingham, and desired her to tell him what could have possessed her to change the character of her evening-parties.

It had been agreed between Deborah and Lady Bellingham that nothing should be told Kit about the mortgage on the house, or Mr Ravenscar's threats to foreclose, but her ladyship divulged the rest of the story, not omitting the scandalous bill for green peas, or the inclusion in the household of Phœbe Laxton. Kit was quite bewildered, he had the greatest difficulty in unravelling the story. His sense of propriety, offended at the outset by the discovery that his aunt's select card-parties had sadly deteriorated, was still more severely tried by the knowledge that an attempt had been made to bribe his sister into relinquishing her claims to Lord Mablethorpe's title and fortune; but he said, in a fair-minded way, that if she had been allowed for the past year to preside over the saloons of what had become no better than a common gaming-house, he was not at all surprised, and could not blame Mablethorpe's relations for misliking the connection.

Lady Bellingham wept, and never thought of telling him that his own expensive habits had had much to do in making it necessary for her to turn her home into a gaming-house. She said that it was all very unlucky, but indeed she had not known where to turn for money to pay the tradesmen. As for Deb, if only she could be brought to marry Mablethorpe, there would be no harm done, but, on the contrary, a great deal of good. 'For she met him at the faro-table, you know, Kit, and even if he is a little young for her, it would be a splendid match!'

'I cannot think what can possess her to refuse such an eligible offer!' exclaimed Mr Grantham. 'Particularly *now*, when it would mean everything to me to have my sister in a position of consequence! However, she knows nothing of that yet, and I daresay she will change her mind when I tell her.'

'Tell her what, dear boy?' asked his aunt, drying her eyes. 'I assure you, she will listen to no one! Indeed, I think she has taken leave of her senses!'

Mr Grantham coloured, stammered, and then said in a self-conscious voice: 'The fact is, ma'am, I expect—that is, I hope—I believe I may say that I have every reason to think that—that—in short, aunt, I am in the expectation of being married myself shortly. You will recall that I mentioned the subject to you in a letter.'

'Oh, yes!' said her ladyship, sighing. 'But Deb says you cannot possibly be meaning to get married yet, and indeed, Kit, you are very young to be thinking of such a thing!'

'Deb is a great deal too busy!' said Kit, affronted. '*She* has never been in love, so *I* may not be either! But if you could only see her, aunt!'

'But I do see her!' objected her ladyship. 'What can you be thinking of, Kit?'

'Not Deb! Arabella!' said Mr Grantham, pronouncing the name in a reverent tone.

'Oh!' said his aunt. 'But it will cost you far more to be married than if you were to stay single, dearest. You can have no notion what housekeeping bills are like! Only fancy! Seventy pounds for green peas!'

'Well, as to that,' said Mr Grantham, reddening still more, 'Arabella is quite an heiress. Not that I mean to live upon *her* fortune, which is one reason why I should like to exchange, ma'am. But she comes of one of the best families, and all hinges upon my being found acceptable by her guardian! It would be above anything great if Deb were to become Lady Mablethorpe! Only think what a difference it would make to *me*!'

'Very true, my dear, but you will never prevail with her,' said his aunt gloomily. 'It would make a great difference to me too.'

'And instead of this,' pursued Mr Grantham, with a

157

strong sense of injury, 'I find that this house has become little better than a gaming-hell! Nothing could be more unfortunate! I do think you should have been more careful, ma'am!'

Lady Bellingham was quite crushed by this severity, but she could not feel that Kit had entirely grasped the exigencies of her situation. She tried, in a half-hearted way, to make him understand how difficult it was for a widow with expensive tastes and a nephew and a niece dependent upon her to live on a restricted income, but as his mind seemed to be almost wholly taken up with his own problems, it was doubtful if he attended to much that she said. At the first pause in her rambling explanation, he favoured her with a description of his Arabella's manifold charms, and expressed his conviction that if anything were to stand between him and marriage to the lady, he should find himself unable to support life, and might just as well blow his brains out and be done with it.

Lady Bellingham was horrified to hear such sentiments on his lips, and begged him to consider her nerves. His sister, when the conversation was reported to her, merely replied that she had listened to much the same stuff from Lord Mablethorpe, who was now falling in love with Phœbe as fast as he could.

'But Kit is so impulsive!' sighed Lady Bellingham. 'I must say, it would be a splendid thing if he were to marry an heiress, my love, and I am very sorry if anything I have done should put a spoke in his wheel.'

'How dare Kit say such a thing to you?' exclaimed Deborah. 'I never heard of anything so ungrateful in my life! If he talks in that vein to me, he shall soon hear what I think of his folly! As for his marrying an heiress, pooh! It will come to nothing, ma'am, for he has been in love a dozen times before, and will doubtless be in love a dozen times again. Who is the girl?'

'Oh, I don't know! He did not tell me, and I was too distracted to ask! My dearest love, he is not at all pleased with us for keeping a gaming-house, and what will he say if he hears of the mortgage, and that horrid man's foreclosing on me, I shudder to think!'

'You have nothing to worry about on that score, aunt: there will be no foreclosure.'

Miss Grantham spoke with a note of certainty in her voice, for she had received a note, brought round by hand from Mr Kennet's lodging, reminding her to prepare her cellar for a guest. She had implicit faith in Kennet, and felt perfectly sure that he would contrive to deliver the arch-enemy into her hands by nightfall. Lady Bellingham was expecting a fairly numerous gathering of people in her saloons that evening, and the only question now troubling Miss Grantham was how Kennet and Silas would manage to carry their prisoner into the cellar unobserved. As she could think of no way by which she might assist them, and supposed they must have taken this problem into account, she very sensibly put it out of her head, and went upstairs to change her green saque for an evening-gown of dull yellow brocade.

Lady Bellingham had meanwhile presented her nephew to Miss Laxton, first impressing on him that he must not divulge her presence in the house to a living soul. His sister had already explained to him the circumstances leading up to Phœbe's arrival in St James's Square, and although he was inclined to think it was excessively imprudent of her to have interfered in what was no concern of hers, he was not proof against the appeal of Phœbe's soft brown eyes, and air of fragility, and soon began to think Deborah had acted in a very proper manner.

He had very little opportunity to converse privately with Deborah before she went up to change her dress, but he did catch her alone for a few minutes on her way down again to the dining-room, and begged her to tell him whether it was true that she had refused a very advantageous offer of marriage. She replied truthfully that she had not done so, but when she saw how his face brightened she added that she had no real intention of marrying Mablethorpe, although she did not at present wish this known.

'You are the strangest girl!' he exclaimed. 'Why don't you mean to marry him? I am sure you cannot hope for a better offer! They say he will come into a very pretty fortune, and my aunt tells me he is perfectly amiable. I do not know what can ail you!'

'I am not in love with him,' replied Deborah, adding with rather a saucy smile: 'You will understand *that*, I am persuaded!'

He sighed. 'Yes, indeed I do, but the cases are not the same. You do not love anyone else, do you?'

'Certainly not, but I am not too old yet to fall in love, I hope.'

He looked at her rather anxiously. 'My aunt mentioned a Lord Ormskirk, Deb. I could not well make out what she meant: you know how she will run on! But it did not sound to me—— In short, you are not contemplating anything of a clandestine nature, are you?'

'No, no!' she assured him. 'You need have no fears!'

'I was sure you could not be! But everything seems to me so topsy-turvy here now—— But I can trust you!'

'I hope so indeed. But can *I* trust *you*, Kit? This is very shocking news, that you are meaning to be married!'

He laughed, and squeezed her arm. 'You will always be funning! Wait until you see her! You will understand then! She is the tiniest, daintiest little darling you can imagine, and with such a countenance! such pretty, taking ways! Only ten to one they will not let her marry me, more particularly since my aunt has allowed her house to become a haunt of gamesters! I was never so vexed!'

'If you do not like it, let me advise you to be less expensive!' said Deborah roundly. 'It is not for you to reproach Aunt Lizzie, after all! You cannot suppose that she keeps a gaming-house from her own choice.'

He looked a good deal mortified, and muttered something about having had no idea that things had come to this pass. 'I suppose it was Lucius who put the idea into my aunt's head. I wonder that he should have encouraged *you* to lend yourself to it!'

'My dear Kit, Lucius has no such nice notions! I could not leave my aunt to struggle alone. You must understand too that I am considered an attraction in the saloons!'

'How can you talk so! I declare, it makes me inclined to sell out! I do not like to have my sister playing hostess to a set of gamesters! Where is Lucius? Shall I see him to-night?'

'Undoubtedly,' replied Deborah, thinking that Lucius Kennet ought by now to be on his way to the house, and hoping very much that he had not failed to accomplish his task.

CHAPTER XI

MR RAVENSCAR came to the rendezvous in the Park alone, and on foot, as Kennet had hoped he would, when he appointed a meeting-place at no great distance from his house, and in one of the walks a little way away from the carriage-road. He knew that unless he drove himself Ravenscar either walked, or took a hackney, and it was not likely that he would have his curricle out so late in the day. He had himself hired a closed vehicle whose owner, a villainous-looking individual with a cauliflower ear, was vouched for by Silas. For five guineas, he was ready, he said jovially, to assist in a murder, and if it were a mere matter of abduction he counted it a very slight piece of work, and was happy to be of service. He bit the gold pieces that were given him, and said that he liked to have to do with honest culls. He engaged to hold his carriage in readiness in the Park, and to be deaf and blind to his employers' activities.

Mr Ravenscar saw the carriage as he crossed the road towards the path where he expected to meet Miss Grantham, and he supposed it to be hers. It was already dusk, and the Park was almost deserted. What reason Deborah could have for appointing a meeting-place in such secrecy, and at such an hour, he could not imagine. He would not have been surprised to find that there was some trick brewing, and was prepared to encounter all the feminine weapons of tears, cajolery, pleadings, and vapours. That she hoped to induce him to relent he was sure; he suspected, with a cynical twist to his mouth, that she was regretting her rejection of his fantastic offer of twenty thousand pounds, and determined that no arts of hers should prevail upon him to repeat the offer, or even the half of it. She might think herself fortunate to get the mortgage and the bills into her hands.

The path down which he was wending his way lay between beds of autumn flowers and was screened from the road by a belt of trees, which made it so dark, in the failing light, that he could not see many yards ahead. A rustic seat, where Miss Grantham should have met him, loomed vaguely ahead, beside a clump of flowering shrubs. No one was in sight. Ravenscar paused, frowning, and suddenly suspicious. It was no longer fashionable to wear a sword, and he carried nothing but his walking-cane in his hand. Some instinct of danger made him tighten his grip on this, but before he had well grasped that Miss Grantham had not kept her appointment with him, Silas

Wantage had sprung out from behind the bush with a club in his hand, and came at him in a rush.

Ravenscar escaped the blow aimed at his head only by the swiftness with which he ducked. The blow missed him, and he sprang back, holding his cane like a rapier. It was too dark to enable him to recognize Wantage; his first thought was that he had been set upon by a footpad. When Wantage came on again, the cane caught him so shrewdly across the elbow-joint that his club-hand dropped, and he let a grunt of pain. In that moment Ravenscar saw his chance, dropped his cane, and went in with a left and a right to the jaw. Silas's head went back, but he had not spent ten years in the Ring for nothing, and he recovered quickly, abandoning his club, and covering up in the manner of an experienced bruiser. 'Come on then!' he growled, pleased that it should have come to a turn-up after all.

Mr Ravenscar did come on, but Lucius Kennet, anxious to finish the business, and fearing that they might at any moment be surprised by a Park keeper, or some late wayfarer, ran out from his hiding-place behind Ravenscar, and clubbed him before he realized that he had two opponents instead of only one.

Mr Ravenscar dropped where he stood. Silas Wantage said angrily: 'You hadn't ought to have done that! Hitting of him from behind, and spoiling the prettiest set-to I've had in years! That was a foul blow, Mr Kennet, sir, and I don't hold with such!'

'Don't stand there chattering, you fool!' said Kennet, kneeling down beside Ravenscar's inert body. 'He'll come to himself in a minute! Help me to tie him up!'

Silas somewhat sulkily produced two lengths of whip-cord, and began to bind one about Ravenscar's ankles, while Kennet lashed his wrists behind his back, and gagged him with a handkerchief, and a scarf.

'I said he'd peel to advantage, and so he would,' said Silas. 'Did you see the right he landed to my jaw? Ah, he knows his way about, *he* does! Fair rattled my bone-box, I can tell you. And then you goes and lays him out before I've had time to do so much as draw his cork!'

'I'm thinking it was your own cork would have been drawn,' retorted Kennet, making his knots fast. 'Take you his legs, man, and I'll take his head. We'll have him safe hidden in the carriage before he comes round.'

'I don't deny he's fast,' admitted Silas, helping to raise Mr Ravenscar from the ground. 'But it goes against the grain with me to see as likely a bruiser knocked out by a foul, Mr Kennet, and that's the truth!'

By the time they had borne Mr Ravenscar's body to the waiting carriage, both men were somewhat out of breath, and extremely glad to be able to dump their burden on the back seat. Mr Ravenscar was no lightweight.

The carriage had left the Park, and was rumbling over the cobbled streets when Ravenscar stirred, and opened his eyes. He was conscious first of a swimming head that ached and throbbed, and next of his bonds. He made one convulsive attempt to free his hands.

'Ah, now, be easy!' said Kennet in his ear. 'There's no harm will come to you at all if you're sensible, Mr Ravenscar.'

Mr Ravenscar was dizzy, and bewildered, but he knew that voice. He became still, rigid with anger: anger at Miss Grantham's perfidy, anger at his own folly in allowing himself to be led into such a trap.

Another, and deeper voice spoke in the darkness of the carriage. 'You went down to a foul,' it said apologetically. 'That weren't none of my doing, for milling a cove down from behind is what I don't hold with, and never did, 'specially a cove as stands up as well as you do, sir, and shows such a handy bunch of fives. But you hadn't ought to have gone a-persecuting of Miss Deb, when all's said.'

Mr Ravenscar did not recognize this voice, but the language informed him that he was in the company of a bruiser. He closed his eyes, trying to overcome his dizziness, and to collect his wits.

By the time the carriage drew up outside Lady Bellingham's house, it was dark enough to enable the conspirators to smuggle their prisoner down the area-steps without being observed either by a man who was walking away in the direction of Pall Mall, or by two chairmen waiting outside a house farther down the square.

The basement of Lady Bellingham's house was very large, very ill-lit, and rambling enough to resemble a labyrinth more nearly than the kitchen-quarters of a well-appointed mansion. The cellar destined for Mr Ravenscar's temporary occupation was reached at the end of a stone-paved corridor, and contained, besides a quantity of store-cupboards, most of Lady Bellingham's trunks and cloak-bags; a collection of empty bandboxes, stacked up against one wall; and a Windsor chair, thoughtfully placed there by Miss Grantham.

Mr Ravenscar was set down on the chair by his panting bearers. Silas Wantage, who had provided himself with the lantern that stood on a table just inside the area-door, critically surveyed him, and gave it as his opinion that he would do. Mr Kennet shook out his ruffles, and smiled upon the victim in a way that made Mr Ravenscar long to have his hands free for only two minutes.

'I'm thinking the second round goes to Deb, Mr Ravenscar. Don't you be worrying your head, however, for it's not for long she means to keep you here ! We'll be leaving you now for a while. You will be wanting to think over your situation, I dare swear.'

'Ay, we'd best tell Miss Deb we have him safe,' agreed Silas.

Both men then left the cellar, taking the lantern with them, and locking the heavy door behind them. Mr Ravenscar was left to darkness and reflection.

Abovestairs, dinner was over, but none of the expected visitors to the saloons had yet arrived. Mr Kennet strolled into the little back-parlour on the half-landing, where the three ladies were sitting with Kit Grantham, and directed the ghost of a wink at Deborah before going up to shake hands with her brother. It was a little while before any opportunity for exchanging a private word with him occurred, but when he had greeted Kit, and each had asked the other a number of jovial questions, Lady Bellingham recollected that on the previous evening the E.O. table had not seemed to her to be running true, and desired Kennet to inspect it. As he followed her out of the room, he passed Miss Grantham's chair, smiled down at her, and dropped a large iron key in her lap. She covered it at once with her handkerchief, torn between guilt and triumph, and in a few minutes murmured an excuse, and left the room.

She found Silas Wantage in the front-hall, ready to open the door to the evening's guests. 'Silas! Did you—did you have any trouble?'

'No,' said Wantage. 'Not to say trouble. But he displays to remarkable advantage, I will say, nor I don't hold with hitting him over the head with a cudgel from behind, which was what Kennet done.'

'Oh dear!' exclaimed Miss Grantham, turning pale. 'Has he hurt him?'

'Not to signify, he hasn't. But I would have milled him down, for all he planted me a wisty castor right in the bonebox. What's to be done now, missie?'

'I must see him,' said Miss Grantham resolutely.

'I'd best come with you, then, and fetch a lantern.'

'I will take a branch of candles down. The servants

might notice it if you took the lantern away. But please come with me, Silas!'

'I'll come right enough, but you've no call to be scared, Miss Deb: he's tied up as neat as a spring chicken.'

'I am not scared,' said Miss Grantham coldly.

She fetched one of the branches of candles from the supper-room, and Silas, having instructed one of the waiters to mount guard over the door, led the way down the precipitous stairs to the cellars. He took the big key from her, and flung open the door of Mr Ravenscar's prison. Mr Ravenscar, looking under frowning brows, was gratified by the vision of a tall goddess in a golden dress, holding up a branch of candles whose flaming tongues of light touched her hair with fire. Not being in a mood to appreciate beauty, he regarded this agreeable picture without any change in his expression.

Miss Grantham said indignantly: 'There was no need to leave him with that horrid thing tied round his mouth! No one would hear him in this place, if he shouted for help! Untie it this instant, Silas!'

Mr Wantage grinned, and went to remove the scarf and the gag. Miss Grantham saw that her prisoner was rather pale, and a good deal dishevelled, and said, in a voice of some concern: 'I am afraid they handled you roughly! Silas, please to fetch a glass of wine for Mr Ravenscar!'

'You are too good, ma'am!' said Mr Ravenscar, with bitter emphasis.

'Well, I am sorry if you were hurt, but it was quite your own fault,' said Miss Grantham defensively. 'If you had not done such a shabby thing to me I would not have had you kidnapped. You have behaved in the most odious fashion, and you deserve it all!' A rankling score came into her mind. She added: 'You did me the honour once, Mr Ravenscar, of telling me that I should be whipped at the cart's tail!'

'Do you expect me to beg your pardon?' he demanded. 'You will be disappointed, my fair Cyprian!'

Miss Grantham flushed rosily, and her eyes darted fire. 'If you dare to call me by that name I will hit you!' she said between her teeth.

'You may do what you please—strumpet!' replied Mr Ravenscar.

She took one hasty step towards him, and then checked, saying in a mortified tone: 'You are not above taking an unfair advantage of me. You know very well I can't hit you when you have your hands tied.'

'You amaze me, ma'am! I had not supposed you to be restricted by any consideration of fairness!'

'You have no right to say so!' flashed Miss Grantham.

He laughed harshly. 'Indeed? You go a great deal too fast for me, let me tell you! You got me here by a trick I was fool enough to think even you would not stoop to——'

'It's not true! I used no trick!'

'What then do you call it?' he jeered. 'What of your heart-rending appeals to my generosity, ma'am? What of those affecting letters you wrote to me?'

'I didn't!' she said. 'I would *scorn* to do such a thing!'

'Very fine talking! But it won't answer, Miss Grantham! I have your last billet in my pocket at this moment.'

'I cannot conceive what you mean!' she exclaimed. 'I only sent you one letter in my life, and that I did not write myself, as you must very well know!'

'What?' demanded Ravenscar incredulously. 'Do you stand there telling me you did not beg me to meet you in the Park this evening, because you dared not let it be known by your aunt that you were ready to come to terms with me?'

An expression of horrified dismay came into Miss Grantham's face. 'Show me that letter!' she said, in a stifled voice.

'I am—thanks to your stratagems, ma'am—unable to oblige you. If you want to continue this farce, you may feel for it in the inner pocket of my coat.'

She hestitated for a moment, and then moved forward, and slid her hand into his pocket. 'I do want to see it. If you are not lying to me——'

'Do not judge me by yourself, I beg of you!' snapped Ravenscar.

Her fingers found the letter, and drew it forth. One glance at the superscription was enough to confirm her fears. 'Oh, good God! Lucius!' she said angrily. She spread open the sheet, and ran her eyes down it. 'Infamous!' she ejaculated. 'How *dared* he do such a thing? Oh, I could kill him for this!' She crushed the letter in her hand, and rounded on Ravenscar, the very personification of wrath. 'And you! You thought *I* would write such—such *craven* stuff? I would die rather! You are the most hateful, odious man I ever met in my life, and if you think I would stoop to such shabby tricks as these, you are a fool, besides being insolent, and overbearing, and——'

'Are you asking me to believe that the letters I have had from you were not written by you?' interrupted Ravenscar.

'I don't care what you believe!' replied Miss Grantham, a good deal upset. 'Of course I did not write them! I did not want to write to you at all, only Lucius Kennet persuaded me to let him answer that horrid letter of yours! And he *did* ask me to try to trick you into meeting me, so that he could kidnap you, but I would not do such a thing, and so I told him! Oh, I was never so provoked! I see it all now! That was why he wanted to answer your letter in his own hand, so that you should think it was my writing!' The colour rushed up again into her face; she looked remorsefully down at Ravenscar, and said: 'Indeed, I am very sorry, and I quite see that you might be excessively angry with me. The truth is that I told Lucius Kennet and Silas to kidnap you for me, but I thought they could do it without using any horrid stratagems! *That* was fair enough! There could be no possible objection, for how could I kidnap you myself?'

Mr Ravenscar was sitting in a position of considerable discomfort, with cords cutting into his wrists and ankles; and his head was aching as well, but his lips twitched at this, and he burst out laughing. 'Oh, no objection at all, Miss Grantham!'

'Well, I think it was perfectly fair,' argued Miss Grantham reasonably. 'I am very sorry you have been tricked, but what is to be done? It cannot be helped now.'

'What do you propose to do with me?' enquired Ravenscar.

'I don't mean to hurt you,' she assured him. 'In fact, I told Lucius I did not wish them to hurt you more than was needful, and I do hope they did not?'

'Oh, not at all, ma'am! I like being hit over the head with cudgels!' he said sardonically.

Mr Wantage, who had come back into the cellar in time to hear this remark, said: 'I disremember when I've been more put-about by anything.' He set down the glass he carried, and proceeded to draw the cork out of a dusty bottle. 'I've brought a bottle of the *good* burgundy, Miss Deb.'

'Yes, of course,' Deborah said. 'You will feel more the thing when you have drunk a little of it, Mr Ravenscar.'

'I should feel still more the thing if I had a hand free,' replied Ravenscar grimly.

'Don't you go a-letting of him loose, Miss Deb!' Silas warned her. 'We'll keep them bunches of fives of his fast behind his back, or you'll be having a mill in the cellar, which your aunt won't like. Here you are, sir!'

Mr Ravenscar drank the wine which was being held to

170

his lips, and once more looked Miss Grantham over. 'Well?' he said. 'What now, ma'am?'

'You'd best make haste, Miss Deb,' said Wantage. 'I'll have to get back to the front-door, or we shall have I-dunno-who walking into the house.'

'I don't need you, Silas,' Deborah replied. 'You may go up now, and leave me to tell Mr Ravenscar what I mean to do.'

Silas looked a little doubtful, but when his mistress assured him that she had no intention of releasing Mr Ravenscar from his bonds, he consented to withdraw, reminding her, however, to be sure to lock the door securely when she left the cellar.

'Will you have some more wine, sir?' asked Deborah, apparently conscious of her duties as his hostess.

'No,' said Ravenscar baldly.

'You are not very polite!' she said.

'I do not feel very polite. If you care to untie my ankles, however, I will engage to offer you my chair.'

Miss Grantham looked rather distressed. 'Indeed, I fear you must be very uncomfortable,' she owned.

'I am.'

'Well, I do not see what harm there can be in setting your legs free,' she decided, and knelt down on the stone floor to wrestle with Silas Wantage's knots. 'Oh dear, they have bound you shockingly tightly!'

'I am well aware of that, ma'am.'

She looked up. 'It is of no use to sound so cross. I daresay you would like to murder me, but you should not have tried to threaten me. It was very ungentlemanly of you, let me tell you; and if you thought I could be so easily frightened into giving up your cousin, you see now how mistaken you were! I have brought you here to get that mortgage and those dreadful bills from you.'

He laughed shortly. 'You have missed the mark,

Miss Grantham. I don't carry them upon my person.'

'Oh no! But you can write a letter to your servants, directing them to place the bills in a messenger's hands,' she pointed out.

He looked down at her bent head. 'My good girl, you've mistaken your man! Bring on your thumbscrew and your rack! You will get nothing out of me.'

She tugged at the knot. 'I don't mean you the least harm, sir, I assure you. No one will hurt you in this house. Only you will not leave it until those bills are in my hands.'

'Evidently my stay in your cellar is to be a prolonged one.'

'Oh, I hardly think so!' she said, her eyes glinting up at him for an instant. 'I have not forgotten, if you have, that you are driving in an important race to-morrow.'

He stiffened, his mouth shutting hard. She pulled the last knot undone, and stood up. 'I trust you are more at ease now, sir,' she said kindly. 'But I am persuaded you will not languish for very long in this horrid cellar. So noted a sportsman as Mr Ravenscar will scarcely let it be said of him that he dared not match his famous grays against Sir James Filey's pair! After such a prodigious bet, too!'

'You doxy!' he said deliberately.

She flushed, but shrugged her shoulders. 'Calling hard names won't help you, Mr Ravenscar. You stand to lose twenty-five thousand pounds on to-morrow's race.'

'What do you think I care for that?' he demanded harshly.

'Not very much, perhaps. I think you care a good deal for your reputation, and will not readily lose by default.'

'You may go to the devil!' he said.

'You cannot have considered your position, Mr Ravenscar. No one but myself, and Lucius Kennet, and Silas, knows your whereabouts. If you think to be rescued, you will be disappointed. There is nothing for you to do but to agree to *my* terms.'

'You may have those bills when, and when only, I am satisfied that my cousin has no longer any intention of marrying you,' said Ravenscar. 'There is no pressure you can bring to bear on me that could prevail upon me to yield one inch to such a Jezebel as you are!'

'I feel sure you will change your mind when you have had time to reflect, sir. Only fancy how odious Sir James would be if you failed to keep your appointment to-morrow! I do not think that a man of *your* pride could bear that!'

'More easily than to be worsted by a jade, ma'am!' he retorted, stretching his long legs out before him, and crossing his ankles. 'You will find it very inconvenient to keep me in your cellar indefinitely, I imagine, but I must warn you that I have not the smallest intention of leaving it, except upon my own terms.'

'But you cannot let the race go like that!' cried Deborah, aghast.

'Oh, have you backed me to win?' he said mockingly. 'So much the worse for you, my girl!'

'No, I have not, and I do not care if you win or lose!' said Deborah. 'There is nothing that you can do that I care for in the least, for I find you beneath contempt! But this is folly, and you know it!'

'I can see that it is very inconvenient folly,' he agreed, maddeningly cool.

She stamped her foot. 'You will have the whole town sneering at you!'

'I will bear that for the pleasure of seeing you in Bride-well.'

'You will not see me in Bridewell!' she retorted. 'Do not imagine that I did not take that into account when I had you kidnapped! You may be poltroon enough to threaten a female with ruin, but you are a great deal too stiff-necked to admit to the world that you were done-up by a female, and locked into a cellar, and kept there by her!'

'How well you think you know me!' said Ravenscar.

She checked the hot words that rose to her tongue, and picked up the branch of candles. 'I will leave you to reflect,' she said coldly. 'When you have thought the matter over, you will no doubt see it in another light.'

'Don't raise your hopes, ma'am! I can be quite as obstinate as you.' He watched her ironically, as she moved towards the door. 'Why did you refuse my first offer?' he asked abruptly.

She looked back, magnificent in her scorn. 'Yes! You thought I could be bought off, did you not, Mr Ravenscar? You thought you had only to dangle your money-bags before my eyes, and I should be dazzled! Well, I was not dazzled, and I would not touch one penny of your money!'

'If that is so, why am I here?' he enquired.

'The mortgage and those bills are different,' she replied impatiently.

He looked amused. 'So it seems.'

'Besides, they are not mine, but my aunt's.'

'Then why worry about them?'

'You have a very pretty opinion of me, I declare!' she exclaimed. 'Not only am I the kind of abominable wretch who would entrap a——' She broke off in some confusion, and said hurriedly: 'But there is no talking to you, after all! I shall marry your cousin whenever I choose, and I shall get the mortgage too, and you are at liberty to call me what names you like, for I do not care a button!'

Mr Ravenscar, on whom the first part of this speech had not been lost, sat up, frowning heavily. 'Now, what the devil are you playing at, Miss Grantham? So you are *not* the kind of abominable wretch who would entrap a boy into marriage? Then why, in God's name——'

174

'Certainly not!' Miss Grantham said, making desperate efforts to retrieve her slip. 'There is no question of entrapping Adrian! He is quite devoted to me, I assure you! You will find it very hard to persuade him to give me up.'

'I do not propose to make the attempt,' he replied. 'I rely upon you to do that.'

'I have no notion of doing it. I have a fancy to be my Lady Mablethorpe.'

'To which end, I suppose, you assumed the manners of a trollop at Vauxhall the other night!'

She bit her lip. 'Oh, I did that merely to make you angry! I thought it would do you a great deal of good to see how a *harpy* might behave!'

'So that rankled, did it?' he said, smiling rather grimly. 'I still say you are a harpy, Miss Grantham.'

'If I were, I would have closed with your obliging offer!'

'I fancy you nourished hopes of getting more from me than twenty thousand pounds,' he said. 'Was not your behaviour at Vauxhall designed to convince me that no price would be too great to pay for my unfortunate cousin's redemption?'

She showed him a white face, and very glittering eyes. 'If I were a man,' she said in a shaking voice, 'I would run you through!'

'There is nothing to stop you doing so now, if you can borrow a sword,' he replied.

Miss Grantham swept out of the cellar, too angry to speak, and slammed and locked the door behind her.

Her interview with the prisoner had not followed the lines she had planned, and although she told herself that a period of reflection must bring Ravenscar to his senses, she could not help feeling a considerable degree of uneasiness. There was a look in his eyes, a stubborn jut to his chin, which held out no promise of his weakening. If he really did refuse to capitulate, she would find herself in the most awkward predicament, for not only would it be impossible to keep him bound up in the cellar, but every instinct rebelled against putting her threat into action, and keeping him from his appointment on the morrow. Miss Grantham was too much a gamester herself to regard with anything but horror a failure to make good a wager.

She made her way upstairs to the hall, where she was unfortunate enough to meet her aunt, who had that instant come down from the Yellow Saloon to cast an eye over the supper-tables.

'Good heavens, Deb, where have you been?' she asked. 'What in the world should take you downstairs? Oh, if you have not dirtied your dress! How came you to do that, my love?'

Miss Grantham saw that there was a mark on the skirt of her brocade gown, and tried to brush it off. 'It's nothing, ma'am. I was obliged to step down to the cellar, and I knelt on the floor for a moment. I am sure it is not very noticeable.'

Lady Bellingham looked at her with a lively expression of anxiety in her face. 'Deb, you are at your tricks again!' she said, in a hollow voice. 'I insist on your telling me this instant what it is you are about! What have you got in the cellar? I never knew you go down there before in your life!'

'Dearest Aunt Lizzie, indeed you had much better not ask me!' Deborah said, her lips trembling on the verge of one of her irrepressible smiles. 'It would only bring on your spasms!'

Lady Bellingham gave a small shriek, and pulled her into the supper-room. 'Deb, do not trifle with me, I implore you! You have done something dreadful, I know! Don't say it's murder!'

Miss Grantham laughed. 'No, no, it is not as bad as that ma'am! I promise you, everything will turn out famously. Who is here to-night?'

'Never mind that! I cannot enjoy a moment's peace until I know what you have been about!'

'Well, I am busily employed in getting your bills back, ma'am, and the mortgage too,' Deborah replied.

Instead of showing relief at these tidings, Lady Bellingham turned pale under her rouge. 'How can you possibly do so? Oh, heavens, don't say you have *stolen* them!'

'Nothing of the sort, aunt. Do let us go upstairs! Your guests will wonder what has become of you.'

'You have had Ravenscar murdered, and hidden his body in my cellar!' uttered her ladyship, sinking into a chair. 'We shall all be ruined! I knew it!'

'My dear ma'am, it is no such thing!' Deborah said, amused. 'He is not dead, I assure you!'

Lady Bellingham's eyes seemed to be in imminent danger of starting from their sockets. 'Deb!' she said, in a strangled voice. 'You don't mean that you really have Ravenscar in my cellar?'

'Yes, dearest, but indeed he is alive!'

'We *are* ruined!' said her ladyship, with a calm born of despair. 'The best we can hope for is that they will put you in Bedlam. Oh, what have I ever done to deserve this?'

'But, ma'am, you do not understand! There is nothing for you to fear! I have merely kidnapped him, and mean to hold him until he gives up these bills. Then we may be comfortable again!'

'You know nothing of Bedlam, if you think anyone can be comfortable there! Very likely they will refuse to believe that you are mad, and we shall both be transported.'

'No, we shall not, dearest! Mr Ravenscar will never bring himself to admit to the world that he was worsted by faro's daughter! Whatever vengeance he takes, it will not be that. Only leave it to me!'

Lady Bellingham moaned.

'If you had not caught me coming up the stairs, you would never have known anything about it!' urged Miss Grantham. 'There is nothing you can do, for I have the key of the cellar in my pocket, and I don't mean to give it up. Forget it, Aunt Lizzie! Is Adrian here to-night?'

'What should that signify?' asked her ladyship bitterly. 'You have treated him so roughly that the poor boy flies to Phœbe!'

'Well, that is just what I wanted him to do,' said Miss Grantham cheerfully. 'Let us go upstairs!'

Her ladyship rose, and allowed herself to be escorted up to the saloons, but she was evidently much shaken, and felt quite unequal to taking her usual place at the faro-table, where a sprinkling of people were already seated, but wandered about instead in a distracted way, pausing for a few minutes to watch the E.O. board, and drifting away again as though she did not know where to go next. Miss Grantham, concealing some inward qualms under a gay front, let it be seen that she was in spirits, and became the life and soul of a not very serious game of hazard, in the smaller saloon.

CHAPTER XII

At about nine o'clock, the rooms began to fill up. Sir James Filey arrived with several friends, to play faro, and he had no sooner greeted his hostess than he said: 'You have not seen Ravenscar, have you, Lady Bel?'

Her ladyship gave a start, and faltered: 'No, indeed! How should I?'

Filey put up his glass, and surveyed the room. 'Why, I hear that he was pledged to dine with Crewe, and some others! They waited for him until past eight, and then were obliged to sit down without him. I see he is not here.'

'No, no, he is not here!' said Lady Bellingham, fanning herself with a trembling hand.

'Very odd!' said Filey, with a faint, sneering smile. 'I understand that Crewe sent word to his house, but got no news of him there. I trust he has not forgotten our meeting to-morrow.'

Lord Mablethorpe, who was standing near enough to overhear these remarks, came towards the faro-table, saying: 'You may rest at ease on that score, Sir James. My cousin will not fail to keep his appointment with you.'

'Oh, do you know where he is?' said Filey, looking him over with a lift to his brows.

'No,' said Adrian. 'I do not. But if you mean to imply, sir, that my cousin will not come up to scratch I am happy to be able to set your mind at rest! He has never yet failed to keep a sporting engagement.'

'What an elevating thing is family affection!' said Filey sweetly. 'Does your estimable cousin know that the betting is in my favour, I wonder? He was a little hasty when he laid such odds on himself, was he not? I recall that you were of that opinion at the time, my lord.'

'Was I?' retorted Adrian. 'I must have forgotten the outcome of your previous encounter!'

Sir James continued to smile, with that air of patronage which made Adrian long to hit him. 'But he matches his grays against a very different pair this time, you must remember.'

'True, but you are driving them, are you not?' said Adrian, with deceptive innocence.

Sir James's face darkened, but before he could speak, Miss Grantham, who had joined the group, intervened, exclaiming: 'So it is you, Sir James! I vow, we thought you had deserted us! Do you care to try your hand at faro to-night, or have you a fancy for the bones? Oh, there you

179

are, Adrian! I wish you will fetch my fan from the other room: I have laid it down somewhere there. And what is all this about Mr Ravenscar, Sir James?'

'Merely that he seems to have disappeared, my dear. I hope we may not hear that he is in poor health, or has been called away on important business.'

'I hope not indeed, and do not suppose there is the least likelihood of it. I cannot conceive what should have put such a notion into your head!'

He spread out his hands. 'My information is that he left his house at dusk this evening, and has not been heard of since. You will admit it to be a singular business!'

'I fear any hope you may cherish of winning by Mr Ravenscar's default will have but a short life,' Miss Grantham replied contemptuously.

He coloured angrily, but as her words were received with a good deal of ill-concealed amusement by those who heard them, he merely bowed, and moved away from her.

Lady Bellingham, feeling herself to be in danger of fainting from fright, retired to the buffet, and told the waiter there to pour her out a glass of claret. She was reviving herself with this when her nephew came up to her, and asked in an urgent under-voice: 'What is this they are saying about Ravenscar?'

'Don't mention that name!' begged her ladyship, with a shudder. 'The least thing will bring on my spasms!'

'But are you acquainted with him?' he demanded. 'I had no idea! Will he come here to-night?'

'Ask your sister!' said Lady Bellingham helplessly. 'I have borne enough, and wash my hands of it. But if we are all clapped up for this night's work, don't lay the blame at my door, that's all I ask of you!'

'I do not understand you! What is the matter, my dear ma'am? What can Deb know of Ravenscar?'

'She has him locked up in the cellar, and she means to keep him there,' replied her ladyship.

'What!'

'Oh dear, I ought not to have told you, for Deb said you were to know nothing about the mortgage, but I declare I am so distracted I do not know what I am doing! She has locked him in the cellar to make him surrender some odious bills of mine, and there is his race to be run to-morrow, and I know he will hound us to our graves for this night's work! But there she stands, laughing away as though she had not a care in the world, and for all she knows he will catch his death in the cellar! But she has the key in her pocket, and she says that she doesn't mean to give it up!'

'Does she, by God!' muttered Mr Grantham, and strode away to where his sister was standing. 'Deb! I want a word with you!' he said in her ear. 'Come outside on to the landing for a moment!'

She looked surprised, but called to Kennet to take her place at the E.O. board, and followed Kit out of the room. 'What is it, my dear? You look quite upset! Have you been plunging at hazard, or have you discovered that the wine is corked?'

'Upset! I have reason to be! What is this my aunt tells me about Mr Ravenscar?'

'The devil fly away with Aunt Lizzie!' said Miss Grantham undutifully. 'What has she told you?'

'That you have him locked in the cellar! I cannot credit it!'

'Well, I did not mean you to know of it,' replied Deborah, 'but there is not much harm done, after all. It is just such a joke as you will appreciate, Kit! You must know that Ravenscar is Lord Mablethorpe's cousin, and has been set against my marriage to him. I cannot tell you the insults I have suffered at his hands! But that is nothing, and I don't mean to complain now that I have such a neat revenge on him. He has got into his possession some bills of my aunt's, and tried to threaten me with them. So I had him kidnapped, and brought to this house, and there he is, neatly tied up in the cellar until he chooses to give up the bills! There is nothing for you to worry your head over!'

'Nothing for me to worry my head over!' he repeated, in a stupefied tone. 'Do you know what you have done? It is Arabella Ravenscar whom I hope to marry!'

She stared at him for a moment in the blankest astonishment, but instead of showing any sign of contrition, when the full import of this disclosure had dawned upon her, she burst into a gurgle of laughter. 'Oh no! Oh, Kit, I am very sorry, but you had never the least hope of marrying her! Ravenscar would see her dead at his feet rather!'

'Thanks to your crazy conduct!' he said furiously. 'Upon my soul, I believe you *are* mad! Where is the key to the cellar?'

'In my pocket, where it will stay!' she replied.

'Give it to me this instant! God knows what I can find to say to him! I shall tell him that you are not yourself. Oh, there was never anything so damnably unlucky!'

She was no longer laughing. She laid her hand on his arm, saying seriously: 'You cannot mean to be so disloyal to me!'

'Disloyal! Do you expect me to help you to gaol? That is where you will end, I can tell you, unless I can smooth Ravenscar down! If you wish to talk of disloyalty, pray consider your own conduct in alienating the one man in the world I would give a fortune to be on terms with! Give me the key!'

'I'll do no such thing!' Deborah said, backing away from him. 'How can you be so poor-spirited, Kit? Does Arabella Ravenscar mean more to you than Aunt Lizzie, and me? I am very sure she does not intend to marry you!'

'You know nothing of the matter! Are you going to give me that key?'

'No, I am not!'

'Then I'll take it!' said Kit, closing with her.

Miss Grantham fought desperately, but being no match for him was very soon overcome. He dragged the key from her pocket, and waiting only long enough to say: 'I am sorry if you are hurt, but it is your own fault!' ran down the stairs to the hall.

She would have followed him, to call to Silas to stop him, but the sound of voices below informed her that more guests were arriving. Angry as she was, she could not inaugurate a brawl in front of strangers, and was obliged to go back into the saloon, to hide her rage and her chagrin under the best smile she could muster.

Mr Grantham was also checked by the noise of fresh arrivals, and turned back to make his way down the back-stairs. In the basement he ran into a surprised kitchen-maid, but he told her hastily that he had come down to the cellars to look out a very special wine, and brushed past her. Finding the lantern by the area-door, he picked this up, and after plunging into a coal-cellar, several store-cupboards, and a boot-hole, came upon the locked door at the end of the stone passage. He fitted the key into the lock with trembling fingers, and turned it, and pushed open the door, holding up the lantern.

Its glow illuminated Mr Ravenscar's harsh features, and showed him to be still sitting in the Windsor chair, with his legs crossed, and his hands behind his back.

'Sir!' stammered Kit. 'Sir! Mr Ravenscar?'

'Who the devil are you?' asked Ravenscar.

Kit set the lantern down on the top of a corded trunk. 'Oh, sir, I do not know what you must think! I do not know what to say to you! I am Grantham —Deb's brother, you know! I came as soon as I was aware—I was never more shocked in my life!'

'Her brother? Oh, yes, I seem to remember that there was some talk of a brother! Have you come to try to persuade me in your sister's stead? You will not succeed.'

'No, no!' Kit assured him. 'I never knew—I would never have consented, nor permitted—I am most heartily sorry for it, sir, indeed I am! I have come to set you free! Nothing was ever so disgraceful! But you will forgive Deb, I know! She was always so headstrong that no one could do anything with her, but though she has a quick temper she don't mean any harm!'

Ravenscar, who had been regarding him with a lowering brow, broke in on this to demand: 'Are you aware of the circumstances that have led to my being in this damnably uncomfortable cellar?'

'Yes—at least, not entirely, for I had no time to listen to it all! But it can't signify, and Deb had no right to kidnap you like this! I cannot think how she could be so mad!'

'Let there be no misunderstanding about this!' said Ravenscar. 'Your sister, I suppose, must have told you that I have insulted her in almost every conceivable way?'

'Oh, but I know how she talks when she is angry, and I assure you I set very little store by it!'

'Well, I did insult her,' said Ravenscar.

Kit looked very much taken aback by this, and did not know what to say. After a moment, he stammered: 'I daresay she might have vexed you excessively. I do not rightly understand just what—but you cannot remain here, that is certain! Good God, did she have you tied up? I will have you free in a trice!'

'Keep your distance!' said Ravenscar, holding him off with one elegantly shod foot. 'Why should you want to set me free? If you had come to knock my teeth down my throat I could better understand it!'

'You cannot suppose that I will allow my sister to—to

184

tie people up, and put them in the cellar!' exclaimed Kit. 'I never heard of such a thing! And when I learned that it was *you*—you must know, sir, that I am—that I have the honour of being acquainted with your sister—with Miss Arabella Ravenscar!'

'Oh!' said Ravenscar. 'So you are acquainted with my sister, are you? Are you, I wonder, stationed in Tunbridge Wells?'

'Yes,' said Kit eagerly. 'That is where I met her, sir! I had hoped to have called upon you in town. I wanted very particularly to——'

"To ask for my permission to pay your addresses to her, I infer?'

Kit blushed, and looked rather sheepish. 'Yes. Yes, that was it, sir! You must know that I——'

'I want to know nothing at all about it!' interrupted Ravenscar unkindly. 'There is not the smallest likelihood of my giving you permission to address her, and if you ever dare to come into my house, I'll kick you down the steps!'

Kit turned pale at this brutal speech. 'It was not my fault that you were brought here, sir! You must believe I had nothing to do with it! I was in total ignorance of it until just now! You cannot mean to visit your anger upon me, and upon Arabella! Indeed——'

'Let me tell you, Mr Grantham, that there would have been more hope of winning my consent to your suit if you had come here to quarrel with me!' said Ravenscar cuttingly. 'When my sister marries it will be to a man with some spirit in him! Why, you contemptible little worm, if you had a spark of pride or courage you would be calling me out, not offering to set me free! Your sister is worth a dozen of you! And she is a jade!'

Kit swallowed, and said with what dignity he could summon up: 'You must be aware that I cannot strike a man who is bound. If Deb had only told me what was amiss I would have acted for her, and I hope I know how to protect my own sister! But to have you kidnapped is beyond anything! You are angry, and I cannot wonder at it, but——'

'Go to the devil!' said Ravenscar.

'But—but shan't I untie you?' asked Kit, utterly bewildered. 'You cannot mean to remain here all night!'

'What I mean to do is no concern of yours! How did you come by that key?'

'I took it from Deb,' faltered Kit.

'Then take it back to her—with my compliments! And don't forget to lock the door behind you!' said Mr Ravenscar.

Kit looked at him in a somewhat dazed fashion, but as Mr Ravenscar's countenance wore a most forbidding expression, he picked up the lantern, and backed out of the cellar, obediently locking the door again, and removing the key. It seemed as though Ravenscar as well as Deborah was mad, and he was quite at a loss to know what to do. He went slowly upstairs again, and since there could be no object in retaining the key to a cell whose inmate refused to be set free, he made his way to Deborah's side, and twitched her sleeve to attract her attention.

She cast him a scorching glance, and turned away, but he followed her into the adjoining saloon, saying gruffly: 'Here, you may take this!'

She looked in surprise at the key. 'Why, what do you mean? Have you thought better of it? Is he still there?'

'I think he is mad!' said Kit, in an aggrieved tone. 'I did try to set him free, but he would not let me! He told me to go to the devil, and said I was to give you back the key with his compliments. I do not know what is to be done! You have ruined everything!'

She took the key, almost as astonished as he was.

'He told you to give it back to me?' she repeated. 'He would not let you set him free?'

'No, I tell you! I do not know what is the matter with him. One would say he must be in his cups, but he is not!'

'He means to fight it out with me,' she said, her eyes lighting up. 'Well, and so he shall!'

She lost very little time in making her way down to the basement again, carrying this time one of the bedroom candles set out on a table at the foot of the backstairs, and guarding its frail flame from the draughts in the passage with her cupped hand.

Mr Ravenscar looked at her with a flickering smile as she entered his prison, and rose from his chair. 'Well, Miss Grantham? What now?'

She shut the door, and stood with her back to it. 'Why did you refuse to let my brother release you?'

'Because I would not be so beholden to him! He has not an ounce of spirit in him.'

She sighed, but shook her head. 'I know, but the poor boy found himself in a sad quandary. He is a little spoilt.'

'He wants kicking,' said Mr Ravenscar, 'and he will get it if he comes serenading my sister!'

'I don't think she has the least idea of marrying him,' said Miss Grantham reflectively.

'What do you know of the matter?'

'Nothing!' she said hastily. 'Adrian has told me a little about her, that is all. But I am not here to talk of your sister or of Kit either. Have you thought better of your rash words, sir?'

'If you mean, do I intend to give you back those bills, no!'

'You need not think I shall let you go, just because you would not permit Kit to set you free!' she said in a scolding voice.

'I thought you were not here to talk of your brother? You may forget that incident.'

187

She looked at him rather helplessly. 'You were to have dined with Mr Crewe to-night. It will be all over town by to-morrow that you have disappeared. Already Sir James Filey is letting fall the most odious hints! He is upstairs now.'

'Let him hint!' said Ravenscar indifferently.

'If you do not race to-morrow, what excuse can you make that will not make you appear ridiculous?'

'I have no idea. Have you any suggestion to offer me?'

'No, I have not,' she said crossly. 'You think I do not mean to keep my word, but I do!'

'I hope you mean to bring me a pillow for the night.'

'I don't. I hope you will be excessively uncomfortable!' snapped Miss Grantham. 'If I dared, I would let you starve to death here!'

'Oh, don't you dare?' he asked. 'I had thought there was no limit to your daring—or your effrontery!'

'I have a very good mind to let Silas come down and bring you to reason!' she threatened.

'By all means, if you imagine it would answer.'

'I will allow you half an hour to make up your mind once and for all,' she said, steeling herself. 'If you are still obstinate, you will be sorry!'

'That remains to be seen. I may be sorry, but you will not get your bills, my girl, I promise you.'

'It will be quite your own fault if you catch a cold down here,' she said. 'And I daresay you will, for it may be damp for anything I know!'

'I have an excellent constitution. If you mean to leave me now, do me the favour of allowing me to keep the candle!'

'Why should you want a candle!' she asked suspiciously.

'To frighten away the rats,' he replied.

She cast an involuntary glance round the cellar. 'Good God, are there rats here?' she said nervously.

'Of course there are—dozens of 'em!'

'How horrible!' she shuddered. 'I will leave you the candle, but do not think by that that I shall relent!'

'I won't,' he promised.

Miss Grantham withdrew, feeling baffled.

Upstairs, she found that Lord Mablethorpe had vanished, and guessed that he had slipped away to talk to Phœbe in the back-parlour. Lucius Kennet came strolling up to her, and asked her under his breath how the prisoner was faring. She whispered that he was determined not to surrender. Mr Kennet grimaced. 'You'd best let me reason with him, me darlin'.'

'I will not. You have done enough mischief!' she said, remembering his perfidy. 'How dared you trick him in my name? I told you I would not have it!'

'Ah, now, Deb, don't be squeamish! How was I to kidnap him at all, without he walked into a trap?'

She turned her shoulder, and went away to watch the faro-players, resolutely frustrating an attempt upon her aunt's part to catch her eye.

The half-hour she had promised to allow Mr Ravenscar for final reflection lagged past, and she found herself at the end of it without any very definite idea of how she was to persuade him to submit if he should still prove obstinate. Her aunt was leading the way downstairs to the first supper when she paid her third visit to the cellar, and she could not help thinking that her prisoner must, by this time, be feeling both cold and hungry.

She unlocked the cellar-door, and went in, closing it behind her. Mr Ravenscar was standing beside his chair, leaning his shoulders against the wall. 'Well?' she said, in as implacable a tone as she could.

'I am sorry you did not send your henchman down to me,' said Ravenscar. 'Or your ingenious friend, Mr Kennet. I was rather hoping to see one, or both, of these gentlemen. I meant to shut them up here for the night, but

I suppose I can hardly serve you in the same way, richly though you deserve it!'

He had straightened himself as he spoke, and moved away from the wall. Before Miss Grantham could do more than utter a startled cry, his hands had come from behind his back, and he had grasped her right arm, and calmly wrested the key from her clutch.

'Who let you go?' she demanded, quivering with temper. 'Who contrived to enter this place? How did you get your hands free?'

'No one let me go. Or; rather, *you* did, my girl, when you left me a candle.'

Her eyes flew to his wrist, and a horrified exclamation broke from her. 'Oh, how could you do that? You have burnt yourself dreadfully!'

'Very true, but I shall keep my appointment to-morrow, and you will not get your bills,' he returned.

She paid very little heed to this, being quite taken up by his hurts. 'You must be suffering agonies!' she said remorsefully. 'I would never have left the candle if I had guessed what you meant to do!'

'I do not suppose that you would. Don't waste your sympathy on me! I shall do very well. We will now go upstairs, Miss Grantham, and set Sir James Filey's mind at rest. Unless, of course, you prefer to remain here?'

'For heaven's sake, don't lock me in here with rats!' begged Miss Grantham, for the first time showing alarm. 'Besides, you cannot go into the saloons like that! You will very likely die if nothing is done to your hands! Come up with me immediately! I will put some very good ointment on them, and bind up your wrists, and find you a pair of Kit's ruffles in place of these! Oh dear, what a fool you are to do such a thing! You will never be able to drive to-morrow!'

'I don't advise you to bet against me,' he said, looking

down at her with a good deal of amusement. 'Do you really mean to anoint my hurts?'

'Of course I do! You do not suppose that I am going to have it said that you lost your race through *my* fault, do you?' she said indignantly.

'I was under the impression that that was precisely what you meant me to do.'

'Well, you are wrong. I never thought you would be so stupidly obstinate!'

'Were you going to release me, then?'

'Yes—no! I don't know! You had better come up the backstairs. You may tidy yourself in my brother's room while I fetch the ointment, and some linen. I wish I had never laid eyes on you! You are rude, and stupid, and I was never so plagued by anyone in my life!'

'Permit me to return the compliment!' he said, following her along the passage.

'I will make you sorry you ever dared to cross swords with me!' she flung over her shoulder. 'I'll marry your cousin, and I'll ruin him!'

'To spite me, I suppose,' he said satirically.

'Be quiet! Do you want to bring the servants out upon us?'

'It is a matter of indifference to me.'

'Well, it is not a matter of indifference to me!' she said. He laughed, but said no more until they had reached Kit's room upon the third floor. Miss Grantham left him there with the candle, while she went off to hunt for salves and linen bandages. When she returned, he had pulled off his coat, and discarded the fragments of his charred ruffles, besides straightening his tumbled cravat, and brushing his short black locks. The backs of his hands were badly scorched, and he winced a little when Miss Grantham smeared her ointment over them.

'It serves you right!' she told him. 'I daresay it may hurt you, and I am sure I don't care!'

'Why should you indeed?' he agreed.

She began to wind her bandage round his right hand. 'Is it any easier?'

'Much easier.'

'If I were a man you would not escape so lightly!'

'I daresay I should not. Or even if you had a man to protect you.'

'You need not sneer at Kit! To be sure, it is the height of folly for him to be falling in love with your sister, but he could not help that! Give me your other hand!'

He held it out. 'You are a remarkable woman, Miss Grantham.'

'Thank you, I have heard enough about myself from you!' she retorted.

'Jade and Jezebel,' said Mr Ravenscar, grinning. 'Harpy.'

'Also doxy!' said Miss Grantham, showing her teeth.

'I apologize for that one.'

'Pray do not trouble! It does not matter to me what you think me.' She pulled open one of the drawers in the dressing-table, found a pair of lace ruffles in it, and began swiftly to tack these on to the sleeves of his shirt. 'There! If you pull them down, the bandages will not be so very noticeable. I have left your fingers free.'

'Thank you,' he said, putting on his coat again.

'If you take my advice, you will go home now, and to bed!'

'I shall not take your advice. I am going to play faro.'

'I don't want you in my house!' said Miss Grantham.

'It is not your house. I am very sure your aunt desires nothing more than to see me at her faro-table. She shall have her wish.'

'I cannot stop you behaving imprudently, even if I wished to, which I don't,' said Miss Grantham. 'If you are determined to remain here, you had better go in to supper, for I daresay you must be hungry.'

'Your solicitude overwhelms me,' returned Ravenscar. 'I own I had expected at least a loaf of bread and a jug of water in my dungeon—until I learned, of course, that you had some idea of starving me to death.'

Miss Grantham bit her lip. 'I would like very much to starve you to death,' she said defiantly. 'And let me tell you, Mr Ravenscar, that Lucius Kennet is downstairs, and if you have any notion of starting a vulgar brawl in my house, I will have you thrown out of it! There is Silas, and both the waiters, and my aunt's butler, and my brother too, so do not think I cannot do it!'

'This is very flattering,' he said, 'but I fear my fighting qualities have been exaggerated. It would not take all these people to throw me out of the house.'

'And in any event,' pursued Miss Grantham, ignoring this remark, 'your quarrel is with me, and not with Lucius. *He* merely did what I asked!' She moved towards the door, and opened it. 'Now, if you are ready, I will show you the way down the backstairs, so that no one shall know you have been up here.'

'You think of everything, Miss Grantham. I will go out by the area-door, and come in again by the front-door, picking up my hat and cane on the way, which we were so thoughtless as to leave in my dungeon.'

She made no objection to this, but led the way down the backstairs again. As she was about to let him out of the house, an idea occurred to her, and she asked abruptly: 'How came you to know that Ormskirk held the mortgage, and those bills?'

'He told me so,' replied Mr Ravenscar coolly.

She stared at him. '*He* told you so? Of all the infamous— Well! I have always disliked him excessively, but I did not dream he would behave as shabbily as that, I must say!'

'You have always disliked him?' he repeated, looking rather strangely at her.

She met his look with a kindling eye. 'Yes!' she said. 'But not, believe me, Mr Ravenscar, as much as I dislike you!'

CHAPTER XIII

FIVE minutes later, Mr Ravenscar knocked on the front-door. It was opened to him by Silas Wantage, and he walked into the house with his usual air of calm assurance.

Mr Wantage made a sound as of one choking, and stood stock-still, staring at him with bulging eyes. Mr Ravenscar met this bemused stare with a look of irony, but gave no sign of recognition. He merely held out his hat, and his cane, and waited for Silas to take them.

Mr Wantage found his voice. 'Well, I'll be damned!' he uttered.

'Probably,' said Mr Ravenscar. 'Have the goodness to take my hat and cane!'

Mr Wantage relieved him of these, and said helplessly: 'I dunno how you done it, but I won't say as I'm sorry. It goes against the grain with me to tie up a cove as can plant me as wisty a facer as you did, sir!'

Mr Ravenscar paid no heed to this confession, but glanced at his reflection in the mirror, adjusted the pin in his cravat, smoothed the ruffles over his bandaged hands, and strolled across the hall to the supper-room.

His entrance created quite a stir. His hostess, who was sipping claret in the hope of steadying her nerves, choked, and turned purple in the face; Mr Lucius Kennet, standing by the buffet with a plate of salmon in his hand, said 'Good God!' in a startled voice, and dropped his fork; the Honourable Berkeley Crewe exclaimed, and demanded to be told what had kept Mr Ravenscar from his dinner-engagement; Sir James Filey was thought by those standing nearest to him to have sworn under his breath; and several persons called out to know what had befallen Ravenscar. Only Miss Grantham showed no sign of perturbation, but bade the late-comer a cool good evening.

He bowed over her hand, looked with a little amusement at Lady Bellingham, who was still choking, and said: 'I'm sorry, Crewe. I was unavoidably detained.'

'But what in the world kept you?' asked Crewe. 'I thought you had forgotten you were to dine with me, and sent round to your house to remind you. They said you had set out just after dusk!'

'The truth is, I met with a slight accident,' replied Ravenscar, taking a glass of Burgundy from the tray which a waiter was handing him. As he raised it to his lips, the ruffle fell back from his hand, and his bandages were seen.

'Good God, what have you done to your hand, Max?' asked Lord Mablethorpe, in swift alarm.

'Oh, nothing very much!' Ravenscar replied. 'I told you I had met with a slight accident.'

'Have you been set upon?' demanded Crewe. 'Is that it?'

'Yes, that is it,' said Ravenscar.

'I hope it may not impair your skill with the ribbons!' said Filey.

'I hope not, indeed,' answered Ravenscar, with one of his derisive looks.

'Gad, Ravenscar, do you suppose it was an attempt to stop you driving to-morrow?' exclaimed a gentleman in an old-fashioned bag-wig.

'Something of that nature, I fancy,' said Ravenscar, unable to resist an impulse to glance at Miss Grantham.

'What the devil do you mean by that, Horley?' demanded Sir James belligerently.

The gentleman in the bag-wig looked surprised. 'Why,

only that there has been a great deal of money laid on the race, and such things do happen! What should I mean?'

Filey's high colour faded; he muttered something about having misunderstood, and swung out of the room, saying that he would try his luck at the hazard-table.

'What's the matter with Filey?' enquired Crewe. 'He's become devilish bad-tempered all at once!'

'Oh, haven't you heard?' said a man in an orange-and-white-striped waistcoat. 'You know he was mad to marry one of the Laxton girls? Pretty child, only just out. Well, the Laxtons are trying to hush it up, but I had it from young Arnold himself that the filly's bolted!'

'Bolted?' repeated Crewe.

'Vanished, my dear fellow! Can't be found! No wonder our friend's sore!'

'Well, I don't blame her,' said Crewe. 'Filey and a chit out of the schoolroom! Damme, it's little better than a rape! But where did she bolt to?'

'No one knows. I told you she'd vanished. And the best of it is the Laxtons daren't set the Runners on to her track for fear of the story's leaking out! Wouldn't look well at all: forcing a child of that age into marriage with a man of Filey's reputation!'

'It wouldn't come to that!' objected Mr Horley.

'Oh, wouldn't it, by God? You don't know Lady Laxton, when there's a fortune at stake!' chuckled the man in the orange-striped waistcoat.

Lady Bellingham, feeling that her cup was now full to overflowing, cast a despairing look towards her niece, and wondered why a mouthful of cold partridge should taste of ashes.

'It is not to be supposed,' said Lord Mablethorpe carefully, 'that Filey will wish to marry any female who shows herself so averse from his suit.'

'If you think that, *you* don't know *Filey*!' said Crewe.

'He would think it added a spice to matrimony.'

Under cover of this general conversation, Lucius Kennet had moved across the room to Miss Grantham's side, and now said in her ear: 'Do you tell me you persuaded him to give up the bills, me dear? Sure, you could have knocked me down with a feather when he walked in as cool as you please!'

'I have not got the bills,' she replied.

'You have not got them? Then what the devil ails you to be letting him go, Deb?'

'I didn't. He escaped.'

He looked at her with suspicion. 'He did not, then! I tied his hands meself! It's lying you are, Deb: you set him free!'

'No, I did not. Only he asked me for a candle, and I let him have one, never dreaming what he meant to do! He burned the cord round his wrists, and when I went down to the cellar he was free. There was nothing I could do.'

He gave a low whistle. 'It's the broth of a boy he is, and no mistake! So that's why his hands are bandaged! Will he be able to drive?'

'He says so. I am sure I do not care!'

She was disinclined to converse further on the subject, and moved away, only to fall a victim to Lord Mablethorpe, who drew her into a corner of the room to ask her if she had heard what had been said about Phœbe Laxton's disappearance. She answered rather curtly that she did not know what it should signify, but Mablethorpe was not satisfied, and said the question of Phœbe's future was troubling him very much.

Miss Grantham was pleased to hear this, but she had borne much that evening, and felt disinclined to embark on a discussion of Phœbe's affairs in a crowded supper-room. She answered rather briefly, therefore, and incurred Lord Mablethorpe's censure for the first time in her life.

'It's very well, Deb, but she cannot stay here for ever, and I don't think you are bothering your head much about her,' his lordship said gravely.

'I have other things to think of,' said Deborah.

'I am sure you must, but she has no one but you to think for her, or to take care of her, remember!'

This was said with a gentle dignity which Miss Grantham had not met before in her youthful swain. She reflected that close association with Miss Laxton was investing his lordship with a sense of responsibility, and liked him the better for it. 'It is very hard to know what to do for the best,' she said. 'I quite thought that her parents would have relented. They may still do so.'

A little crease appeared between his brows. 'Even so——!' He paused, and went on again after a moment's hesitation. 'She has confided in me to some extent, Deb. I daresay she may have told you more. But I have heard enough to realize that she can never be happy at home. Those parents——! If it were not Filey it would very likely be someone as bad. Lady Laxton cares for nothing but money. I should feel we had betrayed Phœbe if we let her go back. She is not like you: she needs someone to protect her.'

This naïve pronouncement made Miss Grantham feel much inclined to inform him that to have someone to protect her was every woman's dream, but she refrained, and said instead that she did not know what was to be done. She added that she must go upstairs to the card-rooms, and left him feeling more dissatisfied with her than he would have believed, a week before, that he could be.

If the truth were told, his lordship had been finding his inamorata a little trying ever since the evening they had spent at Vauxhall. Her behaviour then had certainly shocked him, and although he had never again seen her assume such peculiar manners, he could not help wondering sometimes if there might be a recurrence the next time she found herself in elevated circles.

Then there was her manner towards himself, which occasionally chafed him. She was often rather impatient with him, as though she found his youth and inexperience exasperating; and she had developed a habit of ordering him about more than he liked. There had even been moments when the memory of a governess he had had in early childhood most forcibly recurred in his mind. He was by no means a fool, and he had begun to perceive that Miss Grantham's seniority gave her an advantage over him which might well preclude his assuming the mastery over his own establishment. Lord Mablethorpe had a sweetness of temper which made him universally liked; he was very young still, and diffident; but he was no weakling, and he was growing up fast.

Miss Grantham, well aware of these facts, was riding him as hard as she thought proper, allowing the decision and forcefulness of her own character to throw Miss Laxton's gentler and more yielding nature into strong relief. Mablethorpe, she knew, could not fail to make comparison between them; and it would be an odd thing if a young man who was bullied, in a kind way, by one woman, did not find the admiration and dependence of another a refreshing change.

He did find it refreshing. Miss Laxton's fragility, her helplessness, her implicit trust in him, had made an instant appeal to his chivalry. From the first moment of meeting her, when she had clung to his hand, he had felt protective towards her. She had said that she knew herself to be safe with him, and later she had said that she would be guided by his judgment, and had asked for his advice. No one had ever expressed a desire to benefit by Lord Mablethorpe's advice before; and since his mother, his uncle Julius, and his cousin Max were all persons of decided opinions, he had never received any very noticeable encouragement to put forward his own views on subjects of major importance. His life had, naturally enough, been ordered for him, and although he was fast approaching his majority it would be some time before these relatives, who were all so much older and wiser than himself, would be brought to regard him in the light of a responsible adult. Even Deborah, in her most mellow moments, treated him rather as she might be expected to treat a younger brother. She laughed at him, and teased him, and could rarely be brought to take him very seriously.

But Miss Laxton was two years younger than he, and she did not see him as a delightful boy who had not yet found his feet. To her, running away from the advances of one who seemed to her an ogre, he was a tall young knight who had stepped out from the pages of a fairy-story. His knowledge of the world seemed vast to one who had none at all. He was handsome, and strong, and gentle. He instructed her ignorance, and bade her entrust her safety to him. It was not surprising that Miss Laxton should have fallen head over ears in love with him.

She was in no doubt about her feelings; it was some time before he realized the state of his own heart, and longer still before he would admit to himself that he had, incredibly, fallen out of love with one woman headlong into love with another. It seemed appalling to him that he could have done such a thing, and he was inclined to think himself the most fickle and despicable of created beings. But he knew that his love for Phœbe was quite a different emotion from his half-awed adoration of Deborah. He had been swept off his feet by Deborah. She was a goddess to be worshipped, beautiful, wise, and dazzling; always immeasurably superior to himself. He did not think of Phœbe like that at all. He knew quite well that she was not as beautiful as Deborah, not wise, and appealing rather than dazzling. When Deborah had smiled at him, he had felt quite dizzy, and had had wild, romantic notions of kissing the hem of her garment, or performing impossible feats in her honour. When Phœbe smiled, no such thoughts occurred to him, but he was conscious of a strong impulse to catch her up in his arms, and hold her safe there.

He had had just such an impulse when he had said good night to her before coming down to the supper-room that evening. She had looked forlorn, and defenceless, and was frightened, because she knew that Filey was in the house. He felt concerned about her, so Miss Grantham's lack of sympathy struck him forcibly, and he came as near losing his temper with her as he had ever been in his life.

When she left the room, he joined the group round his cousin. Crewe was trying to discover what was the nature of the injury to Ravenscar's hands, and several other persons were discussing the relative points of the two pairs of horses, and the character of the course to be covered. This had been changed from the original stretch past Epsom to a straightforward run from the village of Islington to Hatfield, on the Great North Road. Listening to the talk, Lord Mablethorpe forgot his heart's pre-occupations for a time. 'I wish I were going with you!' he said wistfully. 'I mean to drive out to see the finish, but that's not the same thing.'

Ravenscar set down his empty glass on the table. 'Well, you may come with me if you like,' he answered. 'Only you must carry the yard of tin if you do!'

An eager flush rose to Mablethorpe's cheeks. 'Max! Do you mean it? You'll take me in place of a groom? Oh, by Jupiter, that's beyond anything great!'

Crewe laughed at his enthusiasm, and began to tease him. 'Why, Max, you can't take him in place of Welling! You will be held up at every toll-bar!'

'He will not!' said Mablethorpe indignantly. 'I can handle the yard of tin as well as anyone!'

'You will be so excited you will forget to blow up for the gates until it is too late.'

'I won't! Why, I have often been with Max! I know just what to do!'

'Well,' said Crewe, shaking his head, 'if you really mean to set up that great, lanky creature in Welling's place, Max, I shall have to lay off you, and that is all there is to it.'

This shaft went home. Lord Mablethorpe's face fell ludicrously, and he turned anxious eyes towards his cousin. 'Oh Max, had I better not go with you? Am I too heavy?'

As his lordship, though tall, was boyishly slim, this apprehensive question produced a shout of laughter, which made him blush more hotly than ever. However, as he was quite accustomed to being roasted by his cousin's friends, he took it in very good part, merely prophesying darkly the hideous fate that would one day overtake Berkeley Crewe, and announcing his intention of going home immediately, to be sure of a good night's sleep before the race.

Mr Ravenscar thought this a wise decision, and further suggested that his lordship should refrain from informing his parent that he was to take part in the race. Lord Mablethorpe said: 'Oh, by God, no! I won't say a word to her about it!' and went off, forgetting, for the first time since he had met her, to take his leave of Miss Grantham.

Mr Ravenscar went upstairs to play faro, but if Lady Bellingham was gratified to see him at the table she managed to conceal it, looking at him with the dilating eyes of a trapped rabbit whenever he glanced in her direction, and finding it exceedingly difficult to keep her attention on the game. She had never been so glad to see a table break up; and when the last of her guests had left the house she found herself without strength to climb the stairs to her bedroom, but collapsed upon a yellow satin sofa, and moaned for hartshorn.

'Be easy, ma'am!' said Lucius Kennet, who had stayed to exchange a word with Deborah. 'Now, me darlin', perhaps you'll be telling me what game it is you're after playing!'

Miss Grantham swung her wide skirts defiantly. 'I told you what happened. It was not my fault.'

'What maggot got into your brain to give Ravenscar a candle?'

'I didn't know what he meant to do. How should I guess?'

'What the devil should he be wanting with a candle at all, if not to be up to some mischief? Sure, it's not like you to be gulled, Deb!'

'Well, I should not like to be left in the dark myself,' she said. 'Besides, he said there were rats.'

'He was quite right,' said Lady Bellingham faintly, opening her eyes. 'The servants are for ever complaining about them, but what can one do?'

'Whisht, Deb! Is it the likes of Ravenscar that would be afraid of a rat or two?'

'Mortimer is afraid of them,' said Lady Bellingham. 'He gives me no peace about it! I am sure Ravenscar might well have been afraid of them. Oh, I shall go distracted! He will tell everyone what you did to him, my love, and the end of it will be that no one will dare come to the house again!'

'Who bound up Ravenscar's hands?' demanded Kennet, his eyes fixed on Miss Grantham's face. 'And if he burned the cord, how came his ruffles to escape? Tell me that!'

'They didn't escape,' said Deborah crossly. 'I lent him a pair of Kit's ruffles. Where *is* Kit?'

Kennet grinned. 'Faith, I'm thinking he didn't care for the style of things here, me darlin', for he took himself off before supper. Don't be trying to dodge the issue, now! It was yourself tied Ravenscar's hands up, was it not?'

'Well, what else could I do?' she asked. 'When I discovered that he was free, I was powerless to resist him. Besides, he had more than half a mind to shut me up in the cellar in his stead, and that I could not have borne!'

'Deb, there was Silas in the hall, and meself playing faro abovestairs! And what must you do but let Ravenscar walk out of the house without a soul to hinder him!'

'You are absurd, Lucius!' protested Miss Grantham. 'How could I have a brawl in the middle of a card-party? There was nothing to be done, and in any event I never meant to kidnap him by a hateful trick, which was what you did!'

'And what will you be doing now, me dear, if I may ask, to get the bills out of his hands?' asked Kennet politely.

'I don't know, but you may be sure I shall think of something,' replied Deborah.

'It's my belief,' said Kennet, 'that it's more than half in love with the man you are, Deb!'

'I?' gasped Miss Grantham. 'In love with Ravenscar? Have you taken leave of your senses, Lucius? I detest him! He is the most abominable, the most hateful, the most odious—oh, how can you talk such nonsense? I am in no humour for it, and will bid you a very good night!'

She flounced out of the room as she spoke, almost colliding with her brother in the doorway. Mr Grantham seemed out of breath, and exclaimed: 'Deb! I could swear I saw him, just as I was crossing Piccadilly! You let him go after all!'

'I daresay you did see him,' she answered angrily. 'But I did *not* let him go, and I never *would* have let him go, and he holds a very poor opinion of *you*, let me tell you!'

'And what, me dear Kit, may you be knowing about the

business at all?' enquired Mr Kennet, as Deborah slammed the door behind her.

'I know it all! And I will thank you, Lucius, not to encourage Deb in her wildness again! If this night's work has not ruined all my hopes it will be no fault of yours!'

'For the love of heaven, boy, what concern is it of yours?'

'Oh, nothing!' said Kit bitterly. 'Merely, that I love Ravenscar's sister!'

Mr Kennet opened his eyes at this. 'You do, do you? And what has that to say to anything?'

'How can you be such a fool? What hope have I of obtaining Ravenscar's consent to our marriage when my sister can think of nothing better to do than to shut him up in the cellar?'

Lady Bellingham felt impelled to defend her niece, and said: 'She did it for the best, Kit. She did not know that you were going to be married to Miss Ravenscar!'

Kennet glanced sideways at Kit. 'Married, eh?'

'And why not?' Kit demanded. 'Is it so extraordinary?'

A smile lurked about the corners of Kennet's mouth. 'Faith, I'm thinking it would be!' he said.

'Yes! And I hold you as much to blame as Deb! More, indeed!'

'Maybe you're right at that,' agreed Kennet, still apparently amused by some secret thought.

Lady Bellingham raised her head from the yellow cushion. 'I am sure it has all been most unfortunate,' she said. 'And I can't but feel that since Deb had got Ravenscar in the cellar—not that I approve of such a thing, for I don't, and I never shall—but since he *was* there, it does seem to me a pity to have let him go without getting those dreadful bills from him! Now he will start dunning me, or persecuting us in some odious way, and you know what will happen next! Deb will try to teach him another lesson, and all will end in disaster! Sometimes

I think that I might be happier in a debtors' prison!'

With these gloomy words, she withdrew to her own room, to spend a restless night dreaming of coachmakers' bills; green peas, rats, candle-ends, and cellars teeming with bound men.

Lord Mablethorpe had had the intention, if Miss Grantham were willing, to drive her and Phœbe into the country next morning. A hurried note to Phœbe was brought round by hand at ten o'clock, explaining the sudden change in his plans, and promising to call in St James's Square that evening to report on the result of the curricle race. Miss Laxton gave a startled exclamation when she read this letter, and thrust it into Deborah's hand, saying in a faint voice: 'Oh, he may be killed!'

'Killed? Nonsense!' said Miss Grantham, running her eye down the paper. 'I declare, I am quite tired of hearing about this race! I am sure Adrian has talked of little else for the past week. Thank heaven it will be over by to-morrow, and we need hear no more about it! As though it signified!'

'Gentlemen think so much of those things,' sighed Miss Laxton. 'Oh, I hope Mr Ravenscar will beat Sir James! Adrian says there is not another whip to compare with him, but if Sir James's horses are as good as people say——'

Miss Grantham clapped her hands over her ears. 'You, too!' she said reproachfully. 'Not another word! For my part, I wish they might both contrive to break their necks!'

'Oh, Deb, not when *Adrian* will be in his cousin's curricle!' shuddered Phœbe.

'Well, if Ravenscar is such a fine whip there can be little likelihood of any accident's occurring,' said Miss Grantham.

Phœbe looked at her with wonder. 'You are so brave!' she said humbly. 'I wish I were, but, alas, I am not!'

'Good heavens, child, what have I to be afraid of?' asked Miss Grantham, at a loss.

'But, Deb! Adrian!'

'Oh!' said Miss Grantham, rather blankly. 'To be sure, yes, my dear!'

'I do not know how we are to be at ease until we know that the race is safely over,' sighed Phœbe.

'Very true,' agreed Miss Grantham, preparing to put the matter out of her mind.

She succeeded in this very well, being a good deal taken up with her own problems; but it was evident, from her restlessness, and the anxious pucker between her brows, that Miss Laxton could think of nothing else. When dusk fell and she thought they might reasonably expect to see Lord Mablethorpe, she stationed herself in the saloon in the front of the house, and kept a watch on the darkening square through the lace curtains that shrouded the windows. Dinner was announced before that familiar figure was seen, and she was obliged to go downstairs, and to make a pretence of eating. Miss Grantham, perceiving her unrest, reminded her that the contestants would certainly dine early at Hatfield, and could not be looked for in London again for some time yet. Miss Laxton agreed to it, but felt disinclined to eat her dinner.

Mr Grantham was present, but it was seen that he was not in spirits. He appeared to be brooding over some secret trouble, and although it did not impair his appetite, it rendered him incapable of bearing more than a mono-syllabic part in any conversation. He had contrived, through the connivance of Miss Ravenscar's handmaiden (who was beginning to cherish dreams of retiring from service in the near future on the accumulated bribes she had received from her mistress's numerous admirers), to arrange an assignation with the volatile Arabella. He had reached the rendezvous a full half-hour too soon, Miss Ravenscar had joined him half-an-hour late, and with ap-parently no recollection of the promises of eternal fidelity exchanged a bare week before, at Tunbridge Wells. She was perfectly ready to flirt with him, hoped to meet him at the Pantheon Ball, but said that she thought, after all, that it would be stuffy to be married. Mr Grantham suspected her strongly of having transferred her affections to another, and taxed her with this treachery. Miss Ravenscar laughed mischievously, and refused to answer. Mr Grantham then put forward a very daring plan he had formed, of taking her to the masquerade at Ranelagh on the following evening. To escape from chaperonage, under pretence of going to bed with the headache, and to spend a stolen evening at a masked ball with a forbidden suitor, was just such an adventure as might have been certain of making an instant appeal to Miss Ravenscar, but, greatly to Kit's chagrin, she cast down her eyes demurely, and said she must not think of such a thing. From the quiver at the corners of her mouth, Kit suspected that she had already thought of it, and was indeed going to the masquerade, though not in his company. It was no wonder that he should have returned to his aunt's house in low spirits.

There was no card-party that evening. Kit went out soon after dinner, and the three ladies prepared to spend a quiet hour or two with the blinds drawn, and a snug fire burning in the Yellow Saloon. Lady Bellingham, however, soon retired to bed, complaining that the stress of the past week had quite worn her down; and while Miss Laxton pretended to be busy with some sewing, but in reality set very few stitches, Miss Grantham flicked over the pages of a romance, and tried to hit upon an infallible plan for gaining possession of her aunt's bills which would not entail surrendering to the enemy, but which would, on the contrary, place him in a position of the greatest discomfiture.

At ten o'clock the knock which Miss Laxton had been waiting to hear at last fell upon the front-door, and she let her needlework drop to the floor. 'That must be he!'

Miss Grantham looked up. 'I won't receive him!' she said.

Phœbe started at her in alarm. 'Deb! Why, what has he done?' she faltered, turning quite pale.

'What has he done? Oh, you are talking of Mable-thorpe!'

'But, dearest Deb, whom else should I be talking about?' asked Miss Laxton, puzzled.

Miss Grantham blushed. 'I was thinking of something different,' she excused herself.

Light footsteps were heard running up the stairs; the next instant Lord Mablethorpe stood on the threshold, flushed, and a little dishevelled, and still dressed in a drab driving coat, and top-boots, both generously splashed with mud. 'We won!' he announced, his eyes sparkling.

Phœbe clapped her hands. 'Oh, I knew you would! I am so glad! And you are safe!'

He laughed. 'Safe? Of course I am! There never was such a race! It was beyond anything great! I do not know when I have enjoyed anything so much! Oh, Deb, do you mind me in all my dirt? I thought you would not: I knew you would want to hear all about it! May I come in?'

'Of course you may come in,' she said, picking up Phœbe's work, and folding it neatly. 'Have you dined, or would you like some supper?'

'Oh, no, thank you! We dined early in Hatfield, and I had supper with Max, at his house, just now. It was touch and go once or twice—only fancy our falling in behind an Accommodation coach on the narrow part of the road this side of Potter's Bar! I thought all was over with us, for you must know that Filey led for the first part of the way, and was ahead of the coach. But there was never anyone like Max! You know where the road divides, at the Hadley Highstone, the Holyhead way going off to the left? Oh, I daresay you might not! but I can tell you it is as tricky a place as you may wish for, and any number of coaches and wagons on the road! Well, before I knew what he would be about, Max had dropped his hands, and let the grays shoot! It was our only chance, but there was a gig coming in from the Holyhead road, and I give you my word we cleared the Accommodation coach, with no more than a couple of inches to spare between it and the gig! I own, I shut my eyes, and said my prayers"

'You might have been killed!' breathed Phœbe.

'So I might, with any other man holding the reins, but Max knows what his grays will do to a nicety.'

'I collect that Sir James's pair was inferior?' said Deborah, despising herself for betraying any interest in the race.

He turned his glowing face towards her. 'Oh, as to that, I would not say so by any means! It was all in the handling. When we came to Islington we found him with as bang-up a set-out of blood and bone as you could wish for: small heads, good necks, broad chests and thighs, pure Welsh bred! Beautifully matched too! But the instant Max laid eyes on them, he said to me that they were poled up too tight, and so they were. I could see Filey's groom thought so too, but that's Filey all over! He must always know best, and he is so cursed obstinate there's no telling him anything! Well, there was quite a crowd gathered at the start, as you may suppose, and a good deal of betting going on. Some of the green 'uns were plunging pretty heavily on Filey, because there's no denying the bays are the showiest pair you'll see in a twelvemonth; but the knowing ones put their money on Max, and, by Jupiter, they were right! Well, we were off to a good start, and Filey went ahead, just as Max thought he would. Max held the grays in all the way to Barnet, no more than keeping Filey in sight. I wish you might have seen Filey driving his cattle up

Highgate Hill, as though it had been the last lap of the race, instead of the first! We went up behind him, just larking, you know: keeping her alive, at a gentle trot. Of course Filey did not take the hill in time, driving up it at that pace, and his near horse precious nearly stumbled as they went over the crest. When Max saw it, he said the race was our own. But that was before we got held up by that Accommodation coach! But I told you of that! We had a splendid run across Finchley Common, going good, very little traffic on the road. I would have passed Filey then, but Max said no: he would pass him in Barnet.' His lordship laughed at the memory. 'In Barnet, of all places! But that is just like Max! I thought we should never be able to do it, for Barnet is always crowded. Filey can't manage well in a street full of carts and chaises, and you could see he was fretting his cattle. They were sweating freely, and only half the course run! There was a chaise on one side of the road, and the Mail pulling out from the Red Lion, and a phæton drawn up outside some shop or other. Not enough room to allow a cat to squeeze through, you'd have said! At all events that's what Filey must have thought, for he made no attempt to clear the chaise. Max saw his chance, and we went through, as neatly as you please, at a spanking trot, threading our way! I wondered if we were going to take the phæton's off-wheel, but we never so much as grazed it. Max has the lightest hands! He says the only thing is, Filey may have ruined the bays' mouths—oh, I did not tell you!—Max told Filey to name his price for his pair at the end, and has bought them. Filey was as mad as fire, because of course Max's offering to buy the tits showed that he thought it was Filey and not they who had lost the race. But he was so angry with them for losing that he would have sold them to the first man who offered for them! They were hanging on his hands when he brought them into Hatfield, but that was his fault. Berkeley says he always drives his worst against Max, because he is so devilish anxious to win, and knows, though he won't admit it, that Max is the better whip. We never lost the lead after Potter's Bar.'

'You seem to have lost it after Barnet,' observed Miss Grantham dryly. 'How was that?'

His lordship chuckled. 'Oh, short of Hadley Green! I told Max that Filey was going to try to pass, and he said he might do so with his goodwill, for he would not spring the grays at that stage. He only passed him at Barnet to fret him a trifle. There never was such a fool! Max says——'

'My dear Adrian, Max seems to have said a great deal, but I wish you will try not to introduce those two words so often into your story!' said Miss Grantham blightingly.

His lordship flushed, and looked so hurt that Miss Grantham was sorry, and might have unsaid her words had she not recollected in time that it was no part of her policy to appear in an amiable light to him. She got up, saying in a cool voice: 'I must go down to speak to Silas for a minute. Do you tell the rest of the tale to Phœbe! I am afraid I am very stupid, and care nothing for driving, or curricle-racing, or horses. I shall come back presently, when you will be able to talk of something else, I hope!'

Lord Mablethorpe rose, and opened the door for her. When she had passed out of the room, Phœbe said shyly: 'Don't be offended! I think she is a little worried over something. I am sure she did not mean it! She is so kind, and good!'

'I am afraid I have been very tedious,' he said. 'The thing is, I found it so exciting——But it is different for you, naturally!'

'Oh no!' she said involuntarily. 'I think it is the most exciting thing I ever heard! Indeed, I do! Please, please tell me the rest!'

Almost without knowing what she did, she stretched out her hand to him as she spoke. He came across the room

212

towards her, and took her hand, and held it, looking at her with such a warm, loving expression in his eyes that her heart stood still. 'Oh, Phœbe, you are so very sweet!' he said. 'I do love you so dearly!'

CHAPTER XIV

Two large tears welled up in Miss Laxton's eyes, and rolled down her cheeks. 'Oh, Adrian!' she said brokenly.

The next instant she was in his arms, and his lordship had forgotten both the race and his betrothal to Miss Grantham, but was wholly occupied in kissing Phœbe, drying her wet cheeks, and assuring her that she should never be unhappy or frightened again. It was she who came to earth first, raising her head from his shoulder, relinquishing her clutch on the cape of his coat, and saying in a drowned voice: 'We must not! *Deborah!*'

His lordship let her go. She sat up, swallowing a sob, and they looked at one another, two troubled young people caught up by fate and unable to see the way to free themselves. His lordship gave a groan, and dropped his head between his clenched fists. 'I must have been mad!'

'Oh no!' Phœbe said, dabbing at her eyes with a small handkerchief. 'She is so very lovely, and kind, and—and—oh dear!'

'I thought I loved her. But I don't. I love you, Phœbe! What are we to do?'

Miss Laxton's eyes brimmed over again. 'You will marry her, and I shall g-go into a nunnery, or s-something. You will soon f-forget me,' she said bravely.

This frightful picture of the future made Adrian raise his head, and say forcefully: 'No!'

'But what can we do?' asked Phœbe.

'I cannot marry Deb.'

Miss Laxton turned pale. 'Oh, you can never tell her so!'

An appalled silence fell. His lordship got up, and began to pace about the room. 'If I don't tell her, we shall all three of us be made unhappy.'

'No, no! She will never know, and you will forget this!'

'I shall never forget!' said Adrian fiercely. 'And I could not pretend to Deb. She would guess the truth.'

'But it would be such a dreadful thing for you to do!' whispered Phœbe.

His lordship was almost as pale as she. 'Yes. I know,' he said. 'But she has not said yet that she will marry me. Perhaps—perhaps she does not mean to.'

She looked astonished. 'But I thought—you told me——'

'Yes, yes, but it was never said in so many words! She used to laugh at me when I asked her to marry me. Then— then it did seem to me that she had changed towards me, and I thought too—— But it is true that she has never yet said it. Phœbe, do you think that she cares for me?'

'Oh, how can she not?' Phœbe exclaimed.

'Well, I do not think that she does. Lately she has been—oh, not cross, but—but different!'

A shocking thought presented itself to Miss Laxton. 'Adrian, can it be that she suspects, and is jealous, or—or hurt?'

Their eyes met; his lordship's chin seemed to harden.

'We must tell her the truth.'

Phœbe sprang up in some agitation. 'No, no, I implore you! Only consider how frightful it must appear! She invited me to her house, and has been everything that is kind! How could I possibly steal you from her? I would rather die!'

His lordship quite saw the force of this argument, but he

was not satisfied with it. 'Yes, but you did not steal me,' he said. 'We did not mean to fall in love! We could not help ourselves, and *that* she will surely understand! *You* are blameless at least! It is I who deserve to be horse-whipped!'

It was not to be expected that Miss Laxton could agree with this judgment. She began to argue the point, laying the blame at her own door, and finding all manner of excuses for his lordship. He would not allow it, and the next few minutes were spent in a singularly profitless discussion, which might, indeed, have lasted for hours, had not his lordship perceived the uselessness of it, and silenced Miss Laxton by kissing her.

'Oh!' said Miss Laxton, burying her face in his coat. 'If you do that, how *can* I behave as I ought? You must not, Adrian! Oh, please, you must not!'

'My conduct has been everything of the most damnable!' said his lordship, determined not to understate the case. 'But it would be worse if I were to marry Deb. I have no doubts on *that* score. I must confess the whole to her, and throw myself on her generosity. If there had been an acknowledged engagement, the case would be hopeless indeed, for as a man of honour I could not draw back, exposing her to the world as a female who had been jilted. But it is not so! No one knows of the engagement but my mother and cousin. I cannot deceive Deb. I *will* not, indeed! She must be told the truth, and at once.'

'I am ready to sink!' declared Miss Laxton, grasping a chairback for support. 'What will she think of me?'

'What will she think of *me*?' asked his lordship.

Happily for them both, Miss Grantham chose that moment to come back into the room. 'Well, and is the race over?' she asked. 'Have you come to the end of all your hairbreadth escapes, or am I too soon?'

Miss Laxton turned away to stare into the fire. Lord

Mablethorpe braced himself, and said resolutely: 'We have not been talking about the race, Deb. There is something I must say to you.'

'No!' whispered Miss Laxton faintly, as one in honour bound.

His lordship ignored this small protest. 'I do not know what you will think of me, Deb. There can be no words bad enough to describe my conduct!'

'No, no! Mine!' gasped Miss Laxton.

'Phœbe is blameless,' said his lordship manfully. 'You will realize that, I know, however hardly you may think of me! *She* would have had you remain in ignorance of the whole! But I cannot! I am determined to tell you the truth, for I am persuaded that nothing but misery could come of keeping it from you!'

Miss Grantham's sense of humour got the better of her at this point, and, tottering towards a chair, she sank into it, exclaiming in tragic accents: 'Oh heavens! I am betrayed!'

His lordship blenched; both he and Miss Laxton regarded her with guilty dismay.

Miss Grantham buried her face in her handkerchief, and uttered one shattering word: 'Wretch!'

His lordship swallowed, and squared his shoulders. 'I am aware in what an odious light my conduct must appear to you, and I cannot attempt to excuse it,' he said. 'Only, I did not mean to do it: it was something I could not help, Deb, indeed it was! And I thought you had rather I told you than—than——'

Miss Grantham gave a shriek. 'You have trifled with me!' she said, into the folds of her handkerchief. 'You promised me marriage, and now you mean to cast me off for Another!'

Lord Mablethorpe and Miss Laxton exchanged stricken glances.

'I never thought I should live to be slighted!' pursued

216

Miss Grantham. 'Oh, was ever any defenceless female so deceived?'

Lord Mablethorpe and Miss Laxton instinctively held hands for mutual support. 'Oh no, do not say so!' implored Phœbe. 'He will soon forget me!'

'Do not let him deceive you, my unhappy child!' said Miss Grantham. 'He will cast you aside as he has cast me! Oh, to think that I should have given my poor heart to a rake!'

'Deb!' exclaimed his lordship, horrified. 'I'm *not*! Indeed, I'm not! And you never *said* you would marry me! It is not as though——'

'My whole life is blighted!' said Miss Grantham, in a hollow voice. 'I shall very likely go into a decline!'

'Deb!' said his lordship, in quite a different voice. 'Well, upon my word! Deb, if you don't st p this instant, I'll—I'll shake you!'

Miss Grantham raised her head, and mopped her streaming eyes. 'Oh Adrian, you foolish boy!' she said. 'What in the world did you think I threw you together for, if not for this? I never had the least intention of marrying you!'

This disclosure astonished Miss Laxton so much that she was quite unable to do more than gaze at her hostess. Lord Mablethorpe, however, drew a sigh of heartfelt relief, and grinned. 'It's just like you to roast me! Somehow, I could not help thinking that you did care for me. But I have behaved very badly to you, and I know it.'

'My poor boy, I fear that it is you who have been the victim. Don't give it another thought! I wish you both very happy, and I am sure you were made for one another. Indeed, I feel that I have made up an unexceptionable match between you! We have now only to consider what is to be done next.'

Miss Laxton, recovering from her stupor, cast herself

upon Deborah's bosom, crying: 'Oh, you are so good to me! I feel so dreadfully at having done such a thing! How can you not wish to marry him?'

'It is very bad taste on my part, indeed,' admitted Miss Grantham. 'Perhaps I was born to be a spinster. But do not let us talk about me, for I shall do very well, I assure you. We must decide what is best to be done with you. Your parents can have no objection, I imagine, to your marriage with Adrian.'

'I am not as rich as Filey. I have not the half of his wealth,' said his lordship, looking anxious.

'You are not precisely a pauper, however. I call it a very good match, and so, I am persuaded, will Lord Laxton.'

'My brother Arnold told me that Sir James would do something very handsome for the family,' faltered Phœbe. 'I do not know what it is, but I fancy Papa has sustained severe losses lately, besides what my brothers owe.'

'Well, so will I do something handsome,' said his lordship stoutly. A shade of uneasiness crept across his face. 'When I am of age,' he added, in a rather flattened voice.

'Nonsense!' said Miss Grantham. 'I do not wish to offend you, Phœbe, but I am not at all in favour of anything's being done for your family. I see no reason why Adrian should be made to pay for the follies of your Papa and your brothers.'

This aspect of the case had not previously occurred to Miss Laxton, but upon reflection she found herself to be in complete agreement with it. 'No, indeed! It would be very bad! I could not consent to such a thing. But what is to be done? My Papa will not care a fig for anything but the money!'

Lord Mablethorpe felt at this point that the discussion could better be continued in Miss Laxton's absence. He said that it was too late to think of ways and means that evening, but that he should call in St James's Square next day, and talk the matter over thoroughly. Miss Grantham, catching a significant glance thrown in her direction, rose instantly to the occasion, and said that this was a wise decision, and that she thought it was high time Phœbe was in bed. She then left the young couple to bid one another a fond good night, only returning to the saloon when she had seen Phœbe to her room, and put her into the hands of the abigail.

She found Lord Mablethorpe walking about the room, his brow clouded with thought. She shut the door, and came to the fire, seating herself by it, and saying in her sensible way: 'Well, now, let us contrive a little! Do you fancy the engagement will not be received with pleasure by the Laxtons? I cannot credit it!'

He looked a little rueful. 'I fear it, Deb. I have been setting a few enquiries afoot, and there seems to be no doubt that Laxton is pretty well done-up.'

'Very true. Those brothers, too, are as an expensive a pair as you may meet! I was talking to Horley about them, and received a very ill account of them. Tell me, my dear boy: do you feel yourself in honour bound to support Phœbe's family?'

'No, I do not,' said his lordship bluntly. 'They have all of them behaved damnably to her, and it is my intention to have nothing more to do with them, after we are married, than we must. I might do something for the younger girls, if Phœbe liked,' he added magniloquently.

'Famous! I was beginning to fear that I had served you an ill turn by casting you into Phœbe's arms. But this is excellent!'

'Yes, but the thing is, Deb, that the Laxtons are not likely to consider my offer beside Filey's. I could not, if I would, do what he might for the family. It means nothing to him: he has almost as much money as Max!'

'That may be, but if Phœbe refuses to marry Filey her parents will be only too glad to discover that she has another, and very eligible suitor at hand.'

Lord Mablethorpe looked rather sceptical, and took another turn about the room. After a pause, he said with some hesitation: 'There is another thing, Deb. I did not tell you, but my mother has always had a notion that I might marry my cousin Arabella one day. She is a great heiress, you know. She won't like it at all if she learns that I mean instead to marry Phœbe Laxton. Phœbe has no more than three or four thousand pounds coming to her, I daresay: not that that would signify to my mother once she has put the idea of my marrying Arabella out of her head: but she don't like Lady Laxton, and I am very much afraid that she will not like the match at all. I don't mean that she won't come round when she knows Phœbe, but—well, it may take a little time, because once she takes a notion into her head.... Well, I daresay you know what I mean! When I am of age, I can do as I please, but until then I don't see how I am to offer for Phœbe, in the proper way, when my mother will very likely oppose the match. I was thinking of Max, too.'

'Pray, what has he to say to it?' demanded Miss Grantham.

'He is not my guardian, but he is one of my trustees, and the thing is that my mother usually attends to him, and although he is the best fellow in the world, I do feel that he will not at all approve of this, on account of the Laxtons being so done-up, you know. He will be afraid that I shall be bled by them, and it will be of no avail for me to assure him that I don't mean to be, because he thinks I am just a boy, and can be imposed upon.'

Miss Grantham was silent for a moment. Privately, she thought that Lady Mablethorpe and Mr Ravenscar would be too relieved to hear that Adrian no longer meant to marry herself to raise any very serious objection to his proposed alliance with a young lady of good birth, and unexceptionable manners; but she was by no means anxious that Mr Ravenscar should learn of Adrian's escape from her toils before she had recovered her aunt's bills, or adequately punished him for his odious conduct. She said, therefore: 'You mean that the matter must be kept secret until you come of age?'

'I think it would be less disagreeable for Phœbe,' he said. 'I might talk my mother over, but I dread the thought of what Phœbe might be made to undergo at Lady Laxton's hands if I did not. I mean to offer for her with all the propriety in the world, but if I am refused permission to address her I shall marry her out of hand, even if it means running all the way to Gretna Green to do it!'

She smiled. 'Bravo! Meanwhile, what is to be done? Am I to keep her with me, or do we send her to stay with her aunt?'

He stopped short in his tracks, an arrested expression in his face. 'I had forgot her aunt! Deb, I believe I should journey into Wales to see her, and to beg for her support! What do you think?'

'It seems to me an excellent plan. She may well be able to assist you. In the meantime, I will keep Phœbe here, where she will be quite safe, depend upon it! You will not mention the matter to your mother, or to your cousin, until things are in a way to be settled.'

He grasped her hands gratefully. 'You are the best of creatures, Deb! I do not know where we should be without you! I will come round to-morrow to talk the thing over with Phœbe, and to learn her aunt's direction.'

She agreed to this, and he then took his leave of her, going home with his head in the clouds, so divorced from earthly considerations that he quite forgot to think out a convincing reason to account for his absence all day to his anxious parent. The result of this oversight was that he blurted out the truth when she questioned him, and then felt very guilty, because Lady Mablethorpe at once expressed her intention of calling in Grosvenor Square the very next morning to favour Mr Ravenscar with her opinion of his wicked callousness in exposing her only son to all the risks of curricle-racing.

On the following day, Miss Laxton stationed herself soon after breakfast at the window in the Yellow Saloon, to watch for Lord Mablethorpe's arrival, while Miss Grantham went to her aunt's dressing-room to see how that afflicted lady did.

Lady Bellingham's spirits had undergone a further buffet by the arrival of a bill from her milliner. She had just thrust this iniquitous document into Deborah's hands when her black page scratched on the door, and, upon being told to come in, handed a packet to Miss Grantham on a silver tray.

She picked it up, recognizing Mr Ravenscar's bold fist, and observing that it had been brought round by hand, asked the boy if an answer was expected. No, he said: the messenger had not waited for any answer.

She dismissed him, and broke the seal, spreading open the stiff sheet of paper. A slim sheaf of bills was disclosed and, attached to them, one of Mr Ravenscar's visiting-cards, with a curt message written across the top of it.

'*With my compliments,*' she read, and sat staring at the card in stunned silence.

Lady Bellingham eyed her with misgiving. 'What is it, my love?' she asked uneasily. 'Who is it from?'

Miss Grantham said, in a voice which did not seem to belong to her: 'It is from Mr Ravenscar.'

Lady Bellingham gave a moan, and reached for her smelling-salts. 'I knew it! Tell me the worst at once! He is going to have us all arrested!'

'No,' said Miss Grantham. 'No.' She handed the packet to her aunt, feeling quite unable to say anything more.

Lady Bellingham took the packet in a gingerly fashion, but when she saw what it contained, she dropped her smelling salts, and ejaculated: 'Deb! Deb, he has sent them!'

'I know,' said Miss Grantham.

'They are all here!' declared her ladyship, sorting them with trembling fingers. 'Even the mortgage, my love! Oh, was there ever anything so providential? But—but why has he done it? Don't tell me you have been teaching him anything dreadful!'

Miss Grantham shook her head. 'I can't think why he has done it, aunt.'

'Did you tell him you would not marry Mablethorpe, and don't care to own it to me? That is it!'

'It is not, ma'am. I told him I would marry Mablethorpe. I said I would ruin him, too.'

'Then I don't understand it at all,' said Lady Bellingham, laying the packet down on her dressing-table. 'You don't suppose, do you, my love, that he can have misunderstood you?'

'I am very sure he did not. But what is to be done?'

'Done, my dear?' repeated her ladyship. 'Well, I think you should write him a pretty letter, thanking him for his goodness in restoring my bills, I must say. It is most obliging of him! I never supposed that he would do so, for they say he is abominably close! But I shall tell anyone who says that to me again that it is not so at all!'

Miss Grantham pressed her hands to her cheeks. 'My dear ma'am, you cannot think that I would accept this generosity! It is impossible! What am I to do?'

Lady Bellingham's eyes started with horror. She caught up the packet and clasped it to her bosom. 'Not accept it?' she gasped. 'After all the trouble you have been to to get these horrid things away from him? Oh, I shall go mad!'

'But that was different!' Miss Grantham said impatiently. 'I never thought he would give them to me merely for the asking!'

'But, my love, you were trying to take them from him by force!' wailed her ladyship.

'Yes, and so I would have,' agreed Miss Grantham. 'But to be beholden to him in this manner is intolerable!'

'Deb, they are my bills, and *I* don't find it intolerable!' said her ladyship in imploring tones.

'It puts me in the most odious position! I can never lift my head again! Besides, he does not even like me! You must see, ma'am, that I cannot endure this! It is not as though I had behaved nicely to him: I have done everything I could to make him hate and despise me!'

'Yes, my love, indeed you have, and that is what makes it so particularly obliging of him! I daresay he must think you are mad, and that is why he has done it, because he is sorry for you.'

This suggestion found no favour at all with Miss Grantham. She fired up at once, saying: 'He must know very well that I am nothing of the kind! I don't want him to be sorry for me! There is no reason why he should be!'

'Well, my love, perhaps he is sorry for me, and I am sure there is plenty of reason for that!'

Miss Grantham got up, kneading her hands together. 'He must be paid!' she said.

'*Paid?*' gasped her aunt. 'I can never pay the half of such a sum!'

'Yes, yes, we always meant to pay the mortgage, my dear ma'am! It must be done!'

'I call it flying in the face of providence!' said Lady Bellingham, with strong feeling. 'With all these other horrid bills for wine, and carriages, and green peas, and candles! I declare, Deb, you are enough to try the patience of a saint!'

'Dear Aunt Lizzie, a run of luck, a little economy, and the thing is done!'

'You know we decided that it was impossible to live more cheaply than we do now, my love! Besides, there is Kit's exchange to be thought of! Do but consider! If you do not like to write to Ravenscar I am very willing to do it for you.'

'Certainly not! I will write to him myself. I will ask him to come to see me, and I will—yes, I will thank him, of course, but I will make it plain to him that he shall be paid back every penny.'

'Next you will be wanting to pay him the interest!' said her ladyship.

'The interest! I had forgotten that! Oh, ought we to pay that too?' said Miss Grantham, appalled.

Lady Bellingham flung up her hands. 'Deb, you *are* mad! I do not know what has come over you! It was bad enough when you wantonly threw away twenty thousand pounds—and I can scarcely bear to think of that, when I remember all these shocking bills!—but when it comes to refusing to accept this dreadful mortgage, which you have spent a week trying to get from Ravenscar, it goes beyond all bounds! Anyone would have supposed that you would be thankful to get the wretched thing so easily! But not at all! I do believe you would have preferred to have wrested it from Ravenscar by main force!'

'Yes, I would,' replied Miss Grantham earnestly. 'Much rather! *That* would have been my wits against his! This—oh, I wonder you cannot see how impossible it is!'

'I cannot, and I never shall,' said her aunt. 'At least, I hope I shall not, but sometimes I feel as though I were going mad too. I wish you will let me call in the doctor to you! I am sure you have caught a touch of the sun, or contracted some horrid disease which is sending you out of your mind!'

Before Miss Grantham could repudiate this suggestion, there was a hurried tap on the door, followed immediately by the entrance of Miss Laxton into the room, looking as white as her tucker.

'Good God, child, what is the matter with you?' exclaimed Lady Bellingham.

Miss Laxton took a wavering step towards Deborah. 'Sir James!' she managed to utter, and crumpled up where she stood, in a dead faint.

'Oh, heavens, if it is not one thing it is another!' wailed her ladyship, looking round wildly for the vinaigrette. 'Untie her laces! Where are those salts? Why is nothing ever where it is wanted? Ring the bell! Oh no, the harts-horn is in that cupboard! I shall go distracted! You ought to burn some feathers under her nose, but there are only the new ostrich plumes in my best hat, and really——However, take them if you like! I am sure I do not grudge them!'

Deborah, who had dropped on to her knees beside Miss Laxton's inanimate form, raised her head to say: 'My dear ma'am, it is quite unnecessary! Have the goodness to bring me a little water, and I will engage for it that she will soon come round! Poor child, what can have happened, I wonder? Did she say Sir James was here?'

'She said *Sir James*, but I heard nothing more. If this is his doing, I will step downstairs immediately, and give him a piece of my mind! This may be a gaming-house, but if he thinks to come to it simply to terrify stupid girls he is very much mistaken, and so he will find before he is a day older!'

Deborah took the glass of water from her, and sprinkled a little on Miss Laxton's face. 'Hush, ma'am! She is coming to herself! There, my dear! You are better now, are you not?'

Phœbe's eyes opened, and stared blankly up into Miss

Grantham's face for a bewildered moment. Then, as realization came, she shuddered convulsively, and clutched at Miss Grantham's arm. 'Oh, don't let him come in!'

'No one shall come in whom you don't wish to see, my dear,' replied Miss Grantham calmly. 'Do not agitate yourself so! you are quite safe! Come, I want you to drink this hartshorn-and-water, and then you will be better!'

Miss Laxton swallowed the mixture obediently, and burst into tears, Lady Bellingham said: 'For heaven's sake, child, don't start crying! If Sir James is downstairs, I will very soon send him about his business! His mother was a very vulgar, low kind of a woman, so that I am sure one cannot be surprised at anything!'

Miss Grantham helped Phœbe to rise from the floor, and put her into a large armchair. 'Is he downstairs, Phœbe?'

'No! Oh, no, I think not! He walked away. He will have gone to my father. I am utterly undone! What shall I do? Where can I go? I dare not stay here another minute!'

Lady Bellingham sighed, and shook her head. 'I declare I cannot make head or tail of what she means! I daresay she is going mad too, if we only knew, and who shall wonder at it?'

Phœbe clasped Miss Grantham's hand feebly, and said that indeed she was not mad. 'It was my fault. It was all my folly! I never thought—I went into the front saloon, to watch for Adrian, and I didn't think that anyone would see me. I pulled back the blinds, to see better, and he was there!'

'Who was there? Who was *where*?' demanded Lady Bellingham.

'Sir James, in the Square, walking by the house in the direction of St James's Street!'

'I daresay he was on his way to White's,' said her ladyship.

'But he saw me! I know he saw me, and knew me too! I did not immediately perceive him, and when I did look towards him he was standing quite still, staring up at me! I thought I should have died of fright! I ran away from the window, and came directly in search of you, Deb! Oh, what is to be done? I won't go back, I won't, but I know Papa will come to fetch me, and Mama too, very likely!'

'Well, if Augusta Laxton comes into this house I shall know what to do!' said Lady Bellingham, with unwonted pugnacity. 'I do not wish to speak ill of your Mama, Phœbe, but she is an odious, mercenary, cheating wretch! She used to play faro at my parties, when we lived in the smaller house, and three times did I catch her cocking her card! Let her attempt to force her way in here, that is all I have to say!'

Miss Laxton, however, refused to be comforted. She was quite sure that she would be wrested from her friends' protection, and compelled to marry Sir James Filey. No representations which Miss Grantham could make of the impossibility of her being compelled to marry anyone bore any weight with her; she seemed to be determined to give herself up for lost. It was with considerable relief that Miss Grantham learned, a few minutes later, that Lord Mablethorpe was belowstairs.

'Desire him to come up!' she said. 'You will not object to his coming into your dressing-room, aunt?'

'Oh no, let him come!' said her ladyship, quite exhausted by her efforts to reassure Phœbe. 'I do not care who comes, if only they can put some sense into this stupid girl's head! I will say this for you, Deb: you may lock people up in the cellar, and fling thousands of pounds in their faces as though it was mud, but you don't cry! Nothing could be more tiresome, when all is said and done! If that is you at the door, Mablethorpe, come in this instant, and *do* something!'

Lord Mablethorpe came in, looking a little shy, and rather startled. He began to apologize for intruding upon Lady Bellingham in her dressing-room, but stopped short at the sight of Miss Laxton, and started forward, exclaiming: 'Good God, what is the matter?'

Miss Laxton, who had been lying with her eyes closed, apparently on the verge of yet another swoon, revived sufficiently to sit up, and to cast herself into his lordship's arms. Miss Grantham then abandoned her own attempts to bring relief to her suffering protégée, and stood back to see what success his lordship's efforts might meet with.

'What a fool that woman is never to have told her daughter that *nothing* can be more fatal than to weep all down a man's waistcoat!' whispered Lady Bellingham, quite exasperated. 'They can't bear it, and I'm sure I don't wonder!'

But Lord Mablethorpe did not seem to mind being wept over. Miss Grantham could not but admire his handling of a situation which she frankly acknowledged to be beyond her power to mend. In a remarkably short time, Miss Laxton had stopped crying, and was even able to smile tremulously up at his lordship, and to beg his pardon for having been such a goose. Now that he had come, she said, she knew that she would be safe.

Lord Mablethorpe then demanded to be told the cause of her distress. When it had been explained to him, once (unintelligibly) by Phœbe, and once by Deborah, his brows drew together across the bridge of his beautiful nose, and he said with more decision than Deborah had ever before heard in his voice: 'That settles it, then!'

Miss Laxton heaved a huge sigh, and tucked her hand in his. 'I knew you would know what to do!'

'Well, it's to be hoped he does,' said Lady Bellingham, with some asperity. 'If I had known that all you wanted was to hear someone say *that settles it*, I would have said it myself, for I am sure it is easy enough to say, and doesn't signify in the least!'

'I do know what to do,' said his lordship, laying Phœbe back against the sofa-cushions, and rising to his feet.

'Don't leave me!' implored Phœbe.

He smiled warmly down at her. 'I am never going to leave you again, my sweet.'

'You can't come and stay here!' interpolated Lady Bellingham. 'I should be very pleased to have you, of course, but now that Kit is home, we have no room.'

'I don't mean to stay here, ma'am. I am going to take Phœbe to her aunt in Wales. Deb, I shall need you too!'

Miss Grantham could not help laughing at his air of authority. 'The devil you will! What do you mean to do, you absurd creature?'

'I mean to marry Phœbe out of hand, if her aunt will permit. I shall take her to Wales, lay the whole case before her aunt, and——'

'And what if her aunt does not permit? I suppose you will abide by her decision?'

He grinned. 'No. I shan't. But I hope she may give her countenance to the marriage. If the worst comes to the worst, I shall have a special licence with me, and we shall be married. But these runaway matches are not at all the thing, and I should prefer to have the marriage performed with the greatest possible degree of propriety, to save Phœbe the embarrassment of any scandal.'

'Quite right!' said Lady Bellingham approvingly. 'I never thought you had so much sense, Adrian! It will answer very well. You will be able to put a notice in the *Morning Post*, saying that Phœbe was married from the house of her aunt, and although it may seem a trifle odd, it will be much better than to have it known that it was a horrid clandestine affair. Where does your aunt live, my dear?'

Miss Laxton, on whom these arbitrary plans for her future had acted like a strong tonic, sat up, and replied that her aunt was a widow, and lived at Welshpool, in Montgomery. She added that she knew her aunt would approve of her marriage to Adrian.

'That means the Holyhead road,' said his lordship. 'I shall inform my mother that I am going into the country for a few days' shooting, with some friends. I often do so: it will occasion not the least remark! Deb, I have no right to expect it of you, but I do beg that you will go with Phœbe in the chaise, which I shall hire! I mean to ride beside you, of course.'

'What, am I to go with you to play propriety?' asked Miss Grantham, amused. 'And pray what is to become of me at the journey's end?'

'I shall bring you safely back to town,' promised his lordship. 'I have thought it all out. Once the knot is tied, I shall leave Phœbe in her aunt's care, and return to London to inform her parents, and my own mother of the event. When that is done, and they are ready to receive Phœbe with the attention and the courtesy which is due to my wife, I shall fetch her to town again. After that, I daresay we shall go down to Mablethorpe.'

'I see that you have it all planned,' said Miss Grantham admiringly. 'But I cannot perceive the least use in my going upon your bridal trip.'

But Miss Laxton at once caught her hand, and begged her not to desert her; and his lordship said, with a touch of austerity, that her presence was necessary to remove from the journey any flavour of elopement. Lady Bellingham, possibly reflecting that the excitement of the adventure might drive the thought of the mortgage out of her niece's head, gave it as her opinion that Deborah ought certainly to go. Miss Grantham submitted, therefore, and promised to have herself and her protégée in readiness to set forward on the journey in an hour's time. Lord Mablethorpe then left the house, to make his own arrangements. He would, he said, have a post-chaise at the door within the hour. The two ladies were to drive away in it, and he engaged himself to overtake them a few miles out of London.

In all the bustle of preparation, Miss Grantham had time only to scribble a hasty note to Mr Ravenscar, in which she informed him that she had received his very obliging communication, and would be grateful for an opportunity of meeting him upon her return from the country, further to discuss the matter. She added that she expected to be in London again within a few days, and gave the letter to Silas, with instructions to deliver it by hand at once.

Miss Laxton spent the hour before her departure in an agony of dread, but the post-chaise-and-four was at the door before the arrival of an avenging parent could frustrate all Lord Mablethorpe's schemes. Lady Bellingham bade farewell to the travellers, announcing herself to be perfectly able to fob off Augusta Laxton, and a dozen like her; the two ladies climbed into the chaise; the post-boys cracked their whips; the equipage lurched forward over the cobbles; and Miss Laxton was able to let her breath go at last.

CHAPTER XV

LADY BELLINGHAM was not called upon to sustain a visit from Lady Laxton, but not long after the chaise had driven away from St James's Square Lord Laxton arrived at the house, and sent in his card.

Lady Bellingham received him in the Yellow Saloon,

and was shrewd enough to perceive at the first glance that he was extremely ill-at-ease. The truth was that his lord-ship believed Sir James Filey to have been mistaken in thinking he had seen Phœbe at one of the windows in Lady Bellingham's house, and much resented having been sent to enquire into the matter. He was positive that his daughter was quite unacquainted with her ladyship, so that when Lady Bellingham received his tentative questions with a look of the blankest bewilderment he was not at all surprised, but reflected that it was just like Augusta to have driven him out on a fool's errand. Lady Bellingham said that she had thought for some time that Sir James was drinking too heavily. She supposed that he must have caught sight of her niece's school-friend, Miss Smith, who had certainly been staying in the house, as his lordship might verify for himself, if he cared to question the servants. This was said with a sarcastic inflexion which embarrassed his lordship. He said that he had no wish to question the servants, and was sure that a mistake had been made. Lady Bellingham then enjoyed herself very much by asking him a great many awkward questions about his daughter's disappear-ance, so that he was glad to make his escape as soon as he could. He was not allowed to depart, however, without being asked how his wife did, and whether her luck at cards continued to hold good; and as he was well aware of the circumstances which had led up to Lady Laxton's ceasing to receive cards of invitation to Lady Bellingham's card-parties, he finally left the house in considerable dis-order. Augusta, he decided, might do what she pleased, but for his part he was not going to be sent on any more such errands. His own belief was that his daughter had fled to her aunt in Wales, which was an exceedingly awkward business, since he supposed he would be obliged to go there to fetch the girl away. As this would entail meeting his redoubtable sister, and enduring the lightning of her extremely forked tongue, it was not a prospect to which he looked forward with any pleasure.

Lady Bellingham's next visitor was Lucius Kennet, who strolled in to see her at about noon. He had come to tell her that he had an engagement that evening, and so would not be able to deal for her at the faro-table, as he usually did. When he heard of Deborah's departure into Wales with Phœbe and Lord Mablethorpe, he was at first amused, and then as exasperated as a man of his easy-going temperament could be.

'So she's going to marry the young sprig to the Laxton chit, is she?' he said. 'I'm thinking that when Ravenscar gets to hear of this the game will be up, ma'am.'

'Oh, if I had not forgot to tell you!' exclaimed her lady-ship. 'Ravenscar has given the mortgage and the bills to her! I had not thought to find him so complaisant!'

He pursed up his lips. 'That's the way it is, is it? I'd a strong notion our friend was a deal more taken up with Deb's charms than she guessed.'

Lady Bellingham sighed. 'I own, I thought the same, and I daresay it is quite true. But it is useless to talk to Deb, Lucius! She has taken such a dislike to the man that nothing will overcome it!'

'It was in me mind, ma'am, that she was more than half in love with the fellow.'

'Oh no, nothing of the kind!' said her ladyship. 'She can't abide him. I can vouch for *that*! And if you are thinking that he might offer for her, I believe he is too proud. If anything of that nature has entered his head, you may depend upon it it is not *marriage* he means!'

He agreed with this, and sat for a few moments, idly casting his dice on to the table at his elbow. After a frowning pause, he raised his eyes to her ladyship's face, and said bluntly: 'How do your accounts stand, ma'am?'

She shuddered. 'Don't ask me that! Of course, it is a relief to get that mortgage into my hands, but when I think of the twenty thousand pounds he offered to give Deb, I declare I could weep!'

'I was thinking much the same meself,' he said. 'This is a bird that lays golden eggs, ma'am, and it would be a pity, so it would, to let it slip through our fingers before we have one of those same eggs.'

'I see no need for you to talk in that vulgar way, Lucius,' said her ladyship, with dignity. 'But in the main I agree with what you say. Only Deb is so proud she will not take a penny from anyone, so you may as well stop thinking of that twenty thousand.'

He grinned. 'And has your ladyship stopped thinking of it?' he enquired.

'No one,' said her ladyship severely, 'can stop thinking of such a sum all in a trice, but I assure you it does not creep into my mind now above once or twice in a day.'

'If I could lay my hands on it, it's not meself that would be forgetting an old friend,' he observed, watching the fall of his dice.

'I am sure you would not,' replied her ladyship, gratified by this kind thought, 'and if *I* had such a sum *I* would not forget you. But Deb is determined not to touch a penny of Ravenscar's money, so there is nothing for us to do but to put it out of our minds.'

'Faith, I'm disappointed in the darlin'!' said Mr Kennet. 'I'm thinking I'll be taking a hand in the game meself.'

'I do not see what you can do,' objected Lady Bellingham. 'As soon as he knows that Mablethorpe is safely tied to Phœbe Laxton, there will no longer be the least reason why he should give us any money at all.'

'Well,' drawled Kennet, rising to his feet, and pocketing his dice, 'Mablethorpe is not the only weapon to our hands, after all. I'll be bidding you a very good day, ma'am.'

He went off, leaving her ladyship rather bewildered, but, on the whole, unimpressed.

Mr Ravenscar, in the meantime, had received Miss Grantham's hurried note, and had read it with some amusement. It was plain that he had taken her by surprise, which was what he had meant to do; and equally plain that she had been thrown into a considerable degree of embarrassment. He more than half suspected her of having told him that she was going into the country merely to gain time to decide on her next course of action. He wondered what this would be, and, having by this time formed a fairly accurate estimate of the lady's character, would not have been surprised to have had the bills flung back at him without an instant's delay on her part.

He folded her letter, and put it away. The various exigencies of the past week had precluded his paying very much attention to his half-sister, but he had noticed a certain saintliness of demeanour about that young lady which he had learnt from experience to mistrust, and thought that it might be as well to devote a little of his time to her. With this end in view, he sent up a message to her, asking whether she cared to drive out with him in the Park.

Upon receiving this message, Miss Ravenscar came down to the library, dressed for walking, and eyed him rather doubtfully. 'Why do you want to take me out driving?' she asked.

'Why shouldn't I want to?' he replied, looking up from the letter he was reading.

'Well, I don't know,' said Arabella cautiously. 'Whenever Aunt Selina invites me drive out with her, in that stuffy barouche, it is always because she wants to read me a lecture.'

He laughed. 'Belle, when have I ever done such a thing?'

'There is no saying when you might take it into your head to do so,' she answered dimpling.

'It won't be today. Do you mean to come with me, or not?'

'Well, I had meant to walk in the Park, with my maid, but if you would like me to come with you I will do so,' said Miss Ravenscar handsomely.

He looked at her with a sardonic gleam of comprehension in his eye. 'An assignation, Belle?'

Miss Ravenscar said airily: 'Oh dear me, no!'

'Little liar,' said Ravenscar, without heat.

She seemed flattered by this, and gave a gurgle.

Ravenscar had had his perch-phæton brought round to the door, with a showy pair of chestnuts harnessed to it. His sister was delighted to find that she was to drive out in this sporting vehicle and skipped up into it, begging Ravenscar to waste no time in starting, since, if her Mama were to look out of the window she would be bound to say that it was too dangerous, and forbid her to go, for fear she might be overturned. Ravenscar took this aspersion on his driving with equanimity, and they drove off in the direction of the Park. As soon as they were within the gates, Miss Ravenscar demanded to be allowed to take the ribbons. Since he had taught her to drive himself, her brother raised no objection to this, and handed them over. Perfect harmony being thus established between them, he felt it safe to ask her whether her affections were irrevocably set on Mr Grantham, of the 14th Foot. Arabella said, in accents of considerable surprise: 'Kit Grantham? Good gracious, Max, no! That was a long time go!'

'So it was,' he agreed. 'At least ten days. I met the young gentleman the other night. I am glad you don't mean to marry him. He would not do for you at all.'

'No, he is *far* too young,' said Arabella. 'I do not think I like very young men nearly as much as older ones. Not too old, of course.'

Mr Ravenscar cast rapidly round in his mind, but was unable to think of any male between the ages of thirty and forty with whom Arabella might have come into contact. He waited, hoping for a further clue.

'I like men who have been about the world a little,' said Arabella reflectively. 'They are more exciting, if you know what I mean, Max.'

Mr Ravenscar thought gloomily that he knew very well what she meant. 'True, but such men do not make good husbands for very young women,' he said.

Arabella turned her innocent eyes upon him. 'Why don't they, Max?'

'Well, they grow old too fast,' he explained. 'Think! Before you well knew where you were you would find your husband a martyr to gout, no longer ready to go out to parties, but wanting always to sit at home over the fire.'

Miss Ravenscar looked much struck by this view of the matter. 'All of them?' she asked anxiously.

'*All* of them,' said her brother, with great firmness.

'Oh!' Miss Ravenscar drove on in silence, evidently digesting this dictum. A barouche ahead of her, drawn by two sluggish brown horses, attracted her attention. She said, pouting a little: 'Aunt Selina! Shall I go past, and pretend we did not see her?'

'Better not,' he said. 'Go past, and draw up by the trees.'

She looped a rein, as he had taught her, and shot past the barouche in a very dashing style, to the evident admiration of a gentleman driving a phæton towards them.

'I did that well, did I not?' she asked, with naïve pleasure in her own skill.

'Very well.'

She drew up by a clump of trees, and waited for the barouche to come alongside. Lady Mablethorpe, impressive in a lavender bonnet, with upstanding plumes, leaned forward to exclaim: 'My dear, surely that is a very dangerous carriage for you to be driving! I wonder you will let her, Max!'

'She will come to no harm,' he replied carelessly.

'I suppose you thought the same about Adrian, when you took him racing with you yesterday!' said her ladyship tartly.

His rare smile lighted his eyes suddenly. 'Why, yes, ma'am, I did!'

'I think it was abominable of you! He might have been killed! I know what these curricle-races are! Next we shall have him wanting to drive in one himself!'

'I should not be at all surprised. You cannot keep him on leading-strings all his life, you know.'

She sighed. 'No, but——Well, it does not signify! I must tell you, Max, that I am in hopes that a certain affair is waning.'

'Indeed! I am very glad to hear it, but what leads you to think so?'

'He has gone off to Tom Waring's place in Berkshire for some shooting. He was in spirits too; I could see he was glad to be going. You may guess how thankful I feel!'

'He said nothing to me about this when he was with me yesterday,' remarked Ravenscar, looking rather surprised.

'It was settled only this morning. I collect that he met Tom at White's, or some such place, and Tom asked him then.'

'I had no idea Waring was in town. In fact, I thought he was fixed in Berkshire until next month.'

'I daresay he was obliged to come up to attend to some business. I do not see what concern it is of ours. The main thing is that Adrian has been persuaded to go out of town for a few days. I regard it as a most encouraging sign!'

'I hope it may be found so,' Ravenscar said. 'Arabella, we must not keep Aunt Selina!'

'No, indeed!' said Arabella promptly.

'You mean you do not wish to keep your horses standing,' said Lady Mablethorpe dryly. 'Drive on, then, but pray take care of that child, Max!'

'As though I had never handled the ribbons before!' said Arabella, as they moved forward. 'Max, was she talking about Adrian's engagement to Miss Grantham?'

'I am not aware of any engagement.'

'Oh, don't be stuffy, Max! Adrian told me of it himself! Is my aunt still set against it?'

'Certainly she is.'

'Because she behaved so oddly at Vauxhall?'

'That, and other reasons.'

'Well, I will tell you something,' said Arabella resolutely. 'I like her.'

He turned his head to look at her. 'Indeed! I should not have thought that you had had time to make up your mind in the short while you were in her company.'

'As a matter of fact,' confided Miss Ravenscar, 'I met her on another occasion. Don't be cross!'

'I am not cross. Where did you meet her?'

She cast him a look, half-mischievous, half-deprecating. 'I wanted to see her for myself. So I went to visit her at her home.'

'The devil you did!' he said. 'And you decided that you liked her?'

'Yes, for she was not in the least vulgar! And it is just as I told you at Vauxhall: she has the most laughing eyes!'

'They do laugh sometimes,' admitted Mr Ravenscar. 'May I ask if you are in the habit of visiting her?'

'No, because she said I must not while you and my aunt disliked her so amazingly.'

'Oh, she said that, did she?'

'Yes, but I told her I should come often to see her when she was married to Adrian, and she said I might.'

'She is not going to marry Adrian.'

'I do not see why she should not. I think you are silly, and fusty, and full of prejudice!'

'I daresay you do.'

'And I may as well tell you at once, Max, that nothing would induce *me* to marry Adrian!'

'I never supposed that you would marry him.'

'You did not?' she exclaimed. 'I quite thought that you expected it! Mama and Aunt Selina do.'

'Very likely. If you take my advice, you will not marry anyone for a year or two yet.'

She wrinkled her brow. 'But I shall be almost on the shelf! Besides, I think I should like to be married.'

'When you think that you would like to be married to the same man for more than a month, Belle, tell me!' he said, smiling.

She shook her head. 'It is a very awkward circumstance, my falling in love so often, Max. However, I am much wiser now than I used to be, and I daresay I shall very soon settle down.'

He said nothing for several minutes, but when they reached the gates of the Park again, he took the reins from her. 'You know, Belle,' he said, 'you will have a considerable fortune when you come of age.'

'I know I shall. I shall enjoy that,' replied Miss Ravenscar.

'Certainly. But take care you do not marry a man who wants to enjoy it too.'

Miss Ravenscar thought this over. 'That's horrid, Max.'

'It is unfortunately the way of a great part of the world.'

'Do you mean—do you mean that all the men who have wanted me to marry them only wanted my fortune?'

'I am afraid I do, Belle.'

Miss Ravenscar swallowed. 'It is a very lowering thought,' she said, in a small voice.

'It would be if there were not plenty of men to whom your fortune will not matter a jot.'

'Rich men?'

'Not necessarily.'

'Oh!' Miss Ravenscar sounded more hopeful. 'But how shall I know, Max?'

'Well, there might be several ways of knowing, but I can give you one certain way. If you should meet any man who would like to persuade you to elope with him, you may depend upon it that he is after your money, and nothing else. An honest man will rather ask permission to call in Grosvenor Square.'

'But, Max, they are all afraid of you!' objected Arabella.

'Depend upon it, you will one day meet a man who is not in the least afraid of me.'

'Yes, but—it is all so respectable, Max, and not exciting, or romantic! Besides, they have not *all* wanted to elope with me!'

'I should hope not indeed! Listen, Belle! I am asking no questions, and I don't mean to spy on you, but I fancy you meet more men than your Mama or I know of. Before you decide to lose your absurd heart to one of them, consider whether you would care to present him to me, or to Adrian.'

'And if I would not, will he be the wrong sort of man?'

'He will.'

'Well, I'll do that,' promised Miss Ravenscar, brightening. 'It will be a very good kind of a game!'

Her brother drove her home, feeling that the morning had not been wasted.

He dined at Brooks's that evening, and played faro afterwards, at the fifty-guinea table. When he rose from it, shortly after midnight, he saw that Ormskirk had walked into the card-room, and was standing watching the fall of the dice at the hazard-table. Ormskirk looked up quickly as Ravenscar put back his chair, and moved across the room towards him.

'I thought you visited Brooks's as seldom as I visit White's,' remarked Ravenscar.

'Quite true,' Ormskirk drawled. 'You, I fancy, came to White's the other evening merely to find me.'

Ravenscar lifted an eyebrow.

'I,' said Ormskirk, flicking a speck of snuff from his sleeve, 'came to Brooks's in the hopes of finding you, my dear Ravenscar.'

'Ought I to be flattered?'

'Well, I must own that it is not my intention to flatter you,' replied his lordship, his thin lips curling into an unpleasant smile.

Ravenscar looked at him, slightly frowning. 'How am I to take that, my lord?'

'I hope you may take it to heart. Let me tell you that I cannot congratulate you on the use you made of certain bills which I sold you. I must confess I am disappointed in you, my dear Ravenscar.'

'May I know how you are aware of what use I made of them?'

His lordship shrugged. 'Inference, just inference!' he said sweetly.

'I suppose I must be extremely dull-witted, but I am still far from understanding what you mean. May I suggest that we step into the next room?'

'By all means,' bowed Ormskirk. 'I can appreciate the delicacy of feeling which prompts you to shrink from discussing your cousin's wife in such a public spot.'

Ravenscar strode over to the door that led into a small writing-room, and held it open. 'I should certainly be loth to do so,' he replied. 'My cousin, however, is not married nor is he likely to be.'

'You think not?' smiled Ormskirk.

Ravenscar shut the door. 'I am quite sure of it.'

Ormskirk took out his snuff-box, and helped himself to a delicate pinch. 'My dear Ravenscar, I am afraid you have been duped,' he said.

Ravenscar stood still by the door, stiffening a little. 'In what way have I been duped?'

Ormskirk shut his snuff-box. 'I must suppose that you have not encountered Stillingfleet, my dear sir.'

'I did not know that he was in town.'

'He arrived this morning. He has been staying at Hertford.'

'Well?'

'He drove to town by way of the Great North Road,' remarked Ormskirk pensively.

'So I should suppose. I do not yet perceive how his movements concern me.'

'But you will, my dear Ravenscar, you will! Stillingfleet, you must know, changed horses at the Green Man at Barnet. When he pulled out from the yard, he was in time to obtain an excellent view of a post-chaise-and-four, which was passing up the street at that moment. Ah, heading north, you understand!'

Mr Ravenscar was looking a little pale, and his mouth had hardened. 'Go on!' he said harshly.

'He was much struck by the appearance of the lady in the chaise. He is not acquainted with Deb Grantham, but I could hardly mistake, from his admirable description of the lady's charms! She had a young woman beside her —her maid, one supposes—and there was a quantity of baggage strapped on behind the chaise.'

Ravenscar smiled contemptuously. 'Very possibly. Miss Grantham has gone into the country for a few days. I was aware that she had that intention.'

'And were you also aware that your cousin had

the intention to accompany her?' enquired Ormskirk.

'I was not!'

'No, I thought not,' said Ormskirk gently.

'Are you serious?' Ravenscar demanded. 'Do you tell me that Mablethorpe was with Miss Grantham?'

'That,' replied his lordship, 'is what Stillingfleet told me. And he is, I fancy, fairly well-acquainted with your cousin. He informed me that Mablethorpe was riding beside the chaise. Ah, I did mention that they were travelling in a northerly direction, did I not?'

'Oh, yes!' said Ravenscar. 'You mentioned that at the outset, my lord. I may be dull-witted, but I collect that you wish me to infer that my cousin was eloping with Miss Grantham to Gretna Green.'

'It seems a fair inference,' murmured his lordship.

'It is a damned lie!' said Mr Ravenscar.

His lordship raised his brows in faint hauteur. 'You should know better than I, my dear sir.'

'I think so indeed! I have known Mablethorpe since he was in short coats, and nothing would astonish me more than to learn that he had taken part in anything so vulgar as an elopement to Gretna. It is not in his character, my lord, believe me! Furthermore, I do not think that Miss Grantham has any more intention of marrying him than she has of becoming your mistress!'

'You would appear to be in the lady's confidence,' said Ormskirk. 'Or has she succeeded in deceiving you, I wonder?'

'She has certainly tried her best to do so, but I can assure you that she failed!' replied Ravenscar, with a short laugh. 'I think I know Miss Grantham now, however mistaken I may have been in her at the outset! If Stillingfleet saw my cousin beside her chaise to-day, I imagine that he was escorting her to her friends in the country. That would certainly be in keeping with what I know of him.'

Lord Ormskirk made a graceful gesture of acceptance. 'If that explanation satisfies you, my dear Ravenscar, who am I to cavil at it? I do hope that you will not suffer a rude awakening! You must not think that I do not find your faith in your cousin's sense of propriety edifying: believe me, I do! For myself, I fear I am a cynic. No doubt we shall discover in time which of us was right.'

CHAPTER XVI

Mr Ravenscar strode home in a mood of some uneasiness. Lord Ormskirk's story had alarmed him quite as much as it had angered him, and although he did indeed believe Mablethorpe to be incapable of so far forgetting what was due to his name as to elope with Miss Grantham to the Border, he could not but recall his own faint surprise at hearing, that morning, that his cousin had suddenly taken it into his head to retire into the country for a few days' shooting. Mr Ravenscar was well aware that his youthful relative, far from showing any sign of recovery from his passion for Miss Grantham, had been haunting St James's Square for the past week. He bore all the marks of a man deeply in love, and nothing, Ravenscar was persuaded, had been farther from his intentions, when he had last seen his cousin, than a removal from town. Miss Grantham's decision to visit friends in the country might, of course, have altered his lordship's plans; and it certainly would have been very like him to have escorted her to her destination before himself travelling into Berkshire. Mr Ravenscar did his best to satisfy his own unquiet mind with this explanation, but could not quite succeed. He could not leave out of his calculations the inconvenient circumstance of his having relinquished the one sure hold he had over Miss Grantham. He thought he had gauged Miss Grantham's character correctly, but the unwelcome suspicion that he might after all have been wrong would not be banished entirely from his brain. This possibility was so exceedingly unpalatable that it set him striding on at a greater rate than ever, his hand rather tightly clenched on his walking-cane, and his face set in more than ordinarily grim lines. At no time did Mr Ravenscar care to find himself mistaken; in this instance he had his own reasons for being doubly anxious that his judgment should not be found to have been at fault.

He reached his house soon after one in the morning, and was surprised, and not best pleased, to be met by his stepmother, swathed in a wrapper, and evidently labouring under a considerable degree of agitation. Long experience had made it unnecessary for him to enquire the cause of her being out of bed at such an hour, and he said, before she could speak: 'Well, what has she been doing this time?'

'Oh, my dear Max!' said Mrs Ravenscar, in a weak voice. 'I ought to have suspected when she said she had the headache that she was planning some mischief!'

'Of course you ought!' replied Ravenscar. 'Out, is she?'

'Her bed has not been slept in!' announced Mrs Ravenscar dramatically. 'I went in, just to see how she did, a couple of hours ago, for you must know that I myself am quite unable to sleep in all the racket of town— not that I mean to complain, I am sure, but so it is! And she was not in her room, and not a word can I get out of that wicked maid of hers, who, I am positive, is in the plot! She will do nothing but cry, and say that she knows nothing!'

'You had better get rid of the girl,' said Ravenscar unemotionally.

'It is all very well for you to dismiss the matter so lightly,

Max, but if you *knew* the number of abigails I have engaged to wait on Arabella, and each one of them less fit to be trusted than the last! Besides, how will that help us in our present predicament?'

'It won't,' he replied. 'Nor will anything help us in any future predicaments of the same nature except your forgetting all these megrims of yours, Olivia, and taking Belle to the balls and masquerades her heart craves for. Where has she gone to-night?'

'How should I know? I do not know how you can stand there, speaking to me in that brutal fashion, when you know how the least thing oversets my poor nerves! It is unfeeling of you, and I did not look for such usage at your hands, though to be sure I might well, for your father was just such another! I will tell you what it is, Max: if you had the smallest consideration for me, or for your poor sister—who is your ward, let me remind you!—you would have married years ago, and provided the child with a chaperon who might have escorted her to parties without being prostrated by exhaustion for days after!'

'Of all the reasons I ever heard for embarking on the married state, that one appeals the least to me!' said Ravenscar roundly. 'You had better go up to bed, ma'am: I have little doubt that already your nerves will suffer from the effects of this night.'

'I have had the most dreadful palpitations this past hour and more. But where can that dreadful child be?'

'I have no idea, and nothing is farther from my intention than to scour London in search of her. She will return presently.'

'If anyone were to hear of these pranks of hers, it would ruin all her chances of making a good match!' mourned Mrs Ravenscar, drifting towards the stairs.

'Nonsense!' said Ravenscar. 'Nothing can ruin the chances of an heiress of making a good match!'

Mrs Ravenscar said that she hoped he would be found to know what he was talking about, but that for her part she wished the child were safely married, so that she herself might retire to the peace of Bath. She then went upstairs, leaning heavily on the bannister-rail, and, after swallowing some laudanum-drops, and soaking her handkerchief in lavender-water, very soon fell asleep.

Miss Ravenscar, knocking softly on the door an hour later, was disconcerted at being admitted, not by her faithful abigail, as had been arranged, but by an exasperated half-brother. 'Oh!' she exclaimed, letting fall her reticule. 'W-what a start you gave me, Max, to be sure!'

'Who,' demanded Ravenscar, 'is your cavalier?'

'He has gone,' said Arabella hastily, seeing that he was about to step out into the porch.

'Just as well for him!' said Ravenscar. 'You are a cursed nuisance, Arabella! Where have you been?'

'Only to the masquerade at Ranelagh,' replied Arabella, in cajoling accents. 'I did want so much to go, and Mama would not take me, and you said it was not good *ton*, so what was I to do?'

'Stay at home,' said Ravenscar uncompromisingly. 'If you don't take care, Belle, I'll send you down to Chamfreys with a devilish strict governess to watch over you!'

'I'd run away,' responded Arabella, unperturbed by this threat, and slipping a small, coaxing hand in his arm. 'Don't be cross with me, dearest Max! It was such an adventure! And I did not once take off my mask, so no one will ever know.'

'Who took you there?'

'Well, I think I won't tell you that, because ten to one you do not know him, and if you do you would say something disagreeable to him,' said Arabella. 'But I will tell you one thing, Max!'

'I suppose I should be grateful! What is it?'

'Why, only that I remembered what you said to me to-day and you were *quite* right! At least, I am very nearly sure that you are, but I shall know more certainly in a day or two, I daresay.'

He looked down at her with misgiving. 'What mischief are you brewing? Come, out with it, Belle!'

Her eyes danced. 'No, I shan't tell you! You would spoil it all! I *think* someone is trying to impose upon me, though I am not quite sure yet. It is the most enchanting sport!'

'Oh, my God!' said Ravenscar.

She pinched his arm. 'Now don't, I implore you, Max, put on that *fusty* face! I promise you I shall not do anything you would not like. And if you are sensible, and don't let Mama plague me, I shall very likely tell you all about it presently.'

'I suppose you imagine that I like your running off to a public masquerade with an adventurer?' said her brother caustically.

'Well, you should have taken me to it yourself, so it is quite your own fault,' said Arabella, dismissing the matter.

'Go up to bed, you baggage!' commanded Ravenscar, never proof against his half-sister's wiles. 'I wish to God I had not been saddled with the care of you! Let me tell you that when you do get married your husband will very likely beat you!'

Miss Ravenscar paused on the staircase, and looked back, the picture of mischief. 'Oh, if *that* were to happen, I should fly back to my dear, kind, fusty, respectable brother!' she promised, and fled.

She bore her mother's gentle complaints, when she met her later in the morning, with docility but not much sign of penitence. Except for warning her that if she again played truant at unseasonable hours he should send her into the country, her brother paid no further attention to her escapade. She was relieved, for she had quite expected him to probe a good deal deeper into the matter, and felt some surprise at his forbearance. She thought, peeping at him over the coffee-pot at the breakfast-table, that he looked preoccupied, but she would have been more than surprised had she known the cause of the faint frown between his brows.

Mr Ravenscar, if the truth were told, was toying with the idea of driving down to Berkshire, to pay a flying visit to his friend Waring. Twice he was on the point of ordering his curricle to be brought round to the door, and twice he refrained. 'Damn it all!' he told the bell-pull, 'I'm not going to spy on the boy!'

He compromised by calling in St James's Square that evening. The rooms were rather thin of company, and the want of Miss Grantham's presence was generally felt. Several dowagers were there, looking remarkably like birds of prey; and Lady Bellingham, who had started the evening by routing Sir James Filey, seemed to be in a belligerent mood. Sir James had got nothing out of her but a selection of home-truths which had made him fling out of the house in a rage; and, emboldened by this victory, she was able to face Mr Ravenscar with scarcely a tremor. He arrived only a few minutes before supper, and begged the honour of taking her down to it. This made her ladyship look a little wary, but she accepted his proffered arm, and descended the broad staircase with him in tolerable composure. He found a seat for her in the supper-room, supplied her with some lobster patties, and a glass of iced champagne-punch, and sat down opposite to her.

Lady Bellingham summoned up her courage, and said: 'I am glad to have the opportunity of speaking to you, Mr Ravenscar. I do not know what my niece may have written to you on the subject of those horrid bills, but for my part I am very grateful to you for restoring them to me.'

'Pray do not give the matter a thought, ma'am! How long does Miss Grantham expect to be out of town?'

'As to that, I do not precisely know,' replied her ladyship vaguely. 'She has gone to stay with friends, and there is no knowing how long they may persuade her to remain with them.'

'In what part of the country is she staying, I wonder?'

'Oh, I don't—that is to say, not very far away! I don't suppose you would know the place,' said her ladyship firmly. 'It is in the north somewhere.'

'Indeed? You must miss her, I feel sure.'

'Yes, certainly I do! No one ever had a better niece! Of course, you must not think that I approved of her putting you in the cellar, and I do hope she begged your pardon for it! But in the main she is a very good girl, I assure you!'

'I fear that the fault was mine. I had grievously offended Miss Grantham.'

Lady Bellingham regarded him with increasing favour. 'I declare it is very handsome of you to say so, sir! To be sure, she was excessively put out by your wanting to give her twenty thousand pounds, not that I shall ever understand——however, that is neither here nor there!'

'I imagine,' he said, looking rather amused, 'that the expenses of keeping up an establishment of this style must be heavy?'

'Crushing!' said her ladyship, not mincing matters. 'You would find it hard to believe the shocking sum I spend on candles alone!'

'Is it worth it?' he asked curiously.

'That is just the tiresome part of it,' confided her ladyship. 'I quite thought it would be when I moved from Green Street, but nothing has gone right with us since we came to this house.'

'Do you like the life?'

'Not at all. I am getting a deal too old for it, I daresay, but what is one to do? One must hope for a run of luck to set all to rights.' An idea occurred to her. She laid down her fork, and looked speculatively at the dark countenance opposite to her. 'Of course, I know that Deb would not accept any money from you. You must know that I am far from considering her an ineligible wife for your cousin.'

'On that subject, then, we are unlikely to agree, ma'am.'

'Yes, but I assure you I am very broadminded,' said Lady Bellingham. 'You will never make the least impression on Deb, you know. I daresay she will marry Mablethorpe just to spite you.' She paused to observe the effect of these words, but Mr Ravenscar's face betrayed nothing but polite interest. 'You must not think I do not appreciate your feelings in the matter,' she continued. 'I am sure there is much to be said for your not wishing the marriage to take place. I might help you. There is not the least reason why Deb should ever know anything about it.'

He raised his brows. 'Are you suggesting that I should bribe you to use your influence with Miss Grantham?' he enquired. 'I should not think of insulting you so, ma'am!'

'When there is no turning round for the bills which clutter the whole house, I do not feel that it is the time to be talking of insults,' said her ladyship. 'If you liked to hand me the twenty thousand pounds you were so obliging as to offer to Deb, I will engage for it that she shall not marry Mablethorpe, if I can prevent her!'

He laughed, and got up. 'No, I think not, ma'am. After all, you might not be able to prevent her, you know; in which event I should have wasted my money.'

Lady Bellingham sighed. 'It would not be wasted,' she said sadly. 'However, I did not suppose that you would consent to do it.'

'Don't despair, ma'am! I may yet lose a fortune at your faro-bank.'

'I wish you may, but I daresay you will break the bank instead,' said her ladyship pessimistically.

Mr Ravenscar did not go to these lengths, but his luck was decidedly in that evening, and Lady Bellingham could only feel glad when he finally rose from the table, and went away.

He was somewhat reassured by what she had said to him, for he could not suppose that she would have offered to prevent her niece's marrying Mablethorpe if Miss Grantham had been even then on her way to Gretna Green. He tried to put the whole affair out of mind, and if he did not entirely succeed, at least he was not conscious of feeling much anxiety on his cousin's behalf. He was merely conscious of a strong desire to see Miss Grantham again.

He had some days to wait before this wish could be gratified. Though a great many letters and invitation-cards were delivered at his house, none of them bore Miss Grantham's handwriting on them. Mr Ravenscar developed a habit of tossing over his correspondence with an impatient hand, and his servants noticed that whenever they brought him a note on a tray he would pick it up with much more eagerness than he was in the habit of betraying, and then look out of reason cross. They drew their own conclusions, and shook their heads over it.

It was a week before Mr Ravenscar received any tidings of Miss Grantham's whereabouts. He was driving himself home from the village of Kensington one afternoon when he came slap upon Lord Mablethorpe, riding along Piccadilly towards him. His lordship bore signs of travel upon his slim person, his top-boots being generously splashed with mud, and his horse's legs mired to the knees. He saw his cousin's curricle approaching him, and waved.

The street was rather crowded, but Mr Ravenscar pulled up his grays, and waited for Mablethorpe to come up to the curricle. It struck him that his lordship was looking radiantly happy, and it was in rather a sharp tone that he said: 'So you are back at last!'

'Yes, this instant!' Adrian said, curbing his horse's wish to shy at a top-heavy wagon which was coming down the street. 'I have just set Deb down in St James's Square, and am on my way to Brook Street. I must not stay: I must see my mother immediately! Oh, Max, I am the happiest man alive! I have so much to tell you! You will never guess where I have been!'

'I was informed,' said Ravenscar, his brow as black as thunder, 'that you had gone to stay with Tom Waring!'

Adrian laughed, and brought his sidling horse round again. 'I know, but it was not so! Max, I am married!'

'Married!'

Mr Ravenscar must have jobbed at the grays' sensitive mouths, for they began to plunge, and his lordship was obliged to rein back out of the way.

'I knew I should surprise you!' he called. 'I will come round to tell you about it later! It is too long a story, and there is no telling it here! Besides, I must see my mother first! Goodbye! I will see you presently!'

He waved his whip, and rode on; Mr Ravenscar, very white about the mouth, drove straight to St James's Square. Arrived at Lady Bellingham's house, he thrust the reins into his groom's hands, said curtly: 'Keep them moving!' jumped down from the box, and strode up the steps to Lady Bellingham's door.

It was opened to him by Silas Wantage, who grinned, and said: 'It's wonderful, so it is, the way you do keep coming to the house, sir, as though there hadn't never been what you might call unpleasantness!'

'Desire Miss——' Ravenscar stopped. His grim mouth

255

hardened. 'Desire *Miss Grantham* to accord me the favour of a few words with her—alone!' he said.

Mr Wantage eyed him shrewdly, and stroked his chin. 'Ay, but I'm not sure as Miss Deb is receiving visitors to-day,' he said.

'Take my message to her!' Ravenscar said fiercely.

Mr Wantage opened his eyes very wide at this, but apparently decided to obey. He showed Mr Ravenscar into the small parlour at the back of the hall, and left him there while he went to deliver his message to Miss Grantham.

Deborah was in her bedchamber, having just taken off her hat and her travelling-cloak. She was giving her aunt a lively description of her journey when Silas scratched on the door, but when she heard who was below, she hesitated, blushed, and said: 'Very well, I will come down.'

'If you were to ask me, Miss Deb, I should have to tell you that if ever I saw a cove in the devil's own temper I've seen it just now, when I opened the door to Mr Ravenscar,' Silas warned her.

'Oh dear! He must have heard the news!' said Miss Grantham ruefully. 'I did hope he would not mind so very much!'

'Maybe I'd better come with you,' suggested Wantage, who had not yet given up hope of enjoying a bout of fisti-cuffs with Mr Ravenscar.

'Certainly not! He cannot eat me, after all!'

'I wouldn't be so sure,' said Mr Wantage darkly.

But Miss Grantham only laughed, and dismissed him, turning to arrange her hair in the mirror, and to straighten the fall of lace over her bosom. She then told her aunt she expected to be back directly, and went downstairs to the back-parlour.

Mr Ravenscar, who was standing staring out of the window, jerking his driving-gloves between his hands, swung round at her entrance, and looked across at her with wrath and the most bitter contempt in his face. 'So!' he said bitingly. 'Stand there, ma'am! Let me take a good look at you! You have tricked me finely, have you not?'

'Well, yes, I suppose I did trick you a little,' confessed Miss Grantham. 'But it is not so very bad, after all!'

'I thought I had been mistaken in you! By God, the only mistake I made was in giving you credit for a little common honesty!' he flung at her. 'You are a cheating baggage, ma'am! Do not put on that air of outraged innocence, I beg of you! A drab from the stews would have scorned to behave as you have! I came to take a look at you, knowing you for the jade you are! You have a beautiful face, I will grant, and you are false to the bottom of your heart—if heart you possess!'

Miss Grantham blinked and gasped under this hail of words, and could only stammer: 'Are you m-mad? If I deceived you, at least I have done nothing to provoke you to such anger as this! It may not be a brilliant match for Adrian, and I own he is a trifle young to be setting up his establishment, but you will see how well it will answer!'

'No, that I shall not!' he retorted. 'Mine is one foot that will not cross the threshold, be sure!'

'Oh, this is nothing but the stupidest prejudice!' she exclaimed. 'I warn you, you had better not talk to Adrian in this vein, if you value his regard for you, for he is as deep in love as can be, and will very likely call you out for saying such things of his wife!'

'His wife!' he ejaculated bitterly. 'My God, his wife!'

Miss Grantham came forward into the middle of the room. 'I see no reason for all this scorn,' she said. 'You are angry because you were hoodwinked, but that was as much Adrian's doing as mine. Do not think to come browbeating me, Mr Ravenscar! I will not bear such treatment! And if you dare to call me by one more vile name I will hit you!

As for the bills, and the mortgage which you were so obliging as to send me, you shall have them back, and you shall be paid every penny!'

'Yes! By Mablethorpe!' he said, with a short laugh. 'I thank you, ma'am, I want none of them back! But if Mablethorpe had known the full story, do you think that he would have married you? Do you?'

Miss Grantham stood as though turned to stone, colour flooding her cheeks as the sense of his words dawned upon her. He did not fail to mark this flush, and said: 'I am happy to see that you can blush, ma'am! I had not thought it possible!'

A pulse throbbed in Miss Grantham's throat; her eyes narrowed to slits of light; she made a strong effort to control her voice, and managed to say: 'And how, may I ask, did you know that I had married Mablethorpe?'

'I have this instant met him. He told me himself. It may interest you to know, ma'am, that a week ago I was told that you had been seen travelling northward with your maid beside you in the chaise, and my cousin riding as escort. The fool that I was I would not believe that you could have been base enough to persuade that boy into eloping with you! I assumed him to be accompanying you merely to your destination, to protect you upon the journey! But to-day I learned the truth. I should have known better than to expect honest dealing from a wench out of a gaming-house!'

If Miss Grantham had been red before, she was now as white as her lace. 'You should be grateful to me for having enlarged your experience! But I would remind you, Mr Ravenscar, that I told you when I had you in my power that I should marry your cousin when I chose!'

'I have not forgotten! I remember something else which you said upon that occasion, and which will prove as true a prophecy! You promised to ruin him! You did so when you let him put his ring upon your finger!'

Miss Grantham thrust her left hand into the folds of her skirt. 'You will be sorry that you ever dared to speak to me in these terms!' she said through her teeth. 'There is nothing I will not do to punish you! I have never been so sorry that I was not born a man! I would kill you if I could! I disliked you at first setting eyes on you: I have learned to detest you!'

'And I thought I had learned to love you, ma'am!' he said. 'You do not understand the meaning of that word, but when you have squandered Adrian's fortune, as I make no doubt you will do soon enough, you may reflect that had you played your cards more cleverly you might have had my wealth to spend, and my name to call your own! You stare! Is it possible that you did not guess it, ma'am? So clever as you are you yet failed to snare a richer prize than Adrian! A much richer prize, Miss Grantham! Take that thought to bed with you, and may you dream of it often! For myself, I count myself fortunate to have escaped so narrowly from the toils of a harpy!'

Miss Grantham's voice shook uncontrollably, and she was forced to grasp a chairback to steady herself. 'Go!' she gasped. 'Marry *you*? I would rather die in the worst agony you can conceive! Don't dare—don't *dare* to enter this house again! I wish I may never see you again as long as I live!'

'You cannot wish that more heartily than I do!' he retorted, and strode from the room.

Miss Grantham stayed where she was for a full minute, her breast heaving, and angry tears starting in her eyes. The slam of the front-door recalled her to herself. She dashed a hand across her eyes, and rushed out of the room, straight upstairs to her bedchamber. Lady Bellingham was still seated there, but at sight of her niece's ravaged countenance she almost jumped out of her chair, exclaiming: 'Good God, my love, what is amiss?'

'That man!' choked Miss Grantham. 'That *devil*!'

'Oh, heavens, you have quarrelled with Ravenscar again!' cried her ladyship. 'Don't tell me you have had him put in the cellar! I can't bear it!'

'He shall never enter this house again!' stormed Miss Grantham. 'He dared to think—he *dared* to think—Oh, I shall go mad!'

'I know you will, and it has been troubling me very much,' said her aunt. 'I never knew you to behave so in all your life! What did he think?'

'He thought—oh, I cannot bring myself to speak of it! *That* is what he thinks me! I have never been insulted so, never! I wish I had called to Silas to *fling* him out of the house! If ever he dares to show his face here again that is what I shall do! I would like to boil him in oil! Nothing could be too bad for him, and if I could see my way to ruining him I would do it, and dance for joy!'

'But, Deb, what has he *done*?' wailed her aunt.

'He believes me to be the lowest kind of creature on this earth! He has insulted me in the worst way any—oh, go away, Aunt Lizzie, go away! And don't let anyone come up to me, for I won't see a soul!'

She looked so fierce that Lady Bellingham did not attempt to remonstrate with her, but tottered from the room, feeling that her days were numbered. She heard the key turn in the lock behind her, and went downstairs to her boudoir, intending to recuperate her own strength by sipping hartshorn-and-water, and lying down on the sofa, with her smelling-salts to hand.

She had barely settled herself comfortably, however, when Lucius Kennet walked into the room, saying cheerfully: 'I hear that Deb has come home. Where is the darlin'?'

'Shut up in her room, and stark mad!' moaned Lady Bellingham.

He stared. 'The divil she is! Now, what ails her?'

'I don't know. Ravenscar has been here, and she says she has never been so insulted in her life! I have never known her to be so angry! She could barely speak!'

'But what has the miserable spalpeen been saying to her at all?'

'It is no use asking me, for I don't know, but I fear he must have made her an improper proposal. She says she would like to boil him in oil. But understand me, Lucius, if you help her to do any such thing you do not enter this house again!'

'Faith, I have a better way of punishing Mr Ravenscar than that! I wish you will inform Deb I am here, ma'am: I'll tell her what will gladden her heart!'

'She said she would not see a soul, and you know what she is! Besides, she has locked the door. Do, I implore you, go away and leave me in peace! I am sure my head is like to split!'

'Ah, now, be easy, ma'am!' he said. 'I'll go, and maybe you'll not be seeing me for a while, but I give you my word I have as pretty a revenge brewing for Ravenscar as even Deb could wish for! You may tell her so with my love—or maybe I'll be writing her a note to raise her spirits.'

'Do anything you please, only go away!' begged her ladyship, closing her eyes, and making a feeble gesture towards the door.

CHAPTER XVII

WHEN Mr Ravenscar stalked inside his house, twenty minutes after he had flung out of the back-parlour in St

James's Square, he was still in a towering rage, which showed itself plainly in his scowling brow, and thinned lips. His butler, unwise enough to make an innocuous remark about the weather when he admitted him to the house, had his head bitten off for his pains, and retired, much shaken, to the nether regions, where he informed his colleagues that if the master had not been crossed in love he did not know the signs.

Mr Ravenscar, throwing his gloves on to one chair, and his long, drab coat across another, shut himself up in his library, and spent an hour pacing up and down its length, a prey to the most violent and confused emotions he had ever experienced. He did not know whom he was most furious with, himself or Miss Grantham, and was dwelling savagely on this quite unimportant problem when he discovered that his bitterest anger was directed against Mablethorpe. He realized that it would afford him considerable pleasure to be able to take his cousin by the throat, and to choke the life out of him. This discovery enraged him still further, and he told himself savagely that he was well rid of a mercenary, heartless, unprincipled baggage. This brought no relief to his feelings; and although the wanton smashing of a Sèvres figure which he had always detested, and which some nameless fool had dared to place upon the mantelpiece, afforded him a momentary gratification, its beneficial effects did not prove to be lasting. He continued to pace the floor, torn between a desire to strangle Miss Grantham and throw her body to the dogs, and an equally strong desire to serve Mablethorpe in this way instead, and to think out a fitting punishment for Miss Grantham which would, in some mysterious manner, entail her remaining in his power for the rest of her life.

It was not to be supposed that this ferocity could endure for long. It wore itself out presently, leaving Mr Ravenscar with a sense of corroding disillusionment, and a conviction that life held nothing further for him. In this painful mood, he went upstairs to change his clothes for dinner, vouchsafing not one word to his valet (who, after one swift glance at his face, was thankful for this forbearance), and attending so little to what he was doing that he allowed himself to be assisted into a coat which he had decided on the previous night that he would never wear again.

His stepmother and Arabella were dining out, a circumstance which relieved him of the necessity of going out himself; and he sat down in solitary state at the head of his long dining-table, and ate perhaps three mouthfuls of every dish which was presented to him, until he came to the syllabub, which he rejected with every evidence of loathing. The only thing he partook of freely was the port. His butler had had the forethought to bring up a bottle of the best from the cellar.

Mr Ravenscar, lost in a brown study, was still sitting at the dinner-table, his half-empty wine-glass in his hand, when the butler brought him a note, which had been delivered by hand. Mr Ravenscar glanced at it indifferently, recognized Lady Mablethorpe's writing, and picked it up, his lips tightening. It was brief, and to the point. It requested him to call in Brook Street at his earliest convenience.

There was scarcely any person whom Mr Ravenscar would not have preferred to confront that evening, but he was not one to put off a disagreeable task, and after tossing off the rest of his port, he told the butler to fetch his hat and cloak and walking-cane.

He went on foot to Brook Street, and was ushered immediately into the drawing-room on the first floor. Here he found his aunt, seated alone by the small fire, looking as though she had sustained a severe shock.

She waited only until the servant had withdrawn before exclaiming: 'Oh, Max, have you heard what has happened?'

He had fully expected to be met by an outburst of wrath, and could only suppose that her ladyship's first rage, like his own, had worn itself out. 'Yes,' he replied curtly. 'I know. I am sorry, aunt.'

'It is not your fault,' she said. 'I was never so taken aback in my life!'

'It was my fault,' Ravenscar said. 'I had the means to stop it, and I was fool enough not to use them.'

She stared at him. 'Good heavens, Max, you never said a word to me about it! Do you tell me you knew all along what he really meant to do?'

He came to the fire, and stood with his back to it, looking down at her with a puzzled frown. 'I don't understand you, ma'am. Surely we both knew?'

'But I never knew of the girl's existence until to-day!' cried Lady Mablethorpe, in the liveliest astonishment.

'Never knew of her existence?' he repeated blankly. 'What in God's name are you talking about, aunt?'

'I am talking about this child whom Adrian says he has married! What are *you* talking about, pray?'

'Child! Am I mad, or are you?' demanded Ravenscar. 'Adrian has married Deborah Grantham!'

'But he has not!' said her ladyship. 'He has married one of the Laxton girls!'

'What?' thundered Ravenscar.

His aunt winced. 'For heaven's sake don't shout at me! I have borne enough this day! So you did *not* know! He threw as much dust in your eyes as in mine!'

Mr Ravenscar seemed to experience some difficulty in speaking, but after a moment's stunned silence he managed to say with tolerable composure: 'I am utterly at a loss, ma'am, and must beg you to enlighten me! Are you sure that you have understood what Adrian told you?'

'Of course I am sure! Do you think I am in my dotage? He has married Phœbe Laxton—a child three years younger than himself, if you please! And that Grantham woman helped him to do it!' Lady Mablethorpe fanned herself in an agitated way, and added: 'It is the most absurd thing ever I heard! A couple of babies to be setting up housekeeping! The girl is as good as portionless, too! Oh, I do not know what to do about it! There is nothing I can do, but to think that I should be obliged to receive Augusta Laxton with an appearance of complaisance when there is no one I dislike more! It does not bear thinking of!'

Mr Ravenscar, who was looking extremely pale, broke in on this to say: 'Have the goodness, ma'am, to be a little more intelligible! This sounds to me like a farrago of nonsense! When did Adrian meet Miss Laxton? How is it possible that he can have married her?'

'He met her at Vauxhall, when he was there with that dreadful woman. It seems that she had run away from Sir James Filey, whom the Laxtons were pressing her to marry. Well, I must say I think she did right to run away from such a satyr! A hateful man, and if you had but known his *mother*———! But that's neither here nor there! What must Adrian do—urged on, of course, by that Grantham woman, though why she should I cannot imagine, for anyone must have guessed what would come of it, with a boy of his romantic notions! Well, what must he do but spirit the girl away to Lady Bellingham's house, where she was kept hidden until Filey chanced to see her looking out of the window one day, and recognized her!'

'Good God!' exclaimed Ravenscar, paler than ever. 'I do recall hearing some talk of the Laxton girl's being missing! She was in St James's Square all the time?'

'Yes, falling in love with my son!' said her ladyship, with a good deal of feeling. 'Under the Grantham woman's nose! She must be a fool, one would think! For what could be more natural than for Adrian to tumble head over ears in love with a child who was calling him her saviour, and thinking him a perfect Sir Galahad, or whoever it was who went about rescuing foolish females! Oh, I can see it all! And I must say, Max, dreadful though it all is, his marriage has improved him already! He seems to have grown up in a flash. If I had not been so angry, I could have laughed to have heard him telling me so sternly how he would have me receive his wife, and how he would not permit anyone to do or say anything that might distress her! He has gone off to call upon Lord Laxton, as cool as you please! A boy of his age! Heaven knows what the Laxtons will say, but they may consider themselves lucky to have married their daughter so well, and so I shall tell Augusta, if she dares to—oh, but, Max, Max, he is too young to be married! I cannot bear it!'

Mr Ravenscar paid no attention to this. 'But the marriage! Do you tell me Adrian took this girl to Gretna Green?'

'No, he was not so lost to all sense of propriety as that, I am thankful to say! When Filey discovered her presence in Lady Bellingham's house, Phœbe was so terrified that she would be dragged back to her parents' house, and forced to marry him, that there was nothing for it, Adrian said, but to take her away immediately. Laxton's sister lives in Wales, and seems to have been a good friend to Phœbe from the outset. Adrian hired a post-chaise, bundled her and the Grantham woman into it, told me he was off to stay with Tom Waring, and set out for Wales! With a special licence in his pocket, Max! Only fancy Adrian's thinking of everything, just as though he were not a perfect greenhorn! One cannot help feeling proud of him! They were married from this aunt's house, and now Adrian says he means to insert a notice in the *Morning Post*!'

'My God, my God, what have I done?' burst from Mr

Ravenscar. He sprang to his feet, and began to pace about the room as though he could not be still another instant.

His aunt regarded him with astonishment. 'I cannot conceive what you should have done! I do not blame you: you could not have guessed that anything so fantastic would happen.'

'You do not know what I have done!' said Ravenscar over his shoulder. 'But never mind that! Where is Adrian's bride?'

'He has left her in Wales. I declare I could have boxed his ears! He had the effrontery to tell me that he means to bring her to London, but would not do so until he was assured that she would be received with the civility due to his wife!'

Mr Ravenscar smiled for the first time since his meeting with his cousin that afternoon. 'Capital! I hope he will come and tell me so too. He told me only that he was married and the happiest man on earth when I met him on his way to break the news to you. I daresay I shall receive a stern warning from him when next I see him.'

'But what is to be done?' demanded Lady Mablethorpe.

'There is nothing to be done, ma'am. It might, after all, have been very much worse.'

'Certainly, if he had married the Grantham creature, but do you tell me I must countenance this match?'

'Unless you wish for a breach with Adrian, undoubtedly,' replied Ravenscar.

'Oh, Max!' said her ladyship, dabbing at the corners of her eyes. 'I don't feel as though I can bear it!'

'It is certainly a severe shock, ma'am, but however much you may dislike the girl's parents there is nothing wrong with her breeding. The greatest ill we have to fear is that Laxton will try to extort money from Adrian, and that he cannot do until the boy comes of age, by which time I must hope to have been able to drum a little sense into his head.'

'That is just what I said, but Adrian vows he does not mean to be bled by a man who has behaved as abominably towards his daughter as Laxton has towards Phœbe. He says he may very likely take care of the younger girls, but there it will end.'

The thought of his cousin's expressing a paternal readiness to take care of the younger girls made Ravenscar burst out laughing. His aunt suddenly perceived the humour of it, and cried and laughed together, and felt very much better for it.

'Send Adrian round to my house in the morning,' Ravenscar said. 'I will talk over the question of settlements with him, and see Laxton myself. We shall have to consult Julius, of course, but you had better persuade him to let me handle the business.'

Lady Mablethorpe had no hesitation in approving of this. Julius, she said, was an old fool, who would allow Laxton to talk him into anything.

'Well, Laxton won't talk me into anything,' promised Ravenscar, and took his leave of her.

When he walked away from the house, it was with the intention of repairing at once to St James's Square, but before he had reached the end of the street he recalled that Lady Bellingham was holding a card-party that night, and stopped. There could be no opportunity of holding any private conversation with Miss Grantham that night, and what he had to say to her could not be said in public. He was obliged to abandon his plan, and to turn homewards, to possess his soul in what patience he could muster until the following day.

His cousin arrived at the house while he was still at breakfast, and for the next hour he was fully occupied in listening to an account of the runaway marriage, accompanied by a rapturous description of young Lady Mablethorpe's manifold charms and virtues, the recital of which led him privately to infer that she was a pretty little creature, without much sense, and certainly no strength of character. He thought she would do very well for Adrian. For himself, he preferred women of more spirit.

When Adrian had talked himself out, and all the business of settlements had been discussed, it was nearly noon. Adrian, who seemed to have taken his father and mother-in-law by storm, and to have cowed them into a dazed acceptance of the situation, was very anxious that his cousin should call immediately at the Laxtons' house. Ravenscar fobbed him off, however, by saying that he must first consult his fellow-trustees; thrust him upstairs to regale Arabella and Mrs Ravenscar with the story of his marriage; and himself made good his escape from the house, and set off for St James's Square.

The door was opened to him by Mr Wantage, who at once barred his passage. 'No good!' he said briefly. 'The orders is I'm not to admit you, sir, and that's all there is to it.'

'Take my card up to Miss Grantham,' said Ravenscar, 'and tell her that I must beg her to see me, if only for five minutes.'

'It wouldn't do a mite of good if I did,' replied Silas pityingly. 'She won't have you inside the house, and if I was to let you in she'd very likely murder me.'

'If you try to keep me from entering the house, it's not Miss Grantham who will murder you!' said Ravenscar.

A joyful light sprang to Mr Wantage's eyes. 'If that's the way it is, put up your dabblers, guv'nor!' he said simply.

Mr Ravenscar did more than this. Before Silas well knew what he was about, he had planted a flush hit to the face, followed it up by a lightning doubler which sent Silas staggering back, and was inside the house, with the door kicked to behind him.

Mr Wantage came boring in, trying to bustle his man, received a heavy facer, popped in over his guard, which drew his cork; threw in a body-blow; tried to job Mr Ravenscar in the face; was thrown on Ravenscar's hip; and went crashing to the floor, where he remained, winded, and bleeding copiously at the nose.

'I owed you that!' said Ravenscar, panting a little.

From the head of the stairs an arctic voice said: 'Have the goodness to leave this house immediately!'

Mr Ravenscar looked up quickly, saw Miss Grantham standing above him, with an expression of frozen fury on her face, and went up the stairs two at a time. Miss Grantham's eyes dared him to touch her, but he gripped her wrist in one hand, saying: 'I must and I will speak to you!'

'I have nothing whatsoever to say to you!' flashed Miss Grantham. 'How dare you knock my servant down?'

'You may not have anything to say to me, but I have something which must be said to you!' replied Ravenscar. 'If you won't walk into that room, I shall pick you up and carry you into it!'

Silas Wantage, having recovered his wind by this time, picked himself up, holding his handkerchief to his flowing nose, and offered thickly to mill Mr Ravenscar down, if it took him all the morning to do it.

'No, no, go away and put a key down your back!' commanded Miss Grantham, shuddering. 'If you have anything to say to me, sir, say it, and then go, and never let me see you again!'

Mr Ravenscar, still grasping her wrist, opened the door of the little parlour on the half-landing, and drew her inside. He then released her, and said: 'I have come to beg your pardon, Miss Grantham.'

She looked disdainfully at him. 'You need not have been to so much trouble, I assure you. Your opinion of my character is a matter of the supremest indifference to me.'

'There is no excuse for me. If I had not been crazy with jealousy I should never have said what I did to you. I love you!'

'No doubt I should be flattered, but as I can scarcely conceive of a worse fate than to be married to you, this declaration fills me with repugnance!'

He bit his lip. 'Forgive me!'

'I shall never forgive you as long as I live! If you have now said what you came to say, pray leave me!'

'I tell you I love you!' said Mr Ravenscar, taking a step towards her.

'If you dare to touch me again I shall scream!' announced Miss Grantham. 'I do not know whether you are asking me to marry you, or merely to become your mistress, but whichever it is——'

'I am asking you to marry me!' interrupted Ravenscar.

'I am obliged to you,' said Miss Grantham, dropping him a curtsey, 'but even the thought of squandering such a fortune as yours fails to tempt me. I have met many men in my time whom I thought odious, but none, believe me, whom I hated as I hate you! I trust I make myself plain, sir?'

'Yes,' he replied, in a deeply mortified tone. 'Perfectly plain, ma'am. I will relieve you of the annoyance of my presence. But I beg of you to believe that now and always I am your very obedient servant to command!'

She made no response to this; he bowed to her formally, and left the room. She heard his footsteps descending the stairs, caught the echo of his voice as he spoke to someone in the hall, and the sound of the front door shutting behind him. Then she sat down on a very uncomfortable chair, and enjoyed a bout of weeping which lasted for half-an-hour by the clock, and left her limp, and much inclined to think that she would have done better never to have been born at all.

This melancholy conviction grew upon her steadily as the day wore on. Her aunt was quite alarmed by her listlessness, and began to fear that she might be starting on a decline, until a chance reference to Mr Ravenscar drew from her so scathing a denunciation of that gentleman's manners and morals that Lady Bellingham was relieved to find that she was still not entirely given over to melancholia. She ventured to deliver Mr Kennet's message. It was well received, Miss Grantham remarking with unnecessary emphasis that she hoped Lucius would ruin Mr Ravenscar. This put her in mind of the mortgage, and she at once wrested this from the unfortunate Lady Bellingham, wrapped it up in a packet, with all the bills which had accompanied it, and sent it round by hand to Grosvenor Square. Lady Bellingham threatened to succumb to a combination of palpitations, vapours, and strong hysterics, and was only prevented from taking to her bed by the immediate return of the packet, this time containing the torn fragments of one mortgage and half-a-dozen bills. Miss Grantham then burst into tears again, spoke wistfully of the beneficial qualities of racks, thumbscrews, and boiling oil, and shut herself up in her room, refusing all sustenance or comfort.

She was not again seen until the following morning, when she appeared some time after breakfast in her aunt's dressing-room, pale, but apparently restored to calm. She kissed Lady Bellingham, saying penitently: 'I am sorry to have been so tiresome, dear ma'am! It was very foolish of me, for I am sure Mr Ravenscar is not worth bothering one's head over. We will forget him, if you please, and be comfortable again.'

Lady Bellingham refrained from pointing out to her that there was very little comfort to be found in a debtors' prison, but said instead that a letter had been brought round late on the previous evening from Mr Kennet's lodging.

Miss Grantham took this missive without much interest, and broke open the seal. The single sheet was spread out, and she read with startled eyes the message it contained.

'*Be easy, Deb,*' had written Mr Kennet, '*by the time this comes to your hand you will have all the revenge on Ravenscar you desire. Your humble servant has made a conquest of his little puss of a sister, and if we do not have twenty thousand and maybe more out of my fine gentleman to rescue her from my wicked wiles my name is not Lucius Kennet. I have persuaded the darling to elope with me to Gretna Green, though it's not there I'll be taking her, unless I'm driven to it. I never met but one woman I'd a fancy to marry, and that's yourself, my dear.*

'*Don't you be letting that tender heart of yours get the better of you, now! It's not a mite of harm I'll be doing the chit, but merely holding her to ransom, I give you my word. I'm thinking Ravenscar will pay handsomely to get her safely back, and to keep my mouth shut on me.*'

Miss Grantham's cheeks were perfectly white when she looked up from her perusal of this letter. She said in a strangled voice: 'When did this come? Why was it not brought to me instantly?'

'Well, my love, you had shut yourself up in your room, and I did not think it would be important,' said her ladyship uneasily. 'It was brought round at about midnight, I think. What does it say?'

'I cannot tell you!' said Miss Grantham. 'Lucius has done something so dreadful—Aunt Lizzie, I must go out instantly, and I do not know when I shall return! Pray tell Silas to order the carriage—no, I will take a hackney! I have not a moment to waste!'

'But, Deb!' shrieked her aunt. 'Where are you going?'

'To Mr Ravenscar!' replied Miss Grantham. 'I

cannot explain the reason to you, but it is imperative that I should see him at once! Pray do not try to stop me!'

Lady Bellingham opened her mouth, shut it again, and sank back in her chair as one past human succour.

Twenty minutes later, a hackney-carriage set Miss Grantham down at Mr Ravenscar's door. It was opened to her by a footman, and she demanded, in a voice which she tried hard to steady, to see Mr Ravenscar immediately. The footman looked very much surprised at this request, and asked her doubtfully if it were Mrs Ravenscar she wished to see.

'No, no!' Deborah said. 'My errand is to Mr Ravenscar, and it is most urgent! I desire you will tell him that Miss Grantham begs the favour of a few minutes' speech with him!'

The footman looked more doubtful still, but he admitted her into the house, and led her to the library, saying that he would see if his master were at home. He then went away, and Miss Grantham began to pace about the room, much as its owner had done on the previous evening, clasping and unclasping her gloved hands.

In a very short time the door opened again. 'Miss Grantham!' Ravenscar said, in a voice which betrayed his amazement. 'Good God, what is it?' he exclaimed, as she turned, and he saw her face.

'Have you seen your sister this morning?' she demanded.

'No, she is not up yet. She was out until the small hours, at some ball or other, and has doubtless overslept.'

'Mr Ravenscar, I have this instant received this letter,' she interrupted him, holding out Mr Kennet's note to him. 'It was brought round to the house late last night, but I never had it until this morning! I have come instantly— you must believe that I would have come last night if I had known! Please read it at once! It is vital that you should be

274

in possession of all the facts without another moment's loss of time!'

He took the letter from her. 'I will read it, but will you not sit down, Miss Grantham? Let me first get you a glass of wine! You are dreadfully pale!'

'No, no, I want nothing, I thank you! Only read that letter, I beg of you!' she said, sinking down on to the sofa.

He looked at her with a good deal of concern, but as she merely signed to him to open the sheet of paper he was holding, he did so, and read Mr Kennet's startling message.

He raised his eyes when he had come to the end of the letter, and fixed them on Miss Grantham's face, saying in an odd voice: 'Why have you brought me this, ma'am?'

'Good God, do you not understand?' she cried. 'Your sister has run off with him, believing that he means to marry her! It is all a plot to get money from you! I came at once, because it is my fault! It was at my aunt's house that she met him, but I never dreamed—but there is no excusing my part in this! I said I did not care what Lucius might do to you! I said I hoped he would ruin you! But indeed, indeed I never meant such wicked mischief as this!' She stopped, trying to regain command over her voice, which was shaking pitiably. 'He won't hurt her,' she managed to say. 'He is not as bad as that! You see he says that he does not mean her any harm, but only to hold her to ransom. You must trust me, sir! I can help you, and I will. Silas knows all the places where he might be found. You must do nothing. You must leave it to me! It would be fatal if you were to meet Lucius! The story would be bound to leak out, and whatever happens no one must ever know the truth! Once Silas has found them, I can do the rest. I give you my word Lucius will not dare to breathe a word of it to a soul. If he does, I shall swear that there is no word of truth in it, but that Miss Ravenscar was all the time in my company. But he will not speak! I know things about him that would

275

ruin him if I chose to divulge them, and I will do so if ever he should dare to try to extort money out of you by threatening to publish the story to the world! Oh, do please trust me, sir! I know that none of it would ever have happened if I had not refused to give Adrian up at the outset, just to punish you, and you must, you *must* let me help you now!'

Mr Ravenscar, who had listened to this speech with remarkable composure, now laid Mr Kennet's letter aside, and sat down beside Miss Grantham, calmly possessing himself of both her hands, and holding them in a firm clasp. 'Deb, my darling, there's no need for you to distress yourself like this! Don't tremble so, my poor girl! Arabella is not such a fool as to be taken in by a man of Kennet's kidney.'

'Oh, don't you understand?' she cried, in an agony of impatience. 'He can be very fascinating to a girl of her age! He——'

'My dearest heart, will you *listen* to me?' said Mr Ravenscar. 'Arabella is upstairs, and very likely asleep, and if you don't believe me I will take you up to see her with your own eyes!'

She stared at him in a dazed way. 'Are you sure?' she uttered.

'Yes, I am perfectly sure,' he replied. 'She told me all about it last night.'

'She—she *told* you?' said Miss Grantham, apparently dazed.

'You see,' explained Mr Ravenscar, 'she has always been in the habit of telling me things, and she sometimes even takes my advice. I advised her to beware of the man who tried to persuade her to elope with him, because such a man could only be a fortune-hunter. You will perhaps have noticed that my sister is a minx. I regret to say that it seemed good to her to dupe Kennet into believing that she meant to fly with him last night. I understand that after waiting in the rain for an hour at the appointed rendezvous, he was joined by a link-boy who had been bribed to deliver a note into his hands which can have done nothing, I imagine, to heighten his self-esteem.'

'Oh, thank God!' whispered Miss Grantham, and burst into overwrought tears.

Mr Ravenscar promptly took her in his arms, and held her so tightly that she was quite unable to break free. After making one half-hearted attempt to do so, and uttering a confused protest, to which he paid no heed at all, she subsided in a very weak way, and cried into his shoulder. Mr Ravenscar endured this with great forbearance for several minutes, but when Miss Grantham made various muffled and wholly unintelligible remarks into his coat, he commanded her to look up. Miss Grantham then gulped in an unromantic manner, sniffed, and groped for her handkerchief. Evidently feeling that she was incapable of drying her own cheeks, Mr Ravenscar performed this office for her. After that, he kissed her, and, when she tried to speak, kissed her again, extremely roughly.

'Oh, no!' said Miss Grantham faintly.

'Be quiet!' said Mr Ravenscar, kissing her for the third time.

Quite cowed, Miss Grantham submitted, making no attempt to say anything more for an appreciable time. When she did speak again, she had discarded her bonnet, and was sitting with her head on Mr Ravenscar's shoulder, and her hand tucked in his. Notwithstanding these circumstances, she said: 'You cannot possibly marry me! You know you cannot!'

'My beautiful idiot!' said Mr Ravenscar lovingly.

Deeply pleased by this form of address, Miss Grantham said: 'You have no notion of the money I owe! You are mad even to think of marrying me!'

'I beg your pardon. I have a very good notion of the money you owe.'

'Do but consider what your relatives would say!'

'I have not the slightest interest in anything they may say.'

'You cannot marry a—a wench out of a gaming-house!'

Mr Ravenscar's arm tightened about her. 'I shall marry a wench out of a gaming-house with as much pomp and ceremony as I can contrive.'

She gave a rather watery chuckle. 'Oh, no! Think of your sister!'

'I am thinking of her. I am wholly incapable of controlling her, and trust that you may succeed where I have failed. My stepmother has informed me that it is my duty to marry, to provide Arabella with a suitable chaperon.'

Miss Grantham lifted his hand to her cheek. 'I may ruin you,' she warned him.

'You may try,' retorted Mr Ravenscar.

'I shall expect you to pay all Aunt Lizzie's debts.'

'I mean to do so.'

'And to remove her from that dreadful house.'

'That also.'

'And to be civil to my poor brother.'

'I'll try to be.'

'And *of course* to let me set up a faro-bank of my own!' said Miss Grantham, in a small, provocative voice.

'If I ever find you playing anything but commerce or silver loo, I'll make you sorry you were ever born!' said Mr Ravenscar, kissing her hand. 'Jade!'

Miss Grantham heaved a sigh of satisfaction, and abandoned any further attempt to bring him to a sense of his own folly.

Arabella

'You cannot know what it means to be the object of
every fortune-hunter, courted and odiously flattered
only for your wealth, until you are ready to wish that
you had not a penny in the world'

Impetuosity is Arabella's only besetting fault. And as
the eldest daughter of a country parson and an
enchanting debutante, she should know better than to
allow herself to be provoked by Mr Beaumaris, the
most eligible Nonpareil of the day. For her
outrageous claim commits her to a deception which
becomes increasingly difficult to sustain. As for Mr
Beaumaris, *his* besetting sin is his exquisite
enjoyment of the ridiculous – watching society's most
beautiful impostress become the catch of the season.

'Her heroines are all young, beautiful, spirited . . .
The predicaments are romantic and full of suspense'
Publishers Weekly

The Foundling

It was undoubtedly better to be the seventh Duke of Sale than a sweep's apprentice, but he was much inclined to think that to have been plain Mr. Dash, of Nowhere in Particular, would have been preferable to either of these callings.

The shy young Duke of Sale has never known his parents. Instead, his Grace Adolphus Gillespie Vernon Ware (Gilly for short) has endured twenty-four years of rigorous mollycoddling from his uncle and his valet. But his natural diffidence conceals a rebellious spirit. So when Gilly hears of Belinda, the beautiful foundling who appears to be blackmailing his cousin, he absconds with glee. Only he has no sooner entered this new and dangerous world than he is plunged into a frenzy of intrigue, kidnap and adventure.

The Talisman Ring

'I dare say it will not be so very bad, our marriage, if I can have a house in town, and perhaps a lover.'

'Perhaps a what?' demanded Shield, in a voice that made her jump.

Neither Sir Tristram Shield nor Eustacie, his young French cousin, share the slightest inclination to marry one another. Yet it is Lord Lavenham's dying wish. For there is no one else to provide for the old man's granddaughter while Ludovic, his heir, remains a fugitive from justice. But when Eustacie carries out her threat to run away at the dead of night she uncovers the mystery of the talisman ring – and a murderer in the family.

'Among her best'   *Nottingham Guardian*

Bath Tangle

'Do you imagine that I wish for a wife upon such terms? You mistake the matter, my girl, believe me!'

'Then release me from so intolerable a situation! To be obliged to beg your consent! Something must be done!'

The Earl of Spenborough always had been noted for his eccentricity. Leaving a widow younger than his own daughter was one thing . . . Leaving his fortune to the trusteeship of the Marquis of Rotherham – the one man the same daughter had jilted – was quite another. Yet that is how Lady Serena and Fanny now a dowager Countess, hit upon the brilliant idea of taking a house in Bath. But the two girls, whose beauty is in no way diminished by their being in mourning, can hardly escape the romantic entanglements for which the spa is famous.

'A very absorbing novel ... Georgette Heyer untangles *Bath Tangle* with remarkable skill'   Elizabeth Bowen

A Selected List of Fiction Available from Mandarin

While every effort is made to keep prices low, it is sometimes necessary to increase prices at short notice. Mandarin Paperbacks reserves the right to show new retail prices on covers which may differ from those previously advertised in the text or elsewhere.

The prices shown below were correct at the time of going to press.

☐	7493 0003 5	**Mirage**	James Follett	£3.99
☐	7493 0134 1	**To Kill a Mockingbird**	Harper Lee	£2.99
☐	7493 0076 0	**The Crystal Contract**	Julian Rathbone	£3.99
☐	7493 0145 7	**Talking Oscars**	Simon Williams	£3.50
☐	7493 0118 X	**The Wire**	Nik Gowing	£3.99
☐	7493 0121 X	**Under Cover of Daylight**	James Hall	£3.50
☐	7493 0020 5	**Pratt of the Argus**	David Nobbs	£3.99
☐	7493 0097 3	**Second from Last in the Sack Race**	David Nobbs	£3.50

All these books are available at your bookshop or newsagent, or can be ordered direct from the publisher. Just tick the titles you want and fill in the form below.

Mandarin Paperbacks, Cash Sales Department, PO Box 11, Falmouth, Cornwall TR10 9EN.

Please send cheque or postal order, no currency, for purchase price quoted and allow the following for postage and packing:

UK   80p for the first book, 20p for each additional book ordered to a maximum charge of £2.00.

BFPO   80p for the first book, 20p for each additional book.

Overseas   £1.50 for the first book, £1.00 for the second and 30p for each additional book
including Eire   thereafter.

NAME (Block letters) ....

ADDRESS ....

....

....